Peace, Love, and Murder

A BO FORRESTER MYSTERY

PEACE, LOVE, AND MURDER

NANCY HOLZNER

FIVE STAR
A part of Gale, Cengage Learning

Detroit • New York • San Francisco • New Haven, Conn • Waterville, Maine • London

Five Star Publishing, a part of Gale, Cengage Learning.

Set in 11 pt. Plantin.

Printed on permanent paper.

LIBRARY OF CONGRESS CATALOGING-IN-PUBLICATION DATA

Conner, Nancy, 1961–
Peace, love, and murder : a Bo Forrester mystery / Nancy Holzner. — 1st ed.
p. cm.
ISBN-13: 978-1-59414-775-3 (alk. paper)
ISBN-10: 1-59414-775-2 (alk. paper)
1. Murder—Investigation—Fiction. 2. New York (State)—Fiction. I. Title.
PS3603.O5468P43 2009
813′.6—dc22 2009013150

First Edition. First Printing: August 2009.

Published in 2009 in conjunction with Tekno Books and Ed Gorman.

Printed in the United States of America
1 2 3 4 5 6 7 13 12 11 10 09

Peace, Love, and Murder

Chapter 1

It was Monday morning, and Carl and Ronnie were bickering in the back of my cab. Just like they did every single other day of the week.

"Yeah, but how do you know?" Ronnie said. I glanced in the rearview mirror to see him jab Carl in the arm. "How do you know the Bible is the word of God? I mean, you weren't there. Maybe the Bible was written by a couple of stoned hippies on the beach."

Carl snorted. "They didn't have hippies back then. Or pot to get stoned with, neither."

"Okay, then two drunk shepherds or Pharisees or whatever. They had wine, didn't they? Didn't Jesus, like, invent it or something at some wedding?"

Carl didn't know how to argue with that.

These two lived in the same trailer park and worked at the same quick-change lube shop in town. And they'd both lost their licenses for DUI, which is why I picked them up each morning and drove them to work—they had a standing order with the Sunbeam Taxi Company. But that was all they had in common. Ronnie was a stoned-out slacker with stringy hair whose idea of fun was poking holes in Carl's political and religious beliefs. Carl looked like a trucker, right down to his plaid shirt and Mack bulldog cap. He was easily baffled and hid his bafflement with red-faced belligerence.

"Listen, you skinny punk—" he began.

I glanced in the mirror again to watch him puff up as he tried to formulate a clever insult to Ronnie's personal hygiene. But I forgot about the pair of them when I saw the deputy's car behind me. I checked the speedometer. Damn. Twelve miles over the limit. I eased my foot off the gas pedal, but the cop lights came on anyway.

I pulled onto the shoulder, next to the post-harvest remnants of a cornfield. We were in the central New York farmland about eight miles outside the college town of Rhodes. The gloomy early-November morning had just turned a whole lot gloomier.

"What the hell?" Ronnie said. He twisted around in his seat. "Oh, Jesus, Bo. You're gonna make us late for work."

"Don't take the Lord's name in vain," Carl said, looking back too. "But you've got a point there, Ronnie. We shouldn't have to pay if the driver can't get us there on time."

"Man's right about that," Ronnie said.

Listen to the two of them, I thought, singing harmony all of a sudden. Ronnie and Carl had never agreed on anything in their lives. But with me to gang up on, suddenly they were best buddies.

I watched the patrol car. The deputy fiddled with a clipboard, taking his time. A few cars crawled by, their occupants craning to peer at me like I was some gory accident victim instead of a guy who'd got caught in a speed trap. Some joker in a vintage Camaro grinned and gave me a thumbs-up. *Could've been you, pal.*

This was bad. I'd only been driving the cab for two months—I started a couple of weeks after I came back to town—and I'd already got slapped with one ticket. The fare had been in a hurry, and when that light turned yellow, I'd tapped the accelerator—barely tapped it—to try and make it through before the red. I did make it, too, although the Statie who pulled me over didn't agree. That was one moving violation. Two more, and I'd lose my taxi license.

In the back, Carl and Ronnie turned up the volume of their chorus, now singing the refrain that somehow I owed them money for making them punch in late.

"Shut up," I said. "Here comes the cop."

The deputy was a small guy, slim, not even five-five. The little cops are usually the mean ones, which meant a ticket for sure, not to mention a long delay out of pure spite. Then I looked again. This deputy wasn't a *he*—it was a woman. I sat up a little straighter. Maybe, just maybe, I still had a chance. I rolled down the window, ready to turn on the charm.

Which, I saw a moment later, would be exactly like trying to lavish charm on a slab of marble. She responded to my smile with a flinty-eyed stare, squinting at me from under her broad-brimmed hat. A scowl creased her forehead, and she held her mouth tight, like she'd tasted something bad and was trying not to show it. Her nametag read *T. Hauser.*

"Good morning, Deputy Hauser," I said.

"License and registration." Her voice sounded like a schoolteacher canceling recess. "I'll need to see your cabbie's license, too."

Cabbie. Man, I hate that word. I wondered how Deputy Hauser would like being called a "coppie." But I smiled and said, "Sure thing." I pulled my wallet out of the back pocket of my jeans, handed her my license, then reached across and opened the glove compartment. It was crammed with junk—empty cellophane wrappers, dirty napkins, even a crushed paper coffee cup. Those other drivers were a bunch of damn slobs. Maybe it was the Army training, but I couldn't stand having my personal space full of disorganized junk.

"I'll have it for you in a minute," I said over my shoulder. "This isn't my usual cab."

Stony silence confirmed the terrific impression I was making.

I pulled out handful after handful of trash, tossing it on the floor. At the bottom of the compartment was the registration. I gave it to her. Then I slid my taxi license from its place on the sun visor.

"License, registration, cab license. All there." I tried the charming smile again.

She scowled and walked back to her car.

"Well, Bo," Carl piped up from the back. "Thanks to you, looks like we'll be, oh, 'bout a hour late. That's seven-fifty you owe us. Each."

"Can it, Carl," I said. "This will only take a couple of minutes. She'll write out a ticket, lecture me a little, and we'll be on our way."

"This is terrible," Ronnie said. His voice sounded strange, high-pitched, and he was jiggling his leg against the back of my seat. "What did you have to get pulled over for, huh?"

"Will you please stop?" I said. "I told you, we'll be back on the road in a few minutes."

"No, I mean it—this is *terrible.* I hate cops. They always make me feel like I done something wrong. Now I'm gonna be a nervous wreck all day."

"Not to mention losing pay for being late, no fault of your own," Carl said.

"Did you see the way she looked at me? All squinty-eyed, like I was some kinda criminal."

"You're nuts," Carl said. "She didn't look at you at all."

Ronnie's fidgety leg was going so hard it shook the cab. "I can't take this," he said. He opened the door, lurched out, and took off running across the mowed-down cornfield.

"What the hell does he think he's doing?" I opened the door and got out far enough to shout across the car. "Ronnie! Get back here!"

He kept going, his skinny arms pumping as he hoofed it

across the field. And right behind him, running like an Olympic sprinter, chased Deputy Hauser. I think she yelled "halt" once before she tackled him. For a small woman, she took him down hard. I could almost hear his *oof!* as he hit the ground.

"Crazy," Carl commented.

"You know, I'm starting to think you might be right about that hour. Here," I handed him my cell phone, "why don't you call your boss?"

While Carl phoned in, I watched the scene in the cornfield. Ronnie was face down in the corn stubble, the deputy more or less kneeling on his back as she cuffed him. A moment later, she stood and yanked him to his feet. He looked dazed, like he'd just woken up in an unfamiliar room—or an unfamiliar cornfield. They walked back to the cruiser, Deputy Hauser holding Ronnie's arm. She folded him into the back seat and closed the door. Then she got into the front and started talking on her radio.

I got back in my cab and closed the door. After Ronnie's weird behavior, I wasn't going to give her even half a reason to look funny at me. Carl handed back my phone. "Boss's pretty mad," he said. "Says cars are lining up outside, and just one guy there to do oil changes." He shook his head sorrowfully, then looked out the window and, for once, didn't say another word.

That deputy was taking her time. I looked in the rearview mirror; she was still on her radio. I thought about calling Ryan, my boss, to let him know what was taking so long, but I didn't want to tell him I'd been stopped unless I had to. Maybe, with Ronnie hurling himself out of the cab and into the police car like some greasy-haired sacrificial lamb, I'd get off with a warning. Twelve miles over the limit had to be a lot less interesting than whatever Ronnie thought he was running from.

Deputy Hauser's face materialized at my window. She didn't say anything, just peered inside. Her sharp-eyed gaze swept across the interior—me, Carl, the mess from the glove compartment. I felt like a zoo animal being observed in a mockup of its natural habitat. When she looked behind my seat, where Ronnie had sat, a grim little smile spread itself across her face.

"Out of the cab," she said. "You in the back first."

That set Carl grumbling again. Then he cut himself off with a gasp and said, "Oh, my dear Lord."

"What? What is it, Carl?" I asked, but he heaved himself outside.

"You stay where you are," the deputy said to me. "And keep both your hands on that steering wheel."

Before I could figure out what was going on, a car appeared on the horizon, heading toward us from the direction of town, red lights flashing. Deputy Hauser had called for backup. What did she think she'd pulled over—some getaway taxi full of violent criminals? A bad feeling plunked itself down in my gut as the new patrol car pulled across the road and parked at an angle in front of the cab. A deputy emerged. This one was a big guy, with a double chin and a gut that hung over his belt. He hitched up his pants as he walked toward us.

Carl was spread-eagled against the cab, his hands on the roof, while the female deputy patted him down. I watched his face through the window. His eyes were closed, but his lips moved. I couldn't tell whether he was rehearsing an explanation for his boss or maybe praying.

Carl straightened and stepped back. Deputy Hauser appeared at my window again. "Your turn."

I got out of the cab, assumed the position. She frisked me in her efficient, no-nonsense way, but her hands were surprisingly gentle, making me think, absurdly, of a bird trying out its wings before its first flight. I heard a car go by, slowly. What a great advertisement for Sunbeam Taxi—the bright yellow cab surrounded by cop cars, its driver getting frisked by the side of the road. Ridership would be way up.

"Okay." Deputy Hauser stood up. I went over to join Carl.

"What did you see?" I asked him. "What was on the floor back there?"

He shook his head. "That stupid stoner."

Deputy Hauser was rummaging around on the floor of the cab, where Ronnie had been. When she straightened, she was holding something pinched between her thumb and forefinger, her other fingers sticking straight out, just barely grasping the corner of a plastic baggie about a quarter full of some kind of dried herb. Only this wasn't just some kind of herb. "Stupid stoner" was right. Ronnie had ditched his stash in the cab—my cab—before heading for the hills.

The deputy looked at me, sizing me up. I could almost read what she was thinking: Birkenstocks, jeans, sweatshirt, ponytail—probably another stoner. She smiled for the second time that morning; I decided I preferred the scowl.

"I'm going to have to search this vehicle," she said. "Go back and wait by my cruiser." She pointed the way with her chin. "And don't try anything stupid like your friend did. Deputy Webb here will be keeping an eye on you." The big cop hitched up his pants again and escorted us to the patrol car.

I glared through the window at Ronnie, who kept his head down. His jittery leg was going like the drummer in a speed metal band.

Leaning against the passenger-side fender, I watched Deputy Hauser go through the cab while the other cop stood between us and the cornfield, his hand resting casually on his gun. She crawled across the back seat, looking under the mats, shining her flashlight under the seats. Irritation bubbled up inside me. These cops had no right to treat me like a criminal just because Ronnie got stupid. The whole thing was a colossal waste of time—there was nothing illegal in the cab.

Deputy Hauser pulled something from under the driver's seat and held it up to the light. A pint bottle. Oh, man. Who'd left that in there? Somebody was drinking on duty—Ryan wasn't going to be happy about that.

Then it hit me. I was in bigger trouble than I'd thought. Even though it wasn't my bottle, even though I could pass any breathalyzer test A+ one hundred percent, there was still an empty booze bottle in my cab. If I got hit with a speeding ticket *and* an open container violation, that was it for me. No taxi license, no job.

Deputy Hauser continued her search. Nothing in the trash from the glove compartment seemed to interest her. The big deputy yawned and scratched his neck as she popped the latch to look in the trunk. She walked around to the back of the cab, but the lid seemed stuck. She heaved at it a couple of times before it flew open.

"Jesus Christ!" she yelled. I thought the trunk lid had whacked her in the chin and started forward to see if she was okay. "Stay where you are!" She whirled around to face us, her gun drawn. She held it straight out in front of her, both arms braced, pointing it first at me, then Carl, then back at me. I half-raised my hands, palms out, in what I hoped was a calming gesture.

The big deputy stood there, gaping. He still had his hand on his gun, but he didn't take it out of the holster.

Behind me, Carl was whimpering. She swung the pistol his way, and I took a step to the right, to get between him and the gun. "Take it easy," I said.

"On the ground, now! Both of you! Face down, hands on your heads. Now—I mean it!"

"What the hell, Trudy?" asked the other deputy. He still hadn't pulled his gun.

"All right," I shouted to her. "We're cooperating." From

behind me came more whimpering. "Get down, Carl, like she said," I spoke low over my shoulder, watching the deputy and trying to make my voice soothing. "I'll stand here till you're down safe. Just do what she says and you'll be fine."

"Okay." He sounded like a terrified three-year-old. Seconds passed. I locked eyes with the female cop. Even from twenty feet away, I could see the gun shaking. "Okay, Bo," Carl said. "I'm down."

I dropped to my knees, maintaining eye contact for as long as I could before I stretched out my full length in the dirt and placed my hands on the back of my head. I could hear Carl mumbling; he was definitely praying now: ". . . hallowed be thy name . . ."

Boots appeared in my limited field of vision. "Don't move," said the female cop. "Don't even breathe." She raised her voice. "Mel, what the hell are you, a goddamn scarecrow? Quit standing there and cuff these suspects."

Suspects?

". . . on earth as it is in heaven . . ."

The boots disappeared, and I heard the car door open. A second later one hand, then the other, was jerked roughly behind my back. I felt a cold metal pinch as the cuffs clicked closed.

I shifted my head a little to get my mouth out of the dirt. I couldn't imagine what might be in the trunk to freak her out like this. Not unless whoever owned that pint bottle had a whole bar—or Christ, maybe some kind of illegal pharmacy—in there. Maybe this was what zero tolerance felt like.

The deputy got on her radio. "This is car 26 again. We got a 12-77 out here."

". . . and lead us not into temptation . . ." Carl's mumblings were getting louder; I couldn't hear the dispatcher's reply.

"Yes, damn it, you heard me right. Code twelve-seven-seven."

"For thine is the kingdom and the power and the glory forever . . ." Carl passed *amen* and started right in again. "Our Father, who art in heaven . . ."

"Trudy," said the other cop. "You called in a 12-77? But that's a—"

"That's a goddamn homicide, Mel. Go and look for yourself. There's a dead body in the trunk of that cab!"

Chapter 2

There's nothing like spending an hour in the back of a police car, handcuffed and alone, to make you feel a little paranoid. Outside, cops milled around like ants at a picnic. Reporters set up camp across the road, as close as the police would let them. An ambulance arrived, then still more cops. There were so many flashing lights it looked like the midway at the New York State Fair. I was cold, dirty, and getting damn sick of being cooped up.

At first, I was glad they'd put Carl in the other car with Ronnie—I wasn't exactly in the mood to listen to either of them whine. Carl must've half-chewed Ronnie's ear off for that stunt he'd pulled. But as I watched all those cops going about their jobs—taking photos of the trunk, tearing apart the cab, sifting through the dirt at the side of the road—I started wondering. If they'd left Carl and Ronnie together, it must mean neither of them was a suspect. Of course not. They were just fares catching a ride to work. But could the cops think *I* might have killed whoever was in the trunk?

I closed my eyes, wishing I could stretch my legs. The truth is, I can't stand tight spaces, so being stuck in the patrol car, unable to get out or even crack open a window, was not helping my general state of mind. Soon, the cops would start asking me questions, and I had no answers. Saying "I don't know" over and over again didn't exactly strike me as the world's best alibi. Oh, man. Did I need an alibi? This was worse than bad. They were going to try to pin this thing on me just because I happened to be in the wrong place at the wrong time, looking like a donkey in need of a tail.

At that thought, the door beside me flew open. A hand reached in and grabbed my arm.

"Out." Deputy Hauser tugged at me.

"What's going on?" I asked, but she didn't answer, just looked at me like I was a cockroach she'd found in her soup and tugged again. It's damned awkward getting out of a car when you can't use your hands, and with her pulling at me I almost fell sideways into the dirt. It felt good, though, to unfold my legs after being crammed into that back seat so long. The morning had warmed up some, not much, and the thick clouds looked ready to let go of some icy rain.

A movement across the street caught my attention. One of the reporters had lifted a camera with a foot-long telephoto lens and was pointing it at me. I turned my head. The last thing I needed was a picture of me—handcuffed and being manhandled by a deputy half my size—gracing the front page of tomorrow's *Rhodes Chronicle*.

A cop broke away from the crowd by the cab and sauntered toward us. He was a bulldog of a man, with a barrel chest and bowed legs, and I recognized him from the newspaper: Victor Ianelli, Chief of the City of Rhodes Police Department. What was he doing here, I wondered, way out in the country? We were several miles outside his jurisdiction.

Ianelli came up to us beaming like a politician on the campaign trail. He offered his hand, then grimaced, half-embarrassed, when he realized I couldn't shake it. He glared at the deputy, who was still holding my arm.

"Trudy, why don't you take the cuffs off this gentleman?"

Her grip on my arm turned painful. "But . . ."

"But nothing. At this time, he's a witness, not a suspect."

I was so pleased to be labeled a mere witness and to have a chance to get out of those damn handcuffs that I almost didn't notice the *at this time.*

The deputy didn't say anything else, just heaved an exasperated sigh and complied.

I rolled my shoulders a couple of times and swung my arms back and forth. Ianelli extended his hand again, and this time I shook it, returning his firm, in-charge grip. I glanced across the street to see the reporter lower his camera and turn back to his colleagues.

"We've got a few questions to ask you," the chief said. "I'll leave you in the capable hands of one of my detectives. Shouldn't take more'n a few minutes. Trudy, can you take notes?"

"I—" She scowled, mad he'd asked her to play secretary. Or maybe that scowl was just her natural expression. "Sure, Chief."

Chief Ianelli went over to the cab and spoke to a guy in a mud-brown suit, who nodded and walked back to us alone. The detective was tall and thin, mid-thirties, with sparse brown hair and a pencil moustache that made his mouth look too wide for his face. He introduced himself as Detective Plodnick. He didn't offer to shake hands as the Chief had done, but he didn't seem overtly hostile, either. I was starting to feel a little more relaxed.

Plodnick returned my driver's license and cab license, then started right in with the questions.

"Your license says Bo Forrester. That your full name?"

"Yes."

"Bo's not short for something?"

I looked at him sharply. Had they dug that up already? But there was no trace of laughter in his eyes. "Like what?"

"I don't know. Beaumont, Beauregard?"

"No. Like I told you, that's my full, legal name. No middle name, either."

"Okay. And is the address on these documents current?"

I said it was, stuffing both licenses into my back pocket.

He nodded, then cocked an eyebrow at Deputy Hauser, who produced a notepad from somewhere and began scribbling in it.

"When's the last time you drove this vehicle?" Plodnick asked.

"Couple of weeks ago, I think. At least that."

"So you didn't drive it Saturday?"

"No. I had an afternoon shift that day. But not in this car."

"Any idea who did drive it then?"

"No. You'll have to ask Ryan. Ryan Pullanksy—that's my boss. He keeps a roster of who drives which car each shift."

Plodnick peered at Deputy Hauser's notepad. "You keeping up, Trudy? You need that name spelled out?"

"I got it." She held her mouth in a thin, tight line, like she was trying to dam up more words that threatened to burst out. But I wasn't worrying about her so much any more. I was thinking that I hadn't driven that cab on Saturday—and Ryan's records would prove it.

Plodnick turned back to me. "Who would have access to this cab?"

"Anyone at the taxi company. Anyone walking by, even, who knew how to hot-wire a car. The garage isn't locked, because we're open round the clock, but of course the dispatcher can't always keep an eye on the whole place."

He nodded. "And is it standard procedure to check the cars before you start out? This morning, for example, what did you do?"

"Checked the fluids—gas, oil, wiper fluid—and made sure that the lights and the brakes worked okay."

"So you wouldn't necessarily look in the trunk at the start of a shift?"

I shook my head. "No reason to. I only open the trunk when

a passenger has bags to put in it."

I was liking this line of questioning. It showed that I wasn't the only one who had access to the cab, that I hadn't been responsible for its contents. Question by question, I was getting myself off the hook. Then Plodnick switched topics.

"What were you doing on Saturday evening, say, between six o'clock and midnight?"

"Is that when—?"

"Just answer the question, please."

I thought back. "I was home all evening. Reading a book. I went to bed early—must've been around ten, ten-thirty."

"Was anyone with you? Any friends stop by?"

"No, but if you want someone to confirm I was there you can ask my downstairs neighbor. Irene Boothroyd. She's got ears like a bat." He stared at me like he didn't get it. "You know," I tapped my ear, "supersonic hearing. She'd probably tell you she could hear me turn each page."

As if to illustrate my point, Deputy Hauser flipped a page on her notepad with a loud rustle. Plodnick looked startled for a second, then took another tack.

"Any idea how a dead body could get into the trunk?"

"None at all. If I'd known anything about it, I'd have called you guys, not driven all over Thomson County with a body in the trunk."

The detective nodded and ran a finger along his thin moustache. A van from a Syracuse TV station pulled over near the reporters across the street, and he turned to look at it.

The second he turned, Deputy Hauser launched herself between us. She would have got right in my face if she hadn't been a good nine inches too short. "Can you identify the deceased?" She blurted out the question fast, like one long word.

Plodnick's head snapped back to us. "Damn it, Trudy—" he

started, but I interrupted him. I'd had about enough of this two-bit little deputy acting like she thought she was Dirty Harry.

"Identify? I don't even know whether it's a man or a woman. I've been sitting in that damn patrol car hoping that it wasn't some kid who crawled in playing hide and seek and couldn't get out again."

A shadow of disappointment crossed her face. She'd been trying to catch me with a clever question, tricking me into revealing something I shouldn't know. Probably got the idea from a TV show. She slunk back a step and wrote something on her pad.

Plodnick shot her an annoyed look, then turned to me. "It's a man. Since Trudy here asked," he glared at her again, "would you be willing to take a look at the body, see if you recognize him?"

I had to think about that one for a minute. I've seen my share of dead bodies, but that was in the Army. It's one thing—not a pleasant thing, either—to come across the remains of some sniper in a jungle or crumpled behind a mud wall. But this was home, the town where I grew up. Corpses weren't supposed to appear in your back yard or in the trunk of your car. I wasn't sure I wanted to stare death in the face again. Not here, not in Rhodes. But maybe I could help. Maybe I could make this whole thing go away faster, get life in Rhodes back to its nice, quiet routine.

I nodded.

The EMTs were bringing out the stretcher, getting ready to load the body into the ambulance. We walked over to the cab, and I looked into the open trunk. A gray-haired man lay on his right side, neatly curled into a fetal position, his head pillowed on the spare tire. He wore a white undershirt and boxer shorts, with black socks. That was all. He'd been shot, but there wasn't much blood. A crimson rose of it blossomed on his chest. A little more had trickled from the hole dead center in his forehead. The back of his head, where the bullet had exited, was a pulpy, sticky-looking mess.

I stepped back, shook my head. "I've never seen him before."

The EMTs went to work transferring the body to the stretcher.

Plodnick took the notepad from Deputy Hauser and flipped through its pages. "I think that's all I've got for now. We'll need you to come by the station some time to sign a statement—tomorrow or the next day. That's Rhodes PD, by the way, not the Sheriff's office."

"What do you mean Rhodes PD?" Deputy Hauser grabbed for her notepad, but Plodnick was quicker and she missed it. "This is a county case. I'm the one who found the body."

"That's not your decision, is it? This crime was most likely committed inside city limits. Rhodes is cooperating with the county sheriff, of course, but Chief Ianelli says it's our jurisdiction. And besides," he glanced at me, "I don't think it's appropriate to discuss the matter in front of civilians."

She glared at him, mouth open. Then she snapped her mouth shut, wheeled around, and strode back toward her patrol car.

"Unprofessional." Plodnick shook his head. "We might need to ask you further questions as the investigation proceeds. What's the best way to reach you?" He wrote down my cell phone number as I gave it to him. "You'll be available, I assume. You're not planning to leave Thomson County in the next week or two?"

I wasn't, but I didn't like the idea of having the cops dictate my travel plans. "Are you telling me I'm a suspect?"

"We have no suspects at this time." There it was again: *at this time*. He said it exactly like he was giving a press conference. Then he smiled a colorless smile and went off to question Carl.

★ ★ ★ ★ ★

Chief Ianelli offered Carl and me a ride back to Rhodes. Ronnie remained in the custody of the Sheriff's department, facing charges of marijuana possession. He looked forlorn in the back of the deputy's patrol car, his head down, stringy hair hiding his eyes. I'd have felt sorry for him if he hadn't been stupid enough to bring his pot into my cab. Carl and I got into the back seat of a City of Rhodes patrol car; Chief Ianelli sat in front, and a uniformed cop drove. A plexiglass barrier separated us from the front seat.

Carl started talking before the driver had pulled all four wheels onto the road. "Sure was some morning." He shook his head. "All that trouble, and I'm the only one who's innocent."

I looked at him, doing his best impression of a newborn babe—one with jowls and cheek stubble in a Mack trucker's cap. "What do you mean, 'the only one'?"

"I'm an innocent bystander. Ronnie got caught red-handed with pot—again. And you got a speeding ticket."

"Now that you mention it, that's the only good thing to happen this morning."

"Huh?"

"That deputy forgot to write out a ticket. No black mark on my license." It was a small blessing, but I'd take it.

"That so?" Carl contorted his face into his thinking expression—scrunching up his forehead and pursing his lips, like he was trying to work out a complicated math problem in his head. Then he let out a big sigh.

"I'm gonna tell," he said.

"What are you talking about?"

"About the ticket. I wanna show these officers that I'm a reliable witness. I hold the law in great respect, and I don't hide nothing."

"Carl, don't do that. There's nothing to tell. That deputy had a choice to give me a ticket or not, and she chose not to."

"You said she forgot."

"Hell, how do I know whether she forgot or changed her mind? Maybe she looked deep into my baby-blue eyes and had a change of heart." *Yeah, right.* "Or maybe that dead body made her realize that the law has more important things to do than hand out tickets to someone going a little fast on a clear stretch of straight road."

I couldn't believe I was having this conversation. It was like I'd taken Ronnie's place, like it was physically impossible to sit next to this guy and not get into some idiotic argument. Carl made his math-problem face again, pinching his lower lip between his thumb and forefinger, then turned to me.

"I'm gonna tell."

I wanted to wring his beefy neck, but strangling a fellow witness in the back of a police cruiser didn't seem like my brightest idea.

Carl leaned forward and knocked on the partition. Chief Ianelli slid open the window.

"I want to report a crime," Carl said.

"Oh yes? And what's the nature of this crime?"

"Well, it's not really a crime so much as a . . . whadayacallit . . . a citation?"

"A violation?" the chief suggested.

"Yeah, that's it. Anyway, seeing as I'm a honest, God-fearing citizen and all, I hate to see someone get away with a violation." He sneaked a look at me. "Even if usually he's a pretty good guy."

"Thanks," I said.

"So anyway," said Carl. "Bo here got pulled over for speeding. I don't know how fast he was going, seeing as I was engaged in a thea . . . thea . . . whadayacallit . . . about God and the Bible and stuff?"

"Theological," the chief provided.

"That's it, a theological debate with my fellow passenger." He nodded, liking the way that sounded. "Trouble is, what with the excitement of finding the body and all, the deputy forgot to write up the speeding ticket. And I'm a man that can't abide seeing the law broken."

I thought of pointing out that Carl could be driving himself to work every day if he'd had the same respect for the law against drunk driving, but I just glared at him.

Chief Ianelli nodded. "Well, sir, I appreciate that attitude. We in law enforcement rely upon an alert public to help us uphold the laws of the State of New York. But to tell you the truth, the violation you're reporting is outside my jurisdiction. It's a county matter, not City of Rhodes."

"Oh." This information presented Carl with an obstacle that it took him nearly a whole minute to think his way around. "So I should call the Sheriff?"

The chief shifted his gaze to me, then—I swear—he winked. "Don't worry about that. We'll take care of your report. Thank you for being a concerned citizen." He turned to face the front of the car.

Carl puffed out his chest so far it almost burst the buttons of his flannel shirt. He tried a couple of times to renew the conversation, asking me what the body had looked like and who I thought it was—he was put out that I'd been allowed to look into the trunk and he hadn't. I ignored him, watching the scenery go by. After a mile or so, he started humming to himself, and I was treated to a nasal, off-key rendition of "Amazing Grace" all the way back to Rhodes.

CHAPTER 3

After we dropped off Carl at the Qwikee-Change—he climbed out of the patrol car like the president disembarking from a limo—we headed for the Sunbeam Taxi Company, on a side street just off the main commercial drag. The lot was more crowded than usual; it looked like every cab in the fleet was there. Plus the place was swarming with cops. They were searching cabs, rooting through the trash, going over the ground inch by inch with the care of someone hunting for a lost contact lens.

A couple of them looked at me funny when I got out of the police car, but Chief Ianelli shook my hand again as he said goodbye, and they lost interest. That magic Ianelli handshake—I wished I could save up a couple for future use. The chief went to talk to some guy in a suit—another detective, I guessed—and I climbed the wooden steps to the twelve-year-old "temporary" trailer that housed Ryan's office. I knocked once before I stuck my head inside.

"You're back!" Ryan tossed a crumpled-up piece of paper through the basketball hoop over his trashcan. "What the hell happened?"

He looked tired. Ryan Pullansky's a big guy: six-one, which is about my height, but with linebacker-broad shoulders and a neck the size of a tree trunk. Sitting at the overflowing desk, in the tiny, fake wood-paneled office, he seemed too big for his surroundings, like a grizzly bear in a kid's playhouse.

"It was surreal." I sat down in the wooden chair facing Ryan's desk and related the morning's events, from getting pulled over to being questioned by Detective Plodnick.

"Plodnick, huh? I know him. His big brother Danny was on my football team in high school. Used to play wide receiver. Damn, he was fast. You remember Danny?"

I shook my head. In high school, I'd been pretty much a loner. Definitely not part of the jock crowd.

"Anyway, Phil Plodnick—the one who's a cop now—didn't make the cut first time he went out for football, when he was a freshman. That was my senior year. Phil was kind of a pipsqueak. Still is, now that I think about it. But he was real mad he didn't get on the team—used to make a big deal of sitting on the wrong side of the bleachers and rooting for the other guys. That's the kind of sore loser he was."

"He didn't seem too bad." He'd been a lot easier to deal with than that scowling female deputy.

"Yeah, well, I hope he doesn't show up here. I wouldn't trust the guy farther than I could throw him." Actually, Ryan could probably pick up skinny Detective Plodnick one-handed and toss him halfway across town without pausing for breath.

A uniformed cop passed the window. "What are all those cops doing?" I asked.

"Looking for evidence. They say they want to eliminate the possibility that the guy in your trunk was killed on the premises. That's how they put it: 'eliminate the possibility.' " He craned his neck to look outside. "It seems to me more like they're looking for proof he was murdered right here. There's a ton of cops out there, and they've been here over an hour. How the hell long does it take to find nothing?"

Good question. While I pondered it, he continued. "Not only that, they made me call in all my drivers. Every single one. They want to search all the cabs. Do you realize what that means? I got no one working right now. I can't take any calls. Lakeside must be loving this."

Lakeside Livery and Cab Service was the big transportation company in town, three times the size of Sunbeam. Its owners had been trying for years to buy Ryan out, but he refused to sell the company his father had started.

"Did all the drivers come back?"

"Everybody but Dinesh. He was up in Syracuse, taking a fare to the airport, when the cops arrived." Syracuse was about sixty miles north of Rhodes, half the journey via two-lane country roads that twisted up and down hills, past farms, and through small villages. "I told him to drop off the fare and come straight back. He should be here any minute."

"What else did they ask you? The cops."

"Mostly to stay in here and keep out of their way. I'm bored stiff and mad as hell, both at the same time. Weird feeling." He crumpled another piece of paper and scored another basket. "But they did want to know a couple of things, like what pick-ups we had in the Heights on Saturday night."

The Heights meant Manitoah Heights, a pricey neighborhood of huge old mansions on East Hill near Overton University. It was an enclave of business executives, university administrators, and several celebrity professors. If the victim was from that part of town, no wonder the cops were all over this case. I couldn't help thinking that the manpower wouldn't be quite as intense if the body had belonged to someone from the housing project across the street. "Yeah," I said, "they asked me about Saturday night, too. So who drove the cab that shift?"

Ryan's forehead furrowed. "No one. That's the hell of it. One of the taillights was busted, and Tony was out with flu half the week." Tony was Sunbeam's part-time mechanic. "He came in Saturday afternoon to make up some hours. Fixed it then. But I didn't put the cab back on the roster until this morning. When you took it out of here today, it was the first time anybody had driven that car for a week."

No wonder the cops were combing the garage. Today was Monday. If the cab hadn't been driven since last Monday and the murder was committed on Saturday night, then how did the body get inside?

Dinesh was back from Syracuse. He bounded into the office and dropped his trip sheet on Ryan's desk. Since there wasn't another chair, he lounged against the wall, his black hair brushing a three-year-old calendar from an auto-parts store. Despite the commotion outside, he was smiling. In fact, I can't remember ever seeing the guy without a grin on his face.

Dinesh Mehta graduated a few years back from Overton University, the bigger and more famous of Rhodes's two colleges. Like a lot of Overton grads, he didn't really want to leave after they handed him his diploma, so he'd stuck around, then stuck around a little longer—he was currently on his second master's degree. His parents called every week, demanding he come home to north Jersey and help them run their empire of motels and convenience stores, but they kept on paying his bills. Dinesh drove part-time for some spare cash, but mostly he spent his days trying to squeeze out every last drop of college life before somebody forced him to grow up. I had a dozen years on him, but we got along; we'd go out for a beer a couple of times a week after work. Now, he looked at Ryan and raised his eyebrows. "Quite a scene out there."

"You're not gonna believe—" Ryan began.

Dinesh held up a hand. "You don't have to tell me. I heard all about it on the radio."

"The radio?" Ryan looked alarmed. "Did they mention Sunbeam?"

"Not by name. When you called me in and then I heard the

news report on the way back, I put two and two together and got Sunbeam—the taxi in question had to be one of ours."

"Thank God they didn't mention the company," Ryan said. "That is not the kind of publicity I need."

"What else did the news say?" I asked.

"Not a lot. They gave the dead guy's name. Fred something. Davis, Davidson—no, Davies. It was Fred Davies. They said he lived in Rhodes and ran some foundation for artists. He'd been missing since Saturday night, never showed up at a fundraiser for his own arts foundation."

"Thank God," Ryan said again. Dinesh and I both looked at him.

"Not that he didn't show up. Just that I don't know him."

"So he missed a Saturday-night fundraiser." I looked at Dinesh. "That's the night the cops keep asking about. Did you drive then?" I was wondering if he'd seen anyone near the cabs that were awaiting repairs.

"Me?" Dinesh shook his head. "Heck, no. I was at a frat party. Dozens of witnesses saw me there." He grinned. "That is, if any of them could even remember Saturday night when they woke up Sunday morning. Good party."

A shout sounded outside, and several cops ran past the window, toward the garage.

Dinesh opened the door and went out onto the steps. "Looks like somebody found something."

Ryan and I rushed to the window, bumping heads as we craned to see into the open garage. Cops crowded together just inside the entrance, around a barrel that stored used motor oil. A uniformed cop was holding something over the barrel; thick, sludgy goop dripped off it.

"What the hell is it?" Ryan said.

I put a hand on his shoulder "That, I'm afraid, is a gun."

★ ★ ★ ★ ★

A few hours later I was waiting for Dinesh at the bar in Donovan's, our usual hangout. Donovan's was a popular pub and restaurant housed in a stately Victorian building, and the owners really played up the Olde Worlde look: pressed tin ceiling, marble-topped mahogany bar, brass rails everywhere, even flickering wall sconces that were supposed to look like gaslights. There weren't many customers at quarter to four in the afternoon, which was why I liked to come here. The place got too crowded once they unchained the nine-to-fivers from their desks.

I took a swig of my Saranac Caramel Porter and sighed, glad to be, for the first time that day, out of the vicinity of any and all police officers. Dinesh had taken off soon after the cops had found the gun, but I'd stayed with Ryan at the garage. Around two o'clock, Ryan had started pushing the cops to let him get some cars back on the road, and by two-thirty they'd given him the green light on that. Then Ventura, one of the full-time drivers, didn't show up for his shift at three. Ryan couldn't get in touch with him, so he'd been phoning around looking for someone else to pick up Ventura's shift when I'd left. The cops barely glanced at me as I walked off the site. It felt like a small miracle.

As far as I knew, they hadn't found anything else. And the pistol in the used oil barrel might not even be *the* gun; it could've been dropped in there any time during the last three weeks, since the last time the truck had come by to transport the used motor oil to the recycling facility. Sunbeam was in a busy part of town; people were always passing by, and the garage doors were always open. The gun could be unrelated to the murder. But that felt like wishful thinking.

I'd picked up one important detail: there were no bloodstains on the site. I was sure about that; leaving the lot I'd overheard one cop say to another, "So if there's no blood, then where was he killed?"

That was what I wanted to know, too. I'd ask Ryan to check the mileage on the cab's last trip sheet against what I'd written down at the start of my shift that morning. The two numbers should match. If they didn't, someone had taken that car off the lot since the light was fixed on Saturday—and we'd know how far it had been driven. That would give the cops a radius for finding the murder site, leaving (I hoped) Ryan, Sunbeam—and me—off any hook the cops were looking to hang someone on.

The door opened, and Dinesh entered the bar. He hung his jacket on the coat rack by the door, then came over and clapped me on the back. "I think you've got an admirer," he said in a stage whisper. "Of the female variety."

That was Dinesh. The world could get knocked off its axis, and he wouldn't care—wouldn't even notice—as long as there was a woman in sight. "Give it a rest, Dinesh."

"No, really. There's this cute blonde sitting all by herself at that table in the back, over by the window—and she's looking over here like she's starving and you're made out of food."

I didn't even turn my head. Instead, I hunched over the bar and picked at the label on my beer bottle.

"Buy her a beer," Dinesh urged.

"Listen, I've had a lousy day. Various cops pointed guns at me, threw me in the back of a patrol car, generally jerked me around, and told me not to leave the county. I am not in the mood to make small talk with some woman just because you think maybe she might be looking at me."

"Okay, then buy me one." He sat down and waved to the bartender, who was reading a thick textbook at the far end of the bar.

"Buy your own damn beer."

He did, ordering a Coors. "So," he started, "let me tell you about Saturday night's famous frat party . . ." I'm not sure why a twenty-six-year-old has any desire to go to those things, but he launched into his story with enthusiasm. I tried to listen, but I was distracted by that creepy feeling you get when you know someone's watching you, like three dozen tiny spiders crawling on the back of your neck.

After a couple of minutes, the feeling got to be too much. So I looked. I didn't go for subtlety, just turned to see this woman by the back window.

A second before we made eye contact, she whipped her head around and stared outside. I looked her over: short blonde hair, black turtleneck, jeans. Slim, but not without curves where they should be. She was attractive, but I didn't know her.

And I still wasn't in the mood to make small talk with her. I turned back to the bar.

"See that?" Dinesh was grinning. "She's playing a little flirtation game with you. Go on." He nudged my arm. "Buy her a beer."

"You're awfully eager for me to waste my beer money on other people tonight."

Dinesh shrugged and went back to his story, which involved a chocolate pudding-filled wading pool and several young women in their underwear.

I still had that crawling feeling along the back of my neck. The more I tried to ignore it, the worse it got, assaulting my skin like an itchy wool scarf. This was ridiculous. I turned toward the blonde, twisting on the barstool to make my movement even more obvious this time.

She made another fast head turn and kept her face averted. I returned my attention to my beer bottle. It was empty, so I interrupted the bartender's studying to order another. Maybe Dinesh was right; maybe she was flirting with me. It felt like something out of junior high. All she needed was a giggling girlfriend to come over and ask me if I liked her as a friend or *liked her* liked her.

The third time I turned, she was gone.

"Oh, man," said Dinesh. "You missed your chance. You should've seen her when she stood up and put on her jacket. Nice. And it was a motorcycle jacket, too. She's probably one wild chick."

He shook his head. Dinesh's main ambition in life seemed to be hooking up with "wild chicks." At least that explained his fascination with fraternity parties.

After another twenty minutes, the bar started to get packed with liberated office workers. The bartender closed his textbook and stowed it under the bar as the orders came flying at him. By the second time someone whammed into my back trying to push past, I was ready to go. So was Dinesh; he said he had a hot date with a pudding wrestler.

"I didn't know Monday was a hot date night."

He wiggled his eyebrows. "It is for me."

We went outside. Quarter past five, and already it was almost dark. Dinesh headed for his SUV, offering me a ride. But I didn't feel like going home yet, so I said goodbye and turned south, walking into the heart of the Crossing, Rhodes's downtown shopping district. The Crossing is a two-block stretch of Main Street that's been closed to cars so pedestrians can wander in and out of its boutiques, restaurants, bars, and coffee shops. It's paved with ornamental brick and dotted with benches, a playground, a bandstand, even a fountain in the summer. Tonight, yellow lights glowed from the windows of the shops that were still open and the restaurants that were just gearing up for business.

People were out, despite the chilly evening, rushing home from work or strolling arm in arm and stopping to read restaurant menus. A small crowd had gathered around a couple of musicians perched on the steps of the bandstand. A skinny white kid with dreadlocks and fingerless gloves strummed a guitar, accompanied on the harmonica by a black man old enough to be his grandfather. They sounded good: bluesy but not sad, playing for sheer love of the music. I pulled some coins out of my pocket and tossed them in the donation can. The harmonica player nodded, not missing a note.

While I listened, that prickly feeling crept up my neck again. Someone was watching me. I wheeled around and scanned the Crossing behind me, but I didn't see anyone. Just a man in an overcoat swinging his briefcase as he hurried north toward Borealis Street. As I turned back to the musicians, something caught my eye. A brass plaque on the door to an office building a few feet to my right displayed a familiar-looking name. I went over to get a closer look: The Davies Foundation for the Arts.

This was where the dead man had worked.

On an impulse, I tried the door, but it was locked. I went backward several steps and stared up at the building. Like most buildings on the Crossing, it was late-Victorian brick, flat-fronted with arched windows, four stories tall. A light shone in a third-floor window; the rest of the building was dark.

I thought about the gray-haired man crammed into the trunk of my cab. A few days ago, he'd sat at a desk in that building, perhaps looking out at the comings and goings on the Crossing, doing whatever it is people do at an arts foundation. And now he was lying on a slab in a morgue.

The shiver that ran through my limbs made me want to get out of the cold, and I ducked into a secondhand bookstore, one of the few shops on the Crossing that stayed open past five-thirty.

Maybe a good book would purge that image of Davies's corpse from my mind. I headed to the back of the store, where my two favorite sections were located: military history and travel essays. I spent maybe ten minutes browsing, but nothing caught my eye, so I decided it was time to walk home. I turned to leave.

And there she was. The blonde woman from Donovan's, over in the Reference section. As soon as I spotted her, she grabbed a book off the shelf and buried her face in it. But by her height and the way she stood, I knew who she was. This was too much.

I walked over to her. She held the book in front of her face like a shield. I put one finger on the top edge and lowered it; her eyes followed the pages.

"Deputy Hauser," I said. "Or is it okay to call you Trudy, since you're out of uniform?"

She looked up at me then. Her brown eyes rounded with fake surprise. "Oh," she said, "I didn't see you."

"That's because you keep turning your head every time I glance at you, like—gee, I don't know—like you're trying to avoid eye contact. You remind me of Fatty Dugan."

"Who?" Her face resumed its familiar scowl. Never compare a woman to someone called Fatty if you want to make friends—not that making friends was my goal here.

"This kid I knew growing up. Whenever we played hide and seek, he'd get into his hiding place, then squeeze his eyes tight shut. Seemed to think that if he couldn't see the kid who was 'it,' that kid couldn't see him, either." I caught her gaze and held it. "It doesn't work like that, you know. You don't suddenly become invisible when you look the other way."

She bit her lip and didn't reply. She looked angry, but so was I. I did not need an off-duty deputy tailing me.

"So was there something you wanted to ask me, or is stalking men a hobby of yours?"

"I came into this store to buy a book. I didn't even know you were here."

I gestured at the book in her hand. "That a good one?"

She jutted out her chin. "Yeah. I just might buy it."

"What's it about?"

"It's uh . . . uh . . ." She glanced at the title, then frowned at the strange characters. The book was in Russian.

She tossed it down on a table. "So I was keeping an eye on you. So what? I do want to ask you something." She looked past my shoulder, and I turned. A short guy with a beard and wire-rimmed glasses was watching us like we were a movie. Trudy jerked her head toward the door. "Let's go outside."

I shook my head. "You're not waving a gun at me now. I don't have to do a goddamn thing you want."

Her eyes narrowed, and she crossed her arms. "How'd you like to get a speeding ticket in the mail a day or two from now? Plus an open container citation?"

That shut me up. I didn't know whether she could mail me a ticket after the fact, but given the stakes—my job—I wasn't willing to take the chance. "Okay," I said. "But if I talk to you now, that's it. You've got to promise you won't keep holding that ticket over my head."

"All right. You have my word."

"Good. If you're lying, I swear I'll report you for harassment."

"*I* don't lie." She threw the sentence at me like an accusation, and I wondered what the hell she meant by it.

The guy with the wire-rimmed glasses had edged closer. She glared at him and said, "Get some popcorn, why don't you?" Then she stormed out the front door. I followed, taking my time. Outside, it was cold enough that I could see my breath, but she hadn't bothered to zip her leather jacket. She was sitting on a bench in the middle of the Crossing; I went over and sat beside her.

"All right," I said, "what do you want to know?"

"This morning, when you were going through the glove

compartment for the registration, you said you weren't driving your regular cab. I want to know why not."

"That's the reason you've been following me? Why didn't you just come over and ask? It's no big mystery." Despite myself, relief washed over me. I'd thought she was going to ask—I didn't know what, but something I couldn't answer. "My regular cab was scheduled for an oil change. Tony, the mechanic, was coming in to do a bunch of those today. So I got assigned a different cab. That's it—you can check with Ryan."

"Oh." Her eyes dimmed, like she'd heard disappointing news, which I suppose she had. She'd probably wanted me to tell her I'd switched cabs on purpose to get rid of the body I'd hidden in the trunk.

I stood up. "Any other questions? Let's clear them up now, so I can lose my shadow and try to have a halfway normal evening."

Her eyes regained their defiant look, and she lifted her chin. "Yeah. Why did you lie to Detective Plodnick?"

"Why did I . . . ? I didn't. I didn't lie to anyone."

"You did, and you know it. I know it too, so cut the innocent act."

She was fishing. Just like when she'd tried to trick me into identifying the body. I wasn't going to play this game. I shrugged and started walking back to the bookstore.

She jumped to her feet. "Don't you dare walk away from me!"

I kept going.

"Come back here," she was shouting now. "Rainbow!"

I froze. Wishing I hadn't heard her right. But I knew I had. Goddamn it. I spun around and went back to her, fast. I pulled myself up to my full height. I could see the part in her hair.

"Don't call me that."

"Why not? It's your name, isn't it? That's what it says on

your birth certificate."

"Yeah, that's what it says. But it's not my name."

She smiled an infuriating smile and didn't say a word.

"Just like I told the detective," I said, "my name is Bo Forrester. That's my full, legal name. I changed it. Wouldn't you?"

She poked my chest with her finger. "You held back information from a detective in a murder investigation. To me, that says you have something to hide."

"Oh, come on." I batted her finger away. "He didn't ask for my life history, just my name. Which I gave him."

"Something to hide," she repeated. "And I'm going to find out what it is. I saw you tonight. I saw you try to get into that office building, then stare up at the victim's window. What were you after?"

"Nothing. I just—" Why bother to explain? I was being hounded by a psychotic female deputy suffering under the delusion that she was Sherlock Holmes. She was going to jump at me every chance she got, like she'd jumped at me that morning when Plodnick turned his back. Then I remembered what Plodnick had said to her. "Wait a minute. You've got no right to be questioning me. This isn't even your case."

"It should be." She clenched her fists. "Rhodes PD muscled in on our jurisdiction. But I'm the one who found the body. I know you killed that man, and I'm going to be the one to bring you in. I'm going to follow you, and I'm going to watch you, and when you trip up, I'm going to be the one who slaps the cuffs on you." She poked my chest again. "Better watch your step, Rainbow."

One more poke, then she walked away, turning the corner at the end of the Crossing and disappearing on Manitoah Street. Dinesh had nailed it, I thought. This one was a wild chick, all right—as in crazy pain in the ass.

CHAPTER 4

Johnny Cash used to sing, "Life ain't easy for a boy named Sue." Let me tell you, that would be a piece of cake compared to life for a boy named Rainbow.

I lay in bed, trying unsuccessfully to sleep. I could still feel that deputy's sharp little finger poking my chest, still see the sneer on her face when she called me that name. She must have laughed herself silly when she discovered my birth certificate.

Okay, so it was the sixties and my parents were hippies, living on a commune just beyond the Rhodes city limits. And Rosie (that's my mother) saw a perfect rainbow arcing across a meadow right before the first labor pang hit. It's a nice story, but that doesn't make life any easier when you're a high school freshman and all of a sudden it's the eighties. In that decade, having a name like Rainbow was the equivalent of tattooing *Torment Me* across your forehead.

The nonstop ridicule taught me how to fight, something I never would have learned from the gentle people of the commune.

On my eighteenth birthday, I hitched a ride to the county courthouse in Rhodes and filed the papers to change my name. The clerk said I'd have to come back in a month to appear before a judge. When the time came, I stood in the dark-paneled courtroom, where a bald guy in a black robe sat at his high desk. As the judge put on his reading glasses, he started to ask why a young man like me would want to change his name, but then he saw *Rainbow Windsong Forrester* on my birth certificate. Cut himself off mid-question. He looked over his glasses and saw a tall, muscular kid with a buzzcut and a chip the size of Syracuse welded to his shoulder. Then he turned to my petition: Bo Forrester, no middle name. The judge nodded, signed my papers, and wished me luck.

So I'd been Bo Forrester—legally—a couple of years longer than I'd ever been Rainbow. I hadn't lied, despite what Deputy Trudy Hauser thought. I knew her type: insecure in her job because she wasn't one of the boys—and the boys never quit reminding her of it. So to build herself up, she used her job to bully people. She'd find a weakness and latch on to it, sucking it dry, like a tick on a dog's back, just to get herself all swelled up with someone else's misery.

She thought she'd found my weakness when she unearthed my given name. She was wrong. You don't survive high school with a name like Rainbow if you let it become a weakness. If she came after me again, she'd find that out.

On Tuesdays I work an afternoon shift, so I slept in. When I woke up at eight, my first thought was to get my hands on a newspaper. This was more difficult than you might think.

My downstairs neighbor Mrs. Boothroyd and I have an ongoing dispute over the paper. We both subscribe, but the geniuses in the subscription department of the *Rhodes Chronicle* haven't figured out how to deliver two actual newspapers to the same address. I've called them, Mrs. B. has called them, and we've both received all kinds of promises—but still only one paper. We've each threatened to cancel our subscription, and you'd think one of us would follow through. But that would mean one of us relinquishing our claim to the paper that does show up.

So every day we dance an uneasy newspaper tango. Mrs. B., a fifty-something widow, is the director of food services at the high school—the very image of a no-nonsense, just-so cafeteria lady, complete with hairnet and cat's-eye glasses. To tell the truth, I'm a little scared of her. She can't bear to have the paper's sections out of alignment, so I let her look at it first. Usually she reads it and turns it over to me; I scan the news and the opinion page and return it to her so she can do the crossword. Sometimes she'll forget when it's my turn, though, and more than once I've had to peel carrot parings or potato skins off a story to read it.

Today, I decided to splurge and spring for a copy from the box on the corner. I jogged down the stairs and opened the front door, and there was our paper, nestled on the porch step, all pristine and cozy in its plastic sleeve. I glanced up and down the street. No sign of Mrs. B.'s car. I was in luck. It was unlike her to go to work without our paper, but once in a while she'd leave early to give herself plenty of time to devise new culinary torments for unsuspecting teens. I grabbed the newspaper and took the stairs two at a time to my apartment.

I spread out the paper on the kitchen table. The quarter-page headline shouted *Local Philanthropist Murdered.* There was a photograph, too: I wasn't in it, but the picture showed the cab surrounded by cops, Sunbeam Taxi clearly legible on the side. Ryan would not be happy.

The headline and photo took up more space than the story. The police weren't giving much away. There was no mention of the fact that Davies was wearing only his underwear. No mention of my name, either—was that good or bad? And there was that phrase again: *no suspects at this time.* Reading those words was like hearing the cops say them the day before, their faces closed and neutral. A chill shivered through me.

Davies's wife Felicia had reported him missing Sunday evening. That day, she'd returned from a business trip to an empty house, the answering machine blinking with messages for

Fred, asking why he wasn't at the fundraiser. The poor woman must have been frantic.

The police did state that they suspected the motive for the murder was robbery: A cashier's check, made out to "cash" in the amount of $150,000, was missing. Quite a chunk of change. I've known more than one person who'd kill for a whole lot less.

I turned to the obituaries, careful not to mess up Mrs. B.'s pages. There he was: Frederick Roland Davies. A photo of Davies, dressed in a dark suit and smiling, accompanied the text. He looked like someone important, someone with the kind of presence that would dominate a boardroom. I'd had Fred Davies's type in my cab; he'd open his briefcase, shuffle papers, boot up his laptop, and carry on a cell phone conversation, all at the same time. Always asked for a receipt at the end. Usually a decent tipper.

The obituary gave a brief overview of his life. Davies, fifty-six, was an Overton alum. He'd spent most of his life in Chicago, running his family's media empire, but had taken early retirement and returned to Rhodes in 1998 to establish the Davies Foundation for the Arts. One of the DFA's pet projects was a rural retreat center called FLAiR (for Finger Lakes Artists in Residence), which offered free room and board for up to two months to artists who made it through the tough application process. The obituary listed a bunch of supposedly famous artists who'd been in residence at FLAiR, but none of the names meant anything to me. It ended by mentioning his widow Felicia and two adult children from a previous marriage: a daughter who lived in France and a son in Chicago.

There would be a memorial service the next afternoon, Wednesday, at the retreat center. The family asked that, in lieu of flowers, donations be made to the DFA "to continue Fred's lifelong mission to support and encourage visual artists."

That was it—the story of Fred Davies's life. It didn't seem like enough.

Fred Davies had been one of the lucky ones. He'd led a charmed life; born into money and educated in the best schools, he'd stepped into the high-powered job his family had reserved for him, prospered, then retired early to pursue what he loved. Anybody would've envied him. A life like that wasn't supposed to end in the trunk of a cab.

My cab. Even though I hadn't known him, in a strange way I felt responsible for the guy.

I thought about tomorrow's memorial service. If I went, maybe I could begin to understand what had happened to Fred Davies. I found a notebook in my desk drawer and wrote down the time of the service, the directions to FLAiR. The retreat center was past Brooktondale, way out in the woods. I'd have to get off work an hour early to go.

I was trying to reassemble the newspaper to Mrs. B.'s exacting standards when a pounding erupted on my door. A voice shouted, "Police! Open up!" I swear the first thing that crossed my mind was that Mrs. Boothroyd had called the cops to get her paper back. Then, glancing at the headline as I crammed the thing back into its plastic sleeve, I realized that my visitors were probably here about a different matter.

I ran over to open the door before they broke the damn thing down. On the landing were two guys in suits, four in uniforms. One of the suits was Plodnick, the detective who'd questioned me the day before. He waved a piece of paper in my face. "We have a warrant to search the premises."

No suspects at this time. The words echoed in my head as they filed in. With my name on a search warrant and a half-dozen cops crowding into my apartment, I wondered if "this time" had come. Bo Forrester, murder suspect. I didn't like the sound of it. Then again, I didn't have anything to hide. They could search the place, then go away and leave me the hell alone.

Plodnick barked a few orders, and the uniformed cops spread out and started pawing through my things. It's a small apartment—eat-in kitchen, living room, bath, one bedroom—and I don't have a lot of stuff, thanks to the nomadic lifestyle I'd led for the past dozen years. I hoped this wouldn't take long.

It's a weird sensation to watch strangers handle everything you own. I stood by the kitchen table, as a young cop with a shaved head pulled bags of lentils from a cabinet, and started to wonder whether they'd find anything. Nothing illegal, but something, well, embarrassing. Everyone's got dirty laundry stashed away, but it's not every day you have cops rooting through it. Literally. I pitied the guy who drew that job, going through the hamper in the bathroom. It had been a couple of weeks since I'd been to the laundromat.

Plodnick and the other detective stood in the middle of the living room, like the eye of a storm, while the chaos of the search whirled around them. I was hoping that the cops wouldn't stop to read the ninth-grade love letters from Missy Friedkin buried in my desk—God knows why I'd saved them—when Plodnick came over and picked up my notebook. His eyebrows rose as he read the directions I'd copied to FLAiR.

"You never told us you were acquainted with the deceased," he said.

"I'm not."

"Then why are you so interested in his memorial service?"

"I just wanted to pay my respects."

He dropped the notebook on the table, stretching his lips into a thin line and making his pencil moustache look about a mile long.

"Do you own a gun, Mr. Forrester?"

"No."

"But you do know how to operate one. In fact, you were Eighteen-Bravo in the Army, weren't you?"

So Trudy Hauser wasn't the only one dredging up ancient history. Eighteen-Bravo meant Special Forces weapons sergeant. Not exactly a job for pacifists. "Yes, I was a weapons specialist. Was. Past tense. I've seen a little too much of what guns can do to people."

"Oh, so you're now some big anti-gun liberal, huh? Must be that hippie upbringing. Peace, love, and harmony down on the commune, right?"

I waited for the crack about my name. I was sure it was coming; Plodnick looked like the sort of weasel who'd take pleasure in that. But he shifted gears—I was beginning to get a sense that a fast change of topic was his part of his interrogation style.

"Forensics hasn't finished the tests yet," he said, "but I'm betting we've got the gun."

No big surprise, since the gun was found so close to where the body had been dumped. I shrugged.

"Don't you want to hear about it?" he asked.

"Not really, no. I told you I don't own a gun."

He watched at me, a smirk stretching out beneath that mile-long moustache.

"I haven't touched one since I left the Army," I added.

Then, like I hadn't even spoken, he started telling me about the gun. "Mostly what you'd expect. No prints, thanks to dropping it in that oil barrel. Serial number filed off. But here's the interesting part. It's an M9, a Beretta 92FS. Sound familiar?"

"No." Of course it did, but I wasn't going to admit it.

"Come on, Forrester. You served in the Gulf in '91. You must have been issued one."

"In the first place, I was not the only person to serve in that war. In the second place, I carried a Colt 1911A1."

"Do you think I'm stupid? I was there, too. I know what

pistols they handed out."

"You were there, huh? What division?"

"My reserve unit was activated. We provided support for the twenty-fourth infantry."

"I was Special Forces. Everyone on my team carried a real pistol."

"Oh, yeah? And what's that?"

"A .45 auto, cocked and locked. It's got a hell of a lot more recoil, but it's faster and can drop a target with one solid hit. If you know what you're doing."

Plodnick was stroking his moustache, a faint smile beneath his fingers.

"What," I said, "you don't believe me? I'll give you the name of my CO and you can check it out for yourself."

"I will definitely get in touch with your commanding officer," Plodnick said. "But that's not what I was thinking."

I looked at him.

"I was thinking that you don't sound much like someone who'd never touch a gun."

He was right, damn it. I sounded like some macho idiot with a lifetime subscription to *Guns & Ammo.* The thought made me queasy. As soon as he started talking about guns, all the old habits, the old training kicked in. I didn't like the idea that gun talk, gun skills—anything about guns—was buried in some deep hole of my subconscious.

I must have looked like someone posing for a portrait entitled "Guilt," but I couldn't think of a way to explain. Just as I started to try, the door banged downstairs.

"Bo?" Oh, shit. Mrs. Boothroyd was back. "Have you got my paper?"

"I'll bring it right down," I called.

I grabbed the paper off the table, only to have Plodnick snatch it from my hands. "Nothing leaves this apartment until we're finished."

"Oh, for God's sake. It's just the newspaper. I borrowed it from my neighbor, and she wants it back."

"Bo?" Mrs. B.'s voice quavered up the stairs. "What's going on? I saw police cars. Are there *police* up there?"

"Let me give the lady back her paper," I said. "She doesn't need to see all this."

After a moment, Plodnick handed the paper to one of the uniforms, who pulled it out of the plastic and opened it, page by page, shaking out each sheet, watching for a cashier's check to flutter to the floor.

By the time Mrs. Boothroyd appeared in the doorway, panting a little from the climb, the newspaper was a mass of scattered pages on the floor. She frowned at the scene from behind her glasses as I dropped to my knees to put the sections back in order. "I'll have this for you in a minute, Mrs. B.," I said.

But she was staring past me into the kitchen. "Billy Thomas, is that you?"

The shaved-headed cop froze as if someone had pulled a gun on him. He turned slowly, looking ready to bolt. "Hi, Mrs. B."

"I don't know what you're up to in there, but I can see you're making an awful mess. You be sure to put Mr. Forrester's things back nice and tidy, you hear?"

The kid's Adam's apple bobbed in his throat. "Yes, ma'am."

She turned to Plodnick. "You keep an eye on that boy. He was a troublemaker, started food fights in the high school cafeteria. Just because he's a police officer doesn't mean he's reformed."

Then she held out her hand to me, and I gave her the paper. As she took it, Mrs. B. gave me a look over the top of those glasses. She jerked her head to indicate I should follow her onto the landing.

"You mixed up in drugs?" she whispered loudly enough for every cop in my apartment to hear.

I shook my head.

"Good. I'd be disappointed to hear a thing like that about you." I noticed she didn't go quite so far as to say she wouldn't believe it.

"Then what are they looking for?" she asked.

I nodded toward the paper. "The body of that murder victim was found in my cab. They think I had something to do with his death. I didn't," I added before she could ask.

"Oh, no," she said, patting my arm. "You'd never do a thing like that." Her tone hinted at the multitude of things she thought I *would* do, but at least she drew the line at murder. She started down the stairs, clutching the newspaper. On the third step from the top, she paused and turned around. "You tell your lawyer I'm willing to be a character witness."

"Thanks, Mrs. B."

Great, I thought, walking back into my apartment. Did I need a lawyer? All I had at the moment was a character witness who thought I *probably* didn't do drugs. Then I saw Officer Billy returning cans and boxes to my kitchen cabinets with shaking hands. Maybe Mrs. B. would be an ally worth having on the witness stand.

Chapter 5

The cops finally left, and I had the rest of the morning to clean up. They had no reason to arrest me, but they'd hauled off what felt like half my worldly possessions: my computer, a file drawer full of letters (*not* including those ninth-grade love notes), a couple of almost-due library books, the notebook in which I'd written down the time and place of Davies's memorial service, and, inexplicably, the dirty clothes from my hamper. I had to sign a receipt. Somehow that felt like adding insult to injury, like I was giving them permission to take my stuff.

By the time I got to work, Ryan had left to coach his son's Pop Warner football team. I wrote him a note suggesting he look for that trip sheet, the one from the cab's last shift before I drove it Monday morning. I still hoped that if we could draw a circle to show where the murder must have taken place, the cops would leave us alone. I also told Ryan I needed to get off work an hour early Wednesday for Davies's memorial service.

Next I checked my cab—my usual, safe cab—and began my shift. I began with a round of deliveries, picking up lab specimens from doctors' offices to drop off at the county hospital. Tuesday afternoon is a slow shift, so the delivery contract helps bring in some cash. Plus there's this nurse at a pediatrician's office who has the prettiest smile and who always takes a minute to flirt with me when she hands over the package. It was nice to get smiled at for a change.

After I'd dropped the samples at the hospital lab, I swung by the Qwikee-Change at the usual time, a few minutes past four, to give the boys their lift home. Ronnie was out on bail. "Hi," he said, sliding into his usual seat behind me.

No "sorry for getting you into this mess." Then again, Ronnie had only panicked and run. He hadn't hidden the dead body in the trunk, and that would've been found sooner or later. From the moment I climbed into the driver's seat of that cab, I became a suspect. I couldn't blame Ronnie for that.

Carl came out of the shop, wiping his hands on a grimy rag, then stopped and stared at me. The way his mouth hung open, he looked like a dead fish in a plaid flannel shirt. "You're still driving? I'm not so sure I wanna be riding with you."

I shrugged. "So call Lakeside. They'll only charge you a couple extra bucks each way. Or take the goddamn bus." There was a bus stop near Carl's trailer park, but the schedule was so convoluted that it would take him two hours and three changes to make the thirteen-mile trip. Easier to sleep on the grubby vinyl chairs in the Qwikee-Change waiting room than get home that way.

"Ready to go home, Ronnie?" I put the cab in reverse.

"Wait a minute, wait a minute." Carl waved his arms. "I guess it's okay. But I'm not getting in 'til you can show me that this one's got nothing in the trunk."

I almost kept going, leaving Carl standing there with his arms waving and that dead-fish look on his face. It'd serve him right to take the bus. But I shifted into park and popped the lid, then got out and walked to the back of the car. Carl stood beside me, clutching his collar like a demure schoolmarm. As I opened the trunk, for one second I half-expected to discover another unpleasant surprise, but it was empty except for a toolbox. I even opened the toolbox to prove that nothing sinister lurked in there.

Grumbling, Carl settled himself beside Ronnie in the cab.

For the first time in all my weeks of driving those two guys, they didn't argue. Ronnie stared out the window and kept silent. Carl tried to get a rise out of him a couple of times; when that didn't work, he started hounding me. During the twenty-minute trip, he must've asked at least fifteen times how fast we were going. "You don't want another speeding ticket" was his oh-so-helpful reminder. A thousand responses flashed through my mind, but I kept them to myself, just in case Carl started thinking again about doing his duty and calling up the Sheriff. I'd have to find out if speeding tickets had a statute of limitations.

I kept it to two or three miles under the limit, prompting Carl to complain about how long the trip was taking. "There goes another one," he commented when the fifth pickup truck blasted past us on a double-yellow line.

By the time we reached the trailer park, I was more than ready to kick his butt out of my cab and get the hell out of there. But he came around to my window and stuck out his hand. "Thanks for the ride," he said. Then he handed me a dollar tip. I stared at it. Carl had never tipped anyone in his life.

"Thanks, Carl."

He nodded. "Enjoy it. You go on out and have a little fun. 'Fore you get arrested, I mean."

"No one's going to arrest me over a speeding ticket." Especially one that hadn't been written.

" 'Course not. I was talking about that murder." He shambled off toward his trailer.

I stared after him. What the hell was he talking about? Had he heard something? He climbed the steps and fumbled with the lock. No, I decided. Carl didn't have any inside information. He was just a squinty-eyed pessimist; the world looked okay to him, but everyone else was on an express train to hell. Especially me.

★ ★ ★ ★ ★

When I turned in the cab at the end of my shift, around eight, a light shone in Ryan's office window. I gave my trip sheet and fare money to the night dispatcher, then went to see Ryan. He sat at his desk, which was overflowing with papers. A stack of folders nearly as high as his head wobbled as I closed the door.

"You're here late," I said.

"Looking for that trip sheet."

"So you got my note."

"Yeah, but the cops asked about it first. Yesterday. I can't find the damn thing anywhere."

"You've been looking for it since yesterday?"

"Yeah. It should be in this folder," he took the top folder from the enormous pile, causing the stack to topple over and fan itself across the floor. He didn't even glance at the mess. "When trip sheets come in, I put them into this folder. When Janet gets around to it, she enters them in the computer. Then she draws a line through each sheet and puts them into *this* folder." He picked up another thick folder and waved it at me. "She starts a new one each week. We keep the paper copies on file for about six months, then chuck 'em." He held a folder in each hand, looking from one to the other. "So it should be in one of these. But it's not."

"Janet didn't enter it in the computer?"

"Nope. Checked there, too. It's the damnedest thing. All the trip sheets for that day are missing. Do you think someone stole them?"

"Maybe." But looking at the mess spread across Ryan's desk, floor, and every other surface in the room, I thought it was more likely that the sheets had been lost. In that office, finding one particular piece of paper would be like finding a specific grain of sand on Waikiki Beach.

Damn. We needed that sheet. A cab drives hundreds of miles

in a normal day, so the previous day's trip sheet wouldn't tell us a thing.

Ryan thumbed through the contents of a folder. "You sure you want to go to that memorial service?" he asked.

"I feel like I owe it to the guy."

"Why? You didn't know him. It's gonna look funny to the cops."

"You didn't see him, Ryan." Without wanting to, I pictured that half-dressed, discarded corpse curled up in the trunk: the black socks stark against the gray-white calves, the blood matting his short, neat hair. "I just want to know who he was. The person, not the part that was left over. Not the part that I saw."

He raised his eyebrows, like that was all very well and good, but . . . "I heard the cops searched your apartment this morning."

Man, life in a small town. "I don't know why I even bother to read the paper. You don't need it to get the news. Yeah, they did. But they didn't find anything."

"Of course they didn't. That's not my point. They've got it into their heads that you're a suspect. And until they get that thought *out* of their heads, you should stay as far away from anything to do with Fred Davies as you can."

He was right. I knew that. But I was going to the memorial service, anyway.

On Wednesday, I finished my shift early and traded my cab for my own car, a road-worn but reliable Toyota Corolla. Then I headed toward Brooktondale and the artist's retreat for Davies's memorial service. FLAiR was famous for its remoteness, one of those impossible-to-find places where artists could do their thing without being disturbed. But I had directions, a good map, and plenty of time. I'd find the place.

I hadn't gone more than a mile past the Rhodes city limits

when the whoop of a short siren blast made me jump. Flashing lights spun in the rearview. Goddamn it. Automatically, I checked the speedometer; at least I wasn't speeding this time. I found a place to pull over. Sure enough, Deputy Hauser got out of the cruiser and sidled up to my window.

"License and registration," she said by way of a greeting.

"You had no right to stop me."

"You were driving erratically. You swerved halfway into the oncoming lane back there."

"Like hell I did." I might have maneuvered around a pothole—driving on the cratered Thomson County roads was like driving on the moon—but that was normal driving around here. "You're harassing me. I warned you. I'm going to report you to the Sheriff."

"So, basically, what you're telling me is that you're refusing to cooperate with a direct instruction from a police officer. As in, 'Give me your license and registration.' "

You can't win with cops. You really can't. Even when they're pushing it, you've got to do what they say or else you're the one who's in trouble. I didn't want to be late for the memorial service, so I gave her my license and registration.

She made no move to go back to her car. Instead, she bent over and peered into mine. An uncomfortable feeling of déjà vu washed over me.

"This your car?" she asked.

"This? Nah, I stole it. I wanted to continue my crime spree in style, so I hot-wired a ten-year-old Corolla with 152 thousand miles on the clock." I gave her back one of her own scowls. "Of course it's my car. It says so on the registration you're holding, if you'd bother to read it."

"I don't like your attitude, Forrester."

"Yeah, well, I'm not too fond of yours, either, Deputy."

She grinned at me then, the way a normal woman would

beam if I'd complimented her dress or her hairstyle. For a second, she almost looked like a human being. Then she went back to her cruiser.

She stayed there for nearly fifteen minutes. I know, because I checked my watch seven times. I hate being late, especially for something like a memorial service. For all I knew, she intended to keep me there all afternoon. She could be sitting in her cruiser reading a magazine or doing a goddamn crossword puzzle, just to waste my time.

I was starting to wonder if maybe she'd fallen asleep—giving me the chance to drive away quietly—when she reappeared at the window and returned my documents. I took them and waited for her to tell me I was free to go. Like she was about to do that. She stood there, rubbing the back of her neck and looking up at the sky.

"Is there anything else?" I finally asked. "I've got things to do."

"Where're you headed?"

"I can't see how that's any of your business."

"You're supposed to stay in Thomson County, you know."

"I haven't left the county. If I had, I wouldn't be talking to a Thomson County deputy, would I?"

"I bet you're going to the victim's memorial service."

What was I supposed to do, lie? To a cop? I elected not to say anything.

"So what's your deal, Forrester? You want to gloat? Savor the pain you caused? Or maybe you're trying to figure out how to get your hands on some more of Davies's money."

"If I wanted to do that, I wouldn't be here. I'd be on my way to rob his house while everyone else is at the service." She blinked and looked thoughtful, and immediately I wished I'd kept my mouth shut. Idiot. This deputy had a way of making me say exactly the wrong thing. If some enterprising Rhodes burglar had seen the obituary and was hitting Davies's house at this moment, I'd be on the suspect list for that crime, too.

By the time I drove away, I was running ten minutes late. Normally I could've made up the time, but this goddamn deputy's car followed me through Brooktondale, so I had to take it slow. When I turned off at FLAiR's driveway, she kept going. But she hit the siren for one short blast. It sounded like an accusation.

Okay, so I was ten minutes late. Maybe the memorial service hadn't started on time. Artists are free spirits, like the people I grew up with on the commune. People like that don't pay attention to clocks.

The long driveway, winding through maples, oak, and pines, reminded me of the Homestead—that was what we called the commune. FLAiR was a lot neater—the grounds looked artistic, like Mother Nature had groomed herself to pose. Fallen leaves blanketed the ground, and here and there a picturesque log cabin was set in the woods at a tasteful angle. At the Homestead, folks lived in the peeling farmhouse, slapped-together A-frames, old campers—one guy even stuck it out in a teepee for a couple of years before the blizzard of '78 drove him to Florida. Of course, the Homestead was a working farm, and farms get messy. At FLAiR, the only thing they grew was art. As I took the driveway's final, graceful curve, the big main lodge came into view.

I couldn't believe what I saw.

Some stupid punk kid with an arsenal of spray cans was vandalizing one side of the lodge with graffiti. He wore a black hooded sweatshirt and baggy jeans and kind of danced as he painted fluorescent loops and whorls across the pine logs.

I braked in the middle of the driveway and got out of the car. "Hey!" I said. "What the hell do you think you're doing?"

The kid stepped back to regard his handiwork. Then he turned, slowly, keeping his gaze on the eyesore until the last possible second. He was a pale-faced, scrawny kid, about twenty, wearing a knit cap and an enormous gold medallion. More gold gleamed from unlikely places in his face—a ring through his eyebrow, another through his nose. Wispy hairs of indeterminate color straggled along his chin. He curled his lip at me and said, "Who the hell are you?"

"That doesn't matter. This is private property. You can't come in here and mess it up."

"Mess it up?" he sneered. "Mess it up? Man, what the hell do you know?"

The kid clearly required an attitude adjustment, but I didn't want to cause a scene. Soft classical music floated from the lodge; the service was underway inside. The kid glared at me defiantly. Appeal to his better instincts, I told myself, watching the light glint off his nose ring.

I kept my voice even, reasonable. "Listen, this property belonged to someone who just died. His memorial service is going on in there right now. People who cared about him—friends, family—have come here to honor his memory. They don't want to see that you've trashed the place." I was thinking that maybe, if the paint was still wet, we could wipe most of it off before the mourners emerged.

"I know about the friggin' memorial service," he said. "This," he gestured at the chaos behind him, "is a tribute to the dude."

I'll admit it; I was speechless. The kid saw it and kept talking. "So don't you go giving me shit about shit you don't know nothing about."

"You knew Fred Davies?"

"He only begged me to come up here to his stupid retreat."

"So you're . . . um . . . an artist?" Somehow the word didn't seem right.

"Yeah, I'm a friggin' artist. What the hell did you think? I'm out here tagging walls in the middle of nowhere for fun?" He shot me a disgusted look. "Fred commissioned a piece from me, man, almost two weeks ago. But when I got here, I had no inspiration. Couldn't do a thing. It's this place—creeps me out." He shuddered, looking around. "Too many friggin' trees."

"But now?"

He shrugged. "Somebody offed the dude. All of a sudden it's easy—I know what to paint. And soon as I finish, I'm goin' back to civilization."

Jagged, brightly colored scrawls covered the log wall. It looked like an explosion at a spaghetti factory—if they made spaghetti sauce in Day-Glo colors. "So how is your . . . uh . . . painting about Davies's life?"

He sighed. "Every asshole thinks he's a goddamn critic. It's nonrepresentational, man. It's not about anything. It is what it is."

The kid shook one of his spray cans and went back to work.

Twenty minutes into the memorial service I eased open the lodge's door, praying it wouldn't creak. I shouldn't have worried. The door swung open silently on well-oiled hinges. FLAiR wouldn't let something like a creaky door disrupt its serenity.

The large room was all knotty pine—walls, ceiling, floor—except for a huge stone fireplace and one wall made completely of glass. A podium was set up in front of the fireplace; a man stood behind it reading from a sheet of paper. The room was packed full of folding metal chairs, all occupied. Several people stood in a cluster to my right. I stepped to the left, away from the door, and leaned against the back wall.

Next to me, on a table, were some programs. I picked one up. Looking it over, I guessed that the speaker was Sebastian Hedlund, assistant director of the DFA. Hedlund, a plump, neat man with slicked-back hair and a trim goatee, filled his expensive suit like a well-stuffed pillow. He was reading a letter of condolence from the director of the Whitney Museum, where, according to the program, Davies had been a trustee. The letter wasn't much more than a bland, generic message of sympathy, like a bunch of Hallmark cards strung together. I tuned it out and studied the crowd.

There was Chief Ianelli in his dress blues, the only discernible person in a row of gray suits. A man sitting next to Ianelli—narrow shoulders in a suit jacket that looked two sizes too big—might be Plodnick. Otherwise, there was no one I recognized. Even though we'd both lived in Rhodes for years, Davies's world wasn't my world. I looked at the front row. The woman in black, a veiled hat on her sleek chestnut hair, must be the widow, Felicia Davies.

After he'd finished reading the letter, Hedlund cleared his throat and launched into a eulogy. He spoke of Davies's dedication to the arts, how he'd used his own money to support artists in a culture that undervalued them. He called Davies a great man and an example to us all. He sounded more like he was unveiling a statue than memorializing a friend.

Hedlund descended from the podium, patted the widow's shoulder, and took his seat. Some churchy-sounding music played—Bach, according to the program. Then a short woman with curly brown hair (the program identified her as the Unitarian minister from Rhodes) stood and invited others to come forward and share their memories of Fred Davies.

People stirred in their seats, but no one got up. The minister waited, a smile frozen on her face. Still no one budged. She swept her gaze across the congregation, always smiling. When that gaze moved toward me, I ducked, concentrating on the program in my hand. I had this panicky feeling that she'd ask me to come up and tell everyone my favorite memory of Fred, and what was I supposed to say? He made a good-looking corpse? But then someone across the room went to the podium, and I could breathe again.

The speaker had to be one of FLAiR's artists, with her frizzy gray hair and floaty, gauzy dress—who but an artist would wear hot pink to a funeral? Even though she mentioned Fred's name often, she talked about herself: how he appreciated *her* art, how he recognized *her* potential, how he'd helped *her* career.

Maybe she set the pace by going first; the other speakers were the same. All were grateful to Davies for seeing how brilliant they were, whether they were an artist, a business associate, or a friend. Sheesh, didn't anyone who knew the guy see him as something besides a mirror?

No one from Davies's family spoke. I didn't blame them. If I'd lost a family member to violent death, I wouldn't feel up to public speaking, either.

When all that *me me me*-ing subsided, the minister came forward for the closing prayer. She'd got as far as "Let us pray" when the door flew open, banging against the wall. In strode the graffiti artist, bright smears of paint on his dark clothes. "Yo," he said. "I got something to say."

The minister nodded. "Why don't you come up and introduce yourself?"

The kid sauntered to the podium with that I'm-so-cool walk you see at the mall. He eyeballed the audience. "Hey," he said. "I'm empty."

At first I thought he was announcing that he'd run out of paint. Then a glance at the back of the program, which listed artists in residence at FLAiR, revealed he was saying his name. Not Empty, but Em-T. Some kind of street name.

"I just wanted to say, like, Fred was okay. I mean, he was okay. Especially for an old white dude, know what I'm sayin'?"

Not a clue, but he kept right on talking.

"So like, I finished my tribute to the dude. It's, uh, outside." He stood there for a moment, looking confused, like he'd run out of words and didn't know how to get away from the podium. He made an odd gesture, holding his fingers stiffly and crossing his arms in front of his chest, then said, "Peace."

To my astonishment, everyone in the room applauded. The kid grinned, then remembered he was supposed to look tough, switching to a scowling nod. He flashed his hand signals again and went back outside.

And that was it. The minister uttered a quick prayer, more classical music played, and a young man—Davies's son?—escorted the widow down the aisle. She leaned against him, clutching a white handkerchief, her head bent. Two rows away from me, she stopped. I saw her tug her stepson's arm. Slowly, in time with the somber music, she raised her head and looked straight into my eyes. My God. What a beautiful face. A question—I didn't know what—flared from her green eyes. My face grew hot, and I felt an urge to run. Then she lowered her lashes and let herself be led out to the front porch.

I left by a side door.

Sitting in my car, I had a good view of the receiving line. Felicia Davies smiled, nodded, wiped her eyes, and embraced, over and over again. I wondered whether she found the ritual a comfort or an endurance test. The artist in the hot-pink dress threw herself at the widow, making her stagger back half a step, and sobbed against her shoulder. Mrs. Davies patted her back, then turned and looked at my car so pointedly that I flinched, wondering whether I'd leaned on the horn. Time to go. I put the car in gear and pulled onto the driveway. A glance in the rearview mirror showed her watching me, still patting the hot-pink back.

She couldn't know who I was, I told myself. She must have mistaken me for one of her husband's pet artists. Yet there had been that question in her look, one so agonizing and deeply rooted that it hurt even to consider what it might be.

So I wasn't surprised the next day to find Felicia Davies waiting for me at the end of my shift.

Chapter 6

She was too stunning to be hanging around a garage. Her hair held back in a gold clip, she wore a simple navy sweater and skirt, but her style left no doubt she was rich. The sunglasses perched on her head cost more than I'd make in a week, and her necklace, with its heavy gold spiral pendant, looked like something that belonged in a museum. Felicia Davies was younger than her husband. Mid-forties, probably, but she could easily pass for ten years younger.

She took my hand in her cool fingers. "You're the one, aren't you?"

The way she said it didn't sound like a question. I felt like I'd been chosen for some important mission no one else could perform.

I was still haunted by that questioning stare she'd given me the day before, and for a moment I couldn't make myself look at her. But the longer I avoided her gaze, the more awkward I felt. So I looked her full in the face and asked what she meant.

Glancing around, she asked, "Is there somewhere we could go?" She checked her watch. "I have to be at the Crossing in twenty minutes. Would you walk with me?"

"Sure."

She didn't ask whether it was out of my way. I got the feeling that Felicia Davies was used to having people go out of their way for her.

We headed up Fourth Street toward Cascade, which crosses

the creek it's named after. Just past the bridge, Cascade intersects with Manitoah, a main drag that passes the Crossing's west end. As we walked, the warehouses and projects around the garage gave way to tightly packed frame structures built to house factory workers a century ago. Rhodes is a safe little city, but if there was an iffy part of town, this was it. I lived a few streets over, but Felicia looked like she belonged there the way the crown jewels belong in a 7-Eleven. As she turned to me, I was glad I was there to escort her.

"You're the one who . . . whose cab—where Fred, I mean, his . . ." Her voice trailed off as she stopped to dig in her purse for a handkerchief. She pressed it to her face and turned away. The handkerchief muffled a sharp sob. I wanted to put an arm around her, but I'd barely met the woman. I waited, hands dangling uselessly at my sides.

"I'm sorry," she said. "It's still so new. I find it impossible to say . . . certain things."

"I understand. Yes, I drove the cab that day."

"How terrible." She dabbed again at each eye, then pulled down her sunglasses to cover them. "I can't even imagine."

For one awful second, I thought she was going to ask me to describe the body, to reassure her that he'd looked at peace. It's hard to look peaceful when half your head is missing. But her question went in a different direction.

"You didn't happen to notice, did you, whether he was wearing a ring? Or perhaps whether it had fallen off in the . . . er . . ."

"In the cab?" I finished her sentence to save her from visualizing her husband stuffed into a trunk. One of those unsay-able things.

She nodded, and something like a smile twitched at the corners of her mouth. "It's an unusual ring. Fred called it a finger cuff: half an inch tall, gold, with a squarish green stone."

"Valuable?" I was thinking that a ring worth a few bucks had probably disappeared with the cashier's check.

"Yes, it's a Peruvian artifact. Pre-Colombian. But the real value is sentimental." She turned toward me, the sun glinting off her dark lenses. "I gave it to him at our wedding."

There was something so raw in her voice that I would have given anything to be able to pull that ring out of my pocket and hand it to her. "The police think it was a robbery. I'm sorry, but it was probably stolen."

"The police also seem to think you killed my husband. Did you?"

The sudden directness of her question, its matter-of-fact tone, stopped me cold.

"No, I didn't."

She nodded, and we walked on. "I believe you. When I saw you at the memorial service yesterday, I thought . . . Well, I can't explain it, but somehow I knew you hadn't done it."

"I didn't notice a ring. The police still have the cab, or I'd check for you. You'll have to ask them about it."

"I already have. They were no help at all. One of them had the nerve to suggest that I look through Fred's dresser. That he'd taken it off himself, to hide it." She shook her head like a bewildered child. "They seem to have heard some absurd rumor that Fred was having an affair."

"Really?"

"Oh, but if you only knew with *whom.*" Her laugh had an hysterical edge. "He knew her, of course, through the foundation; he couldn't snub the chair of an art history department, even from that two-bit Hasseltine College. But really. And she knew he was married, so why hide the ring, even if—? But he wouldn't. He wouldn't. Not with her."

I wished I'd known who she was talking about so I could join in her indignation. But the truth was that I didn't know any of these people, didn't have the slightest clue what they might be capable of. Not Davies. Not some art history professor. Not even the woman walking next to me now. I might give any of them a ride in my cab, but they lived on a different planet.

As if in confirmation of that thought, we passed Saturn—a concrete marker representing that planet, part of the permanent outdoor exhibit in memory of a famous Overton astronomer. The Planet Trail is a scale model of the solar system. The sun is located on the Crossing, and there's a marker for each planet all the way out to Pluto at The Science Place, a kids' museum a couple of blocks north of the garage. On the scale used to create the Planet Trail, each step was worth five billion. It felt like Felicia and I had come a long way.

Her question brought me back to earth. "Didn't you wonder how I knew you?"

"I figured you asked for me at the garage."

"No, yesterday I mean. At the memorial service. At FLAiR."

"Now that you mention it, yes."

"A police officer showed me your picture. She wanted to know if I'd ever seen you before. She seemed terribly disappointed when I said no."

That damn deputy. I should have known. "Was she Rhodes PD? Or from the county Sheriff's office?"

"Goodness, I don't think I'd know the difference."

I glanced at Jupiter as we waited to cross Manitoah Street. The light changed, and we walked past the old high school, now a mall for boutiques and a natural food store. Another block and we were on the Crossing. Felicia paused to regard a shiny metal sculpture at the entrance to the pedestrian mall. She lifted her sunglasses to the top of her head.

"Do you like it?" she asked, nodding toward the sculpture.

It looked like a stack of hubcaps to me. "I don't know much about modern art."

She laughed. "Tactfully put. Fred believed that art belongs in the community. To the community. Sometimes he forgot that the community might not appreciate having art bestowed on it." Her smile was wistful. "I agree with you, actually. I prefer the primitive to the postmodern. Tribal art—Inca, Mayan."

"Like that ring."

"In a way, it's all I have left of him."

She extended her hand. As we shook, she pulled me toward her infinitesimally and looked into my eyes, like she was trying to read something there. Her eyes, almond-shaped and green, shone as a tear welled. Then she turned and strode into the crowd on the Crossing. She moved easily, with confidence, but as I watched her go, doubt shimmered in her wake.

Damn it—what was Felicia Davies *really* trying to ask me?

The next several days—right through the weekend—passed almost normally. No widows with pain-filled eyes asking questions I couldn't answer. No cops pounding on my door. I drove my shifts, enjoyed an after-work beer or two at Donovan's, finished reading an account of a solo trek through the Andes. Occasionally I'd get that creepy-crawly feeling up the back of my neck, and once or twice when I looked around I saw a flash of blonde hair, but I never caught Trudy Hauser in the act. If she was still following me, she was keeping her distance.

Ryan hadn't found the missing trip sheets. It looked like someone had stolen them, but it was equally possible that all the sheets for that day had been misfiled in the trash. Given the state of Ryan's office, it wouldn't be the first time something like that had happened. Bottom line: They were gone.

On Sunday, I worked from nine to five. In the morning, I do a lot of church runs, mostly sweet little old ladies who don't drive or college kids who attend services downtown. For the rest of the day, I mostly go back and forth between our two college campuses and the mall. Sunday is a good airport day, too—

again, thanks to the college kids. They fly into the county airport after a weekend at home or in a more exciting city, like New York or Philadelphia or Washington.

At the end of my shift, I was surprised to see Ventura coming on duty. He hadn't shown up for work all week. Ryan had given up on him.

"Hey, Ventura—you still work here? I thought you quit."

"Nah. Not that I love the damn job. Need the money. I've been in the hospital."

"You okay?" He didn't look sick. Ventura is short and stocky, muscled like a bulldog but not quite as pretty. A couple of bruises faded along his forehead and cheek.

"Got in a fight. Last Saturday."

"But I should see the other guy, right?"

He flashed a grin, revealing a gap where a front tooth used to be. "I wish *I'd* seen him. Got jumped from behind. Took my wallet. I got in a couple of good kicks, but then he knocked me out cold. If I'd had half a chance, he'd be in the goddamn hospital right now, instead of out spending my money." I believed him. Ventura was tough.

"Where did it happen?"

"Over on Jefferson." Just a couple of blocks from Sunbeam. "Right in front of my own goddamn apartment."

Fifteen minutes later, I sat down at the bar in Donovan's and ordered an Ithaca Nut Brown Ale. I took a sip, rolled it around my mouth. Damn good stuff.

Rhodes had changed from when I was growing up. Back then, kids slashing tires as a Halloween prank made front-page news. Now, Fred Davies had been murdered, Ventura attacked on the street in front of his own home, both on the same night. And that wasn't all. The most recent front-page story in the *Chronicle* described how a college student and two local teens had OD'd on heroin. One of the local kids had died; the other two were still in the hospital.

Heroin. On the streets of Rhodes. I swallowed more ale and shook my head. Even at the commune, where pot and an occasional tab of acid were considered therapeutic, Homesteaders had stayed away from that stuff.

The times, they were a-changing, all right. And not in a way that Dylan or any of the Homestead idealists ever would have guessed.

Dinesh came in, sat down next to me, and ordered his usual Coors. He took a swig and smacked his lips. "Man, what a weekend."

"Any good frat parties?" I asked.

"Too busy. I spent the whole weekend with Trina."

I didn't recognize the name.

"The pudding wrestler," he supplied.

Ah. "So where is she now?"

"In the library. She's got a paper due tomorrow afternoon and figured she'd better get started on the research."

"Get started? The night before it's due?"

"Yeah. That's one of the things I like about Trina. She's responsible. Doesn't leave stuff until the last minute."

I laughed, but he actually meant it. So I segued to a cough, then gulped some ale.

"How about you?" Dinesh asked. "What'd you do all weekend?"

"I kept busy."

"Huh. That means you drove Friday night and a double shift yesterday. Probably worked today, too. And when you weren't driving, you were here or moping around your apartment."

"I don't mope." Other than that, he'd described my weekend to perfection. So what if I did a lot of driving? I could use the money.

"Bo, you gotta get a life, man. We gotta get you some action. Want me to hook you up with one of Trina's sorority sisters?"

"I've got no desire to get 'hooked up' with someone half my age."

"You're not that old. We're talking more like, um, two-fifths your age. Anyway, lots of those sorority chicks are into older men."

"No thanks. I can take care of my own social life."

"How?"

"What?"

"How you gonna take care of it?"

I sat up straighter on my stool. "It just so happens that I've been thinking about asking someone out."

"Who?"

"A nurse. I see her on my Tuesday hospital run. Her name's Debbie." At least, I thought of her as Debbie. Our flirtation hadn't progressed to an exchange of names.

Dinesh slapped me on the back. "Good man. I knew you had it in you. Wanna double? There's this absolutely insane punk band playing at The Lair next Friday."

"I'm not sure that's her speed." I knew it wasn't mine.

"Okay. But I want to hear all about it. Right here, in one week. Deal?"

"We'll see."

The truth was I *had* been thinking of asking the-nurse-whose-name-might-be-Debbie out. Some day. That smile of hers brightened my Tuesday shift; I looked forward to it all week. But I didn't know whether she was dating someone or what she liked to do. Dinner was an option, but I'm a pretty strict vegetarian. Thanks to growing up on the Homestead, my idea of comfort food was lentil-and-tofu casserole. Which kind of limited where we could go.

As I left Donovan's, I noticed the community bulletin board

at the edge of the Crossing. Maybe there'd be a flyer for a concert or play or something. I went over to study the posters and papers fluttering under the streetlight. A lesbian theater co-operative was performing a "radical feminist reinterpretation of Euripedes' *Medea.*" Um, no. There were a couple of chamber music concerts, which might seem classy until I started snoring in my seat. A lecture by the chair of the Art History department at Hasseltine College was another big ho-hum. And the Committee for World Justice planned a big demonstration on the Crossing to protest U.S. policy in the Middle East. Darn—I preferred to save political demonstrations for a second or third date. I sighed. For an active college town, Rhodes offered very little for a guy like me to do.

I turned to walk home, then nearly gave myself whiplash looking back at the board. Art history at Hasseltine—Felicia Davies had said police thought Fred was having an affair with the head of that department. I looked at the name: Nora Glaser. This was the woman. Had to be. Her lecture was on Monday afternoon—tomorrow—at four P.M. in some auditorium at the college. I wrote the time and place on my hand.

Fred Davies had been found in his underwear. As far as I knew, the police weren't even thinking about that. Underwear suggested intimacy, like Davies's lover had got him half undressed, then shot him.

If I could learn something about this Nora Glaser, maybe I could get the cops on the right track—the one leading away from me. Besides, I had this feeling that I could help Felicia Davies somehow. Her look of pain haunted me. I still hadn't figured out where to ask Debbie-or-not-Debbie to go. But tomorrow afternoon, I was going to learn about art history.

Chapter 7

During the school year, the population of Rhodes doubles as students swarm into town to attend our two colleges. Overton is the one everybody's heard of. A world-class university with picturesque ivy-clad buildings, its campus covers 750 acres and looks down on Rhodes from East Hill. Hasseltine College is on South Hill. It began in the 1800s as a female seminary, training missionaries. In 1965 Hasseltine dropped its religious affiliation; five years later it went coed. But when a national magazine named it a top-ten party school three years running, applications skyrocketed. Locals call the place "Hassel-time," thanks to its young scholars' fondness for weekend block parties.

You had to be hot stuff to be on the faculty at Overton. Hassel-time, on the other hand, knew its second-fiddle status—and was defensive about it. I wasn't sure what to expect from a public lecture from one of its professors.

Nora Glaser's talk was on stage sets for nineteenth-century Shakespeare productions. I wondered if it was possible to come up with a topic I knew less about. Not what you'd call a crowd-pleaser—the auditorium was mostly empty, except for some professorial-looking types who sat near the front and a few college kids sprawled across seats here and there. I sat down in the fourth row. Behind me, some students greeted each other: "Dude, what are you doin' here?"

"Extra credit, man. My grade's in the toilet."

"Hey, me too. Wanna get a brewski afterwards?"

"Definitely. I will so need one."

I heard a slap like a high five.

A bearded man with white hair and a tweed jacket took the stage. He requested that everyone make sure their cell phones were off, then sighed at the shuffling and beeping that ensued. Then he cleared his throat and introduced our speaker. Nora Glaser had earned a PhD at the University of Minnesota, coming to Hasseltine College the following year. She'd been at Hasseltine for a dozen years and currently chaired the Art History department.

He was describing the faculty grant that had made this talk possible when some latecomer picked the wrong door—it slammed shut with a bang that echoed through the hall. The speaker paused to telegraph a disapproving look to the back of the room, and everyone in the audience turned around to see a red-faced Trudy Hauser slink into a back-row seat.

That woman had a real talent for undercover work. I almost gave her a thumbs-up sign, but she looked so embarrassed I turned back to the stage.

The speaker finished his introduction, and Nora Glaser stepped up to the lectern. She was thin—bony, even—with high, sharp cheekbones. Mid-forties. Her red hair stuck out in a wiry halo. I suspected it was dyed, because her eyebrows were dark brown. She wore a black suit and a red blouse that clashed with her hair. The suit's skirt was short, a little too short to look professional, and revealed skinny legs with the knobbliest knees I'd ever seen. I had to agree with Felicia—this woman did not look like a home wrecker.

Professor Glaser adjusted the microphone, leaned into it, then covered her ears as a loud squeal pierced the auditorium.

A couple of students ran up to fiddle with the amplifier knobs and do something to the microphone. When they sat down again, Professor Glaser began her lecture. I'd wanted to observe her as she spoke, get a sense of her body language, but almost immediately the auditorium lights dimmed so she could show slides. Her voice was soft, the room was warm and stuffy, the lights were out—soon I heard snoring from one of the extra-credit kids behind me.

Since I couldn't watch the woman herself, I tried to focus on what she was saying. That way, I could strike up a conversation after the lecture and—and what? How could I possibly bring the conversation around from the storm scene in *King Lear* to her relationship with Fred Davies? I couldn't. This whole thing was a bad idea, a waste of my afternoon.

When the lights came up, we were invited to ask questions. No takers. Professor Glaser's face held a fixed, hopeful look, but crumpled a little when students began clambering over seats to get to the aisles. Faculty members clustered around her. I watched a couple of faces. They were as eager as their students to get out of there and have a brewski—or whatever professors drink after work. It didn't take long for the crowd to thin. When it did, I stood up, stretched, and glanced toward the rear of the hall. Deputy Hauser had gone. I approached Nora Glaser.

"I enjoyed your lecture."

"Thanks." She looked me up and down, making me feel like a naked statue in a museum. "I've never seen you around campus before. You must be from Overton. Grad student?"

"No, I'm not in school."

"Ah, then you must be one of our struggling local artists. Hmm . . ." She took a step back and stroked her chin, inspecting me again. I've known construction workers who were more subtle. "You don't look like the starving variety, anyway. No wedding ring, so no wife to support you. You must have a day job that keeps you fed. Let me guess. You're a waiter who makes monumental sculptures out of scrap metal."

"I'm afraid not. I—"

"No, don't tell me. This is fun. Okay, you grow organic vegetables and sell them at the Farmers' Market alongside your watercolors of sunsets over the lake."

"Not exactly."

"No, no, of course not. Silly of me. You're definitely not the watercolor type. All right, let's nail down the day job. Personal trainer? No, not aggressively muscular enough. Massage therapist? Freelance Web developer?"

I was shaking my head so much I was starting to get dizzy.

"I give up. What's your day job?"

"I'm a driver."

"A driver. I wouldn't have guessed that. Although you would look cute in a chauffeur's cap." She smiled—well, *leered* might be the more appropriate word. "But nobody in Rhodes is just a driver. At least you're an underemployed PhD in cultural studies or something. Come on. What's your passion?"

I was trying to figure out how the heck to answer that one when she asked, half to herself, "So why would a driver be interested in my lecture?" Her eyes widened and she clapped her hands. "You're an actor! Or maybe a set designer. Of course! Which theater company do you volunteer for?"

"I don't. I just—" What was I supposed to say? *I just wanted to get a look at you to decide whether you killed Fred Davies?* "I just like Shakespeare."

It sounded lame even to my ears, so her delighted laugh surprised me. "The truth at last," she said. "You're a writer. I know your type. The aw-shucks regular Joe who'd rather die than admit he spends every night in his garret sweating out page after page of immortal verse."

One more time with that appraising look. "I like Shakespeare, too. How would you like to get together and discuss the old boy over a drink? How about Ambrosia? Tonight, at nine?"

She actually batted her eyelashes at me, leaving little flecks of mascara sprinkled under each eye. So you want to get to know me better, I thought. How could I resist?

Ambrosia sits on the Crossing, facing Donovan's. The restaurant serves food it describes as "Italian-Pacific Rim fusion," and its bar is considered the most sophisticated in town, displaying an array of artfully backlit bottles in all kinds of colors liquor was never meant to be. The next place that feels even vaguely as Manhattanesque is a four-hour drive south.

Aside from the chi-chi ambience, there are two reasons people frequent the bar at Ambrosia: syrupy cocktails in neon colors and million-calorie desserts. I'm not big on sugar, and since the beer list is practically nonexistent, the place never held much attraction. Not that they're desperate for the cab-driver market.

Nora Glaser sat at the bar, wearing the black suit she'd worn for her lecture and toying with the stem of a martini glass. Her drink was a radioactive-looking shade of purple.

"Hi," I said.

"There you are," she replied. "It's about time. I hate drinking alone."

She couldn't mind it too much. I was to-the-second on time, and she looked like she'd already had a couple besides the half-finished drink in her hand. Her mouth was stained bright purple, making the clash between her auburn hair and red blouse even scarier.

"So . . ." I began, taking the stool next to hers. Someone sat down on Nora's far side—none other than the lovely Deputy Hauser. Again. How did she expect to catch me making some dumb crook's mistake if I couldn't take two steps without tripping over her?

"You know," I said to Nora. "It's getting crowded in here. How 'bout we snag a booth for some privacy?"

"Good idea. Hang on one sec." She tossed down her drink

and ordered another. "We'll be over there," she told the bartender, pointing to a booth in the rear corner, the only empty booth in the place.

It was as far as you could get from the bar. No way Trudy Hauser could eavesdrop without inviting herself over and sitting in my lap. I winked as we walked by. She glared at me in return; her stare burned holes in my back all the way to the booth.

I sat against the rear wall, facing the front door. A waitress brought over Nora's purple concoction and took my order for a draught Guinness, which arrived a minute later.

"Alone at last," I said.

"So you wanna talk about Shakespeare, huh?" she asked, slurring her words a little. I wondered exactly how many of those purple drinks she'd had.

"I can read about Shakespeare at the library." I gave my best charming smile. "To tell the truth, I'd rather talk about you."

"Well, well. What would you like to know?"

"You said everyone in Rhodes has a passion besides their day jobs. What's yours? Are you an artist?"

"An artist, me? You've got to be kidding. Those who can't, teach, right?" She laughed as though she'd said something witty and looked at me expectantly. I wasn't sure whether she wanted me to agree with her or contradict her, so I just smiled.

"No, seriously," she continued. "I am involved in the arts. I've been on the juries of competitive shows, that sorta thing. I also authenni . . . autenthi . . ." she licked her lips and then finally got the word out, "*authenticate* paintings."

"What does that mean?"

"People bring me their paintings, and I say whether or not they're genin . . . *genuine*. For insurance." She leaned toward me. "You wouldn't believe how many forgeries are out there."

She glanced around as though forgers lurked on all sides. "I did one last week—insured for $270,000. A Muldoon. D'you know his stuff?"

I shook my head.

"William Muldoon. Nineteenth-century Irish painter. Rural landscapes, fat-cheeked, happy peasants. That sorta thing. Not exactly sexy—not 'til you start talking about how much it's worth." She whistled, or tried to. Mostly she just sprayed purple drops onto the table. "Two-seven-zero K. Do you know how long it takes an art history professor to earn that much?"

"Not as long as it would take a taxi driver."

She threw herself back in her seat, mascara-smeared eyes round. "You drive a taxi? I thought you were a chauffeur. Wait a minute. Oh, God. You don't know the guy who found Fred?"

"We, um, work for the same company."

She shuddered. "How awful. Poor Fred. We were very close."

I made a sympathetic noise. The best thing to do was to let her keep talking.

"Very close. Until he—He was a wunnerful man. Kind. Gen'rous. And he really knew art. I'm married to a man who doesn't unnerstand me. Cliché, I know, but it's true. Fred . . . well, he unnerstood so much. He really did. Even though he had so much on his mind. Like that audit. Said he was worried about it. The audit, I mean. But he was a good man. Good. And then he . . . he . . . Oh, God. I need a drink." She grabbed my Guinness and chugged it like lemonade.

It was fascinating to watch the kaleidoscope of emotions as she spoke. One moment she'd be teary-eyed, then a hardness would pass over her features, followed by something that looked like confusion. Whatever she felt about Davies, it was complicated.

She thunked the glass onto the table. "What was I saying?"

"That Fred was worried about an audit. What was going on, do you know?"

She didn't reply. Her eyes were unfocused, and foam coated

her upper lip. She blinked and looked at me like she was surprised to see me there. "I don't wanna talk about Fred," she said. She leaned forward, and I felt her squeeze my leg just above the knee. "I'm tired of talking."

"Heads up, Rainbow," called Trudy's voice. I turned to glower at her. Instead, I swallowed about half the air in the room in one big gulp.

Bearing down on us from the front of the bar was a very angry giant. At least he looked like a giant from where I was sitting. I started to stand up, jerking my knee away and causing Nora to lurch forward; she landed face down on the table. Halfway to my feet, the guy still looked like a mountain. He was at least six-five, with a massive neck that shortened his tie by several inches. I sat down again.

Frowning, the man spoke to Nora, his voice taut with the effort of maintaining control. "You told me you'd be at the library."

She raised her head and squinted upward. "Perry. Why didn't you come to my lecture?"

"I had a job interview. You *knew* that."

"This is my husband Perry. Perry, this is . . ."

"I don't care who it is. You're coming home. Now."

"*He* came to my lecture."

Glaser took his wife's arm, which disappeared in his meaty hand. She slid out of the booth and stood, wobbling. Her husband looked at me for the first time.

"I don't know who you are, and I don't care who you are, because I'm never going to see you again. Got it?"

I tried to think of a smart response, but the best I could do was gape at him.

"If I ever find you anywhere near my wife again, I'll kill you."

He put his arm around Nora and guided her from the bar. She leaned against him, but when he stopped to open the front door, she turned and waggled her fingers at me.

"Nice going, Romeo." Trudy Hauser slid into the seat Nora had just vacated. Her hair shone golden in the soft light, an odd contrast to the smirk on her face.

"Huh. And here I was thinking you were too far away to eavesdrop."

"What do you mean?"

"You obviously heard us discussing Shakespeare."

"Yeah, right. And you were getting her drunk on Kool-Aid."

"You know, that junk she was drinking *did* look like Kool-Aid."

"Come on, Forrester. What's your angle? Why were you hitting on the lady professor?"

"Two answers come to mind. Number one: I wasn't hitting on her. Number two: Leave me the hell alone."

I got up and left the bar, not looking back until the cold night air hit my face. She sat in the booth, her back to the door. I pulled up my collar, hunched into the wind, and walked toward home.

Hell of an evening. A nymphomaniac art professor, a dangerously jealous husband, the possibility of something funny with the DFA's books—the murder was starting to look more complicated than a simple robbery. The more I learned about Fred Davies, the more reasons I found for someone to kill him.

Chapter 8

The next morning, I picked up Carl and Ronnie at the usual time. Expecting another silent ride—Ronnie surly and Carl ignored—I intended to spend the drive figuring out how to learn more about the audit Nora Glaser had mentioned.

Ronnie surprised me by starting in before we'd even left the parking lot. "So, Carl. I read this article on the Internet last night. It proves that George W. Bush is the Antichrist."

Sputtering noises from Carl's side made me glance in the mirror. His face was a meaty shade of red. "That's . . . that's treason!"

"I dunno," Ronnie said. "Made sense to me. The article said the Bible prophesized it. Something in Revelations."

"Oh, yeah? What?"

"I dunno. Look it up. Something about a great beast and a bottomless pit . . ."

Carl produced a green-covered New Testament from his shirt pocket and thumbed through it furiously. Ronnie watched him with heavy-lidded eyes and a faint smile.

And behind us appeared a police car.

Goddamn it. This had to stop. I was not going to get pulled over every time I ventured outside the Rhodes city limits. I checked the speedometer—my speed was okay. If I came across any potholes, I'd plow right through them. I wasn't going to give Deputy Hauser a single reason to flash those lights at me.

The trouble was, she didn't need a reason. And we both knew it.

Today, though, she left me alone. The cruiser kept back, staying just close enough to let me know she was there. Ronnie and Carl, whose debate had progressed to name-calling and Bible-shaking, never even noticed. When we crossed the Rhodes city line, she pulled a three-point turn and disappeared.

After I'd dropped the boys at the Qwikee-Change, the dispatcher sent me on a pickup to a housing development just north of town. Deputy Hauser had already put me in a bad mood; this made it worse. I hated—really hated—going anywhere near that particular subdivision.

I turned off the main road, determined that this time, I wasn't going to let the place get to me. But it did, right from the moment I saw the low, ornamental wall with its scrolling black letters: "Welcome to Homestead Estates." This subdivision had displaced the commune where I grew up. Not displaced. Obliterated was more like it. Nothing was left of the place I'd called home for the first eighteen years of my life. The meadows where our sheep had grazed, the fields where we grew everything from corn to soybeans to grapes—all gone. Now, oversized brick homes stood on undersized lots, each house turned half away from its neighbor, like someone who didn't want to socialize at a party they'd been forced to attend.

I pulled into a driveway and tooted the horn. A woman in a fur coat came out the front door. Jesus, fur. No one in the Homestead would have killed an animal to make a fashion statement. And it wasn't even cold out—about forty-five, typical for the first week of November. The woman carried some kind of designer bag and clicked down the walk in high heels.

I didn't bother to get out and open the door. She stared at the handle, like she didn't know how to make the thing work. I busied myself with writing her address on my trip sheet and waited to see if she'd try Open Sesame. Eventually, she managed to pull the door open herself.

"Where to?" I asked as she settled in the back seat.

"The Overton faculty club. We're having an important luncheon there today, and I'm helping to set up."

"PETA meeting?"

"What?"

"Nothing."

I backed out of the driveway. The old barn had stood near here. When I was a kid, haying was a highlight of the summer. What a joy to ride in the wagon—breathing that sweet smell of mown grasses, feeling hay tickle my bare legs—then watch as the men used a contraption of hay forks, ropes, and pulleys to pitch it loose into the loft. Throughout the fall, I'd climb up there and lie on my back in the hay, sneezing at the dust and daydreaming while the animals snuffled and munched below. That hayloft was my favorite place in the world. Now it was gone. The whole damn place was gone.

And the worst part was that my parents had disappeared with it. Rosie and Frank, the diehard hippies who'd never dug the authoritarian names *Mom* and *Dad*. You wouldn't catch them living in a subdivision. Over the years we'd lost touch—okay, we'd gotten to the point where we couldn't stand each other and stopped communicating. When I finally came back to Rhodes, after years in the Army and more years of drifting around, I came back to find them. But they'd left without a trace. And in their place were fur-coated, luncheon-giving women in half-million-dollar houses—

"Driver? Driver! I said the faculty club."

I'd sailed right past it.

I pulled over into the bike lane, put on my flashers, and waited for the cars behind me to pass. One of them, a dark sedan, crept by, the heads of its two occupants turning toward me open-mouthed. The sedan pulled off into the first parking lot up the street, a faculty lot for the Physics Department. Wow, these guys were subtle for cops.

When the lane was clear, I backed up half a block on the wrong side of the road, engine whining, as the woman in the back seat gasped. A totally illegal maneuver, but I couldn't let the poor thing tire herself out by walking a few feet.

"Ten-fifty," I said.

She gave me a ten dollar bill, two quarters, and a meaningful look. The kind of look that said, "I wouldn't tip you if I had to give away every cent I own before sundown."

Well, whoever said I wanted her goddamn money?

As I drove off campus, the unmarked car appeared behind me again. Fine. They could follow me around as long as they wanted. Maybe call up Trudy Hauser; we'd make it a parade.

The day didn't get any better. Every fare I picked up either talked to me like I was brain-damaged or acted like I didn't exist, getting annoyed when they had to interrupt a cell phone conversation to tell me where they wanted to go. By early afternoon, even the cops had quit pretending and followed me openly.

Near the end of my shift, I told the dispatcher I was taking a break. Then I drove to police headquarters on Elm Street, parked at a meter, and went inside. Must've surprised the hell out of my two cop friends.

The Rhodes police station was exactly what you'd expect: cracked gray linoleum tiles, dirty green walls, and a beat-up counter. The young cop behind it looked like a kindergartener ready for his afternoon nap. I walked over and leaned across the counter.

"I want to see Detective Plodnick."

"Oh, you do, huh?" His baritone contrasted oddly with the

pink baby face. "And who are you?"

"Bo Forrester. It's about his homicide investigation."

That made him move. He punched some buttons on the phone. "Forrester's out here. Says he wants to see you."

He'd barely hung up before Plodnick came barreling through a side door, pulling on his suit jacket. He looked at me, then around the empty lobby, stroking his caterpillar of a moustache.

"You by yourself?"

It took me a second to realize what he was thinking—that I'd come to confess. "No lawyer. The only thing I'm here to tell you is to quit following me. Your men are so obvious they might as well hop into in my back seat. It'd save gas."

He didn't answer, just stroked that damn moustache.

"Besides," I said, "there's no need. If you want to know where I go during my shift, check the trip sheet. I write everything down."

"Don't worry, we've been doing that. Comparing your actual movements to where you claim to have been. Since you spotted my men, I guess that's no surprise."

No. The surprise was that Ryan had been giving the cops my trip sheets without telling me about it.

Plodnick noted my reaction. "If you're not doing anything wrong, why do you object to being under surveillance?"

"Don't give me that 'innocent have nothing to fear' crap. That's not why I fought for this country. I *am* innocent, but I've been questioned, harassed, searched, followed around like a fox with a pack of bloodhounds at its heels. I can't trust my friends. I can't even drive outside of Rhodes without that damn deputy right behind me."

His fingers stopped in mid-stroke, and he narrowed his eyes. "What deputy?"

"Hauser. The one who found the body. She's been following me everywhere I go—if your guys haven't noticed, they're blind.

And she pulled me over the other day for no reason other than to give me a hard time."

Two red splotches colored his cheeks. "I'll speak to the Sheriff about her. In the meantime, you remember that we're conducting a homicide investigation. If that inconveniences you, too damn bad." He planted his feet and threw me a challenging look. "Now unless you have something useful to tell me, I've got work to do."

We stared at each other, fists clenched. He broke eye contact first. He turned and disappeared into the station's interior.

I checked the clock on the dingy green wall. My shift was almost over. Close enough. I wanted to catch Ryan before he left for the day. I had a question or two to ask my old buddy.

When I skidded into the lot at Sunbeam, Ryan was climbing into his Explorer. I parked behind it, blocking him in.

He got halfway out and waved me off. "Will you quit screwing around? My kids have a game this afternoon."

I got out of my cab and closed the door. "I'm not screwing around. I'm the one who's getting screwed."

"What are you talking about?"

"You. I'm talking about you, Ryan. I'm talking about how you've been reporting to the cops behind my back."

He winced, like I'd punched him in the gut. "I wouldn't do that. You know I wouldn't." His face was broad and open, his eyebrows up in a *who me?* expression. If I didn't know better, I'd almost think he was telling the truth.

"You've been giving them a copy of my trip sheet after each shift."

"I—"

"Don't bullshit me, Ryan. Plodnick told me."

He sighed. "Yeah, okay. You're right. I've been doing that.

But I didn't think it mattered. You're not faking your sheet, right?"

"Of course not. But you could've told me."

"What good would that do? Would you have acted differently? You already know the cops suspect you. I didn't think there was any reason to rub it in."

He had a point. Sort of. But if the roles had been switched, I would've taken him aside and let him know. That's what friends did for each other.

"Anything else?" I asked.

He sagged against his car. "Nothing that should surprise you. That Plodnick pipsqueak has been around a couple of times asking questions. Whether we hung out in high school. What I knew about your stint in the Army. Why you came back to Rhodes. Stuff like that."

"What did you tell him?"

"The same stuff I would've said if you'd been standing right there. Jesus, Bo, I know you're under a lot of pressure here, but you need to get a grip. I'm on your team."

On my team. In high school, Ryan had been a football star, and I'd been the kid with the stupid name from that weird commune. We'd never been on the same team.

Ryan came over and clapped my shoulder. "Listen, if the cops want to know anything else—anything at all—I'll tell you, okay? Even if they say to keep quiet." He gave my shoulder a rough shake. "I promise."

He seemed sincere. So maybe it wouldn't hurt to have somebody on my team. The other side certainly had me outnumbered. I decided to believe him—for now.

A normal day would've seen me on my way to Donovan's by four o'clock to enjoy a quiet beer or two before happy hour made the place uninhabitable. But today wasn't a normal day.

Being followed by cops for eight solid hours had given me an idea.

I walked along the Crossing, past a circle of kids playing hackey sack and shoppers toting bags. Pausing in front of a music store's display window, I glanced around. No one plopped down on a bench or developed a sudden interest in the window of another store. No lurkers in doorways. As far as I could tell, I wasn't being followed. Either Plodnick had reeled in his men or he'd found somebody better at being invisible.

I resumed walking. Halfway along the Crossing was The Organic Bean, a coffee shop owned by a farmers' cooperative. They sold fair-trade coffee and tea, soups made with locally grown produce, and homemade breads and cakes. As I entered, I was surrounded by warm, steamy air that smelled of coffee and curry, with that undertone of lentils that pervades vegetarian restaurants and natural food stores. The menu was written in white and blue chalk on three big blackboards behind the counter. They had fifteen different kinds of coffee—and I don't drink the stuff. I ordered jasmine green tea, wishing to hell they served beer, and received a dented pot and a lopsided pottery mug.

I sat by the window overlooking the Crossing. From here, I could watch the front door of the building that housed the DFA's offices. I was waiting for Sebastian Hedlund to emerge.

If anyone knew anything about the audit, it'd be Hedlund, the foundation's assistant director. The trouble was, I couldn't figure out how to make him talk to me. I couldn't breeze into his office and start asking questions—who the hell was I? So my first step was getting to know a little about the guy, gain some insight into how I might approach him. Today, I wanted to see where he went after work.

Admittedly, he'd probably go straight to his car and drive home. But maybe I'd get lucky and he'd stop somewhere for a drink. If Hedlund went into a bar, he'd be on my turf. I could sit down next to him, strike up a conversation. I was good at that. I'd been told more than once I had the kind of face that made the guy on the next barstool want to narrate his life's story.

I poured a mugful of steaming tea, blew on the surface, then took a sip. Burned my tongue. I put the mug down to cool. The coffee shop door opened, and a man in a dark suit and tan overcoat bustled in. My first thought was "cop," but he walked by, bought a loaf of bread from the bearded guy behind the counter, and left, all without so much as a glance in my direction. I watched him walk down the Crossing and turn onto Manitoah Street, heading toward the parking garage. I scanned the Crossing again; I still didn't see anyone who might be watching me. I focused my attention on the DFA's building.

I looked at the building, then looked at it some more, as the daylight faded, darkening the façade from brick-red almost to black. The Crossing's Victorian-style streetlights came on, one by one. And still nothing happened. My boiling hot tea cooled to tepid, then downright chilly, and Hedlund didn't appear. A few minutes past five, a woman with smooth hair and a wool coat emerged from the building, trotting toward Manitoah. Someone from the DFA? There were two other offices in that building, a law firm and a travel agency. She could have worked for any of them. For the next ten minutes, office workers trickled out in ones and twos. But no Hedlund. Not one plump, shortish man with gleaming hair and goatee.

Customers entered the coffee shop and waited in line while the bearded counter guy hopped around serving them. Some students sat down near me, covered their table with books and notebooks, and started quizzing each other for an anthropology test. Another half-hour passed. A couple of lights still shone in the upper floors of the DFA's building, but by the time I'd been sitting in The Bean for two fruitless hours, I was ready to quit. I stood up and pulled on my jacket.

As if that was the signal he'd been waiting for, Hedlund appeared, carrying a briefcase.

He turned toward Manitoah Street. I let him get ahead by a dozen yards, then went the same way. When he reached Manitoah he cut across the street diagonally, going left. Damn. He was on his way to the parking garage. Sure enough, he turned in at the stairwell and climbed toward the second level. Well, I'd known it was a long shot. I'd wasted two hours, and now Donovan's would be too crowded. The only thing left to do was go home.

I turned back toward the Crossing, waiting at Manitoah for the light to change. I heard footsteps behind me and glanced back to see if the cops had picked up my trail again. But the footsteps belonged to Hedlund, who was puffing in my direction along the sidewalk. Something was different about him, and it took me a second to realize what it was. He no longer carried his briefcase; he must have stowed it in his car.

Now I was in the awkward position of being ahead of the person I wanted to follow. The light changed, so I crossed the street. Hedlund kept going down Manitoah. By now he was even with me on the other side of the street; I strolled in the same direction he was going. Hedlund continued down Manitoah until it intersected with Main, where he turned left. I had to wait to cross the street again. Worried I'd lose him, I darted across against the light, dodging cars and getting honked at by two drivers. When I made it to the other side, he was a good block ahead of me. I sped up to close the distance. Hedlund moved pretty fast for a guy built like a sofa cushion.

A little way down Main, he turned onto a side street. By the time I made the same turn, he'd disappeared.

The side street was mostly residential, crammed with big,

hundred-year-old houses with rickety porches and no yards. Judging from the number of mailboxes tacked onto the front of each house, they'd been chopped up into studio apartments. There was no way to tell which one Hedlund might have gone into. But I couldn't imagine why Hedlund, with his air of money and his expensive suit, would be in this neighborhood at all.

Three-quarters of the way down the block was a rundown neighborhood bar. No name on it, just a couple of neon beer signs in the grimy window. I couldn't see inside, so I pulled open the door.

The small room had a checkerboard floor of black and yellow tiles, green vinyl barstools, and three booths along one wall. Two guys in dirty t-shirts at the bar were the only customers. "Close the damn door," one of them said. "You're letting cold air in." Since there was no sign of Hedlund—and no way I could picture the guy setting foot in this place—I stepped back onto the sidewalk and let the door drop shut.

I'd lost him. I retraced my steps toward Main Street. A TV blared from a cracked, half-open window. Yellow "Caution" tape strung across one porch blocked access to the sagging front steps. On another porch, a woman who must've topped 300 pounds teetered on a plastic chair and smoked a cigarette. The question still tugged at my mind: What was a rich guy like Hedlund doing in a place like this?

Chapter 9

The next night I stashed my car near the parking garage exit, ready to follow Hedlund if he drove off somewhere. But everything happened the same as the day before. Hedlund emerged from his office at six, got rid of his briefcase, and then hurried to the side street. This time, I didn't let him get so far ahead of me, and I saw him go into the bar. I didn't want to step on his heels, so I walked around the block. It was a cold night, dark under heavy clouds, and this part of town wasn't oversupplied with streetlights. At times I could barely see the sidewalk under my feet. By the time I got back to the bar, its neon Budweiser sign shone like an oasis in the desert. I went in.

The same two guys occupied the same two stools. The booths were empty. But Hedlund wasn't there. What the hell? I sat down at the bar and ordered a Bud.

It was the most silent bar I've ever been in. There was no music. No conversation. The TV in the corner was tuned to CNN, but the sound was off. It was so quiet that you could hear the bartender's shoes stick to the floor as he walked back and forth.

I turned to the closest guy, a couple of stools down. "Cold out," I said. He was the one who'd complained when I'd opened the door the night before, so I figured it was a topic he could get into. He grunted, not looking at me. So much for my famous ability to start bar conversations.

Maybe Hedlund was in the men's room. I slid off my stool

and went to the back of the bar, into a short hallway that dead-ended after maybe a dozen feet. On the right were two doors marked with old-fashioned silhouettes: one of a gent in a top hat and the other of a lady with a high collar and a ponytail. Both doors were ajar. I pushed open the one to the men's room and flicked the wall switch, illuminating the single dim bulb overhead. It was one of those one-at-a-time restrooms—toilet, sink, mirror, paper towel dispenser, trash can—you locked the whole room when you wanted to use it. Obviously, Hedlund wasn't in there. I nudged open the ladies' room door, in case he'd needed to powder his nose. He wasn't in there, either.

On the left side of the hallway was another door. Both bathroom doors were the cheap hollow-core kind, their veneer peeling in splinters at top and bottom. This door was metal. I tugged on the handle, but it was locked. I looked around. Nothing else to investigate here. I returned to my barstool.

The bartender watched me cross the room and sit down, his face carefully blank. I nodded at him and said, "I was supposed to meet a, um, business associate here but now I'm wondering if I got the time wrong. Maybe he was in here earlier? About this tall," my hand hovered at Hedlund's approximate height, "a little on the heavy side, has one of those goatee beards?"

The bartender frowned, then shrugged. "Don't see him," he said.

"But he was here?"

"What I said was, 'I don't see him.' You done with your beer?" The bottle was half full, but he took it and dropped it in the trash.

I got the message. What I didn't get was why he wanted me out of there. But now I was even more determined to find out.

I walked home, formulating my plan for seeing what Hedlund was up to in that bar. It seemed easy enough—tomorrow night,

Thursday, I'd be ensconced at the bar when Hedlund arrived. Then I'd greet him like we were old buddies and accompany him through the locked door. That had to be where he disappeared to. Unless he was moonlighting as a dishwasher, there was no other possibility.

At my house, I went up the porch steps and opened the front door, sorting through the bills and ads that had landed in my mailbox. Mrs. Boothroyd was playing swing music at top volume; "In the Mood" bounced along with me up the stairs. I opened my fridge to see what there was for supper. The cupboard was more than bare; it was an echo chamber. If I was going to eat that night, I'd better go to the grocery store. Besides, I needed to pick up some beer.

I climbed into the Corolla and drove the two miles to the store, keeping one eye on the rearview mirror, watching for a tail. I didn't see anyone following me, but I came damn close to rear-ending a minivan at a red light. When I parked at the grocery store, I sat in the car for a few minutes to see who else pulled in. No suits, no Trudy Hauser. Apparently the cops weren't interested in what I was having for dinner that night.

The store was crowded, and everyone there seemed to be rummaging through the produce section. I tried to maneuver my cart around a stout blonde woman in a dark-blue business suit who was blocking all access to the eggplants.

"Bo Forrester!" she exclaimed. "I don't believe it!"

I looked closer. She did seem kind of familiar—in the way any plump, middle-aged female looks completely at home in the produce section of any grocery store. She was smiling at me expectantly, and I couldn't place her at all.

"Hi," I attempted. "It's been a long time."

Her smile broadened, and for a second I thought I'd gotten away with it. Then she laughed. "You don't remember me, do you?"

"Of course," I began, but then I shrugged and admitted it. "You look awfully familiar, but . . ."

She laughed again. "You've forgotten me. I don't blame you one bit. I wasn't very nice to you in high school." She patted her round belly. "And I don't exactly fit into my cheerleader's uniform anymore. Shows what three kids and an office job will do to a girl."

I thought of all the cheerleaders who'd snubbed me in high school. Could have been any of a dozen—the whole squad, in fact. I searched her face for a clue. It was round, with full lips, dimples, and a slight double chin. Her eyes, twinkling in amusement, were a strange shade—not quite green, not quite blue. Oh, God. Was this woman really the sexy senior I'd lusted after my entire sophomore year, dreaming about the way she filled out that cheerleading sweater and short skirt? "Sharon?" I ventured. "Sharon Dupuis?"

She clapped her hands with delight. "Sharon Barton now. Can you believe it? I actually married my high school sweetheart."

Bobby Barton had been captain of the hockey team, a no-neck ape of a guy whose idea of a good joke involved belching, farting, or hitting someone—preferably all three. Those of us who worshiped Sharon prayed she'd wake up one day, take a look at the guy, and regain her senses, but they'd gone steady all through high school.

"How is Bobby?"

"Doing great, ever since he joined the AA. He's an agent over at Kind Insurance."

I could imagine. Instead of shaking a client's hand, he'd punch the guy in the nose and laugh. *Good thing ya just bought hospital insurance. Har. Har.* That was the sort of thing Bobby would do.

"So what are you doing here?" Sharon asked. "I thought

you'd blown this town for good."

"You know how it is with Rhodes. Sooner or later, everyone comes back."

"That's true. I see it all the time. I'm a banker now." She laughed as though the very idea were hilarious. "A loan officer for the Rhodes National Bank. Bobby wanted to get married right out of high school, but I made him wait for a couple of years while I went to MC^2." That was the local nickname for Midstate Community College—a place that wasn't exactly known for its Einsteins. "I got an associates' in accounting, then took a job as a teller. Worked my way up from there." She thrust out her chest, which was still ample, but . . . not quite the same. "I'm gonna make vice president one of these days."

"That's great." I started to make "good to see you" noises and move past her, but she still blocked the aisle, and she was in a mood to chat.

"How are your folks?" she asked.

I thought about saying fine and letting it drop, but she'd probably ask for details I didn't have. "To be honest, I don't know. They weren't too thrilled when I joined the Army. We kind of lost touch. I came back here looking for them, but . . ."

"But the commune was gone, and you couldn't find them. That's sad." She looked at the ceiling, calculating. "The Homestead kept chugging along until . . . oh, about '92, '93. I heard it was back taxes forced 'em to sell. The property taxes in this town are shocking. Just shocking." She made a face of matronly disapproval.

Almost immediately, she brightened again. "Why don't you call me? Come over for dinner some night. Bobby would get a kick out of seeing you, and I'd love to show off my kids. Here's my card." She pulled a pen out of her suitcase-sized purse and wrote her home number on the back, then handed me the card.

"Thanks." I couldn't quite imagine sitting at the family table with this new version of Sharon. Not to mention her kids and Bobby. The only time Bobby had ever spoken to me in high school was to ask whether we really had drug-crazed orgies out at the Homestead every Saturday, hoping to wangle an invitation. I'd told him no, it wasn't true, but he could join us for a game of noncompetitive Scrabble. The poor guy tried to express his disappointment by punching me in the shoulder, but I was too quick for him and he jammed his fist into a locker instead. That was the whole of my relationship with Bobby Barton.

"Now, promise you'll call," Sharon was saying. "You look like you could use a good home-cooked meal."

"Sure," I said, taking out my wallet so she could see me put her card in it. I didn't intend to call, though—the thought was too weird.

"You know," Sharon said, dimpling, "even though I was Bobby's girl, I always thought you were kind of cute." For a moment, I could see a seventeen-year-old cheerleader gazing out of those green-blue eyes.

She wheeled her cart past me and headed toward the bakery, hips gliding as though she were swishing one of those short, swingy cheerleader skirts. More than twenty years later, she still had the moves. There was just a lot more of her moving.

If there's anything more depressing than drinking mediocre beer alone in a silent bar, I don't know what it could be.

I sat on one of those green-vinyl stools at a few minutes before six, waiting for Hedlund to appear. My two companions stared into their drinks. The bartender watched CNN headlines scroll noiselessly across the screen. I thought about Dinesh, probably whipping up a batch of pudding with Trina at that very moment. I could imagine the look on his face—half-disgusted, half-amused—if he could see me now. This bar had to be the last place in town to look for action of any kind. So what was the attraction for Hedlund? He'd be here soon, and I'd find out.

Only Hedlund didn't show up. For the past two nights, he'd been here by six-fifteen. I looked at the wall clock, which proclaimed it was Miller time. At the moment, Miller time was past six-thirty and there was no sign of Hedlund. There was no sign of anything. No one had come in. No one in the place had moved a muscle. It was the Bar of the Living Dead.

This time, the bartender waited until my bottle was empty before he picked it up. "Care for another, Officer?" I stared at him, then turned around to see who he was talking to. No one stood behind me.

"You think I'm a cop?" I started laughing. I couldn't help it. The irony was too much. The bartender regarded me with skeptical eyes. It didn't matter what I said. I could laugh until I fell off my stool. I could deny it until I'd run out of ways to say no. The guy had me pegged as a cop, and nothing would change his mind.

And that meant nothing would happen here tonight.

I got up to leave. But when I saw the bartender staring at me in that smug way, believing he'd blown my cover, I decided to use his mistake to my advantage. I still didn't know where Hedlund disappeared to when he came into this bar.

"That door in the back. Across from the rest rooms. Where does it lead?"

His smile broadened. "Basement. Have a look if you want."

I went to the short hallway. Just before I reached the door, a buzz sounded and the lock clicked. I pulled the door open, then paused. I had no intention of getting locked in the basement. I'd known guys in the Army who'd fantasized about being locked in a bar overnight, but they sure as hell weren't thinking of this place. I studied the inside of the door. There was a horizontal exit bar you pushed to get out when the door was locked on the other side. I pressed it a few times, holding the door open. It seemed to work.

I took one step down and flipped the light switch. The door swung shut behind me. For a second, I couldn't catch a breath, and I almost wished I *was* a cop. Cops have backup, people who know where they are. I could disappear into this basement forever and no one would have a clue what happened to me. Feeling a little shaky, I reached behind me and pressed the exit bar. The door opened.

So it wasn't a trap. But I've got this thing about tight spaces, being closed in. Okay, I'll admit it—I'm claustrophobic. A little. When I was nine years old, I was playing explorer at the Homestead and got stuck in a culvert under a dirt road. I screamed until my throat burned, as invisible *things* crawled over my arms and legs. It was five hours before they found me—and being wedged in a dark, slimy, creepy-crawly culvert is no way to spend five hours.

Neither is being locked in a strange basement.

I let the door swing shut, and immediately my lungs went on strike; again I couldn't breathe. This wasn't working. I'd never learn what was in that damn basement if I couldn't get past the second step down. I pushed the bar (it worked, thank God), exited, and went into the men's room. I grabbed a paper towel from the dispenser and tore off a piece. Tugging on the door handle, I realized my mistake. It was locked from this side.

I stuck my head around the corner, trying to look like a cop. "Buzz me in again."

The bartender raised his eyebrows, but he hit the button.

I opened the door, wadded up the piece of paper towel, and stuffed it into the bolt hole. Then I sat on the top step, holding the door open with my body, and took off my right shoe. I stuck the shoe between the door and the frame, propping the door open. I knew it looked stupid, but if they did try to lock me in, maybe they'd kick the shoe out of the way and overlook the paper jamming the lock. I didn't think that was their plan, but my lungs worked better knowing the door was wedged open a crack.

I went down the wooden stairs to the short hallway at the bottom. The place smelled like mildew and stale beer, and the concrete floor felt cold on my right foot. There were two rooms: one in front of me, the other to my left. The room facing me had no door, and its light had come on when I hit the switch at the top of the stairs. I looked inside.

It was a typical bar storage room: kegs, stacks of boxes, cleaning supplies. A cracked, dusty mirror advertising Michelob Light leaned against one wall. Steps led to a back door on the alley. That door was fastened with a padlock. I couldn't believe that this room held any attraction for Hedlund.

I opened the door on the left, groped for the light—and stared. This room couldn't have been more different from the dusty storage room. The walls were paneled—with real wood, mahogany or something, not the thin, fake stuff you can buy for a few bucks at any home improvement store. A polished brass-and-crystal chandelier hung from the ceiling. The deep blue carpet was so thick that my feet sunk into it. There was no furniture whatsoever. It looked like a country club waiting for the decorators to arrive.

The room smelled of old cigars. Obviously, this was where Hedlund had gone. But why? No trace remained of what the room had held. The only clue was some furniture indentations in the carpet. It looked like three heavy tables had stood in the center of the room, and there were six regularly spaced rectangular dents in the carpet along one wall.

Something had been mounted on the far wall—a flat-panel TV, maybe? I inspected the bracket: a metal plate next to an electrical outlet and cable feed that would be hidden behind whatever had hung there. I went right up to the wall to examine the spot, and felt something under the big toe of my right foot. I looked down. A black plastic disk had been half-pushed under the baseboard and was stuck there. I pinched it and tugged. It was wedged in tight, and it was hard to get my fingers around the bit that protruded, but eventually I got it out.

A poker chip. Hah! I tossed the chip in the air and caught it. Now I knew what Hedlund had been doing here.

I took the stairs two at a time, then stopped short. The door was closed. On the top step was my shoe, with a piece of wadded-up paper towel inside.

Oh, shit.

It was like all the air had been suddenly sucked out of the basement. I couldn't breathe. Dizzy, I had to lean against the wall. It was like I was nine again, trapped in that culvert, concrete squeezing the life out of me. Buried alive. I forced myself to relax, knowing I could breathe again as soon as I shoved the panic out of the way. Relax. Relax. When I felt like I had some control, I closed my eyes for a second, then opened them and pressed the exit bar.

The door swung open, and I took in a big lungful of pure relief. Maybe the bartender was trying to show me what he could have done, or maybe he'd developed a sick sense of humor from working in that damn boring bar. I didn't care which. I shoved my foot into my shoe and went to confront him.

The bartender smirked. "Nice carpet down there. Makes you want to take your shoes off."

I slapped the poker chip on the bar and watched the smirk fall off his face. I grabbed the chip back again before he could snatch it. "You'll be seeing us again—with a search warrant," I said, *us* implying me and all those cops he believed were my buddies.

I left the bar. Man, it felt good to walk out of that place. Now

I knew the angle to use with Hedlund. Time to get busy. In fact, I'd be way too busy to inform the cops about this little gambling club.

I smiled, picturing the bartender making frantic phone calls and shredding records—all for nothing. Too bad if he couldn't take a joke.

Chapter 10

The state of New York has some downright schizophrenic gambling laws. Although it's perfectly legal to play cards for money, it's against the law to promote gambling or to possess any records or devices related to gambling. Exceptions exist: bingo games, Native American-owned casinos, state-approved race tracks and off-track betting facilities. Not to mention the state lottery, whose odds are so terrible that its motto, "Hey, you never know!" ought to be "Hey, you never win!"

So technically, Hedlund wasn't breaking any laws in the basement gambling den of that no-name bar. But the bar itself—its owner, its employees—would be in big trouble if the cops raided. I knew they had poker games going—and maybe something like roulette or baccarat. Those six rectangular indentations along the wall probably marked where six video slot machines had stood.

Rhodes doesn't have any big-time gambling operations—no legal ones, anyway. Neither does Thomson County. No racetracks or OTB, no casinos. You can drive a couple of hours to get to those places, but from what I'd seen, Hedlund was hooked. He needed something accessible.

And that's how I planned to get into the man's office for a chat. On Friday morning, I asked around the garage: did anyone know of any high-stakes games? Taxi drivers are aware of such things—it's often worth their while, even in a small city like Rhodes. The first couple of guys I asked merely shrugged and said the only place they knew of for poker had just got raided by the cops. I shook my head. Man, those cops. They get everywhere.

I tried Ventura, who was filling a thermos at the coffee machine. He'd recovered from his mugging; the bruises were gone. The guy still wouldn't win any beauty contests, but he was probably scaring fewer fares away.

"Hey, Ventura, do you know of any poker games going on this weekend?"

He kept his gaze on the coffee streaming into his thermos. "Why? You got some cash you want to lose?"

"It's not for me. Yesterday I picked up a guy at the county airport who asked about a game. I had no clue, so I lost a big tip. He was coming to town for some weekend conference up at Overton, and I figure there'll be more of 'em arriving today. Somebody else might ask."

Screwing the top onto the thermos, he narrowed his eyes at me. "I did know a place off Main. But they shut down. Weird story. An undercover cop staked it out, but the raid never happened. The owners got nervous and got rid of everything." He shook his head. "Weird, huh?"

I tried not to crack a smile. "So the undercover guy took a bribe. You know how cops are."

"Yeah, but the owners never paid him anything. It wasn't like that. He showed up, threatened a raid, and disappeared. Didn't you hear about it?"

"Not me. I never hear anything." I did a sheepish Mr. Innocence shrug. "I couldn't even find my fare a game yesterday."

Ventura looked hard at me, his dark eyes slits. Then he grinned. He was still missing a front tooth. "Yeah, right. But okay. I know about a game. All-night tournament at a private home. Here's the address." He scribbled on a napkin and handed it to me. I glanced at the address—it was in Manitoah

Heights, the rich part of town.

"Hey—Forrester, Ventura!" Ryan stood in the garage doorway. "You're not supposed to take a coffee break before you start your shift. Hit the road, guys."

I turned my back on him, stashing the napkin in my pocket, and said to Ventura in a low voice, "Don't tell Ryan I asked, okay?"

Ventura gave me another hard look, then nodded. "Nobody's business." He carried his thermos to his cab and left.

I had to walk past Ryan to get to my cab. As I approached him, I hoped my smile didn't look as fake as it felt. "Man, what a slave driver." I started to pass him, but Ryan put a hand on my arm.

"I was thinking about our conversation the other day," he said. "You were right. I should've told you."

"Forget it." I made to get by him again, but he held my arm. He looked over my shoulder toward the coffee station.

"I didn't know you were buddies with Ventura." A question lurked behind his words, but he didn't ask it. I wondered if he'd seen Ventura hand me the napkin.

"Just bullshitting."

Ryan didn't answer, and we stared at each other for a minute. A line creased the space between his eyebrows, and he frowned slightly, like something worried him.

"What?" I said. "I thought you wanted me to get to work."

"I—nothing. It's nothing." He tried to smile but only managed to look like he had gas. "Better get out to Enfield before Carl starts calling to see where you are."

He dropped my arm, and I walked past him and got into my cab. So Ryan didn't like me talking to Ventura. Well, tough. At least Ventura gave me information when I asked for it.

I figured a guy with Hedlund's nighttime habit wouldn't start work much before ten, so around 10:30 I told the dispatcher I was taking a break and parked in the Mohawk Street public garage. The sun was out for the first time in two weeks, and it was one of those perfect Rhodes days—blue sky, sunshine everywhere—that get you through the other 300 cloudy or rainy or snowy ones. Being out in the cool, crisp air felt so good that I almost forgot to check for a tail. When I got to the Crossing, I turned left, even though my goal was to the right, and strolled around the block, stopping frequently to look in shop windows and survey my surroundings. I sat on a bench for a couple of minutes. People hurried past, intent on their business. If someone was following me, I didn't see him.

As I headed for the DFA building, I thought about Trudy Hauser. I hadn't seen her for three or four days—no deputy's car following me when I drove Carl and Ronnie to work, no blonde in a motorcycle jacket eyeing me in bars. Amazing that Plodnick had managed to rein her in. If I hadn't been the main suspect in his murder investigation, I'd have felt like I owed him one.

I opened the door of the DFA's building and went inside. Despite the fancy Victorian brick front, the lobby was scruffy—grubby yellow walls and an ancient tile floor. The place smelled like bleach and could've used some higher-watt lighting. I checked the directory, which hung crookedly next to the elevator; the DFA was on the third floor. I hit the up button, and the elevator groaned to life, clanking and moaning and banging. I decided to take the stairs.

As I climbed two flights of creaky, rubber mat-covered stairs, I thought about the audit and wondered if the DFA was in financial trouble. Square footage was pricey on the Crossing, but this seemed like a low-rent building.

Walking past the glass-paned door into the DFA's reception area, however, told a different story. I felt like I'd stepped into

Oz, like my surroundings had morphed from black and white to glorious Technicolor. The foundation had money, no doubt about it. You could practically smell it in the tufted leather of the club chairs, hear it in the soft classical music playing through the state-of-the art sound system. Oriental carpets covered the polished hardwood floors; oil paintings in gilt frames, discreetly lit, graced the walls. A receptionist, looking as polished as the brass wall sconces, smiled at me from behind her desk. I recognized her from my stakeout at The Organic Bean.

"Good morning. May I help you?"

"Nice place. In that lobby downstairs, you'd never guess this building held anything so classy."

Even her laugh was expensive, ringing like crystal. "I know what you mean. Mr. Davies chose these offices for their view of the Crossing. He liked to watch people come and go."

"Good boss?" I asked.

"The best. A wonderful man." Her smile grew a shade fainter, then she blinked and it brightened again. "What may I do for you today?"

"I'm here to see Sebastian Hedlund."

"Very good. Is he expecting you?" She flipped a page in her appointment book.

"No. A friend told me to look him up. It'll only take a minute."

"I'll just buzz him and see whether he's available. May I have your name?"

A name. Why hadn't I thought of that? I didn't want to give Hedlund my real name. "Um, Smith." Jesus, how lame could you possibly get? "Bo—er, Joe Smith." That lame.

She picked up the phone and hit a button. "Mr. Hedlund, a Mr. . . . ah . . . Mr. Bojo Smith is here to see you." She paused. "No, he said a friend asked him to drop by." She listened a moment, then cupped her hand over the phone and looked at me.

"What's your friend's name, please?"

I didn't know the bartender's name. What was I supposed to say now, John Doe? "Just say he's a mutual acquaintance from a bar off Main Street."

She gave me a quizzical look, but she repeated my words into the phone. She hung up and smiled as though nothing could be more delightful than dealing with a guy with a fake name and no appointment on a dubious mission. "He'll be right with you, Mr. Smith. Please have a—"

Hedlund's office door flew open, and there stood the man himself. His small eyes gleamed in his doughy face. "Come in, come in," he said.

He held open the door for me. His office was like an extension of the reception area: a massive leather-topped desk with a new-looking computer, a deep red Oriental carpet, leather chairs. Several paintings hung on each wall; one of them reminded me of the fat, happy peasants Nora Glaser had described. I wondered if this one was worth $270K.

Hedlund walked around his desk, sat down, and smoothed his goatee. "I'll be right with you," he said. "Let me just finish saving this file." He took out his keys, which were attached to the loop of one of those high-capacity flash drives. He stuck the flash drive into the computer's USB port, tapped at the keyboard, and hummed tunelessly while he waited for the computer to do its stuff. He didn't look at me, just watched the screen. Then he removed the flash drive and, keys jingling, slid it into his pocket.

"All right." Now he looked over, his eyes shining like he expected good news. "You have some information for me?"

I sat in one of the leather chairs. It was less comfortable than it looked—slippery and stiff. "Some people are getting a game together tonight."

He let out a big lungful of air and sat back in his chair.

"Good. I'm in."

"Not so fast."

He blinked and straightened. "Whatever do you mean?"

"See, the guys who are putting it together, they're pretty serious. We're talking high stakes." I hoped I sounded like a gambler and not a bad imitation of a tall James Cagney in jeans.

"Well, that's good," Hedlund said. Light glinted off a gold signet ring on his right hand. "The higher the stakes, the bigger the payoff, right?"

I was sliding down the slippery chair and had to scoot myself back up. "That's the thing, see. There's some question about your ability to participate. Ever since your boss died, there's been a rumor going around that this setup," I gestured to include his office, the reception area, the whole DFA, "is in trouble. Moneywise, I mean. Something about an audit . . ." I let my voice trail off.

Hedlund's forehead shone with a sudden sweat. He pulled out a handkerchief and swiped at it. "I see. I can assure you there's nothing to worry about. The finances of the DFA are in order. Anyway, that's beside the point. I've got the money. I'll put up my stake in cash."

"Of course you will. We wouldn't expect anything less. It's just that this audit rumor has caused some concern."

"It hasn't even happened yet!" Hedlund leaned forward over his desk, his bulging eyes ready to pop out of his head. "Fred's death postponed the damn thing." He swiped at his forehead again, his crisp white handkerchief looking limp. "Everything will be fine. I promise."

So the audit had been pushed back when Davies died. Interesting.

"All right, Hedlund. You're in." I stood and handed him the napkin with the address Ventura had given me. He grabbed it like it was a life preserver and he'd been treading water for a week.

"Don't forget to bring cash," I said and turned to leave. I had the door half-open when Hedlund gasped behind me.

"Is this a joke?"

He was around the desk in two seconds, waving the napkin in my face.

"Who put you up to this? Was it Tommy? Or was it your own idea to have a laugh at my expense? Very funny. Ha ha ha." Each *ha* hit me with a moist blast of sour-smelling breath.

I backed out of the office. "I don't know what you're talking about."

"Oh, you don't? And I suppose you don't know that this—" he balled up the napkin and threw it at me "—is *my* address."

His address? I must have looked as flabbergasted as Hedlund did furious. Either Ventura was seriously misinformed or—or what? What the hell was Ventura playing at?

I backed into the reception area. The receptionist half rose from her chair, her eyes and mouth round. Her boss was red-faced, pop-eyed, looking ready to keel over from a heart attack. Spittle sprayed as his yelling rose toward screaming.

"Get out of my office. Now! If I ever see you again, I'll . . . I'll . . ."

I never got to hear the rest of his threat. I turned to get the hell out of there—and bumped smack into Felicia Davies.

She looked gorgeous. Even though I'd nearly knocked her over, Felicia was as poised and put-together as a model stepping off the runway. She wore a black-and-white jacket with slim black pants. She straightened the jacket, then smiled as though finding me being thrown out of her late husband's office was the best thing that had happened to her all day.

In the short time I'd known her, I hadn't seen much of Felicia's smile. It was like a flower blossoming, the way it opened up her whole face.

"Hello," she said. "I didn't expect to see you here."

"Felicia!" Hedlund sputtered. He came around to stand between us. "Don't tell me you *know* this person. Is he—?"

"Sebastian," she said sharply, "don't be rude. Of course I know Mr. Forrester. He's—"

"Forrester? He said his name was—"

Felicia raised her voice, talking over him. "He's been a great comfort to me since Fred died, and I expect you to treat him as my friend. Do you understand?"

Hedlund gaped at her, perspiration gleaming on his forehead. Then he lowered his eyes and nodded. He mopped his face with his handkerchief.

"I apologize for Sebastian's behavior," Felicia said. She laid her hand on my arm; her green eyes bore into mine. "I need to discuss DFA business with Sebastian. Will you wait for me? I'd like to talk to you."

The flower blossomed again, and I was ready to promise I'd wait all day. But I was on break, and I'd already taken too long. "I'm working," I managed to say. "Can we talk after my shift?"

"What if I engage you in your professional capacity? I need a ride, and you can save me the trouble of calling for a cab." She squeezed my arm gently. "Please? I won't be more than a few minutes."

"All right." With those eyes burning into mine, there was no way I could say no.

"Good." Another squeeze, and she turned away. "Sebastian, a word, please."

She took Hedlund's arm and led him into his office. He practically twisted his head off gaping at me over his shoulder. The heavy oak door closed behind them. Warmth tingled along my arm, where her hand had rested.

I glanced at the receptionist, whose polished appearance had melted into barefaced curiosity. I gave her a *who knows?* shrug. Her veneer of friendly efficiency returned, and she started typing on her computer.

I sat in another of those slippery leather chairs and thought about Felicia. She was attractive—I'd have to be blind to miss it—but she was so far out of my league we might as well be different species. It was like Nick at the Homestead, who'd had a thing for Jackie Onassis when I was a kid. He papered the walls of his room with cut-out magazine photographs—Jackie in oversize sunglasses on Ari's yacht, Jackie posing in a sparkling gown at a charity ball, Jackie in Monte Carlo, Jackie on horseback. Hundreds of photos. I asked Nick once why he had so many pictures of someone he didn't have a prayer of meeting. He sighed and said, "Class, Rainbow. The lady defines class." Now, for the first time, I understood what he'd meant.

Felicia possessed the kind of class a guy like me could admire from a distance. But today, the way she'd touched me and looked into my eyes made me wonder. And as soon as I started wondering, I pushed the thought away. For God's sake, the woman's husband had been murdered. She was in mourning. What kind of a jerk was I to even think—

I picked up a magazine, *ARToday,* and flipped through the pages. An article went into raptures over a huge canvas that looked like someone had pelted it with mud balls, then attacked it with a knife. Would Felicia find something like that artistic? Would she hang it over the fireplace? I didn't get it at all.

The next article showed a performance artist in a business suit hanging himself from a diamond-encrusted ladder. It was the same all the way through. A solid black painting. A frame holding sixteen severed doll's heads. A thirty-foot sculpture of an apple core that had sold for $40,000. Too bad. I had the perfect spot for it in my back yard, next to the composter. Jesus, forty thousand bucks. Every article, every piece of so-called art, reminded me again that Felicia's world was not mine.

I turned another page and stopped cold, staring at a full-page photo of that kid from FLAiR, the one who'd sprayed graffiti all over the lodge at Davies's memorial service. In the photo, he held a can of spray paint in one hand—and a pistol in the other. He aimed both at the viewer.

And this was the kid who'd said he couldn't paint until he found inspiration in Davies's murder. Was that a reason to kill him? From what I'd seen in this magazine, artists were capable of just about anything.

The story, an interview, was titled "Graffiti Gangsta." I hadn't read beyond the first sentence when Hedlund's door opened and Felicia emerged. She closed the door behind her, leaving Hedlund inside. Then she turned to me and smiled. "I hope I haven't kept you waiting too long. Shall we go?"

In the beacon of that smile, the magazine dangled from my hand, then dropped to the table. I had to rouse myself to note the issue date: April 2005. I did want to read about what's-his-name, the graffiti kid. I'd snag a copy at the library later.

Felicia slipped her arm into mine, and together we went outside. From the DFA to my cab, I found myself hoping that someone, anyone—even Plodnick's detectives—would notice that Felicia Davies walked by my side.

Chapter 11

"Did you know," Felicia said, "that this is the most-painted view in Thomson County?"

We sat in the parking lot at Lakeshore Park, at the southern end of Manitoah Lake, Felicia beside me in the front seat of the cab. She'd asked me to drive her here but made no move to get out when we arrived. Together, we watched the lake. Canada geese flew over West Hill in V-formation. Sunshine sparkled on the water. And I felt as awkward as a sixteen-year-old in his dad's car on a first date.

"Fred loved it here," she said. "I think Lakeshore Park was his favorite place in the world. In fact, I almost came here to look for him that Sunday. When I got home from my trip and he wasn't there, this was the first place I thought of. But then I checked the answering machine: five calls from five different people asking why he wasn't at the fundraiser. That's when I knew something had happened to him. Fred would never have done anything to jeopardize his foundation. The DFA was the real love of his life."

Did I hear bitterness in her tone? Her face didn't look bitter, just sad, with a sort of fragile wistfulness as she watched the lake.

She stirred, looked over at me, smiled. "I wasn't jealous, not really. Each of us had our own passions. That's what made our marriage work. Fred had the DFA. I have my gallery."

"An art gallery?"

"Art and antiquities. It's called MetroPrimitif."

I'd never heard of it. "It's in Rhodes?"

"Manhattan. I live there about half the time. I import pre-Colombian artifacts and contemporary art from Central and South America. My assistant Angelica pretty much runs the place, but I enjoy keeping a hand in. And I go on buying trips. I was in Quito when—" She broke off and gazed at the lake.

The dispatcher chose that moment to squawk a question over the radio, asking if I could pick up a fare in Collegeville.

"No." I turned the thing off.

"I'm sorry," Felicia said. "I'm monopolizing your time."

"No, it's fine."

"Everyone I know is so *careful* around me. Sitting here with you, I feel like maybe some day things will be all right again." The way she said it, I had this crazy urge to take her hand. But I hesitated. She tucked her hair behind her ear, then folded her arms and turned to me. "I miss him," she said simply.

Tears gathered in her eyes, and I wanted to wipe them away. I wanted to protect her from the sudden violence that had shattered her world. But it had already happened. She'd lost her husband suddenly, violently. There was nothing I could do to fix things.

"We only had two years together," she said, dabbing at her eyes. "Not quite two. We met in New York, at a fundraiser for the Guggenheim, and married a month later. To the day. Sounds reckless, doesn't it? But we knew. We both knew. Have you ever felt like that?"

I shook my head.

She twisted a ring on her left hand—her wedding ring, a broad silver band with a deep blue stone. When she saw me looking at it, she spread out her fingers. "I don't suppose you've had any news about Fred's ring?"

"No, I'm sorry."

"The police never found it. I've looked everywhere. I even inquired at that pawn shop out on West Main." She sighed. "I suppose I'll never see it again. It's like you said before, if the motive was robbery, the ring must be gone."

Her spread fingers curled into a fist, then relaxed. "It would mean so much to me to have that ring back," she said. "I don't care about the check. It's DFA money, and recovering it would be good for the foundation, but the foundation will get along all right. Except for the house and a few bequests, Fred's entire estate goes to the DFA."

I wondered how she felt about that. As if reading the question in my thoughts, she said, "That's as it should be. I don't need the money, and neither do his children. They're grown and doing quite well on their own. Fred's legacy shouldn't be to his family. It should be to the arts. As I said, the DFA was his passion."

"Will you take over now?"

"Me? No, no—I have nothing to do with the DFA. I'm executrix of Fred's will, which is why I stopped in to talk to Sebastian this morning. So many legal details." She shook her head. "And I apologize again for the way Sebastian acted. He's been under a lot of stress lately—we all have—but to blow up like that . . ." Another sigh. "What happened? Sebastian wouldn't tell me."

I debated how much to say. If Hedlund was embezzling DFA funds to support his gambling habit, Felicia should know. But all I had were suspicions, and it didn't seem fair to start tossing accusations around without any proof. Felicia had enough on her mind; I didn't want to add to her worries.

"It was a misunderstanding," I said. "No big deal. Somebody gave me some information for him. But I had either the wrong guy or the wrong info. I think the person who gave me the information was playing a stupid joke."

"I see." Her look said, *So you're not going to tell me, either,* making me feel like the latest in a long line of people who'd stepped up to hurt her.

"That's all I know," I lied.

"Well." She reached over and patted my hand like I was a child. "You and I both have things to do. Would you please drop me off back at the Crossing?"

We drove the couple of miles downtown in silence, me feeling like I'd let her down. She paid the fare, adding ten dollars extra for the time we'd spent at the park, and gave me another ten dollars for a tip. I started to argue, but she waved away my objections.

"I hope I'll see you again," she said, treating me to another of those smiles. Then she sailed into the crowd, which parted magically around her. You were wrong, Nick, I thought. When it came to class, Jackie O. had nothing on Felicia Davies.

For the rest of my shift, Felicia's presence lingered in the cab, like a trace of her perfume. Every time I glanced to my right, I half-expected to see her there, smoothing her hair or twisting her wedding ring.

I couldn't shake the feeling I'd disappointed her. She'd said that I comforted her—but I couldn't help her. I couldn't bring her husband back. I couldn't give her the missing ring. And I even lied to her about my encounter with Hedlund, holding things back. The more I thought about it, the angrier I got at Ventura for putting me in that position in the first place. What the hell was he doing, giving me Hedlund's address? Who was he trying to get at—Hedlund or me? Ventura had set me up, and I wanted to know why.

My shift ended at three, but I got to the garage early. I didn't want to let Ventura slip past me. He was going to explain what was so damn funny about making me look like a fool in front of

Felicia Davies. I slammed the door of the cab and shoved my paperwork at the dispatcher. "Ventura in yet?"

The dispatcher shrugged. "Better ask Ryan."

Well, that was helpful. The guy couldn't even be bothered to say yes or no. I shot him a look and went to Ryan's office.

He looked up, started to smile, then cut it off when he saw my expression.

"Where's Ventura?" I demanded.

"Why?"

"Jesus, can't anyone answer a simple question around here? Because I want to wring his neck—how's that for a reason?"

"What's up with you two?"

"Nothing. Did he come back yet or not?"

"Yeah, he came back."

Damn it all—I'd missed him. I started to ask for his address, but from the weird look on Ryan's face I decided to get it from the phone book. I pushed open the door, but Ryan kept talking.

"He came back halfway through his shift. Quit right on the spot. Said he had something better lined up and he was leaving town."

I stood there until I realized my mouth was hanging open. I shut it. Ryan asked again, "Bo, what's going on with you and Ventura?" I ignored him and took off. Ventura had quit in the middle of a shift to leave town. Why? What the hell was he up to? The questions were piling up, and I had a feeling that Ventura would disappear before I had the chance to ask a single one.

Ventura and I were practically neighbors—he lived about three blocks from my place. Since it was so close, I walked. The day was still sunny, but the light was already dimming, at twenty past three.

The building was one of those big Victorians—with turrets

and gingerbread trim and a wraparound porch that must have really been something in its day. But its day had dawned and set at least eighty years ago. Now, the paint was peeling, the trim was missing or falling off, and the porch had lost part of its railing. The building held half a dozen apartments. I studied the multitude of doorbells until I found the one labeled *R. Ventura.* I pressed the button, but I couldn't hear whether it buzzed inside. I waited. No one came to the door.

I tried again—still no response. So I pressed the button marked *Superintendent.* A minute later I heard a window scrape open.

"Yeah?" A voice floated up from the basement level. "Somebody want something?"

I backed down the porch steps and scanned the half-sized windows near the ground. A woman in a bandana, cigarette dangling from her mouth, squinted up at me.

"Hello," I said. "I'm looking for Ray Ventura."

She snorted, sending smoke billowing from her nostrils. "Well, you'll have to look for him someplace else. He don't live here no more."

"He moved out today?"

"Move? Hah. I kicked him out. The bum was two months behind on his rent. Landlord sent him an eviction notice a month ago. Thought we was going to have to take him to court, but he up and cleared out this afternoon. Packed all his junk into two suitcases, and that was that. Wish all my problems got solved so nice and tidy."

"Do you know where he went?"

"Maybe he moved in with one of them girlfriends. Fancy women coming by, all times of day and night." She squinted at me through a haze of smoke. "You a friend of his?"

"Not exactly."

"Good. He's a bum. His friends are bums. Stay away from

them types or you'll be a bum, too."

As if that were the last possible word on Ventura, she slammed the window shut. A cloud of blue smoke drifted across the rhododendrons, then faded into the late afternoon shadows.

So Ventura was gone. I'd ask around at the garage, see if anyone knew anything about a girlfriend he might've moved in with, but I didn't hold out much hope. A guy who takes off that fast doesn't want to be found.

Now what? As I walked home, my thoughts returned to the audit. Davies had been worried about it; Davies's death had postponed it. What exactly had he been worried about? No way Hedlund would tell me. Instead, I'd go back to the source: Nora Glaser. If I could catch her sober, maybe she'd tell me what had bothered Davies. Besides, I felt a little guilty for not checking up on her after her husband had hauled her out of that bar.

From my apartment, I called Hasseltine's Art History department. The secretary told me that Professor Glaser had office hours until five. I checked my watch. Four o'clock. I was in luck. Even in afternoon traffic, I could get there in fifteen minutes, easy. I revved up my Corolla and headed for South Hill.

But a mile from the college, as I turned onto Elm Street, traffic jerked to a halt. Some kind of disturbance was going on, up by the police station. People waved signs and shouted.

Somebody's always protesting something in Rhodes. It's that kind of town. They might as well issue you your own personal soapbox when you move in. Usually, the protests happen on the Crossing or up at Overton University, but this one spilled down the front steps of the police station and into the streets. The protesters blocked traffic, standing several deep in each intersection to create gridlock on Elm and its side streets. Horns blared in competition with whatever the protestors were chanting. I looked around. Cars idled bumper to bumper in front of me, behind me, and in the other lane. No place to turn off, no way to turn around. Damn. I wondered if I'd be stuck here long enough to miss Nora Glaser. There was nothing I could do about it, though, so I got out of the car to see what was happening.

Judging from the ages of the protesters, this was a student group. A guy on the steps of the police station shouted Spanish through a megaphone. Many of the signs were in Spanish, too. I walked over to a young woman who was wearing a colorful jacket that looked like a woven blanket. She carried a Spanish placard; I asked her what the demonstration was about.

"We are protesting the racist assumptions of the ignorant Rhodes police."

"What did they assume, exactly?"

She looked at me like I'd just admitted I didn't know the alphabet. "Chief Ianelli is racist against the peoples of Latin America," she explained. "He blames our Latino brothers and Latina sisters for Rhodes's drug problem."

So that was it. An article in yesterday's *Rhodes Chronicle* described the recent influx of drugs into the city, especially heroin and cocaine, which had led to several overdoses. Between the college students and the old hippies, Rhodes has always had its share of pot smokers, but a sharp increase in the hard stuff worried police. The article quoted Ianelli as saying that they were trying to trace the supply line back to its origins in Bolivia, Colombia, Peru, "or one of those countries." Had to be that last phrase that got him in trouble—like a politician saying "those people" to refer to an ethnic group other than his own. Now, protesters were calling for Ianelli's head on a platter—*su cabeza en un disco,* if I remembered my high-school Spanish.

The speaker said something in Spanish, and the young

woman raised her fist and shouted, "Si!" She turned back to me. "Do you understand what he's saying?"

I shook my head, and she wrinkled her nose in disgust at my ignorance. "Drugs are an Anglo problem. The United States keeps the Latino nations in poverty for its own profit, then blames the peasants it exploits for the decadence of U.S. citizens. We will not have blame for Anglo greed and depravity laid on Latino doorsteps. We are demanding a written apology and Chief Ianelli's resignation."

Well, at least Ianelli would have something other than the Davies murder on his plate for a while. Maybe he'd pull Plodnick off my back and sic him on the drug dealers.

All at once, from all sides, the police arrived. Some burst out of the station; others came running up Elm and its side streets. A uniformed officer with a bullhorn (not Ianelli, I noticed), ordered the crowd to disperse—first in English, then in Spanish. The protestors booed and jeered, then one by one lay down in the street. As the police moved in to clear them out, I decided now would be a good time to return to my car.

I watched the cops carry protesters into the station and waited for traffic to start flowing again. The protest struck me as oversensitive, demanding the chief's resignation over a poor choice of words. On the other hand, maybe those kids had a point. There wouldn't be drugs flowing in from south of the border without demand for them here. Someone was making a lot of money, and it sure wasn't the peasant farmers who lived in "those countries."

Two cops went by, lugging my friend in the colorful jacket between them. She sagged as though trying to make her body as heavy as possible—all 110 pounds of it. Another cop stepped into the intersection to direct traffic. Within minutes, I was on my way up the hill. As I left the protesters behind, I shook off thoughts of drugs, cops, and overdoses. Rhodes had a big-city drug problem—maybe bigger than it could handle—but that was Ianelli's problem. Right now, my problem was Nora Glaser. After our interrupted "date" the other night, I wondered whether the good professor would be happy to see me. Or willing to see me at all.

Chapter 12

Hasseltine's Art History department was on the third floor of the Humanities building. I sprinted up the stairs and emerged in a long, narrow hallway paved with cracked linoleum squares and lined with cinderblocks painted a dingy off-white. Every few yards, bulletin boards displayed colorful notices about exhibits, competitions, fellowships, and graduate programs. A directory across from the elevator listed faculty offices in white letters pegged crookedly into a black background. I scanned the list: Glaser, N., 304.

The office was to the left, three doors past the elevator. I stood in front of the closed door, my hand poised to knock, when the door jerked itself open and two grim-faced men in dark suits emerged. They appeared so suddenly I nearly rapped the first one on the lapel. He frowned at me, then glanced at his friend. The two of them proceeded down the hall without a word.

They'd left the door open. I stepped forward and tapped on the frame.

"Anybody home?"

Nora sat at her desk with her head in her hands, but she looked up quickly at the sound of my voice. A bright red circle glowed in the middle of each cheek, and she wiped at her eyes with the back of her hand.

"Oh, it's you."

"I wanted to make sure you were all right."

For some reason, my expression of concern annoyed her. "All right? Why wouldn't I be all right? I'm just sitting here in my office trying to get some work done."

"Well, the other night. Your husband seemed pretty angry."

"Oh, that." She made a gesture like batting away a mosquito. "I can handle Perry."

It would take a matador's red cape and a stun gun to handle that guy, I thought, nodding sympathetically. I tried to figure out a natural way to bring up the audit, but I couldn't, so I just blurted it out.

"So, um, the other night at Ambrosia you said that Fred Davies was worried about an audit. Do you know what worried him about it?"

"Fred?" She pronounced the name as though she'd never heard it before. "What are you talking about?"

"The audit. At the DFA."

"I don't know. He thought there was something funny with the books. He didn't go into details. I'm not an accountant, you know." She stopped, a puzzled scowl creasing her sharp features. "Why are you asking?"

Why *was* I asking? Several ostensible reasons flashed through my mind, all of them lame, so I decided a quick change of subject was the best strategy.

"Who were those men visiting you? Not students. They want you to verify another expensive painting?"

She jumped in her chair and looked at me with wide eyes. Then she narrowed them and started shuffling papers on her desk. The edges of the pages trembled.

"I can't talk now," she said. "I've got a lecture to write and three sets of papers to grade. I assure you that I'm fine. Perry didn't drag me home by the hair and beat me up. But I really don't think that it's a good idea for us to see each other. In fact," she glanced at the clock on the wall, "my husband will be coming by any minute now, and I can't guarantee he won't beat *you* up if you're still here."

I raised both hands, palms out. But she didn't see because at this point she was crashing things around on her desk with the intensity of a tornado. I left the office, closing the door behind me. It didn't square with its frame, and I had to give an extra tug to get it closed.

The elevator dinged as soon as I stepped into the stairwell. Peering around the corner, I saw a back as broad as a cornfield heading down the hall. Either I'd just avoided Perry Glaser or Nora's next visitor was a professional linebacker. He opened her door without knocking and went inside. I stole down the hallway. The door was ajar. I hesitated half a second before pressing my ear to the crack.

"You ready?" Perry asked.

"Not quite." The tornado still slammed books and papers around full force. After a particularly loud crash, there was silence, then Nora's voice asked, "How did it go?"

"What?"

"The job interview. How did it go?"

"Oh. Fine, I guess."

"Tell me about it. Where was it again?"

"The Center for Community Diversity."

"Was it? I thought you told me it was the Clean Lakes Coalition."

"Did I say—? No, the CLC was last week."

"Well, Rhodes is overflowing with non-profits. And they all need fundraisers and grant writers and that sort of thing. You'll get something, dear."

Perry mumbled something that I didn't catch.

"Have you been drinking?" Nora's voice was sharp.

"The interview finished early. I stopped off for a quick one on the way here."

"Oh, Perry."

"What? What's 'Oh, Perry' supposed to mean?"

"You'll never get a job if you go around smelling like a distillery."

"You're a fine one to talk."

"Don't project your inadequacies onto me."

"Anyway, what the hell difference does it make? I could go an interview drunk, naked, and with my ass painted blue, and it wouldn't hurt a thing. As soon as they get to that little box on the application—*ever been convicted of a crime?*—I'm out the damn door. You try finding a job with a felony on your record."

"Me?" Nora's voice cracked, and she cleared her throat. "Don't be absurd."

"Of course not. Not you. Little Miss Perfect. You're a bigger drunk than I am. At least I don't make a pass at whatever walks by—"

"No, you throw a punch at it." There was a pause, and I imagined them glaring at each other, the desk between them, Perry's fists clenched. I'd want more than a desk between me and that guy when he was mad. Something more the size of the state of New York.

Nora broke the silence. Her voice sounded tired. "I don't want to argue now. I need to get my notes in order for my conference paper."

"That's another thing," Perry was in no mood to let go of his belligerence. "I don't want you going to that conference."

"Of course I'm going. I'm chairing a session and giving a talk."

"I know what goes on at those meetings. A bunch of horny professors let out of the library for a few days, getting drunk at receptions, and—"

"Stop it right now. It's a professional conference. And since *my* profession supports us both, I have to go."

"Then I'm going with you."

"For heaven's sake, will you please stop? You'd be bored out of your mind. You imagine drunken orgies, but it's really just a bunch of stuffy academics babbling on to each other about obscure subjects no one else has the slightest interest in."

"I'm going."

"You can't." There was triumph in her tone. "I registered months ago, and the reservation can't be changed now."

"You don't want me there."

"Honey, of course I do," Nora's voice melted all over him and oozed past the door. "I just wish you'd told me before now that you wanted to go. When I could have made the arrangements." She stirred in a little more sugar. "I'll only be gone a few days. After I get back, maybe you and I can go somewhere together."

Perry grunted, then muttered something I didn't catch.

"Remember those two weeks in San Carlos?" Nora said. "Wouldn't you adore going back to Mexico?"

Perry laughed, a rumbling sound halfway between exasperation and amusement. "You're crazy, you know that? Jim would never OK it."

"So who'd tell him? You've been such a good boy all through your parole. He wouldn't have to find out."

"There'd just be hell to pay when we got back."

"Why come back? Wouldn't it be grand to spend the rest of our lives lying on a Mexican beach, living like royalty? Or Cuba. Think of it—Old Havana, mojitos at the Tropicana, the ghost of Hemingway. We could retire there right now. You wouldn't need a job."

Perry's laugh sounded more relaxed this time. "If only you meant that," he said.

"Maybe I do. Come on, let's go home."

I beat it down the hallway and into the stairwell. I ran up one flight, then watched at the window until I saw the Glasers emerge, arm in arm, walking together toward the parking lot.

It was a little after six when I got home. It felt good to get inside my warm apartment—as night fell, the clear day had turned cold and clouds had banked up, threatening snow. I went to the kitchen and reached into the fridge for a porter. Nothing like a strong, dark beer to warm you up on a cold night.

I had half a vegetarian pizza left over from the day before, and I ate it out of the box, washing it down with the porter. I nearly wolfed the whole thing down standing over the sink, but then I thought about Dinesh and his taunts about my non-existent social life. Eating cold pizza over the sink was probably his exact image of how I spent my Friday nights. So I carried what was left of the pizza and my beer over to the kitchen table and sat down. There. Much more civilized. Besides, I wanted to think. I'd learned a lot in the past few days about the people around Fred Davies. One of those people, I was sure, had killed him.

Sebastian Hedlund seemed like the number one suspect. The guy was a gambler, and he was in charge of the DFA's books. With millions of dollars sitting at his itchy fingertips, the temptation to skim a little off the top had to be tough to resist. Gamblers never believe they're really losing, and Hedlund probably convinced himself he could pay back the money before anyone noticed. Maybe he'd "borrowed" more than he'd intended, and the upcoming audit was about to reveal his self-approved loan. Or maybe Davies had learned that Hedlund was embezzling funds and confronted him—Hedlund could have panicked and shot Davies.

The problem with this theory, of course, was zero evidence. It was just a guess—though a good one—that Hedlund was an embezzler. And I didn't know how to find the proof. After leaving the Army, I'd taken a few community college classes, and I'd slept right through Accounting. All those numbers flying around was like counting sheep to me. So even if I could get access to the DFA's books—an impossibility right there—I wouldn't know how to read them. Besides, Davies's death had postponed the audit, which probably gave Hedlund ample time to cover his tracks.

Of course, the mere fact someone likes to play poker doesn't automatically make him a thief and a murderer. Other people had motives, too. Like the Glasers. What a charming couple. Nora saw herself as some kind of femme fatale. If Davies wasn't interested—and how could he be interested in Nora with a woman like Felicia at home—would that make her angry enough to kill him? The woman was unstable. I wouldn't want to be there if she started waving a gun around, especially after a few drinks. And the husband, Perry, was no better. Insane jealousy, possible alcoholism, and a criminal record—bad combination. I'd have to learn more about his felony conviction. Maybe I could look through back issues of the *Rhodes Chronicle* in the library to find out why he'd gone to prison.

That reminded me: I wanted to look up the *ARToday* article about that Em-T kid. He seemed like a long shot, but there was something disturbing about that photo of him with the gun. Probably just a pose, but the kid obviously bought into that whole hiphop culture thing—and the stars in that sky were always shooting at each other and bragging about their bullet scars and prison time. Was it possible for a skinny white kid to go too far, trying to fit in?

I rose and got another porter, opened it, then stood there with the bottle in my hand as I thought things through. Even if any of these people had committed the murder, how the hell did Davies's body get into the back of that cab? What was the connection with Sunbeam?

The doorbell buzzed, interrupting my thoughts. *Bzzzt.* My apartment is in a 100-year-old house, converted into a duplex, and missing some of the modern conveniences of newer buildings. *Bzzzt.* So there was no intercom. *Bzzzt.* If I wanted to stop that annoying buzzing and find out who wanted to see me so badly, I had to go downstairs to the front door. *Bzzzt.* I went out onto the landing, jogged down the stairs, and opened the door.

On the porch stood Carl, clutching a fistful of red carnations.

It took me a second to recognize him, probably because it was the first time I'd ever seen him without his Mack trucker's cap. He'd slicked down his sparse gray hair, which winged out over his ears in exactly the same way it would if the cap were in place. Under his denim jacket, which was pretty darn close to clean, he'd buttoned his plaid shirt all the way up to his chin.

Carl's mouth dropped open when he saw me. His eyebrows squeezed together, he looked at the flowers in his hand, then back at me, then whipped the flowers behind his back. A petal fluttered to the floor. "What are you doing here?" he asked accusingly.

"Spending a quiet evening at home. You?"

"You live here? But I thought—"

A door opened and closed behind me, and I turned to see Mrs. Boothroyd cross the front hall. She was dressed for a night on the town—she wore some kind of shawl over a dress with lace at the neck and a full skirt that swung as she walked. Her cats-eye glasses flashed in the light. She'd removed her habitual hairnet and even found a pair of stockings that didn't sag into wrinkles around her ankles. Mrs. B. was hot to trot.

She looked toward the porch and smiled, dimpling. "Good evening, Carl."

"Irene! There you are. Thank the Lord. I thought I had the

wrong house." He glared at me, and I could almost see him thinking that I had no business living under the same roof as his woman.

Mrs. B. stepped past me onto the porch. "Shall we go?"

Carl lurched forward to offer his arm. He must have forgotten he was holding a bunch of flowers, because he nearly lashed Mrs. B.'s face with carnations as he brought his arm around. Two or three flowers landed at her feet, several more heaved over on broken stems.

"Oh, Carl," she said. "How thoughtful. Let me put these in water before we go."

I bent and picked up the flowers that had fallen on the porch. It looked like it was going to take more than water to revive them—something more on the order of divine intervention—but Mrs. B. beamed all over, fussing with the bouquet as she carried it into her apartment.

While she was inside, Carl rocked back on his heels and whistled tunelessly, looking at the night sky.

"So," I said, feeling like a dad on prom night, "where are you two headed?"

"Dance over at the Y," Carl replied. "That's how we met, Irene and me—in one of them recreational-type classes they got there. Swing dancing for 50 and older. They partnered us up together to learn the Lindy Hop, and Lord, how that woman can move. All those times I stepped on her foot, she didn't complain once." He shook his head in wonder. "Not even once."

Mrs. B. returned and managed to take Carl's arm without further incident. "Have fun," I said as they went down the porch steps together.

"Oh, we will," Mrs. B. replied. Even though her back was to me, I could hear her dimples in her voice.

They crossed the street to Mrs. B.'s ancient ocean liner of a Chrysler. Carl opened the driver's side door for his date, then clomped around to the passenger side and climbed in.

For her sake, I hoped Mrs. B.'s dancing shoes had steel toes.

Still in father-of-the-prom-queen mode, I waved from the porch as the car pulled away from the curb. The taillights faded as the Chrysler disappeared down the block.

The night air felt heavy with snow. You could smell it, mixed with the tang of wood smoke from someone's chimney. I stood on the porch, staring in the direction the Chrysler had gone. Along my street, a few lights lit up windows here and there, but most of the houses were dark—just porch lights on to welcome Friday-night partiers home. It was eerily quiet: no voices, no music, not even a television murmur or flickering blue light. Downtown would be another story. The bars and restaurants of the Crossing would be jammed, people laughing and shouting over the music that spilled out onto the sidewalk. Up in Collegeville, bordering Overton University, students would be getting a head start on their weekend goal of drinking themselves into oblivion and waking up next to a (hopefully attractive) stranger. Dinesh would be up there in the thick of it. Everyone was out having a good time. Even Mrs. B. had a date tonight. Hell, even Carl did.

I wondered what Felicia was doing, and the best I could come up with was a blurry image of cocktails, country clubs, and people swanning around in designer clothes. I imagined her in a black dress, hair up in a sort of Audrey Hepburn style; she was laughing and holding a martini glass. I looked at the bottle still in my hand, took a swig. Probably not many beer drinkers in that crowd. Anyway, what was I doing, thinking about Felicia? In fact, what the hell was I doing still hanging around Rhodes? I'd come back to town looking for my parents; my parents weren't here. I'd probably never see Frank or Rosie again—might as well admit it. And here I was, spending my days driving a taxi through a city and a landscape that had changed almost beyond recognition. Whatever I was looking for—my parents, the Homestead, a way of life that had made more sense the farther away I'd traveled—it wasn't here.

As soon as this murder investigation was cleared up, it would be time for me to move on. Where, I didn't know. Some place, maybe, where it wouldn't bother me so damn much to spend Friday night at home, alone.

I shivered—time to go inside. I took another swallow of beer and cast one more glance down the street. A flash of movement inside a big pickup truck parked under a streetlight caught my eye. I looked again. All was still. I could've sworn that I'd seen someone in the driver's seat take a sideways dive. Someone, now that I thought of it, with short blonde hair.

Forgetting the cold, I went across the street and rapped on the driver's window. No response. I hopped up on the running board to get a better view inside. A woman lay across the seat, face down, her arms folded over her head. She wore a leather motorcycle jacket. I rapped again.

Slowly, Trudy Hauser sat upright. Her expression, a cross between sheepish and mad as hell, was kind of cute. If your definition of cute included kittens, big-eyed children, and psychotic deputies.

I stepped back off the running board as she rolled down the window. "What?" she snapped.

"The official word is you're supposed to leave me alone."

"This is a public street. I can sit here if I want to."

"How would you like me to call Plodnick and tell him you're still following me?"

"Following you?" Her snort was not what you'd call ladylike. "I'm not following you. I'm sitting here minding my own business."

I gestured at the empty street. "Yeah, this is a popular hangout on the weekend."

She didn't answer, just set her jaw into a mule-like expression. That's when I noticed that her teeth were chattering, and she was trying like hell not to let it show.

"Look," I said, "it's cold out. The forecast says it's going to get colder. Snow, maybe. It can't be much fun sitting out here freezing. So let me save you the trouble. I'm not going to go out and do any crimes tonight, okay? I'm going to go back into my nice warm house, climb the stairs to my apartment, enjoy another fine microbrew, and then go to bed." She glared at me, sitting there stiffly and trying not to shiver. I felt a little sorry for her, but that stubborn set of her chin spurred me on. "In fact, tell you what. If I get a sudden urge for a crime spree, I'll call you. You'll be the first to know. In the meantime, you can go and do whatever it is that off-duty deputies are supposed to do on a Friday night—which I doubt includes harassing innocent citizens."

I tilted the bottle to drain the last dregs of porter. Her face lit up like fireworks.

"I could give you a ticket for that, you know. There's an ordinance against public drinking. Soon as you stepped off that porch with an open bottle in your hand, you were in violation."

"Oh, for Christ's sake, will you lay off? This is stupid. Why don't we call a truce? Come on up to my place, have a beer. Quit playing undercover agent or whatever the hell you think you're doing. Just for an hour."

She bit her lower lip, like she was thinking it over, like she might actually say yes. Of course she'd love to get into my place and nose around. She was probably fantasizing right now how she could get me drunk and wring a confession out of me. What the hell was I thinking? The last thing I wanted was to have this woman violate the sanctity of my apartment. Friday night or no Friday night. I must be losing it.

"Yeah, I thought not," I said, before she could answer.

"Consorting with the enemy and all that, huh? Well, stay warm, Deputy." I walked across the street, up the porch steps, and into the house, all without looking back.

Half an hour later, I thought I'd just glance out the window, see if the snow had started. I nudged apart two slats of the miniblinds and peered outside. No snow, but an empty space gaped under the streetlight where the pickup truck had been. Good. I let the miniblinds fall together. So Trudy Hauser had taken my advice and found a better way to spend her time. Why that depressed me, I had no clue.

Chapter 13

It was getting toward the end of my Saturday shift. I'd just dropped a couple of college kids at the mall when this guy came over and banged on my window. Made me jump a mile—man, I hate that. Especially when I've got fifteen different things to be jumpy about.

"I need a ride to the Towers," he said. He fidgeted with his necktie, wrapping it around his finger and then unwinding it.

"Sorry. I'm going off duty. And it's out of my way." Okay, so it was out of my way by maybe two miles. But the guy had annoyed me.

I was about to peel away, when he did something that made me hit the brakes. He said *please*.

"Please—it's urgent. I'll make it worth your while. Please."

Driving a cab, you forget that folks actually say things like "please" and "thank you." Or at least you forget they can say them to you. *Please* made me stop and look the guy in the face.

What he looked like was desperate. And hopeful. And scared. All at once. There was kind of earnestness in his expression, like he was trying to convince me of some complex argument using only his eyes.

"Get in."

As he opened the door, I listened for the "thanks." No dice.

I picked up the radio and told the dispatcher I was dropping off a fare at the Towers then heading back to the garage. "Wait," the voice said. "You're at the mall? We just got a call up there.

Do you see another fare anywhere?"

"That was me," the man said quickly. "I called. There's no one else."

I scanned the area in front of the glass doors. A few kids waited at the bus stop, but no one seemed to be watching for a cab. "Just the one fare," I told the dispatcher. I pulled a U-turn and headed to the exit.

The fare jabbered at me all the way to the hotel. He talked about local politics, national politics, college sports, and Thomson County's high taxes, the whole time winding and unwinding that damn tie. After a couple of miles, I was ready to yank the thing from his neck and toss it out the window. *Please* wasn't worth this crap.

We pulled up in front of the hotel, and he leaned forward. I could feel his breath on my neck. He thrust a bill at me before I'd even told him how much.

"Hang on, I can't make change for a hundred—"

"Just shut up and listen. Or don't you want to find out who killed Fred Davies?"

That shut me up for sure.

"You know the Speakeasy, right?"

A biker bar seven or eight miles west of town. I nodded.

"Go there. In the men's room, on the far wall by the broken hand dryer, there's a phone number. Call it."

He was out of the cab and through the hotel's revolving doors before I had a chance to ask him what the hell he was talking about.

I signed out at the garage and asked Dinesh if he wanted to get a beer.

"Sure, but I've got a couple of errands to run first. Meet you at Donovan's in twenty minutes?"

"Not Donovan's. I need a change of scenery. How about the

Speakeasy?"

He stared at me like I'd just suggested performing a blood ritual on the Crossing. "You're kidding, right?"

I shrugged. "Why not? I'm sick of hanging around town all the time."

"Bo, the Speakeasy is the kind of place Ventura hangs out. They'll eat you alive out there. It's a biker bar, for chrissakes. Hippies are their favorite bar snack."

"I'm not a hippie."

"But you look like one with that hair. And what do you think I'll look like to them? You, they'll eat for lunch. They'll just kill me."

"Come on. I'll even treat. I just got a ninety-dollar tip." I waved a wad of bills in his face.

His eyes bugged out, but he shook his head. "No way, man. Standing here right now, I'm exactly as close to the Speakeasy as I ever want to be."

Me too, I thought. But I was going there anyway.

The Speakeasy wasn't the kind of place I'd normally choose to spend my leisure hours. Watered-down beer served warm from the tap in a cloudy glass. A bar sticky with spilled drinks and a seventies-vintage jukebox. And on a Saturday night, you stood an excellent chance of getting into a fight with some switchblade-wielding maniac. But it was early, and I planned to get in and out quickly, before the regulars got rowdy.

The jukebox blared ZZ Top as I crossed the concrete floor toward the men's room.

"Hey! You gonna order something?" The bartender, bald except for a bristly salt-and-pepper moustache, looked like he started most of the fights himself. "Bathrooms are for customers only."

"Give me . . ." I tried to imagine what kind of beer they

served here. "Oh, hell, give me a Budweiser. In a bottle." I slapped a five on the bar. "I'll be right back."

The men's room looked like it had last been cleaned during the Carter administration. The fluorescent light was on the fritz, flashing and sputtering like the lighting in a slasher film. A line of hand dryers adorned the far wall. The one on the left looked like it had been recently serviced with a baseball bat—that would be the broken one. I headed toward it, then stopped in my tracks. All around the dryer, all over the whole goddamn wall, were dozens and dozens of scrawled phone numbers. It looked like half the Thomson County phone book.

I'm gonna kill that guy, I thought. I'm gonna find out who he is and then kill him.

Bad choice of words. Because the next morning, the same face that had peered into my cab window was staring out from the front page of the newspaper under the headline, "Local Banker Found Dead."

His name was George Boutros. He was single, forty-six, and a vice president at Rhodes National Bank. When he missed an important meeting without phoning in and coworkers couldn't get hold of him, they called the police. The cops had found Boutros in his home, tucked into bed and dead as a burned-out lightbulb. No autopsy yet, but drug paraphernalia had been found "beside the bed and elsewhere in the residence." There was yet another quote from Chief Ianelli decrying the tidal wave of hard drugs washing over Rhodes.

So the guy who'd jumped in my cab was a druggie. That would explain his fidgety behavior. Maybe he was tripping, with his talk of broken hand dryers and mysterious phone numbers. But his chatter had sounded lucid enough, and he knew who I was. What if he knew something? I wished to hell he'd just come out and told me whatever he had to say, instead of playing cloak-and-dagger games.

I read the article again. Rhodes National Bank was the DFA's bank, the one that issued the stolen cashier's check. That was one connection between Davies and Boutros. Maybe there were others, connections I couldn't find in the newspaper. Maybe Hedlund wasn't the embezzler, after all. What if Boutros had been skimming money from DFA accounts to support his drug habit? His picture smiled out at me from the front page. He was clean shaven, his short hair receding a little on top and around the temples. He didn't look like an addict, but outside of the movies, who does? Still, I couldn't shake the feeling that he'd known something but—for some reason I couldn't guess at—he'd been afraid to tell me.

Damn it. Even though Boutros was dead, I wasn't done with him yet. He was still my only lead. After my shift, I'd have to pay another visit to the Speakeasy.

The same bartender was working, and he gave me the same evil look as he had the day before. Man, what was it with bartenders lately? Usually I got along great with them. Under his glare, I stopped at the bar to order.

"You gonna drink this one?"

"What?"

"Last time you were in here you ran out without even touching the beer you ordered. If you're planning on doing the same thing today, I thought I'd save a wasted beer and just throw you out now." He smiled, showing me a mouth in need of serious dental work.

"Just give me the goddamn Bud. And I need some quarters in the change."

I paid with a twenty. He gave me a ten, some singles, and—to my surprise—over two dollars' worth of quarters. I made a big show of taking a swig of my Bud, straight out of the bottle. The bartender grunted and moved down the bar to wipe beer mugs with a dirty rag.

"Free Bird" came over the sound system. As soon as I noticed the bartender singing along—was that a tear slithering toward his moustache?—I slipped off the barstool and headed for the men's room.

I pulled a notepad from my back pocket and walked over to the dented-up dryer hanging halfway off the wall. Just as I remembered, there were dozens of phone numbers scribbled all around it. Most of them promised a good time if you called some woman. Starting on the left side and working in a circle, I copied down the dozen phone numbers closest to the dryer. When there was a name attached, I wrote that down, too. Boutros never actually said that the number I wanted was the one *closest* to the broken hand dryer, but I had to start somewhere. There must have been a hundred phone numbers on that wall.

I was bent practically upside down, copying a number written beneath the dryer, when the door opened and a voice said, "Looking for a date, huh?"

I jumped up and spun around, whacking my head in the process.

A man stood grinning at me. He was obviously proud of his beer gut, the way he let it peek between the buttons of his flannel shirt. I rubbed my head and stared at him. What can you say when someone catches you copying phone numbers off a bathroom wall?

"Call Cherree, man, she is fine. But make sure you get the right girl. Two *r*'s, two *e*'s: C-H-E-R-R-E-E. I guess that's three *e*'s, ain't it? Here, it's the one in red pen. I wrote it in myself."

He started forward to show me.

"Um, thanks. I got what I needed."

I dodged around him and went out. The payphone was right

outside the men's room door, but I figured I'd better put in another appearance at the bar so as not to hurt the bartender's delicate feelings.

My beer was gone. So was the ten-dollar bill I'd stupidly left beside it.

"Hey, thanks for the tip." The bartender treated me to another of his dingy 10-watt smiles. "Your beer was getting warm, so I took the liberty of disposing of it for you. I guess you'll be wanting another."

What I wanted was to tell him to go to hell and find somewhere else to make my phone calls, but I figured I might have to keep trying for a while before I found the right number. *If* I found it. So I assured him that another Bud was just what I wanted. This time, I paid a nickel over the cost. "Keep the change," I said.

He scowled, and I went to use the phone. The guy in the flannel shirt came out of the men's room and gave me a thumbs-up. "Say hi to Cherree for me."

I turned my back to him, to the bartender, to the whole damn place, and dropped in a quarter. I punched in the first number on my list.

"Hellooo?" a woman said, her voice rising about an octave by the end of the word.

I realized I had no clue what to say. "Uh . . . uh . . ."

"Who is this?"

I tried to clear my throat to stall for time, but this set off a coughing fit. The woman on the line got angrier.

"Is this another of them sicko calls? 'Cause lemme tell you, I've had about enough of them lately. I don't know where you perverts get this number. But you just hang on. I got a police whistle 'round here somewhere . . ."

I hung up before she could find it. Great start. I stared at the list for a full minute before I tried the next number.

This number had a name with it. When a woman answered, I asked for Marge.

"This is Marge. What can I do for you, sugar?"

"I'm calling about Fred Davies."

"Sorry, honey. No one by that name here."

"No, what I mean is—"

"You have an awful nice-sounding voice. What's your name?"

"Uh, that doesn't really matter." I wondered if I should just hang up. How much information could this woman have if she didn't even know Davies was dead? But maybe that was just a cover. Could there be some kind of code word? Damn that Boutros. Then inspiration hit. "George told me to call you."

She caught her breath. Bingo! I thought. Then she cursed, her voice hard and angry. "You mean George Rakowski? That no-good bum owes me fifty dollars! You tell that goddamn George his credit is no good with me. And you tell him not to give out my number to his lousy friends until he forks over my money!" *Click. Buzz.*

Ten minutes later, I'd gone through the whole list and used up most of my quarters. I got two answering machines. One number kept ringing and ringing; another was disconnected, and the rest claimed ignorance of anyone named Fred Davies or George. One man threatened to impair my future ability to have children if I ever called his wife again. He sounded like he meant it.

"You sure do enjoy our men's room," said the bartender when I sat back down at the bar. "I never seen anyone spend as much time in there as you do."

More men had come in while I was on the phone. Some of them turned to gape at me. I heard a snicker.

"You know," continued the bartender loudly, "up in Collegeville, where all them goddamn liberals live, they got bars for your kind." He held up his arm, making his hand flop over like his wrist was too weak to support it. The guys at the bar guffawed.

"I was making some phone calls," I said through my teeth. "In fact, I could use some more quarters."

"Yeah, sure you were." He turned to the other guys at the bar. "Better be careful if you need to take a piss tonight, boys. Might be some long-haired pretty boy wants to play peek-a-boo." He sneered at me. "Quarters, huh? Sorry I can't help you. All I got is a goddamn *nickel.*"

The hell with it. I wasn't going to sit there and be laughed at by a bunch of bikers. "I'm making a phone call," I announced, wading through their hoots and catcalls to the phone.

I still had two quarters, but I didn't have any numbers left to call. Hoping no one could see me go in, I pushed open the door of the men's room and headed straight for the beat-up dryer, but someone blocked my way. Someone who stood there drying his hands.

"What the hell?" How could he possibly be using *that* one?

The biker turned to stare at me. He was big and mean-looking, with long greasy hair and tattoos all the way up his arms to where his shoulders disappeared into his leather vest. He didn't look like he ever washed at all, yet there he was drying his hands. At the broken dryer.

"You got a problem?" he asked.

"Yeah. No. I mean, I thought that dryer was broken."

He turned back to the dryer, rubbing his hands in the air stream. When he was finished, it took him three steps to put himself in my face. "What are you, some kind of freak?"

"No, not at all." I twisted my head around to study the wall beyond him. There were three dryers on it. "Well, look at it. Doesn't it look broken to you? Somebody beat it all to hell."

He turned and inspected the wall. "Yup," he said, "but it works." Then he walked past me, bumping me hard on the shoulder, and went into the bar.

I rushed over and hit the buttons on all three dryers. The two on the left hummed and spewed out air. The one on the right, although it looked okay, didn't turn on. I hit the button again, then one more time. Nothing. And next to this dryer, pressed almost into the corner and written in thick black marker, was a single phone number.

Chapter 14

I went back to the payphone and tried the number—busy signal. I tried again, two, three, four, five times. It figured I'd be calling the only number in America without voice mail—not that I was about to leave a message. After a few minutes, I gave up and left, glad to get out of that damn bar and into the early twilight.

Half an hour later, I was back in Rhodes, at a gas-station payphone on Route 13. I'd chosen this station because the phone sat at the edge of the lot, away from the pumps, the convenience store, the parking spaces. I didn't know who I was about to talk to, but I didn't need anyone overhearing. And I sure didn't need the call on my cell phone record.

I'd just picked up the receiver when a car pulled up behind me, tires crunching gravel. A second later, red lights flashed rhythmically across me, the phone, the piece of paper in my hand. I turned around to see Trudy Hauser get out of her cruiser. Goddamn it. I knew I should've set Plodnick on her. For one minute, I'd felt sorry for her, given her a break, and now she was stalking me again.

Hand on her gun, she swaggered toward me. I stuffed the paper with the phone number into my jacket pocket.

"Who're you calling?" She gave me a smile that would have been sweet if it weren't so damn sarcastic. "Because if you're calling me to confess, I'm not home right now."

"You know, you've got a real tendency to show up at all the wrong times. Where were you earlier? I could have used a pain-in-the-ass deputy with a gun."

"You mean out at the Speakeasy? No, thanks—not my kind of place. You know," she leaned in close, her voice confidential, "illegal drugs have been known to change hands there."

"No!"

She nodded. "I figured that's what you were up to. Didn't want to cramp your style, so I waited in the parking lot. I'd hate to have to haul you in for possession."

"I thought it was your most cherished dream to arrest me."

"Not for possession. For murder." She squinted down Route 13, rubbing her neck, then turned back to me. "Want to know what I figure?"

"No."

"I figure you were trying to get yourself arrested. You know I'm keeping an eye on you, so you go and buy a joint or two. That's a class B misdemeanor—get you a couple of months. While you're on the inside, all nice and cozy, the case is cooling off. You've got that money stashed somewhere good, some place you're sure we won't find it. You're just biding your time." She tapped her temple with her forefinger. "Pretty smart."

"You know, if I were as smart as you think I am," I said, as she looked at me all smug, "I'd be pretty damn stupid." She blinked, and I kept going before she could think of some smart-ass answer. "You think I intend to sit in some jail cell while you and your cop buddies build a phony case against me? Uh-uh."

I turned my back to her and picked up the phone. I'd call the goddamn time and temperature number just to ignore the woman. A moment later the cop lights stopped flashing. I listened for her car to leave, but the next thing I heard was her voice—quiet, menacing, and right in my ear.

"You gave George Boutros a ride yesterday."

I whirled around to face her. How the hell did she know that? Now it was my turn to gape.

She smiled, knowing she'd scored a hit. "It occurred to me to wonder where Boutros got ahold of those bad drugs. And then I find out you gave the guy a ride, and next thing you know, Boutros is dead. Hmm . . ." She put a finger on her chin in a pantomime of thinking deeply. "So now what I'm wondering is—did you know the drugs you sold him were bad? Or were you purposely supplying Boutros with bad drugs to shut him up about something?"

I shook my head, unable even to begin to explain how wrong she was.

"Catch you later, Rainbow." She grinned like an evil Cheshire cat, then sauntered to her patrol car. She backed up, one arm across the seat, turned toward the exit, and left.

Her car merged into the flow of traffic on Route 13, heading south. Damn, that woman was tenacious. Behind those big brown puppy-dog eyes was a pit bull that bit down hard and refused to let go. One that blamed me for every recent unnatural death in Thomson County.

When I was sure she was gone, I dialed the number. A man answered on the first ring. "Yeah?"

I clenched the phone. "George told me to call you."

There was a pause. I thought I heard muffled voices and maybe music in the background, but a semi chose that moment to roar past on 13, so I couldn't be sure. Then the voice came back on the line.

"George is dead." My heart started pounding. This was it—this was the right number.

"Yeah, I know. But I'm calling anyway."

Another pause. I waited, straining to hear the background noises. Music, yeah. And two voices.

"Okay," the voice said. "We'll cut you the same deal as George. Three thousand, cash. Can you handle that?"

"Sure." No, but I'd worry about that later.

"You got it now?"

"What, you think I carry around three G's in my wallet? I'll have it by this time tomorrow."

"Tomorrow night. Two A.M. We'll meet you in the parking lot by the overlook at Oneida Falls. Got it?"

"I'll be there."

He hung up.

I stood looking at the phone in my hand. What the hell had I gotten myself into? In just over twenty-four hours, I was going to show up, short of cash, in an out-of-the-way place to meet some seriously dangerous people for a transaction that could easily send me to prison for as long as Trudy Hauser would like to put me there—if they didn't kill me first.

I had no intention, of course, of participating in any drug deal. Neither was I itching for a formal introduction to the men who'd put George Boutros out of commission. Maybe Trudy was right, maybe Boutros had been murdered. And these guys were offering me the "same deal." Big joke—no way was I going to let myself become the punch line.

My plan was simple, which is why I thought it could work. The most complicated part was keeping Trudy Hauser off my trail. Dinesh agreed to help out there. He would come over to my apartment in the evening for a couple of beers, parking his huge, shiny, Tonka-truck yellow SUV—fondly nicknamed the Big Banana—on the street out front. He could do the drinking for both of us, since he was going to crash at my place. Around midnight, I'd put on his jacket and tuck my hair up into his trademark Yankees cap, then go outside and drive off in the Banana. I'm about three inches taller than Dinesh, but the streetlight in front of my building was burned out, and if I hunched a little, I'd get away with the impersonation. Anyone who knows me knows I'd never be caught dead in a baseball cap.

After that, the good deputy could sit and stare at my apartment all night if she wanted to. I had the keys to Dinesh's apartment in Collegeville and would return there after my rendezvous.

Except there wasn't going to be any rendezvous.

Dinesh arrived, hitting his horn a couple of times and parking exactly below the burned-out streetlight. Perfect. He made a big show of getting out of the Banana, waving at me and shouting, "Party time!" He lifted two six packs, one in each hand, for my approval.

"What the hell was that performance?" I asked him at the front door.

He grinned. "Just making sure that cute little deputy knows I'm here."

We were headed up the stairs to my apartment when Mrs. Boothroyd stuck her head out her door, scowling. "I hope you boys won't be making a ruckus," she said. "It's a school night, you know."

"We won't, Mrs. B.," I promised. "Sorry if my friend was a little loud."

She harrumphed and shut her door.

"Why do I feel like I've been sent to the principal's office?" Dinesh asked.

"She's *worse* than the principal, man. She's the head cafeteria lady. She's also president of the North End Tenants' Association. So behave yourself. I don't want to get kicked out of my apartment."

"You mean you live upstairs from the person who's responsible for putting mystery meat on a soggy English muffin?" He shuddered. "And you expect me to *sleep* here tonight?"

★ ★ ★ ★ ★

"Okay," Dinesh said once we were upstairs. "Here's my camera. Let me show you how to use the night setting."

He turned on the digital camera, glanced at the LCD, and grinned. "Hey, did I show you these pictures?"

I looked over his shoulder as he scrolled through the photos. Two women dressed in skimpy bras and panties attacked each other in a wading pool—twisting arms, pulling hair, getting covered with green goop. The last one showed the winner striking a pose.

"Trina?" I asked.

"Yeah, she really rubbed her opponent's face in the pudding that time." He pressed a button and the LCD went blank. "Be careful with the camera, okay? I haven't uploaded all of these yet."

He went back to showing me how to set the camera to take night shots. I intended to get to the rendezvous site early, hide, then snap as many photos as I could of whoever showed up. No meeting, just some evidence I could use to identify the voice on the phone. If I had a name, I thought, everything else would fall into place.

Dinesh cracked open a beer. "You want one? Steady your nerves?"

"Nerves? Mine are rock solid." But that wasn't how I felt. My stomach was queasy, my heart pumped, and my focus felt off. A lot of years had passed since my last mission; I wasn't used to this shit anymore.

It was about 11:40 when Dinesh handed me his jacket and keys. "Be careful," he said. "Those are nasty people."

"Nothing to worry about. They'll never see me. Worst case: They won't show up, and I'll freeze my butt off in the woods." We'd just watched the eleven o'clock news; the weatherman was predicting another cold night.

"You taking a gun?"

"You know I'm not."

"Thought you might change your mind. The other side probably isn't quite so fastidious."

"I swore off guns in '92. Anyway, they won't see me to shoot at."

He looked at me doubtfully.

"Hey," I said, "Special Forces, remember? I'm a trained soldier, man."

"Last time I checked, soldiers carried guns."

I put on the Yankees cap and grimaced at my reflection in the mirror. Definitely not my style.

"Too cool for words," Dinesh said. "You should get yourself one of those. Turn you into an instant chick magnet."

He stayed upstairs while I let myself out. For the first time in a month, I was glad the city hadn't got around to replacing that streetlight as I got into the Big Banana and closed the door.

I drove to the stop sign at the end of the street. No car appeared behind me—no sign of any movement at all. So far, so good. I grinned and gunned the engine as I headed out of town.

Parking was a problem. Dinesh's SUV was big and noticeable—great for distracting nosy deputies, but not so great now. I couldn't leave it on the side of the road in the middle of nowhere at two in the morning. Then I remembered the campground near the base of the falls. There were likely to be a few intrepid souls sleeping in tents down there, even in November. A vehicle parked near a campsite wouldn't look out of place.

I parked away from the road, next to the log building that served as park office and camp store. The office was closed, the building locked up tight. Across the campground, I could make out the shapes of a couple of tents and an RV. Everything was quiet.

A bright moon lit up the path, which twisted steeply uphill to the falls overlook. The night was cold, and I must have been tired; I still felt queasy and off-balance as I climbed. When I reached the rendezvous point, I skirted the parking area, keeping well back in the woods. There was no sign of anyone: not a car in the lot, not a rustle of leaves. I paused every few minutes to look and listen, but each time all I heard was the blood beating in my temples.

A low rock where I could lie down and see the whole parking lot made a good vantage point. I heaped up a pile of leaves and climbed inside them, lying on my stomach. It took a few minutes to get the camera into position and arrange myself in something approximating comfort. Then I was still, and the night settled around me. I waited.

It was going to be a long wait. I was more than an hour early for our two o'clock meeting. I must have dozed off because suddenly I lurched awake, blinded by headlights on the road. The car passed the lot, didn't even slow down. I checked my watch: ten to two. Okay, boys, let's go. I'm ready for you.

Anticipation stretched out each minute that ticked by. A hundred times I tensed, feeling this was it; a hundred times I was wrong. I was so tensed up that it took excruciating physical effort just to lie still. Any second, I thought, any second now. Two o'clock came, then went. Nothing happened.

By two-thirty, I knew they weren't going to show. I waited until three.

When I finally got up, I was stiff and sore and aching with the cold. I brushed off the leaves that clung to my clothes, stamping my feet to restore circulation. I thought the hike back to the car would warm me, but as I walked I couldn't stop shivering. The frosty night, all that tension coming to nothing—it felt like the cold had taken up residence inside my skin. All I wanted was to get in the Big Banana and turn up the heat full blast. At the SUV's door, my fingers were stiff, and I dropped the keys. They landed in the shadows with a metallic clatter.

Cursing, I bent to retrieve them. As I did, I heard a pop and the crash of glass shattering—glass that rained down on my head and shoulders. It took me a second to realize that someone was shooting at me.

I dropped to the ground and rolled under the SUV. I was trapped. I had no clear idea of where the shot came from or how many gunmen there might be. But they sure as hell knew where I was.

I held my breath and strained to listen. I could just make out the sound of footsteps approaching across the gravel parking lot. My best chance—hell, my *only* chance—would be to roll out on the other side of the SUV and disappear into the woods. Unless another gunman was waiting for me there.

The footsteps stopped. I could see a pair of tan work boots a few feet away from the car. I got ready to run for my life.

With roaring engine and squealing tires, a car peeled off the road. A horn blared. Headlights swept the ground. I heard shouting and another engine. Tires on the gravel close by. A door slammed; a car took off. I heard engines revving, tires screaming, some bangs that might have been more shots. The cars—how many were there?—took off down the road. Within seconds, all that noise faded into silence.

I crawled out from under the SUV, on the far side from where I'd seen the boots. I crouched by the car, listening, then stood up cautiously. The parking lot was deserted. A haze of dust or exhaust hung in the light of the streetlamp by the exit.

"Hey!" a voiced shouted. I jumped and spun around at the cry. Thank God I didn't have a gun, or I swear I would have fired. A jowl-faced man in longjohns jogged toward me from the direction of the tents. "What the hell's going on?"

"Beats me," I said. "Kids, maybe. Or a couple of drunk hunters."

"I thought I heard shots." The guy shook his head. "The sport's gone all to hell. Any lunatic with a gun thinks he can blast away at anything that moves." He came up beside the SUV and realized he was stepping on safety glass. He peered at the vehicle. The bullet had passed through the driver's side window and ripped across some upholstery before shattering another window on the passenger's side.

"Jesus!" he said. "They do that? You're lucky they didn't kill you."

Yeah, I thought glumly, because when Dinesh sees his car, he's going to want the honor of doing that himself.

Driving with two shot-out windows didn't help me get warm. Even with the heat blasting, I shivered all the way back to town. All I wanted was to crawl into my own bed. Too bad for me I couldn't. Dinesh was fast asleep by now, and even if he wasn't, I didn't have the energy to explain what had happened to his car. I knew a guy who ran an auto body shop in Enfield who might cut me a deal, and I wanted to be armed with an estimate before I showed Dinesh the damage.

Funny I was so worried about the car when someone had very nearly done damage of a more permanent sort to my head. What the hell had gone wrong out there? The events of the past few hours came back in jagged flashes—shattered glass, tan work boots, a fat guy in longjohns. Where had the second car come from? Why did the shooter take off? My head hurt thinking about it.

Dinesh lived in one of Collegeville's new high-rise apartment buildings. I drove up the steep, tranquil street through the predawn quiet. My joints ached. I was so stiff I could barely drag myself up the stairs from the garage to the lobby. I felt like I was walking through a long, dark tunnel, and the walls and floor seemed to pulse through flashes of bright light. Thank God there was an elevator to get me to the eighth floor. I was shivering so badly that I had to keep stopping to lean against the wall as I shuffled down the hallway. Somehow, I made it into the apartment, where I cranked up the thermostat and fell into bed.

CHAPTER 15

I must have turned the heat too high because when I woke up I was sweating, the blankets tangled around my feet. The room was too bright; I couldn't see through the glare. My head throbbed. I became aware of a cool hand on my forehead, one that reminded me of my mother.

"Rosie?"

"Uh, no. Sorry."

It was a woman's voice. I squinted toward the sound. Gradually, a face came into focus.

"What the hell are you doing here?" I struggled to sit up.

"Hush." Trudy Hauser put a hand on my chest, trying to make me lie down. "You're sick. You've got a fever."

"This is private property. You can't come barging in."

"Dinesh let me in."

"Why in hell would he do a stupid thing like that?"

"Because he—"

"Just stop, okay? I can't deal with you right now." The pounding in my head added to my sense of aggravation. "I feel like crap. I got shot at last night. Go away. I am *not* the goddamned killer."

The outburst left me exhausted. I collapsed against the pillows, my heart a jackhammer in my chest. I wanted her gone, but I wanted even more for her to shut up and put that soothing hand back on my forehead.

"I believe you."

Great. Now I was hallucinating. Maybe we could swing by a hospital on the way to the Sheriff's office.

"Bo," she said, and her hand on my forehead felt like the answer to a prayer, "I know what happened last night. I was there."

It was too much. I had to be dreaming. I heard her voice, all echo-y and far away, telling me that we'd talk later, that now I should sleep. It seemed like excellent advice, so I took it.

The next time I awoke, I felt better. Dinesh sprawled in a chair by the bed, reading *Playboy.* I started to tell him about the crazy dream I'd had—Trudy Hauser as ministering angel—then remembered I had some less amusing news for him.

"Um, about the Big Banana," I began.

"I saw it." His eyes were still on the magazine. I couldn't read his expression. "You parked in my neighbor's space. She was pretty pissed off."

"I know this guy out in Enfield—"

"With an auto body shop? I've already talked to him." Dinesh looked up; amazingly, he was smiling. "He's fixing it for free. Owes me a favor."

"I guess I owe you a couple of favors by now."

"A couple?" He snorted as he put the magazine on the nightstand. "At least."

"You're not mad about the car?"

"I'm mad as hell—at whoever did the damage. That wasn't you, by the way. But I'd be a whole lot madder if that asshole had been a better shot."

"He was a good shot, all right. I dropped your keys at just the right moment."

"Man."

He shook his head, and we sat there for a minute. Last night had been too close. There were killers out there who'd had me—literally—in their sights. I'd survived thanks only to dumb, clumsy luck. If they came after me again—well, I couldn't see any way of stacking the odds in my favor. I still had no clue who they were.

The doorbell rang, and Dinesh went to answer it. He reappeared a moment later. "You, ah, have a visitor," he said. I could see Trudy Hauser's face peering past his shoulder. She stepped around him and into the room.

"Are we feeling better?" She said it all bright and cheerful, like a nurse on a children's ward, but she was wearing her deputy's uniform, complete with gun. The effect was surreal.

"We think we might live."

She was carrying a thermos, and she thrust it out in front of her with both hands. "Chicken soup."

What was I supposed to do, start playing nice all of a sudden? I did not want this woman around me. Who the hell did she think she was, bringing me chicken soup like some kindly old grandma? She didn't know what "kindly" meant. I shook my head. "I'm a vegetarian."

"I'm not." Dinesh relieved her of the thermos and unscrewed the lid. "Smells good. I'm starving." Using that as his exit line, he retreated to the kitchen. Thanks, bud.

"Vegetarian, huh? And I thought I knew everything about you. I should have guessed."

"Why are you here, Deputy?"

"Truce, okay? Like you said the other night. And call me Trudy. This is an unofficial visit."

"Yeah, I could tell by your casual attire."

"I'm in the middle of a shift. This is my lunch break." She sat in the bedside chair. "Like I told you before, I saw what happened last night. And I thought—"

"What do you mean, you saw what happened? You couldn't have. You were watching my apartment all night."

"Oh, come on. Did you really think you'd fool me by putting on a baseball cap? You and Dinesh are nothing alike—different builds, different ways of walking. I knew right away it was you."

"I didn't see anyone following me."

"If I'm doing it right, you're not *supposed* to see me."

Okay, so she'd done it again. I was impressed, but the smirk on her face prevented me from admitting it.

"So suddenly you're on my side, huh? Why should I believe you? You think you're some hotshot undercover superdetective, but you're just a pain in the ass. Why should I believe anything you say?"

"Because I saved your life last night, Rainbow. Who do you think came in like the cavalry and scared the shooter off? That was me."

"Yeah? Did you catch them?"

She sagged like a leaky balloon. "No. They got away."

"And why was that?"

"I hit a pothole. Damn thing must've been a foot deep. Blew out a tire and wrecked the wheel rim."

The admission embarrassed her. Watching her blush, I found myself glad that those crooks had kept going, instead of turning around to have a word with her.

"Do you know who shot at me?"

She shook her head. "No plates on the car. I saw the shooter when I pulled into the parking lot, but I didn't get a good look at him. He was wearing a pea coat and a knitted cap. White guy, about five-seven, five-eight. I didn't get much of a look at his face." Again she blushed. She didn't like admitting to failure. She'd been so close to catching those guys—also to getting herself shot. It seemed like some kind of miracle that both of us had survived the night and were sitting here now, more or less unscathed.

She smiled at me—encouraging, almost friendly—as the

blush faded from her cheeks. "What I wanted to ask you, off the record, is what you were doing there last night."

Since this wasn't her case, on or off the record didn't apply. But for some reason it didn't matter. Her face was open, completely without sarcasm. Her gaze reminded me of that cool hand stroking away my fever.

I talked. I told her about Boutros's cab ride and cryptic message, about my trips to the Speakeasy, about how I set up the meeting. I even told her about last night's brilliant plan without any embarrassment at how it had almost got me killed. She listened, nodding from time to time, refraining from any wise-ass comments. When I was through, she sat silent for a moment, her lips pursed.

"Do you still have that phone number?" she asked.

"Yeah. It's in my jacket pocket." But I'd come back wearing Dinesh's jacket. We called him out of the kitchen. He'd brought my own jacket; now he retrieved the paper from its pocket. Trudy snatched it.

"Great. I'll find out who the phone number belongs to." She went to make a call.

A few minutes later, she returned, a funny expression on her face.

"You sure this is right?"

"Yeah. Why, whose is it?"

"It's the number for the payphone at the Speakeasy."

I gaped at her, feeling like I was sinking back into delirium. "The Speakeasy? Are you sure?"

She nodded.

Jesus, what an idiot I'd been, standing at that very payphone, dialing it over and over to get a busy signal—because I was the one on the phone, calling myself.

"Why in hell would Boutros tell me to call the payphone at the Speakeasy? I can't believe I wasted all that time playing his stupid game."

"Not necessarily. Think about it. When you called that number from a different phone, somebody answered—and then tried to kill you. You touched a nerve." She had a point. There had been more to my attempts to call that number than a constant busy signal—like a bullet whizzing past my head. "We know that Boutros was mixed up with drugs. And we know that drugs are sold at the Speakeasy. I've heard rumors there's a big operation run out of the place, even though we've only been able to make a couple of minor busts so far. What if Boutros was trying to tell you that Davies was involved in whatever's going on out there?"

"And that's what got him killed." Maybe got both of them killed.

"Sounds like a theory." She checked her watch. "I've got to get back to work. Listen, though, I have a proposition for you."

Suddenly I remembered who I was talking to. There she was, in her deputy's uniform, getting ready to tell me what to do. I eyed her warily. But there was something different about her—the scowl was gone, replaced by a look of wide-eyed earnestness.

"How 'bout we pool our resources?" she asked.

"You want to work together? You and me?"

"Why not? Neither of us is supposed to be investigating this case, but neither of us is going to quit any time soon, right?" She sat on the edge of the bed. "I've got access to police resources you don't, including," for some reason, a blush spread across her face, "a source inside Rhodes PD. And you've been checking out people who knew Davies. So you can bring me up to speed on what you've learned—like who else might've had a motive. What do you say?"

She leaned toward me, eyes still wide, the image of sincerity. But part of me couldn't help wondering what she was up to.

Was she trying to gain my trust so she could nail me later? I wouldn't put it past her. On the other hand, she'd saved my life the night before. I couldn't argue with that. And she might have information that would help me. I decided to risk it.

"All right. When do you want to compare notes?"

"How about tonight, after my shift?" A look of concern crossed her face. She made a movement like she was going to put her hand on my forehead, then checked herself. "Or do you want to get more rest? You were pretty feverish this morning."

"I'll be fine." I wouldn't have minded that light touch on my forehead one more time. "You want to meet at Donovan's?"

"I'd rather make sure that no one listens in on us. Plodnick's still got men on you, you know." Jesus. Half of Rhodes still following me around, and I'd given in to wishful thinking that Plodnick would leave me alone. "How 'bout you come out to my place? Eight o'clock?"

"I'll be there."

She said she lived in a trailer—"not in a park, it's on my own lot, out in the woods"—and gave me directions. Then she checked her watch again, swore under her breath, and left.

I lay back against the pillows and closed my eyes. So Deputy Hauser and I would be working together. Snow fell in Hell and pigs flew past the window. I wondered how much stranger reality would look when I finally managed to wake up.

I figured I'd intruded on Dinesh's hospitality long enough, so as soon as I could stand without the room spinning, I thanked him for his help and went back to my place. Good thing I had the day off. I'd slept through what would've been my shift. Plus it was hard to drive, the way the ground kept tilting.

Dinesh had left my Corolla in a visitor's space. I pulled onto College Street, into another cold, damp November day, so dark that it seemed like night was falling. I looked at my watch—only three-thirty. I'd have some time to pull myself together before meeting Trudy at eight.

In my apartment, I thought to check my phone for messages. I turned it on—one new voicemail. Okay, let's see who'd called.

"Bo, hi, it's Sharon Barton. We bumped into each other last week, in the grocery store? I got your number from Ryan Pullansky; he said you wouldn't mind."

Thanks, Ryan, I thought. Why don't you just put out a newsletter? *The Bo Forrester Gazette.* Publish my trip sheets, my contact info, high school grades, shoe size . . .

"I haven't seen Ryan," Sharon was saying, "since . . . good Lord, since the class reunion two years ago. Funny how you can live in the same town and never bump into each other. Anyway, the reason I'm calling is someone came into the bank today. You used to know him. Leonard Ehrlich—"

Lenny Early! From the Homestead. He'd earned that nickname because he was always the first one up each morning, watching the sun rise over the east field. Lenny almost burned down the barn trying to build a still. He'd also taught me to skip stones, spinning a flat stone so it would skitter nearly all the way to the pond's far shore before it sank.

"Len has an organic farm now," Sharon was saying, "out in Van Etten. He's doing well. He came in to apply for a mortgage to buy a couple of neighboring fields. Of course, I *had* to tell him I'd seen you. And, well, the upshot is that Len said he knows someone who might know where your parents moved to. So call me back when you get a chance. And don't forget, you're coming over for dinner soon. Bobby can't wait to see you. Well, he claims he doesn't remember you, but I'm sure once you're here . . . Anyway, bye for now." A computerized voice informed me she'd called the day before at seven-oh-six P.M.

A lead on my parents—I found Sharon's business card and snatched up the phone. Then, phone in hand, I stared at the card: *Sharon Barton, Senior Loan Officer, Rhodes National Bank.* The same bank Boutros had worked for. Suddenly, I had two reasons to call Sharon: maybe, just maybe, she could put me on the trail of Rosie and Frank. That was more than I'd hoped for since I'd returned to Rhodes. But Sharon had worked with Boutros. Maybe she'd even worked on the DFA's accounts.

I dialed her number, thinking that a home-cooked meal—even in the home of superjerk Bobby Barton—was sounding awfully good.

CHAPTER 16

A little before eight I was on my way to see Trudy Hauser, bumping down a dirt road and wondering what the hell I was going to say to the woman I'd been trying to shove out of my life for the past two weeks. Trudy's trailer was out past Jacksonville, a couple of turns off Route 96 and down one of those long, narrow roads you could drive past a hundred times without ever wondering where it went. After a mile, fields gave way to thick woods. Then a sharp bend to the right and there it was: Trudy's trailer, in a grove of pine trees, her pickup truck parked to one side. A light shone by the front door.

I walked across a carpet of pine needles and up three steps. I took a deep breath and rang the bell.

The door flew open like she'd been standing there waiting.

"Hi," she said.

"Hi."

She stood in the doorway, a smile pasted on her face, probably just like the one pasted on mine. Neither of us moved. We stayed that way, with our fixed smiles, the yellow light pouring over us, like bugs trapped in amber.

"Um, do you mind if I come in?"

She laughed nervously as she stepped back. "Sorry. It's just . . . a little strange to see you here."

"Tell me about it."

I stood on the postage stamp of linoleum that made up the entryway, feeling big and awkward in the singlewide. Trudy went right, into the galley-sized kitchen. I followed. She pulled open the refrigerator door. "Would you like a beer?"

I looked past her into the fridge, which held a six-pack of Miller Light.

"Better not. I'm still getting over that bug."

"Orange juice? For the vitamin C."

"Thanks, that'd be great."

She filled a big glass and handed it to me. In the bright light of the kitchen, Trudy looked different. She'd fluffed up her short hair, and done something with makeup to make her eyes look big and round. Lipstick, even—there was a little cloud of red at the corner of her mouth where it had smudged. To tell the truth, I thought she looked better without the gunk on her face. But there was a softness to her looks—a prettiness, almost—that I'd never noticed all those times I'd seen her in uniform.

"I thought you might be hungry," she said. "So I'm putting together some snacks. Nothing fancy. Oh, and one-hundred-percent vegetarian."

"Thanks, but you didn't—"

Her eyes got even rounder, and she cut me off. "Omigosh. You do eat cheese, right? God, please don't tell me you're one of those raw-food vegans."

I assured her that cheese was fine.

Her laugh, still nervous, was high-pitched and flute-y. "Nachos. I made the salsa from scratch. All organic veggies—I got organic avocadoes for the guacamole, too. I thought, you know, being vegetarian and all, you probably went for that stuff."

I didn't know what to say. A couple of days ago, this woman had been determined to arrest me. Then she'd saved my life. Now, not only had she invited me to her home, she'd gone to a lot of trouble to play hostess. Never in a million years would I have expected any of this from Trudy Hauser.

"Thanks. Can I help?"

"No, kitchen's too small for more than one cook. It's almost ready. You go on into the living room and relax. It's just down that hall." She gave me a little push to get me moving in the right direction.

I entered the paneled living room and found myself nose-to-nose with the antlered head of a huge buck mounted over the sofa. In fact, the entire decorating scheme revolved around dead animals' body parts. A smaller doe's head stared at me from a side wall. Two lamps had been fashioned from antlers, and there was a candy dish, piled high with peppermints, made out of a bear's paw. A scruffy-looking stuffed squirrel in a glass case perched on top of the entertainment center. Its glass eyes gleamed at me like it expected an acorn.

I looked at the expensive-looking CD player a couple of shelves beneath the squirrel. Maybe a little music would make the place feel less creepy. "Okay if I put on a CD?" I called.

The whirring of some kitchen appliance obscured Trudy's reply.

I raised an eyebrow at the antlered deer head. "What do you think, Buck? That a yes?"

I took Buck's silence as agreement.

Behind one of the glass doors of the entertainment center was a crammed-full CD rack. I flipped through the titles, praying I'd find something I could listen to: please, God, let there be classic rock, blues, even jazz—anything but country. I favored guitar-heavy rock from the late sixties and early seventies, and I liked classic country from that period. I just couldn't listen to the stuff that came out of Nashville nowadays.

Trudy's collection seemed to have lots of Mozart. Funny—I wouldn't have pegged Deputy Hauser as a classical music fan. Then I realized it was *all* Mozart. Nothing else. The guy's name appeared on every single disc. There were fifteen different recordings of *Don Giovanni* alone. I was just beginning to count how many there were of something called *Idomeneo* when she came up behind me and looked over my shoulder.

"Not opera," she said. "Too distracting. Here. I like this one for background music."

She reached past me, pulled out a disc, and handed it to me. Piano sonatas. What the hell was a sonata, anyway? I was about to find out. Here goes, I thought, and slipped it into the CD player. Notes raced up and down a keyboard with the glee of kids just let out of school.

"You, uh, sure like Mozart."

"Anything wrong with that?" She looked at me like maybe I was insulting her somehow.

"No, of course not. It's just . . ." I glanced at Buck for help, but he stared back at me all glassy-eyed. "It's just not what I expected."

"Oh, I get it. People who live in trailers aren't supposed to like classical music. You think Mozart's out of my league."

"No, that's not—"

"You wouldn't have been a bit surprised if all I had in there was Travis Tritt or Alan Jackson or some shit like that. But Mozart? That's *weird*, isn't it?"

I could feel myself blushing because she was so exactly right—damn it—but I felt honor-bound to deny it. "That's not it. Really. I was just trying to make conversation. If I offended you, I'm sorry."

She let about a quarter-inch of her tension go, watching me closely. I smiled in what I hoped was a reassuring way; after a moment, she relaxed and smiled back. She had a nice face when she smiled. We both sat down—me on the plaid sofa and Trudy in the matching chair under the doe's head. Piano notes ricocheted around the room.

I was about to bring up Davies when Trudy said, "He was my

great, great, great, great-grandfather. Give or take a few greats."

Wait. Fred Davies was her—?

"I know what you're thinking," she continued. "Mozart had no direct descendants. Neither of his surviving sons ever married."

Mozart? Actually, I wasn't thinking anything of the kind since I knew exactly zilch about Mozart or classical music. If she'd paused for breath, I'd have told her so.

"Well, so what? Everyone knows how much Mozart liked a good time. I'll bet he had affairs all over Vienna. Vienna and Salzburg and Paris and Prague. One of them was with my great, great, great" she rolled her hand to indicate the *greats* should go on, "grandmother. Maria Renata Hauser. Maria sang in the chorus of the Viennese company that premiered *Figaro* in 1786. In 1787, she had a son out of wedlock. Know what she named him?"

I shook my head.

"Amadeus." She sat back, looking triumphant.

I stared at her, my face probably as blank as my thoughts.

"Don't you get it? Amadeus was Mozart's middle name."

"Huh." I didn't know what else to say.

She regarded me, chewing her lip, like she was trying to make a decision about me. "I want to show you something."

She rose and disappeared into another room but returned a moment later holding a long, narrow box covered in gray velvet, the kind you'd get from a jewelry store. She handed it to me. "Look inside."

I flipped open the box to see a long, tattered piece of faded blue ribbon.

"Careful! Don't touch it," she said. "It's fragile. The oil on your fingers is bad for it."

I studied the thing for a minute. Just an old piece of blue ribbon.

"That," she said, and I swear it must have been tears that made her eyes so shiny, "is a hair ribbon that belonged to Wolfgang Amadeus Mozart. The greatest musical genius of all time. He gave it to Maria as a love token." She blinked a couple of times and then swiped at one eye with the back of her hand. "It's been in my family ever since. Look—you can still see some flecks of powder from one of his fancy wigs."

A buzzer sounded in the kitchen, and Trudy hurried out of the room. I looked at the ribbon lying limply in its box. Pretty flimsy evidence of paternity, I thought, but what the heck. Who cared about Mozart? What amazed me was that she'd shown this to me at all. I closed the box carefully and put it on the coffee table, beside the bear-paw candy dish.

She returned carrying a tray almost as big as she was, overloaded with food. I jumped up to help, but she scowled at me as fiercely as she had the first time she pulled me over, so I sat down and let her do the hostess thing.

"Wow," I said, surveying the assortment of Mexican food, "it looks great."

"Dig in."

I scooped up a nacho and wolfed it down. Two seconds later, my mouth, my esophagus—hell, my whole body—was engulfed in fire. My eyes streamed water in a feeble attempt to put out the flames. I chugged what was left of my orange juice.

"Too hot, huh?" She'd squeezed both hands into fists. "Damn. I knew it. They didn't have organic jalapenos, so I bought habaneras instead. I *knew* I should've adjusted the recipe."

"No, it's fine. I like spicy food." I just prayed I wouldn't have to eat any more of it.

"Try the guacamole."

I did. It didn't singe my eyelashes like the nachos but it tasted . . . different. Like maybe the avocadoes weren't ripe.

And salty. Way salty.

"It's good," I said, reaching for my glass. Empty. And I was going to need about a gallon of orange juice to get through the evening. "Mind if I get a refill? That vitamin C is really helping."

In the kitchen, I filled the glass with water, drank it down, then refilled it with orange juice. While I was pouring, I decided the best thing to do was shift the conversation away from the food—to Fred Davies's murder. That was why I was there, after all.

"So," I said, coming back into the living room. I noticed that Trudy hadn't touched any of the snacks. "Let me tell you what I've learned about Davies's inner circle."

I told her about Hedlund's gambling and my ideas about embezzlement and the audit. "The thing is, though, I don't see how that ties in with this new information about drugs."

"Guy's addicted to gambling. Maybe he's a drug addict, too."

"I don't know. You need a clear head to play poker."

"If he's skimming money from the DFA to play, he's probably not such a terrific player."

"Good point."

"Something else bothers me, though—when would Hedlund see Davies in his underwear?" She rubbed her chin, thinking. "Davies wasn't wearing a stitch of anything more than what we found him in when he died. The autopsy said that there were no other fibers in the chest wound. So why would Davies be hanging around with his work buddy in his drawers?"

"Maybe Hedlund forced him to get undressed first. To scare or humiliate him."

"Maybe." She sounded doubtful, drumming her fingers on the table. "But I keep wondering—who'd see the guy in his underwear? His wife or his lover."

"But Felicia was out of the country when it happened."

"She could have hired someone. I bet she inherits a bundle."

"No, she doesn't. Just the house they lived in. Most of his money goes to the DFA."

"How do you know that?"

"She told me."

Trudy shot me a look, like she didn't believe Felicia Davies would give somebody like me the time of day.

"What about Nora Glaser?" I asked. "Where was she on the night of the murder?"

"At the fundraiser, the one Davies didn't show up for. But that started at eight, so she could have killed him before then. She went to the fundraiser alone, by the way. We don't know where her husband was. He started drinking at a west-side dive around four in the afternoon. He left there before six, but nobody knows where he went."

"Maybe he found his wife and Davies in bed together."

She nodded. "He's done that before—not Davies, but he attacked his wife's shrink and beat the guy up real bad. Then did time for aggravated battery."

"Nora had an affair with her shrink?"

"Yup. Glaser went to prison for a year and something. Cost him his job. He used to work in development up at Overton—writing grant proposals and letters begging alumni to cough up donations."

"He's not working now," I said. "I heard him talking about job interviews."

"Must be tough, with a violent felony on your record. The thing about Glaser, though—guns aren't his style. He's the kind of man who expresses his feelings with his fists."

"Yeah, but if he had a gun, don't you think he'd shoot first and apologize later?"

" 'Course. All I'm saying is that he seems like the type who's, well, afraid of guns."

I told Trudy about Sharon Barton, her job at Rhodes National Bank. "I'm having dinner with her family tomorrow. So maybe I can learn something useful about George Boutros."

Mentioning food was a mistake. Trudy's eyes narrowed as she surveyed the untouched snacks.

"You're not eating much."

"I'm, uh, still recovering. I was pretty sick this morning, remember?"

"I'm a terrible cook. I try to follow a recipe, and it's like the directions are in Swahili. I think I'm doing it right, but . . ." She shrugged. "I should've got stuff out of a jar."

"No, it's not that—"

"Don't lie to me, okay? You don't have to worry about my tender feelings. I've got taste buds, too. I tried it while you were in the kitchen. Blech. Hang on a minute." She got up, went to the kitchen, and came back with a bag of tortilla chips. "It's impossible to screw these up straight out of the bag." She grabbed a fistful and passed the bag to me.

"You know who I don't like?" she said, munching on a chip. "Em-T. That so-called graffiti artist. How can they call that mess he makes art?"

Her tone of outrage seemed excessive. I wouldn't have thought Trudy had such strong feelings about art. But then, I hadn't guessed she was a Mozart fanatic, either.

"You won't believe this," she said. "I pulled the kid over for speeding. He was going almost ninety in a fifty-five mile an hour zone. Ninety! Big fancy Ferrari. Red, real flashy, with a bass-heavy stereo blasting that rap shit. Kid gave me all kinds of lip. Real arrogant, like he's above the law. Later, I find out he *is*. The Sheriff made the ticket go away. Just like that." She snapped her fingers.

"Why?"

She shrugged. "Who knows? Kid has some kind of connections. All I know is I was told to make sure he enjoyed his stay in our fair county. He's back in New York City now. But I hate that kind of spoiled brat. He pulls crap like that with a speeding ticket—driving really dangerously, no penalty at all—why should he respect the law?"

I could imagine the details Trudy was leaving out of her story. The kid sneering and swearing at her, the Sheriff telling her to quit being a hypersensitive female. Man, if Trudy ever crossed paths with the kid again, especially outside of Thomson County—well, I wouldn't want to be Em-T.

"So all the while," she was saying, "even when I thought you did it, I had the kid in the back of my mind. I found this about him." She went over to her desk and came back with some pages torn from a magazine. "An interview."

It was the *ARToday* interview I'd seen at the DFA. The article spewed all kinds of pseudo-intellectual junk about the "existential nihilism" of Em-T's art, how his name signified the emptiness of modern culture and his scrawls, "like howls of postmodern urban angst, sublimated petty street crime to an art form." Yeah, right.

"Look at this part," Trudy said, turning over the page.

She'd highlighted several paragraphs.

ARToday: Doesn't it disturb you that your art is, essentially, vandalism? That to create art you're breaking the law?

Em-T: You can't draw some bullshit line between crime and art. They're both protests. Me, not you. My rules, not yours. Your property? Shit, property don't mean anything. You think it's your building, your truck, your wall, but it's my canvas.

ARToday: So crime is an art form? Even stealing?

Em-T: I told you, man. Property don't mean shit. So there's no such thing as stealing. Who's got it, who uses it, owns it. It's theirs.

ARToday: What about murder?

Em-T: Murder (laughs). Think about it. My art is an assault. It leaps out at you, grabs you by the throat, forces you to pay attention. But that's it. You still walk away, move on to other things. Now murder, that's something else. You can't walk away from it. It rips your heart out like no dumbass painting ever could. The way I see it, murder is the ultimate art form.

ARToday: So would you kill someone for your art?

Em-T (laughs): Let's just say I got no plans to do my painting in prison.

I flipped back to the photo, the one where Em-T pointed a spray can and a gun at the camera. Trudy sat beside me on the sofa to look at it, too.

"What do you think?" she asked.

"I don't know. At Davies's memorial service, Em-T told me he'd been blocked. But after Davies was murdered, he suddenly knew what to paint. That's what he said."

"This article makes you wonder, doesn't it? Most of it seems like a stupid pose. Like he says he doesn't care about property, but I bet he'd go crying to the cops in a minute if somebody stole his Ferrari. So how do you read all that talk about murder? Is it bullshit, or did the interviewer give him an idea? Something to make his art even more out there."

Murder is the ultimate art form. Strangest motive I'd ever heard of. But, like all the other possibilities—drugs, money, sex, jealousy—we couldn't discount it yet.

Chapter 17

Old hippies never die; they just toke away.

I was sitting in the parlor of Lenny Early's 1840 farmhouse, squinting at the old man through a haze of smoke. I doubted I'd have recognized Lenny if I'd passed him on the street. For one thing, he'd lost most of his hair, and the few strands that remained were pure white. Years spent outdoors had etched lines across his forehead and around his eyes. His son Dylan—younger than me, he'd been in kindergarten when I left the Homestead—sat next to his dad on the sofa. They passed the joint back and forth between them, solemn as priests.

I'd woken up that morning feeling almost back to normal and made it through my shift okay. Ryan even let me off an hour early—no questions asked, for once—so I could drive out here to Van Etten, a little farming town about twenty miles south of Rhodes, and make it back to town in time for my dinner with the Bartons.

Now, I perched on a spindly Victorian chair across from Lenny and Dylan, who shared the hard-looking sofa. Lenny gestured toward me with the joint. I shook my head—I hardly ever smoked pot anymore, and anyway, I wanted a clear head for talking to Sharon later. Lenny sighed. "Yeah," he said, "your folks said you went straight." He shook his head and handed the joint to his son. Dylan, now about twenty-five, was the spitting image of Lenny as I remembered him: strong-looking, bearded, scruffy, a little shy. It was like the smoke filling the parlor was the mists of time: through them I could see two Lennies, young and old.

"You look like your old man," Lenny said. At first I thought he said it to Dylan, but then I realized he was looking at me.

"When's the last time you saw Frank?" I asked.

Lenny took the joint. He sucked on it, held his breath as he considered, then expelled a stream of smoke. "Must've been . . . six, seven years ago. Your folks were passing through here, headed west, they said."

"West? Where?"

Lenny exhaled more smoke, shaking his head. "Just west. But the reason they came around, they were looking for Snake."

"Snake." Was that someone's name or an exotic form of marijuana I'd never heard of?

"Yeah, you probably don't remember him. Radical dude. He got himself in some trouble back in '69, trying to blow up a police station down around New York City somewheres. The bomb went off in the face of a bomb squad cop was trying to defuse it, so Snake got slapped with a murder charge. Been underground ever since. We hid him out for a coupla months at the Homestead in '70." He blinked at me. " 'Course you wouldn't remember. You were only a coupla years old." He shook his head. "You look so damn much like your old man. It's hard to remember you were just a little kid back then. You could be Frank, sitting here now." He cocked his head to one side. "Or maybe Frank's older brother."

Jesus. What a thought. I looked older than my own father. Then it hit me: I was exactly the age Frank had been when I left home. I'd never thought about that before. How could that even happen? Lenny passed the joint to Dylan, and I nearly reached for the damn thing. Better not. Remember the Bartons.

"Let me show you something." Lenny got up and left the room. Dylan smiled through the smoke but didn't say anything.

He was sprawled on the sofa, as though his spine got softer with each hit.

Lenny reappeared with a photo album, flipping through the stiff pages. "Here it is," he said, handing me the book. "Look at this."

It was a small, black-and-white snapshot, about three by three, held to the page with those little black corners. Me and my parents, circa 1974, '75. I was a skinny kid of seven or eight, clowning around. My hair was longer than it was now, down past my shoulders. I wore shorts but no shirt, and I was striking a he-man pose, showing off nonexistent biceps. Rosie, bending toward me, probably trying to get me to stand still and smile, wore a long sundress. Her dress looked gray in the picture but in real life it was yellow and smelled of patchouli. And there was Frank. Jesus, Lenny was right. He did look like me. Or I looked like him. I rubbed my cheek. If I grew a beard, I'd be seeing my father every time I glanced in a mirror.

I looked up, tried to speak, but my voice got stuck. I swallowed, cleared my throat. "Where are they, Lenny?"

"I don't know. I wish I did. But Snake might. Now you gotta understand, Bo, the only reason I think so is they were asking for him last time they came through here."

"So where's this Snake?"

"I'm working on that. He's underground, remember. Probably nobody's even looking for him any more, but he keeps himself hidden. I know somebody who knows some people. I'm working on it."

Working on it. Which meant he didn't even know where Snake was. Shit. It was great to see Lenny, but I'd come all the way out here expecting—what, that Frank and Rosie would be here waiting for me? I looked at the photo album, still open on my lap, and blinked hard. Maybe Lenny would think it was the smoke.

"I should be able to locate him in a few days," Lenny said. "A week tops. Here's what you gotta do. Give me a number where he can reach you. You got a cell phone?"

I nodded, my eyes still on the snapshot.

"Good. Keep it on. Snake might call anytime, night or day. And if he misses you once, he probably won't call back. Now when he does call, he'll ask for a code word, one he knows you got from me. You know it, he'll talk to you. From there on out, 'course, I can't make any guarantees. I don't know whether he's still in touch with your folks—don't even know whether they found him when they were looking for him."

"So what's the code word?"

"You wanna write it down? Make sure you don't forget?" He patted his pocket like he was looking for a pencil.

"I'll remember."

"Okay. The code word," he leaned toward me and dropped his voice to a whisper, "is *musical chairs.*"

"So Snake'll say, 'What's the code word?' and I'll say, 'Musical chairs.' "

Lenny nodded. "And then he'll talk to you."

"Thanks, Lenny." I pulled a pen and a taxi receipt out of my own pocket and wrote down my cell number.

Lenny took the number and read it over, his lips moving, then nodded. "Might be a long shot, but what the hell. It's a place to start."

The clock on the mantle struck five. I had to go—I was supposed to be at the Bartons' by six, and I still had to stop and pick up something for the dessert I'd promised to bring. I took one more look at the photograph. I wanted to reach inside it, take Rosie by the hand and pull her to me, smell her incense-scented dress. To look Frank in the eye and shake his hand. To say, "You're the people I came from."

Lenny came over to me. He reached down, I thought to take

the album, but he pulled gently on the photo until it popped out of the corners that kept it on the page.

"Something tells me you don't have a lot of pictures of your folks."

He was right. I didn't have a single one.

"Go on, take it."

I nodded, unable to get any words past the lump in my throat. Lenny gave me a bear hug and thumped me on the back. Neither of us spoke. From the sofa, Dylan waved and nodded.

I put the photo in the inner pocket of my jacket. I could feel it there all the way back to Rhodes.

Sharon and Bobby Barton lived in a split-level house in one of the subdivisions that had sprung up in the northeast part of town like mushrooms after a heavy rain. When I'd left Rhodes, this had all been farmland. Now it was cul-de-sacs and look-alike houses with basketball hoops over the garages and toys scattered across front lawns.

I rang the doorbell, clutching a store-bought carrot cake in one hand and a carton of ice cream in the other. I sniffed at my sleeve, hoping my clothes didn't smell from all that pot smoke at Lenny's place. My eyes still stung a little from it. The door was opened by a wiry boy half my height, with white-blonde hair and Sharon's eyes. He stared at me, open-mouthed, then asked, "Are you a goddamn commie hippie freak?"

"Robbie!" Sharon shooed him away from the door and opened it to let me in. She wore an apron over a bluish-greenish blouse tucked into a black skirt. The blouse brought out the color of her eyes. She pushed a strand of hair off her face and smiled. "I don't know where he picks up these things," she said.

"But Daddy said—" Robbie objected. Sharon swatted him on the rear with an order to go back to his video game. "Daddy said . . ." he mumbled sulkily, then stuck out his tongue and ran from the room.

"That's Robert, Junior," Sharon laughed. "He's in kindergarten this year."

"He looks like you."

"And he acts like his father." She laughed again. "Goodness, where are my manners? Let me take those things. Thanks for bringing them. Would you mind hanging up your jacket in the closet over there?"

I put away my jacket and followed her into the kitchen, which looked like it had recently been bombed. A stack of dirty bowls towered out of the sink, and every square inch of counter space was taken up with canisters, pots, pans, jars, spoons, knives—you name it. If it was ever used in a kitchen, it was on one of those counters. Sharon stowed the ice cream in the freezer, glanced around for a place to put the cake, then laughed. "I'm a messy cook," she admitted, stretching up to store the cake on top of the refrigerator. I stepped over to help. "Lucky for me, Bobby and the kids clean up. Well, sometimes."

I made a mental note to offer my help after dinner.

"Did you talk to Len's friend? Does he know where your parents are?"

"Well, it's complicated. But I hope to find out soon."

"That's nice." A timer dinged, and Sharon flew to the oven and peeked inside. "I hope there'll be enough for you. I made a roast for Bobby and the children—Bobby wouldn't call it a meal without meat—but there's salad and broccoli and potatoes and green beans, and I tried this recipe for a lentil ragout, oh, and I got the really good French bread." She paused for breath.

"Sounds like a feast."

She smiled. Maybe even blushed a little. "I can't abide having you see my messy kitchen," she said. "Let's go find the girls."

Sharon's daughters were in the family room, draped across

the furniture and watching MTV on a huge flat screen that took up most of one wall.

"That's Tiffany on the sofa, and this is Amber. Girls, this is my friend Mr. Forrester." Both girls glanced over and mumbled something that might have been "hi," then turned their attention back to the television.

By a cruel twist of fate, both of Sharon's daughters had inherited their father's looks. They were stocky with meaty chins and dark, thick eyebrows. Robbie, on the other hand, looked like the angel in a Christmas pageant—as long as angels weren't expected to stand still for more than two seconds. He made an appearance now, darting in one door and out another, screaming, "YAAAAAAAHHH!" as he whizzed through the room.

"He's showing off because we've got company," his mother said, smiling. "But you haven't seen Bobby yet. Tiff, where's your dad?"

The girl on the sofa shrugged, without looking away from the television. Some rapper with baggy pants and a bare chest chanted, while half-naked—whoa, make that nine-tenths-naked—women gyrated around him.

"YAAAAAAHHHH!" Robbie ran through in the other direction.

Sharon sighed. "Bobby must be in his den, reading the paper. He probably didn't hear the doorbell. Come on." We walked down a short hall, where Sharon knocked at a closed door. At a rumble from the other side, we entered.

Bobby Barton peered at me over his paper, then laid it down on the desk and stood to shake my hand. All that muscle had gone to fat, and I was surprised that he was shorter than me. I'd always thought of him as a big guy in high school. For some reason, I'd imagined he'd be bald now, combing the last, precious strands of hair over a shiny scalp, but I was wrong. His hair was thick, curly, and shoe-polish black. He looked like a short, fat Jay Leno in a Tom Jones wig.

"I'll let you boys talk," Sharon said. "So I can get the food on the table." She disappeared, leaving me alone with Bobby. Lucky me.

I sat down. Bobby and I stared at each other across his desk. I couldn't think of a thing to say, so I looked around the room. A display case held high school hockey trophies; his old stick was mounted on the wall above it. In the corner leaned a golf bag.

He spoke first. "Sharon's been all excited to meet up with you again, but damned if I remember you. What sport did you play?"

Oh, man. How would I explain this one? "I wasn't really into sports." The truth was I'd spent four years dying to play basketball, but my parents refused to sign the permission slip. They didn't "groove on the competition vibe," as Frank had put it.

"So I guess you don't golf." The words were an accusation. I shook my head.

We resumed our mutual staring, all possible topics of conversation exhausted. After a while, Bobby cleared his throat.

"So how are you fixed for insurance—" he began. The door flew open, and Robbie slammed into the room. He leaped onto the empty chair and jumped up and down.

"Daddy Daddy Daddy Daddy Daddy Daddy Daddy," he chanted with each bounce.

Bobby didn't seem to notice him. "These days, you know, with so much litigation going on, you've gotta—"

"Daddy Daddy Daddy." Bounce bounce bounce. The volume got louder. "DADDY DADDY DADDY DADDY!"

Bobby finally turned his head. "What, Robbie?"

"MommysaysdinnersreadycomeRIGHTNOW!" Robbie

leaped from the chair with a floor-shaking thud and ran out of the room.

"Boy loves attention," Bobby commented.

"I guess we'd better go eat," I said, getting up before Bobby could return to his sales pitch.

Sharon stood in the dining room, beaming. A white cloth covered the table. At each place was a brimming-full salad bowl, and serving bowls and platters were artfully arranged. It looked like Thanksgiving, a couple of weeks early. We sat where Sharon directed us—she was at one end, Bobby at the other. I sat on Sharon's right, Robbie across from me. The two girls sat to my right, across from each other.

Robbie stared at the table in horror. "Why are there so many vegetables?"

"Mr. Forrester is a vegetarian," Sharon answered.

"What's that?"

"It means he doesn't eat meat."

Robbie eyed me with as much suspicion as if I'd been described as a Martian. "You mean he only eats vegetables? He can have mine!" The kid shoved his salad bowl toward me, but it tipped over halfway across the table, scattering lettuce leaves and leaving a puddle of French dressing to form an orange stain on the tablecloth.

"Robbie, stop being a brat," scolded Tiffany. Or maybe it was Amber. Whichever one didn't have both ears connected to an MP3 player.

"Children! Just this once, can we please have a civilized meal?" said Sharon.

Nobody responded but the girl with the earphones, who nodded, then nodded again—and again, in time to the bass line I could hear throbbing from across the table.

Bobby, ignoring his family, pushed aside his empty salad bowl and helped himself to several slabs of roast beef. When there was a small mountain of meat on his plate, he looked up. "Armour Mutual announced today it's pulling out of New York. That's the third major insurance carrier we've lost this year. Goddamn Albany makes it impossible to do business in this state."

"That's a pity, dear. But I've got some good news," Sharon said, glancing toward me. "I've been invited to apply for George's job."

"That's terrific, Sharon," I said, pleased she'd brought up the bank. "You mean the vice president position?"

"That's right. Of course, I have to submit a résumé and be interviewed, but all that's a formality. I've been there longer than any of the other loan officers. I know that bank as well as I know my own family." She passed me the mashed potatoes.

"You can't have that! That's not a vegetable!" Robbie yelled as I spooned some onto my plate.

"Potatoes are so a vegetable, junior moron." This nutrition lesson came from his sister.

"Oh yeah? Then how come they taste good?" Robbie stuck out his tongue, his logic irrefutable.

I needed to get the conversation back on track. I turned to Sharon. "Were you surprised about George? I mean, what happened to him?" I wasn't sure drug overdoses were an appropriate topic of discussion at the family dinner table, but no one blinked an eye.

"Well, I wouldn't have guessed he was a drug addict, if that's what you mean. Although looking back now, I can see the signs. George wasn't my favorite person. Not easy to work for, I mean. He was the kind of boss who couldn't handle pressure—'When the going gets tough, George gets yelling,' we always said. The man fell to pieces whenever the heat was on."

"Lousy golfer, too," Bobby said.

"But he seemed competent in his job. He was a quiet man

when he wasn't screaming at us. He didn't get drunk at staff parties or grope the tellers or anything like that. Betsy—she's a teller—Betsy claimed he had a secret girlfriend, a married woman, but I never believed it. You know what office gossip's like. I mean, who'd want to fool around with *George?*"

Bobby laughed through a mouthful of food.

Robbie threw his napkin to get my attention.

"How come you don't eat meat?"

"Well, I—"

"Because he thinks it's wrong to kill animals for food," his sister cut in. "So do I." She sent me a glance that was almost flirtatious. The look, coming from a 15-year-old female version of Bobby Barton, almost put an end to my dinner. "I'm thinking of becoming a vegetarian," she said.

Robbie laughed hysterically, as if this was the funniest thing he'd ever heard. He laughed so hard he fell out of his chair. Literally. He got up off the floor, then ran to the end of the table and pretended to be a cow. "Oh, no, Mr. Farmer. Please don't shoot me," he pleaded. "No! No! No! No! ARRRGHHH!" He collapsed onto the floor again and bellowed out the agonizing death cries of a slaughtered cow. Except slaughtered cows don't giggle between moans.

His parents ignored him. Sharon merely raised her voice to be heard over the racket. "As I told the children, what happened to George should be a warning to them. Drugs aren't cool. They should just say no."

The would-be vegetarian daughter, who was pouring gravy over her roast beef, rolled her eyes and shot me another eyelash-heavy look.

"That's right," Bobby said in a voice weighted with parental authority. "Drugs make you crazy." On the other hand, his son's loud, writhing imitation of a dying cow—still going on—was perfectly normal behavior.

"So much upheaval at the bank," Sharon said. "First Fred Davies—George personally handled all his accounts, you know—and that business with the stolen cashier's check. And now George."

"Didn't they stop that check?" Bobby said.

"Oh, you can't. Not with a cashier's check. The DFA reported it as stolen, of course. But it takes ninety days for the claim to take effect. So whoever stole that check has more than two months to try to cash it."

So Boutros was Davies's banker. "You don't think there's any connection, do you," I had to shout to be heard over the still-expiring cow, "between George's death and Fred Davies's murder?" Robbie quit dying during that sentence, so the last few words boomed across the dining room and seemed to echo through silence that followed. Everyone stared at me.

"I'm sorry, Bo," Sharon finally said. "We don't discuss murder at the dinner table."

"Sorry." I felt someone yanking on my sleeve and looked over. Robbie.

"Now I'll be the farmer," he said, "and you be Mr. Cow."

"I don't think so. I'm trying to eat dinner."

The kid made a gun with his fingers and stuck it in my face. "Pow! Pow! Pow!"

"Robbie, you are *such* a moron," said his sister.

I tried to ignore both of them, but it's impossible to eat when someone is firing a finger gun two inches from your nose. I closed my hand gently around Robbie's and moved it away.

"Hey! You're supposed to fall down dead!"

"Not me, Robbie. I'm Mr. Supercow. Bullets bounce right off my hide." I leaned over and lowered my voice to a menacing whisper. "And if you don't sit down and eat your dinner, me and all the other farm animals—the pigs and the chickens and the sheep—we're going to creep into your bedroom tonight while you're asleep and eat you alive. See how *you* like being food."

Robbie's eyes widened. He walked around the table and sat down at his place, then picked up his fork and started eating his mashed potatoes.

"I'm a veg'table-tarian, too," he announced. He eyed the broccoli in the serving bowl in front of him. " 'Cept I *only* eat potatoes."

Chapter 18

"The mailbox belonging to Trudy Hauser is full. Please try again later." I snapped my phone shut. I was in the cab, on my way to pick up Carl and Ronnie. Last night, I'd managed to escape the Barton household without buying insurance, receiving any more come-hither glances from would-be vegetarians, or being attacked by another blast from a homicidal farmer's finger gun. Now I wanted to touch base with Trudy about my conversation with Sharon. But she wasn't answering her cell phone.

Carl stood at the entrance to his trailer park, blowing on his hands in the cold, clear morning. Steam puffed from his nostrils as he opened the back passenger-side door.

"Do me a favor, huh?" I asked as Carl started to climb in the back. "Go pound on Ronnie's door, get him out here if he's ready. I can't wait around if he overslept again."

"Ronnie's got the day off," Carl said. "He's in court."

Right. The possession charge. Good luck to him, I thought.

I steered the cab back toward Rhodes. I was wondering whether it would be a good idea to try to leave Trudy a message at the Sheriff's office when Carl spoke up.

"So tell me," he said, "what would you say is Irene's favorite color?"

"Irene—oh, Mrs. B." When I thought of Mrs. B., the colors that came to mind were beige stockings and shapeless brown sweaters. "Jeez, Carl, I couldn't really guess."

He nodded, pulling on his lip. "I know what you mean. She's a complicated woman."

We both pondered this statement for a moment. That was when the red lights started flashing across the cab.

Carl yelped like a dog having a nightmare and said, "What'd you do now?"

"Nothing. I was three miles under the limit."

"Shoot, I never even got pulled over this many times when I had my license. Maybe you should let me drive."

We both turned around to watch the cruiser behind us. When Trudy got out, Carl said, "Oh, Lord. Oh, Lord. It's the crazy one." He slid down the seat like he was trying to melt into it. "She waving that gun around?"

"You don't have to worry about that." Or at least I thought not. We were supposed to be on the same side now. So why in hell was she pulling me over?

Trudy tapped on my window, smiling. The smile dimmed a little when she saw my expression. I rolled down the window.

"What's that look for?" she asked.

"This look? You should recognize it by now. It's the one that happens when I get pulled over for no damn reason."

"Oh. Yeah, sorry about the flashers and all. But I need to talk to you." She peered into the back seat and saw Carl. "Hi," she said. "How's it going?" Carl responded with a sort of strangled gurgle. I glanced back at him. He was pressed as far as he could get against the passenger door, his eyes squeezed shut.

I turned back to Trudy. "I've been trying to call you since last night. See this thing?" I pulled out my cell phone and waved it in her face. "Handy little device. It lets you talk to people, and you don't even have to pull them over."

She squinted at the phone, then shrugged. "I forgot mine. Somewhere. Anyway, I don't have it on me. But the point is, we need to get together. As soon as possible. Tonight, if not sooner.

I'll have something to show you."

"What?"

She glanced back at Carl. "Not here."

"All right. I get off at three."

"Me too. So let's say four."

"Your place again?"

She shook her head. "I've got something to do in town, so let's make it yours this time."

"Okay. Four o'clock. But no more goddamn traffic stops. It gets on a guy's nerves."

She shrugged. "Sure. By the way, you missed a call."

"Huh?"

"Your phone. It says 'one missed call.' "

I looked at the screen; she was right. A call had come in when I'd been trying to call her. Shit, had Snake tried to call already? Lenny had said it'd take a few days, but maybe he got lucky. I checked the number. Dinesh. Probably continuing his campaign to set me up with a sorority girl in time for the weekend. I'd call him later—"no thanks" wasn't all that urgent. At least I hadn't missed Snake's call.

"I hope you don't talk on that thing while you're driving," Trudy said. "It's a violation of Article 33, section 1225-c. Fine's a hundred-fifty dollars."

Typical. "I'm not talking on it now, am I? I'm not even driving now—which I should be, if my fare's gonna get to work on time."

She looked at Carl again. "Yeah, okay. I've gotta go, anyway. See you at four."

She went back to her cruiser. The red lights stopped flashing. A minute later, she waved as she roared past. I put the cab in gear and pulled onto the road.

Gradually, Carl began inching back up the seat. I felt kind of sorry for the guy, the way Trudy had scared him. What had we been talking about before she showed up? Oh, yeah. "Mrs. B. sure liked those flowers you brought her the other night. Maybe red's her favorite color."

"I would've thought better of you, Bo."

"What, you got some problem with red? You bought the flowers."

"And right over that sainted woman's very head."

"Okay, Carl, I give up. What the hell are you talking about?"

"You got some kind of hanky-panky going on with that crazy deputy. Her place, your place—all that talk of 'getting together' was making my poor head spin. And at four o'clock in the afternoon, when decent folks are working."

I was so dumbfounded I nearly drove across the center line.

"You like 'em feisty, huh?" Carl continued. "Well, I can understand that, as you probably guessed on account of my admiration for Irene." The image of Carl with a feisty Mrs. B. was one I did not need flashing through my mind. "But there's a difference between feisty and crazy. You better think about your intentions. You don't want to end up married to a lunatic."

"Hang on, hang on. You're way off base. Nobody's getting married to anyone."

"Lord almighty. That's even worse. Aside from committing a mortal sin—and I won't say no more about that, seeing as the state of your soul is between you and the good Lord—but aside from putting your immortal soul in eternal peril, are you sure you want to be taking sexual advantage of a crazy woman with a gun?"

No matter what I said, no matter how I tried to explain, I couldn't convince Carl that I was *not* indulging in the pleasures of the flesh with Trudy Hauser. His sermon lasted all the way to the Qwikee-Change.

The rest of my shift was normal for a Thursday, even a little slow. I didn't notice anyone following me, but I no longer trusted my ability to spot a tail. So I quit worrying about it. If the cops wanted to trace my route on a slow Thursday, they could knock themselves out with the excitement of the chase. When I turned in the cab at three, the dispatcher said Ryan wanted to see me.

Ryan was in his office, doing something on his computer. He looked up as I entered. He wore a Patriots sweatshirt that showed a scowling Minuteman getting ready to hike a football. The image contrasted with Ryan's grin, but then so did the dark circles under his eyes.

"What's up, Boss?"

"Hey, how's it going? I thought you might wanna grab a beer."

I shook my head. "Can't. Not today. I'm—" I hesitated. No need to advertise that Trudy and I were working together. "I've got a hot date."

"Jesus, you sound like Dinesh. Just don't start going to frat parties, okay?"

"Hell, at my age, I'd be nodding off before the party got rolling."

"Your age?" Ryan snorted. "You're two years younger than me."

We smiled for a second. There seemed to be nothing else to say; I reached for the doorknob. "Well," I said. "I've got some things to do . . ."

"Listen, Bo, I did want to tell you something."

He cleared his throat, then pushed up the sleeves of his sweatshirt. I waited.

"Plodnick came by today." I knew it, I thought. Ryan was still in close contact with the cops. "He was asking about you and Ventura."

Ventura—and me? "What did you tell him?"

"Nothing. Nothing to tell, as far as I know. I just wondered about last week. First you seem all buddy-buddy with the guy, then you come tearing in here shouting about how you want to wring his neck. I didn't say anything, 'cause I didn't know what was going on, but . . ."

"I hardly know the guy. He played a dumb practical joke on me, and I wanted to ask him why. That's the full extent of my relationship with Ventura. I don't know where he took off to or anything." I wondered if one of Plodnick's men had seen me at Ventura's house. "I don't suppose Plodnick dropped any hints why he was asking."

Ryan shook his head. "He's a closed-mouthed little pipsqueak. He likes to be the one asking the questions."

I opened the office door. I was halfway outside when I realized that Ryan had no obligation to tell me about Plodnick's visit. He might even have stuck his neck out a little. "Hey, thanks, man." I said. "Let's get that beer soon. For real."

I walked home, wondering what trail Plodnick thought he was sniffing. Why was he looking for Ventura? Could be some other case, of course. But what would that have to do with me?

When I turned onto my block, Trudy paced my front porch, half an hour early, looking pretty damn good in jeans and that motorcycle jacket. She paused and pressed the buzzer, tapping her foot with impatience. Man, she was really eager to see me. I grinned. Poor old Carl would be shocked.

"Look at this." We'd barely got inside my apartment when Trudy slapped a manila envelope against my chest, then stepped back. I just managed to grab the thing before it fell to the floor.

"Hurry up, hurry up." Her eyes shone like she'd had a vision of heaven. "This is a big break. This is *it*, Bo—I can feel it."

I bent the metal prongs to open the flap and pulled out four glossy eight-by-ten photographs. They were black and white, taken from above, and showed grainy images of someone standing at a counter.

"What are these?"

"Someone tried to cash the missing check yesterday." She nodded at the photos. "That guy. The photos are stills from the bank's security camera."

I looked at the blurry figure. He was wearing sunglasses, a dark knit cap, and a heavy pea coat. His head was tilted downward, face turned away from the camera, like he knew right where it was and wanted to avoid it.

"You can't tell much from these." A thought struck me. "How do you even know it's a guy?"

"Of course it's a guy. There's more than the photos. There's an affidavit from the teller. I read it, but I don't have it with me."

"So what happened?"

"This guy came in to cash the check, and the teller told him she had to get a manager to authorize it. She said the guy was all cool, relaxed, like he had all the time in the world. But it took her a while to find the manager, and then they called the bank up here because the check was for so much. Soon as they found out it was stolen, they called the cops. Bank security went to nab the guy and keep him company 'til the cops arrived, but he'd already taken off." She gave an impatient sigh. "He was right there," she jabbed a finger at the photo in my hand, "right there, and he just walked away. At least someone was smart enough to save the security video."

"You said they called the bank 'up here.' Where were these photos taken?"

"New York City. Some fancy bank in Manhattan—he probably figured they cash big checks like that all the time. The cops down there overnighted these stills to Rhodes PD."

"So how did you get them?"

Trudy's face flushed an almost fluorescent shade of pink. "I . . . uh . . . borrowed them."

"I'm not sure it's a good idea to steal from the police, even if you are a deputy."

"I didn't steal them! They were sort of . . . loaned to me."

I raised an eyebrow and waited. She ruffled her hair, then gave an exaggerated sigh.

"There's this guy named Mike. He works in Records. Every so often he does me a favor."

"Ah, I get it. Mike in Records has the hots for you. And you milk the poor guy for information." She was cute when she blushed. "You should tell him that champagne and roses are the true way to a girl's heart."

She socked me in the arm. "I've got less than an hour to get these back to the station. So let's at least look at them while we've got them, okay?"

I rubbed my arm—for a small woman, she threw a pretty good punch—as I sat down at my desk. I spread the photos in a square. Trudy leaned over my shoulder. "Do you think it could be that Em-T kid?" she asked. "He's from New York."

"Hard to tell. Height's about right, but with that coat, you can't see his build. He wore a knit cap, but so do a lot of people in November."

I bent forward to look more closely, wishing I had a magnifying glass. But it just wasn't possible to get a clear look at the face, not with the hat and sunglasses. Then something else caught my attention. "Wait a minute. Check this out. Do you notice anything on his hand? The right one." I held up a photo, the only one where both hands were visible.

"Like a tattoo?" She snatched the photo and studied it, pulling it right up to the tip of her nose, then holding it almost at arm's length before taking another close-up look. "There's something on the index finger. What is it, a Band-Aid or something?"

"I think it's a ring. I never saw it, but I bet that's the missing ring Felicia Davies described. It's an antique—gold with a green stone. And it's wide, about the width of a Band-Aid. Felicia called it a finger-cuff. Not your average bling."

"Your average *what?*"

"That's what kids call flashy jewelry."

Trudy snorted. "So we've gotta go to New York, find Em-T, and ask him about his blang or bling or whatever you called it."

I grinned. "Great minds are thinking alike today."

My cell phone rang. I picked it up and checked the display; the call was from a number I didn't recognize. My heart took off at a gallop. Maybe this was it.

"Snake?"

No response. Shit, maybe I shouldn't have answered with the guy's name. Fugitives from justice probably didn't like that. I listened. Nothing. God, please don't let him hang up.

"Musical chairs," I said into the phone. "Musical chairs!"

A second later, a woman's voice came on. "I . . . ah . . . think I have the wrong number. I was looking for Shirl's Curls salon. Sorry." The connection broke.

Damn it. I closed the phone.

Trudy was looking at me funny, as though—well, as though I'd just shouted "musical chairs" into the phone and hung up.

"I thought . . ." Hang on. I was talking to Deputy Hauser here. Someone who'd have more than a casual interest, I suspected, in a guy who'd once made the FBI most-wanted list. She didn't need to know about Snake.

"Wrong number," I said. "Wow, look at the time. Didn't you say you have to get those photos back to Mike in Records?"

She gathered up the pictures and stuffed them into the envelope. "You're right. I'm going to make some copies first, so I'd better get moving. While I'm at the station, I'll see if I can get Mike to scare up Em-T's real name and home address."

"You and your feminine wiles."

She ignored me. "Then I've got to pick up my truck from the shop—the guy called and said the wheel was fixed. Be packed and ready to go by seven-thirty. We'll have to find a place to stay en route so we can get an early start tomorrow. Besides finding the graffiti kid, I want to talk to that teller."

"I'm not supposed to leave Thomson County, remember? What if Plodnick finds out?"

"Don't worry about that. You'll be with me."

I wasn't sure I had much faith in Trudy's ability to keep me out of trouble with Plodnick. Wait, though—if someone had tried to cash the check in Manhattan, that shifted the investigation away from me. It had to. For the first time in weeks, I started to believe that life might get back to normal. All we had to do was nail the guy with the check. And the dead man's ring.

After Trudy left, I called Dinesh, nixed the blind date, and wheedled him into taking tomorrow's shift. "Tell Ryan I'm sick," I said. "Tell him I had a relapse of that bug." Then I called back and made it the next two days, just to be safe. I threw some things into my duffel bag and dropped it by the door. I was ready to hit the road.

Chapter 19

Trudy arrived in her truck at seven-thirty; in five minutes we were on our way. To leave Rhodes—wherever you're headed—you have to drive for almost an hour on back roads past farms, woods, and dozen-house villages before you find anything that resembles a highway. We started east on State Route 79, a thirty-mile stretch of two-lane, middle-of-nowhere road, planning to pick up Interstate 81 at Whitney Point.

Before we were past the city limits, Trudy clicked on the CD player and punched a button several times. A blast of classical music blew me back in my seat—some guy was singing with a voice so deep it rattled the windows. I reached over and twisted the knob until I could hear myself think again.

"Do you have to play that so loud? I kind of like having my eardrums intact."

"Sorry. It's a great aria. Gets me pumped. It's all about revenge. *La vendetta*—that's Italian for revenge."

"You're not supposed to blast classical music. It's supposed to be background music for sipping sherry and discussing philosophy or some crap like that."

"Bullshit. What do you know about it? *Figaro* isn't about philosophy. It's about passion. And passion should always be loud as hell."

I blinked, disconcerted by an image of Trudy hollering her head off in the throes of passion. Kind of interesting. Absorbed by the idea, I barely noticed when she cranked up the volume again.

We rode like that for a while, the music blaring as fields, woods, and the yellow rectangles of farmhouse windows whizzed past in the dark. A couple of times some deer, grazing by the side of the road, looked up, panicky in the headlights. I listened to the music, not that I had much choice. I wasn't about to admit it, but some parts of the opera I actually sort of liked. Once in a while, a performer would hit a note or sing a phrase that went straight inside my chest and buzzed around in there. The feeling got all mixed up with that image that wouldn't go away: Trudy, passionate Trudy. I shook my head and stared out the window, although it was so dark out all I could see was my own reflection. We headed sharply downhill into a town that was little more than a cluster of rundown houses. Its main features were a four-way stop and a gas station selling live bait.

As we climbed another hill, Trudy began to sing. I held my breath to listen. Her voice was surprisingly sweet, innocent-sounding, yet there was something sexy in those Italian words emanating from her lips. To my ear, she was way better than the woman on the CD.

When the song ended, I hit the pause button.

"Hey! This is my truck; we listen to what I want."

"I was just going to tell you that I think you missed your calling. You have a beautiful voice."

I thought she'd steer us off the road as she turned her head sharply to see whether I was making fun of her.

"No, I mean it," I said. "What was that song?"

She stared at me—still going seventy—before she answered. *"Non so più cosa son, cosa faccio."* Man, she made that Italian sound good. "This boy sings that he's so crazy about love he doesn't know what he's doing."

"A boy, huh? I thought it was a woman."

"The *character's* a boy—a teenager, really—but the part's always sung by a woman." She pursed her lips. "Kind of like what you said this afternoon. I was wondering whether you might be right about that. What if our mystery man at the bank was really a woman in disguise? That's why I want to talk to the teller, to get a better description. And did the suspect talk to her or just push the check at her? If he—she, it, whatever—didn't talk, maybe the 'guy' was a woman who didn't want her voice to give her away."

"It's possible. Who do you think it was?"

"I was thinking about your girlfriend Professor Glaser." She glanced at me, half-smirking, so I didn't take the *girlfriend* bait. "There's something funny going on with her. I called the Art History department, and the secretary said she was at some conference."

"Yeah, I heard her talking about that. Where is it?"

"They said Boston, but who's to say she really went there? Plus New York's not much farther from Boston than it is from Rhodes. Anyway, Nora's out of town Wednesday through the weekend." She pursed her lips. "So Boston or not, she wasn't in Rhodes yesterday, when someone tried to cash that check."

I was thinking about my last encounter with Nora, in her office. "You know, I went to see Nora during her office hours last week." I told Trudy about the two men in dark suits who were leaving as I arrived. "She was flustered. Didn't want to talk to me."

"Those guys were Feds."

"FBI? Are you kidding?"

"Mike in Records told me that the Feds were in town. Wouldn't say for what, though. He acted like he was in on the investigation and it was all hush-hush, but I'm guessing he doesn't know squat. All he'd tell me is that they interrogated someone up at Hasseltine."

"Someone who's now split town."

She nodded. "Like I said, there's something funny going on with Nora Glaser."

We lapsed into silence. Trudy reached for the CD player, then stopped. "Would you prefer something instrumental? Or we could try the radio, but the only thing that comes in out here is evangelists."

"No, that's okay. Play whatever you like. I'll survive."

She smiled. Once again singing erupted in the truck, but she turned the volume down a little. A few more miles, and we were making good time on 81 south, heading for our encounter with the big city—and maybe with Davies's killer.

It was past eleven, and we were somewhere in New Jersey when Trudy pulled off the highway. "We'd better find a place to stay," she said.

The main road off the exit was lined with fast-food places and seedy-looking motels. She picked one between a bar and an all-night diner, easing the truck over a couple of speed bumps and into a parking space. "This look okay?"

"You mean we're not staying at the Waldorf-Astoria?"

"Ha ha."

I followed her through the glass door into the tiny lobby. The place looked anonymous, like thousands of other small-time motels. Fake wood paneling, a couple of green vinyl chairs, a wire rack stuffed with tourist brochures. The receptionist, a sleepy-looking man around seventy, sat behind a counter with a glass partition. The blue light of a TV glowed behind him. He slid back the window and asked, "Can I help you," sighing out the words liked he'd said them a million times and could barely stand to utter them once more.

"We'd like a couple of rooms," Trudy said.

"Hang on," I said and pulled her to one side—which meant

about two steps to the left in that matchbox of a lobby.

"I'm a little short on cash," I whispered. "And I gave up two shifts to come with you—that's sixteen hours' pay plus tips. Can't we, um, share?"

She stared at me, a little furrow between her eyebrows that deepened as the seconds passed. I began to have visions of sleeping in her truck. Then she wheeled around and went back to the counter.

"Make that one room."

I expected some joke about the change in plans, but the man looked at us with zero interest.

"How many nights?"

"One. Maybe two. Can we stay an extra night if we need to?"

"Check-out time's eleven. Have to let me know before then."

Judging from the number of cars in the nearly deserted parking lot, the place wasn't in much danger of being overbooked.

"Let's say just for tonight, then," Trudy said.

The man hit a few keys on his computer and squinted at the screen. "Looks like all we got's rooms with two doubles. Wait, no, we got one king-sized left." He raised his heavy eyelids to peer at us. "Water bed."

"Two doubles," Trudy said.

She paid cash up front and collected the key, not a card but the old-fashioned kind on a diamond-shaped tag. We got our bags from the truck, and she led the way to the room. When she flipped the light switch, a single forty-watt bulb struggled to life overhead. The room was a study in beige: the walls, the thin grubby carpet, the threadbare bedspreads, even the beachscapes on the walls. Trudy walked around the room, turning on table lamps, but it didn't do much to brighten up the place.

"You hungry?" I asked. I hadn't eaten since lunch.

"Yeah, now that you mention it."

We went to the twenty-four-hour diner next door. Inside, the air was warm and smelled like grease and coffee. It was an old-style diner, all red vinyl and chrome, with spin-around stools at the counter and booths along the wall. Even this late the place was buzzing, with only a couple of empty booths. We took one near the back, next to a window framed by red-and-white striped curtains. A waitress appeared immediately, pulling a pencil from behind her ear. Trudy ordered a hamburger and fries; I opted for two grilled-cheese sandwiches and a salad.

Trudy flipped the cards on the tabletop jukebox.

"I doubt they've got much Mozart," I said.

She smiled. If she was tired from all that driving, her face didn't show it. "I hope it wasn't too much to put up with, listening to opera the whole trip. Mozart was a genius, but I know some people don't like his music."

"It was okay."

"My mother used to listen to Mozart when she was pregnant with me. Before that became fashionable. Now, if I listen to anything else, it sounds so thin. Plus Mozart helps me think."

I pictured Trudy's mother, a big-bellied version of Trudy in seventies-style bell bottoms and long straight hair, dusting furniture and humming along to that song Trudy had sung in the truck. "Do your parents live near Rhodes?"

"No, they took off for Florida about ten seconds after my dad retired. Bought a condo in Naples. This time of year, they like to call either me or my brother in Buffalo and ask if it's snowing, then report on their local weather. Eighty and sunny, every single damn day." She shook her head, smiling like an indulgent parent. "How about you? Your folks still live nearby?"

My parents. There must have been spots with no phone signal, going up and down all those hills. I pulled out my phone to check it. No missed calls.

She waited, watching me with a pleasant, carefully blank expression. I decided to tell her the truth. Most of it. "My parents left Rhodes after the Homestead shut down. I don't know where they are now. They weren't thrilled when I enlisted, and it caused trouble between us. We didn't communicate for years." On the day I'd left home, Rosie hugged me but wouldn't look in my eyes. When I extended my hand to Frank for a farewell handshake, he turned and left the room. I pushed the image away, replacing it with the one in Lenny's photo, still in my pocket.

The waitress slapped plates down on the table, produced a bottle of ketchup from her apron pocket, and bustled off. Trudy slathered ketchup over everything on her plate, then attacked her food like a pack of wolves falling on a freshly killed antelope.

After a minute, she came up for air. "So that's why you joined the Army. Teenage rebellion, huh?" I nodded. "I always wondered. You didn't seem like the type. I mean, you're a vegetarian. You don't like guns. My hunting trophies totally creeped you out. No offense, but if I was a recruiter and I saw you coming, I wouldn't waste the brochure." She bit off a hunk of hamburger, chewed thoughtfully, then swallowed. "Strange way to get back at your parents. Most families would be proud of a son who enlisted."

"Yeah, but think about it. How do other kids rebel? They smoke a little pot or go shoplifting. My parents were hippies who lived in a commune. They believed that private property was a crime—so what if I 'liberated' some eight-tracks from the evil capitalists? As for smoking pot, I might get yelled at if I didn't share, but that'd be it."

"So joining the Army . . ."

"Was the worst thing I could possibly do. My father burned his draft card, risked going to prison. For a while, my parents thought they'd have to run to Canada. Yet there I was, eighteen years later, enlisting of my own free will." Again, I saw my mother's lowered eyes, my father's back disappearing through the doorway. "I'm trying to find them. That's why I keep checking my phone—I'm waiting for a call. A guy from the old days who might know where they are."

"I can help." She leaned forward, her eyes wide. "When we get back to Rhodes, give me their full names. Social Security numbers if you know them. I'll search some databases at work, see if I can track down an address."

Her right hand rested on the table. I reached over and squeezed it, just for a second. Her skin was warm, her bones delicate. "Thank you."

She looked at her hand where I'd touched her, then up at my face. Her lips parted, as if in surprise. For a moment I was afraid I'd overstepped some boundary, then she smiled. "My parents can drive me nuts," she said. "But I don't know what I'd do if I couldn't talk to them once in a while."

Smiling softened her face, and something about the light in that diner made her hair all golden. She looked the way she sounded when she sang, and I wished I could say something in Italian. Right then, it seemed like the only language worth knowing.

She held my gaze, flecks of gold making her brown eyes glow. Then she coughed and straightened, shoving her empty plate to the edge of the table. And she was back: the familiar all-business, no-bullshit Trudy.

"Listen, we've got to figure out our plan of attack. Tomorrow, I want to get into town early, then go straight to Em-T's house. Bank opens at ten, so we'll go there afterwards."

"Sounds good."

"I got the kid's real name, by the way. First name Myron, last name Terepka. Get it? Myron Terepka: M.T. His so-called street name is just a fancy way of spelling out his initials. Nothing to do with all that 'postmodern angst' garbage *ARToday* talked about."

Myron. Yikes. Definitely not a cool name. Not as bad as Rainbow, but still. I could sympathize with the kid for changing it.

The waitress cleared away our plates. Trudy asked for coffee. I opened my wallet and thumbed through the bills. Tomorrow was payday—it would've been nice to get my check before we left town. If I was careful, though, I'd have enough for meals and my half of two nights in a motel.

While I counted my cash, Trudy fished a key chain from her pocket. She pressed a button, and a row of lights lit up. "Yes!" she said. "This is a WiFi hotspot. I was afraid I was going to have to use dialup back in the room."

She pulled a small laptop from her bag and turned it on. The computer clashed with our surroundings—the diner could've been the set for a Fifties film—but as I looked around, I counted five other patrons tapping away on their laptops. *Happy Days* meets the digital age.

"Give me your phone," Trudy said, her eyes on the screen. "I need to make some calls."

"I just told you, I'm expecting a call."

She looked at me, a scowl brewing. "Your parents' friend isn't gonna call at midnight."

Any time, day or night, Lenny had said. And it struck me that the middle of the night was exactly when a fugitive from justice *would* call. But I hadn't told Trudy about the fugitive part. "Where's your phone?" I asked. "And, as you point out, it's late. Who do you think you're going to call this time of night?"

She sighed, then turned her computer screen so I could see it. "This is the Web site for that art history conference in Boston. It lists three hotels. I want to find out if Nora Glaser is staying at any of them." She put out her hand. "Come on, it'll take two minutes." When I still didn't give her my phone, she gestured impatiently. "I don't have mine with me."

"Why not?"

Her face turned half a shade pinker. "I'm not sure where it is."

"So what you're telling me is you lost your cell phone."

"It'll turn up. It always does." She muttered something I couldn't make out.

"What?"

"Eventually. It always turns up eventually."

I passed my phone across the table. "Make it quick."

She pivoted her computer back toward her and peered at the screen, then punched some numbers into my phone. After a few seconds, she asked for Nora Glaser's room. She shook her head, then looked at the computer screen again. On the third try, after asking for Nora, she lifted one finger to show she'd hit pay dirt. "She arrived on Wednesday, right?" A pause. "Oh, I see. Could you connect me with her room, please?" After a few more seconds, Trudy hung up. She handed me my phone.

I checked for missed calls. Nothing. I folded the phone closed.

"Nora Glaser is registered at the Lanesborough House," Trudy said. "She checked in Tuesday night. But she didn't answer her room phone. It rang five times then switched me over to voice mail."

"So she's been in Boston since Tuesday. When's her talk?"

Trudy tapped at her computer a couple of times. "Not yesterday," she said. *Tap, tap.* "Not today." More tapping. "Bingo." She turned the computer toward me. "Down near the bottom."

The screen showed Friday's schedule. The conference consisted of hour-long sessions; in each session, three different scholars read a paper. Papers had titles like "New Readings of Maori Visual Culture" and "Historicizing Aesthetic Intersubjectivity." At the bottom of the page was a session on "Spectacle,

Nostalgia, and Ideology in Late Victorian Art," scheduled for three P.M. Nora was in that session, giving the same talk I'd attended at Hasseltine. Except she wasn't giving it. Next to her name, in bold, red, italic letters, was the notice: *Canceled due to illness.*

I looked up. Trudy grinned at me over her coffee cup. "She's not there," I said.

She swallowed, shaking her head. "Doesn't look like it. Of course, she could be lying in her hotel bed, too sick to answer the phone."

"You believe that?"

"Uh-uh. I think she checked in Tuesday night, then took off for parts unknown. Could've gone anywhere. Maybe," she drained her coffee and thunked her mug on the table, "she went to look for a bank where she could cash a check. A big one."

"Or maybe she went home."

One way or the other, we were going to find out.

It was twelve-thirty when we returned to our motel room.

"I'm setting the alarm for oh-six-hundred," Trudy said. "Can you handle that?"

"Easy." I was tired, but I rarely slept past six, anyway.

She went into the bathroom to change. I lay on top of the bedspread, tucked my hands behind my head, and listened to her moving around on the other side of the door. I wondered what kind of nightgown she'd wear. Definitely not your satin-and-lace type. Flannel with a high neck and long sleeves would be more her style. Still, something shiny and slippery would be nice . . .

The door banged open, and Trudy emerged, wearing a gray sweatshirt with *S.W.A.T.* emblazoned across the front and a pair of too-long black sweatpants. As I watched, she removed a .38 from her suitcase and tucked it under her pillow.

"Jesus! You sleep with a gun?"

She looked up, her eyes round. "What'd you expect? A teddy bear?"

I shook my head and clicked off the light.

Chapter 20

"Hurry up, will you? We're gonna miss him." Trudy was in a foul mood. Not that I blamed her, after what she'd just driven through: an hour of bumper-to-bumper traffic going eighty, then another hour at a standstill, waiting to enter the Holland Tunnel. Not fun, especially when you're used to cruising the wide-open roads of Thomson County. When we'd finally reached Em-T's Upper East Side neighborhood, there was nowhere to park. We circled and circled, finally squeezing into a space five blocks away. Backing in, Trudy had bumped a BMW, setting its alarm shrieking. No one paid any attention, and we trudged down the block, the wind blowing grit in our faces.

Now, past nine, we arrived at a four-story brownstone that looked like it belonged on the cover of an architecture magazine. Trudy marched up the front steps and rang the bell. Chimes rang dimly inside.

A tuxedoed butler opened the door. I didn't know that those monkey suits were even legal before noon. He asked, in a plum-pudding British accent, if he could help us.

"We're looking for Em-T," Trudy said.

He gave us a look that suggested he'd thought as much. "Master Terepka is not expected to rise before noon. He certainly will not receive visitors before one. If you'd be so kind as to leave your names, I shall inform him you called."

"Thanks, anyway. We were just in the neighborhood."

"As you wish," he replied, already closing the door.

"Whoa. Quite the setup," I said as we walked back to the truck. "Do you think that kid makes enough money from those graffiti paintings to afford an English butler?"

"Doubt it, but it's not his house. Kid lives with his parents." Trudy took out a notebook and turned some pages. "Here they are. Dr. Erwin Terepka and Dr. Holly Webster-Terepka. Physicians to the rich and powerful. He's an orthodontist; she's a plastic surgeon."

"Teeth, tits, and tummy tucks, huh?" I gave a low whistle, looking at the black and silver luxury cars—Mercedes, Audi, Lexus, BMW—lining the street. Trudy's pickup stuck out like clown at a morticians' convention. "You and I both are in the wrong business."

She jabbed me with her elbow. "Come on," she said. "The bank will be open by the time we get there. Let's go talk to that teller."

Again we circled endlessly, looking for a place to park. I wondered how New Yorkers put up with it day after day. The traffic. The continual jostle of people. The way the buildings crowded in from all sides. After what felt like an hour, we found a spot on the street, but only because the previous occupant launched into traffic, almost sideswiping us. It took Trudy a couple of tries to parallel park in the space, horns blaring the whole time. When we got out, her face was red, her mouth tight.

The bank—marble fronted with arched windows and gold-chiseled letters over the massive doors—looked like the kind of place where a hundred and fifty grand was pocket change. I could see why the suspect had chosen it.

"Let me do the talking," Trudy said as our footsteps echoed through the lobby. She introduced herself to the security guard in her no-nonsense deputy style. "I need to speak to a manager.

It's about a murder investigation."

She grinned as the guard scurried off. "I love doing that."

"What if the Rhodes cops have already been here?" I asked. "You know, the ones who are *supposed* to be investigating this murder."

"Mike said they'd done everything over the phone and through the NYPD." A look of disdain crossed her face. "Lazy. That's why I'm gonna be the one to crack this case."

"You mean *we*—" I began, but Trudy was looking to the right. A manager approached. Mid-forties, dark suit. Trudy introduced herself and handed him her ID. He glanced at it, then nodded. "What can we do for you?"

"We need to talk to the teller who was presented with the stolen check. We have some photographs of possible suspects to show her."

"Right this way." He studied me for a second, and I wondered if he was going to ask for my ID too, but I must have looked like his favorite rogue cop from TV because he turned abruptly and led us to a meeting room behind the main lobby.

"Please make yourselves comfortable. I'll send her right in."

We were in a staff room, which didn't make the same effort to impress as the lobby. Eight chairs sat at haphazard angles around an oak-laminated oval table. Motivational posters—some rowers demonstrating "teamwork," a guy clinging to a cliff to personify "challenge"—hung crookedly on the walls.

Trudy sat down and motioned me to the seat across from her. "I'll handle the interrogation. You listen." She held her face in a tight, "I'm-not-kidding" way. I was beginning to feel about as necessary as a sixth toe. I glanced at the seat she'd pointed me to, then chose the one next to it.

Trudy shot me a look, but just then the door opened. She turned to it, all smiles.

The teller walked in, chewing gum. She was young, early

twenties, with dark curly hair and eyes that would have been pretty if she hadn't lined them with thick black gunk. Her name tag said *Ashlee.* She glanced at Trudy, pushing the gum around her cheek, then maneuvered past a couple of chairs to sit next to me.

"Hi," she said.

Trudy cleared her throat. "Hello, Ashlee. I'm Deputy Hauser from Thomson County."

"Deputy? What is this, some wild west movie?" She popped her gum and turned to me. "That make you the Sheriff?" She flashed me that smile women give you in a bar when they're hoping you'll buy them a drink.

Trudy cleared her throat. "Ashlee, the stolen cashier's check is a very serious matter. It's evidence in a murder investigation. Your cooperation is important."

Ashlee kept looking at me. "So what do you want to know?" She emphasized the word *you,* putting her hand on my arm.

I reached for the manila folder with our collection of photos. Trudy slapped her hand down and held on. She was furious. In a comic book, flames would be shooting from her eyes. After a moment, she let go, and I picked up the folder.

"As you can see," I said, taking out the security photos, "the bank's camera didn't get very good pictures." Ashlee nodded, leaning in to look. Her breast brushed against my arm, pulled back a little, then reasserted itself.

"We were hoping," I continued, shifting out of brushing range, "that you might give us a better description. Did you get a good look at the guy?"

"Usually it's like, people just come through and I don't even see them. I mean, I check IDs and all, but that's part of the routine. Five minutes later, it's like, who was that, you know?" She popped her gum and laughed. "Unless it's a hot guy or something."

I gestured at the photos. "So this guy wasn't hot?"

She wrinkled her nose. "Eww. Yuck. Total grunge." She paused, thoughtfully shifting the wad of gum from one cheek to the other. "I did a double-take when I saw how big the check was—I was like, Whoa! That's a lot of money to be made out to cash—but he'd kind of, like, turned his head away."

"So you don't remember anything special about him?"

She shook her head and shrugged in the same motion. "Just the gold tooth. I thought it looked dumb. This one." She pulled back her lips and tapped her upper right front tooth. "Like, so tacky."

"Gold tooth?" Trudy sat up straight. "Why didn't you mention that in your statement?"

Ashlee shrugged again.

Now that Trudy was in the conversation, she pressed her advantage. "How about a ring? Was he wearing any jewelry?"

Ashlee was shrugging so much it looked like she had the hiccups.

"How would you describe his voice?" Trudy's own voice might be described as "tight with repressed fury."

"I dunno. He didn't say much. Maybe hi or something." The gum popped. "Anyway, I hate it when customers wanna stand there and chat. It's like, I don't *care* about your life history, just like, hello, goodbye, have a nice day." She turned to me. "You know?"

I opened the folder. "We've got some photos here. I'd like you to study them carefully. If you think it's possible that either of these people presented the check, please say so."

"Okay."

I pulled out the picture of Em-T Trudy had clipped from *ARToday* and gave it to Ashlee, watching her face. Her eyes widened. "Whoa. Who's that?"

"Do you recognize him?" Trudy leaned forward.

Ashlee ignored her, staring at the picture, so I repeated the question.

"Why, is he famous or something? He's, like, so hot."

"So he's not the guy who came into the bank the other day," I said.

"Him? No way. I'd have noticed that hottie for sure." She blew a bubble, making the gesture look lewd.

"What about this person?"

She tore her eyes away from Em-T to glance at a photo of Nora Glaser. "That's a woman," she said.

And here I'd been thinking Ashlee was a little on the dim side.

"Yes, it is. But do you think it's possible that she put on the knit cap and sunglasses and passed herself off as a guy?"

"Why would she do that? Oh, you mean, like a disguise?" The black-rimmed eyes narrowed to slits as she squinted at the photo. "Nuh-uh. It wasn't her. Not unless she's got some kind of hormone problem."

"What do you mean?"

"The guy who came into the bank needed to be introduced to a razor, know what I mean? He had, like, a five o'clock shadow at lunchtime."

"So what do you think? Is Nora off our list?" I asked Trudy as we jogged down the steps.

"No one's off the list. That idiot is worthless as a witness."

"Yeah, but Nora doesn't have a gold tooth. And you can't fake a five o'clock shadow."

"You can buy a phony gold cap at any costume shop. And she could've used makeup."

"I doubt it. Checking out guys is Ashlee's hobby. She'd spot a woman disguised as a man a mile away."

"She's some kind of nymphomaniac, that's all." Trudy made

her voice go all breathy. "Ooh, Mr. Big Strong Sheriff, will you show me your six shooter?"

I laughed. "Can I help it if I'm hot?"

"Oh, please."

"So she wanted to talk to me, not you. Seriously, would you have asked her anything different?"

Trudy didn't answer. Instead, she walked faster, so that even at a jog I was barely keeping up. I couldn't figure out what she was so mad about. We were working as a team. I thought I'd done a damn good job of picking up the ball and keeping it in play. Why the hell was I even tagging along if she didn't want my help?

A parking ticket fluttered under a windshield wiper on Trudy's truck. She tore it in half and threw the pieces in the gutter. "It's too early to go back to Terepka's. You got any brilliant ideas what to do next?"

"Yeah, I do. We could visit Felicia Davies's gallery. Her assistant might be able to ID the ring." I was hoping she could do more than that. If the ring had been in inventory before Felicia gave it to Fred, there might be a picture of it.

Trudy stared at me, then broke into a grin. "You got the address?"

"It's in Soho. MetroPrimitif. I looked it up yesterday, before we left Rhodes."

"Okay, Forrester. I'll give you 'brilliant' on this one."

I grinned back at her; I couldn't help it. She got into her truck and reached across to open the passenger door. "Let's go," she said.

After yet another game of circle-the-block, we parked in a garage that charged fifteen bucks for the first hour. But it was right around the corner from Felicia's gallery. MetroPrimitif announced itself with gold letters on a glass door. The display window showed a huge painting in a turmoil of bright colors, populated with grimacing demons, shining angels, snakes, spiders, and symbols I didn't understand. While I examined it, Trudy opened the door and disappeared inside. Another glance at the painting, then I followed her.

Cases lined each wall, like a museum. Above them were more colorful, chaotic paintings. Trudy bent over a case of jewelry, looking, I guessed, for a ring like the one I'd described. Felicia had said it was one of a kind.

The gallery seemed deserted, but a fashionably dressed woman hurried out from the back.

"May I help you?"

"I hope so," I began, when another woman's voice interrupted from the back room.

"Angelica, I need you to—Oh, it's you." And there stood Felicia Davies in the doorway, holding a sheaf of papers.

I blinked, and she was still there.

She smiled. "You're always surprising me."

"Well, I . . ." I didn't get any further. I was aware of the two women flanking me: Trudy behind, brimming over with energy, Felicia in front, looking sleek and elegant. My face was hot, and I felt like I'd been caught red-handed at . . . something. Then I remembered why we were here. Felicia could help us. And she'd want to know what was going on. "Felicia," I said, "did you know that someone tried to cash the stolen check?"

The papers she'd been holding hit the floor. "Who? Have they arrested him?" She stopped, took a deep breath, smoothed her hair.

"No." Trudy barged over, stepping on some of the papers Felicia had dropped. "The suspect ran off before police arrived. We don't know who it was. But we've got some photos." She started rummaging through her bag.

"Bo?" Felicia inched around Trudy. "This is your friend?"

"Trudy. My friend Trudy Hauser. Sorry, I should've introduced you."

Trudy stopped rummaging and stuck out her hand. "*Deputy* Trudy Hauser. We met once before, but I guess you don't remember. I'm the one who found your husband's body."

Felicia gasped and swayed. I rushed forward to steady her. "Are you all right?" She sagged against me, and I put an arm around her shoulders. She turned her face into my chest.

Trudy stood there with her hand out. I shook my head at her. She raised her eyebrows and shoulders together, like she was asking *what'd I do?* I shook my head again and returned my attention to Felicia, touching her hair lightly.

"Can you get her a glass of water?" I asked Felicia's assistant.

Angelica nodded and left the room.

"I'm all right," Felicia said. She leaned into me a moment longer, then pulled away and turned to Trudy, making an effort to smile. "You have some photographs?"

The bank photos were already in Trudy's hand. She passed them to Felicia. "Do you recognize this person?"

"Just a moment." Felicia went into the back room, passing Angelica, who tried to hand her a glass of water. Felicia ignored her assistant and disappeared. She returned a minute later, reading glasses perched on her nose. She studied the picture for a long time. Finally, she shook her head. "I have no idea," she said. She kept staring at the photo. "And you think this is the man who killed Fred?"

I couldn't read her expression, couldn't imagine how it must feel to look at a picture and think, *This person murdered my husband.*

"Felicia," I said, and when she looked at me I wanted to put my arm around her again, "you told me about a missing ring. In one of the photos, it looks like the suspect is wearing a ring. Do you recognize it?"

She shuffled the photos until she had the right one. She squinted at it. "Oh, dear," she said. "It's hard to make out, isn't it? If you'll just excuse me for another moment." Again, she went into the back room.

I watched the space where she'd disappeared, wishing we hadn't come here. We were asking too much of her. Something hit me in the arm.

"Hey, Rainbow," Trudy said, "I'm talking to you. I said, after this we'll head back over to the East Side and—"

Felicia returned with a jeweler's loupe. She carried the photo to a display case and held it under the light, scrutinizing the image through the magnifier. When she looked up, her face was ashen. "God damn him," she whispered. Her voice gained strength. "You must find this man. There's no doubt—that's the ring I gave Fred on our wedding day."

Felicia found an image of the ring in the gallery's database and printed it out for us. As I took it, she touched my hand. "Thank you," she said. "I'm glad you came." Her green eyes burned into mine.

Outside, Trudy was mad at me again. "Now what did I do?" I asked. She probably thought I was still trying to upstage her.

"You—" The anger drained from her face, and she looked away. "Nothing. Forget it. Let's go talk to Terepka."

Chapter 21

We were on the sidewalk two blocks from the Terepkas' brownstone when Trudy grabbed my arm and said, "Bingo!" Em-T was walking toward us.

He wore a knit cap and a black peacoat, like the ones in the bank photos. His coat was open despite the cold. He had his hands jammed into his pockets and walked with his head down, oblivious to other pedestrians and even to cars as he surged across the street between blocks.

Trudy dropped my arm and ran up to him.

"Excuse me. Excuse me—sir! Aren't you Em-T?"

His head jerked up at the sound of his name. The guy certainly liked his jewelry. He'd lost the nose ring, but several thick gold hoops dangled from each ear, and he wore an eyebrow ring and a stud centered beneath his lower lip. But there was no way to tell whether he was wearing Davies's ring while he kept his hands in his pockets.

He sneered at Trudy. "Yeah. So?"

"It's a pleasure to meet you." Trudy extended her hand. Em-T looked at it, then looked up at her face. He kept his hands—ringed or otherwise—in his pockets.

"Whatever," he said.

Trudy kept smiling as she dropped her hand and dug through her bag. "I'm so excited to see you in person! I was just blown away by your show at the DeMarchis Gallery. Your work is so primal, so powerful. And I read this article about you in *ARTo-*

day. There's no other artist like you. I was wondering if you could . . ."

She held out the article and a pen. Em-T shook his head.

"Sorry, babe. I don't do autographs."

"Um . . ." Trudy bit her lip. She stared at the spot where his sleeves disappeared into his pockets, scowling a little, like she was trying to will herself sudden powers of X-ray vision.

"Later." Em-T moved to go past her.

"Think fast!" she shouted and hurled her bag at him.

He blinked as it bounced off his chest and landed at his feet. "What are you, a psycho?" He kicked the bag out of his way and walked on.

"Hey!" she shouted as she bent to retrieve the bag. That one syllable sizzled with all the fury her five-foot-four frame could hold. Uh-oh, I thought.

"I came here to ask you some questions, and you're going to answer them."

He kept walking.

"Myron!" She sure had powerful lungs. The name bounced off the buildings all around and echoed up and down the street. It seemed to stop everything: the traffic, the bustling pedestrians, even—I had the strange feeling—time itself.

Em-T froze, too. Then he turned around and stalked back several paces to put himself right in Trudy's face.

"Don't fucking call me that," he said.

"Why not? That's your name, isn't it?" Her eyes shot sparks, and she raised her voice again. "Hey, look, everybody, it's Myron! Myron, Myron, Myron. I think it fits. A twerpy little name for a twerpy little punk."

The kid's eyes bulged. For a minute, I thought he was going to hit Trudy, and I stepped forward, fists clenched. Then his cheeks puffed out, and he started bobbing around and making these weird, semi-rhythmic sputtering noises. Oh, God, I thought, reaching for my phone. 911 time. He's having a fit.

Instead, he took a step back, pulled his hands from his pockets, and moved them in stiff-looking gestures as he started rapping. At least I think that's what he was doing. He had no sense of rhythm at all, but the words rhymed, as he shouted them in Trudy's face and stomped around in something like a dance.

"Em-T's the name
And no it ain't no game
'Cause my claim to fame
You'll never find in a frame.
Art pays my bills
With my amazing skill
But if my will's to kill
Then to kill's my thrill . . ."

Trudy's eyes were bulging themselves at this point, and she looked a little dizzy as he hopped around her, shouting and gesturing. Pedestrians stared, some stopping, some turning and walking backward a few paces as they passed. As for me, I was watching his hands. He had a ring on every damn finger, and the way his hands flashed around, it was impossible to make out anything besides a golden, shiny blur. He kept shouting.

"You look in my eyes and see they're EMPTY
You look in my soul and see it's EMPTY
Em-T, Em-T, that's me, that's me—
You mess with me, you'll need an E.M.T.!"

He abruptly cut himself off, panting a little, glaring at Trudy. She was bent double at the waist. I thought he'd hit her. I grabbed the kid around the middle, pinning his arms to his sides, and lifted him off his feet. He struggled, but I was behind him, so he couldn't even see who was holding him there.

Trudy was howling. Jesus, was she hurt that badly? I'd squeeze the guts out of the little creep. Then I realized that the sound coming from Trudy was laughter. She was in hysterics.

I put the kid down. He turned and swore at me, then straightened his coat, brushing at the sleeves like I'd dirtied him.

Trudy gasped and started to straighten, then bent over again, holding her stomach as her whole body quaked with laughter. Finally, she stood up, wiping tears from her eyes. "You think *I'm* a psycho?" she said. "Thanks for the freak show, Myron."

"Bitch." He turned up his collar and walked away. He kept his head down, pretending not to notice the stares and pointed fingers of those who'd stopped to watch.

Trudy smiled as she watched him go.

Nice that she was amused, but why couldn't she keep a lid on her goddamn temper? We were no wiser than we'd been that morning. "I guess we blew that one, huh?" I said *we,* but I was thinking *you.* "The kid will never talk to us now."

"Was that supposed to be rap? I'll stick with Mozart." She wiped her eyes again as a final bubble of laughter escaped. "C'mon, we'd better follow him."

"What the hell for? If he sees me again, he'll probably press assault charges." I could imagine myself trying to explain to some New York cop that I'd attacked the kid because he made Trudy laugh.

But Trudy took off in the direction Em-T had gone. I caught up with her, and she asked for my cell phone, holding out her hand like my whole purpose in life was to supply her with a phone. I checked to see whether I'd missed any calls—still nothing—and gave it to her. She punched in a number, humming to herself. I couldn't see what the hell she was so happy about. She'd done it again. Pushed a little too hard and gone right over the line. It might work dealing with speeders in Thomson County, but it was no way to play detective.

"Chief Ianelli, please. No, I'll hold." She beamed me a sweet smile. "It's too bad I can't make the arrest. Still, those boys'll have to admit that I'm the one who figured it out."

"What are you talking about?"

"Didn't you see? He had it. He was wearing that ring. Same finger as the bank perp. Big as life, clear as day. I'm telling you, Myron's our boy."

"Yes!" Trudy pumped her fist in the air as she handed me back my phone for the fifth time that day. I did a quick check. No missed calls. And that was it—I was not going to let her commandeer my phone again. New York is full of payphones for people like her.

We were camped in a Greek diner somewhere in midtown. She'd been making calls all afternoon, while I sat across from her—first eating a feta-cheese omelet, then staring at my empty plate, then trying to drink a cup of decaf very very slowly so the waitress wouldn't keep threatening to refill it.

Trudy was grinning like she'd just won the lottery. "What's up?" I asked.

"They've picked the kid up and are booking him now. He'll be a guest of the city overnight, and questioning will commence in the morning."

"Mission accomplished, then. What do you say we pay up and head home?" I was glad I wouldn't have to give up another shift. I needed the money.

"Well, um, that's the thing. The cops here want me to give a statement. And also . . ." Her fingers started drumming on the table, and she looked past me out the window. "I've been invited to observe the interrogation."

"And that's tomorrow." So much for driving that shift. "I suppose I can survive another night in that fleabag motel."

The fingers drummed faster. "I was thinking I'd stay in the city tonight. I've got an invitation to sleep on the couch of this female desk sergeant I've been talking to." She finally looked at me, her expression a mixture of pleading and defiance. "There's really no need for you to stay. They won't let a civilian observe the interrogation. You'd just be sitting around the station."

"So I guess I'd better start walking, huh?" I shoved the coffee cup aside. "How the hell am I supposed to get back to Rhodes?"

"I can give you a ride to the bus station. I called to check—there's a bus that leaves in about an hour."

Using my own phone to get rid of me—how had I missed overhearing that call? I stared at her, but she wouldn't meet my eye. I slid out of the booth and walked out the door, leaving Trudy scrambling to pull out her wallet. Let her pay. I, apparently, had a bus ticket to buy.

Neither one of us had a thing to say as we walked block after block to the garage where we'd left the truck. As soon as we pulled into traffic, though, it was like a dam burst. Relieved, I guess, that I wasn't giving her a hard time, Trudy chattered away, her sentences peppered with cop-show jargon like *perp* and *vic* and *M.O.*, about how she'd suspected Terepka all along. Because I was giving her the silent treatment, I didn't remind her how just last night she'd been convinced the murderer was Nora Glaser. Not to mention me before that.

The silent treatment doesn't have much effect when the person you're giving it to won't pause for breath. I tuned Trudy out and stared through the window. A crumpled sheet of newspaper somersaulted down the sidewalk. Man, I'd be glad to get out of this town, back to someplace where I could breathe. I didn't even *want* to stay in New York another night.

Trudy stopped in the taxi stand in front of the bus station. A cab pulled in behind us and blasted its horn. She glanced over her shoulder, then turned to me with a too-bright smile.

"Have a good trip."

"That's it?"

The smile dimmed about a hundred watts, and a frown creased her forehead. "What do you want me to say?"

"How about 'Thanks, Bo'? Or 'I couldn't have done it without you, Bo'? You know, something a little more heartfelt than 'Get the hell out of my way, Bo.' "

"All right. You were a big help, okay?" She gave the steering wheel an impatient slap. "Look, I'll only be here another day. I'll see you back in Rhodes."

"Yeah? Where? At the next Mozart Society meeting? Or at the annual venison dinner of the Deer Hunters' Association?"

I got out and slammed the door, yanked my duffel bag out of the pickup bed. No looking back, I thought as I stormed toward the terminal. I wouldn't give her the satisfaction. Yet once I was inside, I did it. I turned around. The truck was gone; the taxi already in its place. She couldn't even give me a lousy wave before rushing off to play big-city cop.

"The hell with it," I muttered and plunged into the crowd.

The bus was delayed. Of course. I slumped in one of those butt-numbing plastic chairs, feet on my duffel bag, eyes unfocused, staring at nothing as people rushed past to wherever they were going. Not that I cared, sitting there clutching my goddamn one-way ticket.

I wondered what Trudy was doing, then wondered why the hell I was wondering. She'd dumped me at the curb like a sack of garbage. I wasn't going to waste any thoughts on her.

Well, it was over, at any rate. I'd be free to walk the streets of Rhodes without some plainclothes cop following a block behind. No more search-warrant surprise parties. No more goons taking potshots at my head.

But that was what bugged me. I couldn't link up Em-T with the thugs out at the Speakeasy. The kid wanted to prove he was bad, sure, but his whole act was urban street punk—not redneck biker. And the two definitely didn't mix. If Myron Terepka ever set foot in the Speakeasy, calling himself Em-T and showing off with his baggy clothes and mouthy attitude, he'd wake up in the woods the next morning with a lot less gold and a few new holes in his head.

Why had Boutros sent me there? Something was missing.

The kid had the ring. It was one of a kind, and it was a definite link to Davies. But Davies's murder was only one piece of the puzzle. Trudy was looking at the case through a microscope, when we needed binoculars. But every time I tried to take a longer view, the picture got bigger—and uglier. It unfurled into a tableau of murder, money, theft, drugs, and God knew what else. Faceless drug dealers at the Speakeasy. Hedlund and his gambling debts. Nora Glaser and the FBI. Perry Glaser with his ham fists and hair-trigger temper. No matter how hard I looked, all those images jumbled together. Em-T was just too small to be the whole picture.

The hell with it. Let the cops figure it out—that was their job. I was out of it now.

I saw Felicia's sad face, her questioning eyes. How would she feel if the cops arrested the wrong man? Even the slightest doubt—

My phone rang, interrupting my thoughts. It was a number I didn't know. "Hello?"

An unfamiliar man's voice said something. The reception was terrible—two bars. I couldn't make out what the voice was saying, but I thought I heard the name Lenny.

"Hang on!" I shouted. "You're breaking up." I ran to the door of the terminal to see if the reception improved outside.

On the sidewalk it was a little better, but still not great.

"Did you say you're a friend of Lenny Early?" I asked.

"Maybe," the voice said. "You got" *bzzt bzzt* "for me?"

I was on the curb. I stepped onto the street between two

parked cars and the signal seemed a little stronger. "Musical chairs," I said.

"Okay. Now I got a couple questions for you. See if"—the connection cut out—"say you are."

"Go ahead." I went a little way into the street, watching for cars. For the moment, the block was clear.

"What happened when we were planting the soybean field in '70?"

"In 1970? Wait, Snake, you've gotta understand. I wasn't even three years old then." How could I make him believe me? "Don't you remember Frank and Rosie had a little boy? A kid called Rainbow?"

There was a pause. I didn't know whether he was thinking or had hung up, or maybe the reception had gone bad again. I clutched the phone, turned one way, then the other, took another step into the street. His voice came back: "—Rosie's favorite color?"

I thought of the yellow sundress. "Yellow," I said. "She liked yellow."

Out of nowhere a taxi appeared, horn blasting. I dropped my phone as I dodged it. The taxi swerved around me and almost hit a car pulling out of a parking space. Down the block, a tsunami of cars roared my way. I scooped up the phone and sprinted for the curb. "Snake?" I shouted into the phone. Was it broken? Had I lost the call? "Snake, you still there? Listen, man, the connection's really bad."

Dead air. I'd nearly been run over, and I had nothing. Nothing.

Then his voice came over the phone, crystal clear. "I'll be in touch."

"When? If I know when to expect—" But I knew he was gone. I looked at the screen. Call ended.

Chapter 22

Back in the bus terminal, my duffel bag was gone—stolen. Nobody had seen anything, of course. No one even met my eye when I asked about it. Well, fine. If somebody really wanted my toothbrush, shaving gear, and dirty socks, they could have them.

I never should have left Rhodes. That garbled phone call might have been my only chance to find my parents. "I'll be in touch," Snake had said, but what guarantee did I have? Short answer: none.

This whole damn trip had been a disaster. My bag was stolen. I'd nearly been run over. And Trudy had brushed me off to run after a "murderer" who was probably innocent. Last night, in that New Jersey diner, I'd felt like we were together. I'd thought—

It didn't matter what the hell I'd thought. Right now, the last thing I wanted to think about was Trudy Hauser.

I went over to the boarding area. Still no bus. I asked a guy at the information desk how much longer. He shuffled some papers like he was way too busy to talk to a mere passenger, then finally said that the driver had called in to report the bus was stuck in traffic. "Could be another half hour before it gets here. Could be more."

Half an hour. Terrific—like I didn't have anything better to do than hang out in a bus station. Still, it could be worse. Like I could be the one driving that bus, sitting in gridlock, choking on exhaust fumes and listening to grumbling passengers. I couldn't imagine trying to maneuver a bus through these streets. In fact, I couldn't even imagine driving a cab in this town. Ventura had done it, before he moved to Rhodes. In Manhattan, you had to lease your cab from the garage for a hundred bucks a day. Only after you'd paid that plus gas did you start making any money. No wonder the cab drivers around here were a bunch of lunatics—they had to hustle like crazy just to break even. A slow day and you'd lose money. No thanks. I'd stick with my hourly salary plus tips back in Rhodes. It wouldn't make me rich, but I could get by on it.

Ventura, on the other hand, used to head down here every chance he got. Every couple of weeks, someone wanted a ride from Rhodes to JFK or LaGuardia—a full day to make the round-trip—and Ventura always volunteered. I thought he was nuts, but he said he had family around here and it gave him a chance to stop by.

Then it hit me. Ventura. I saw him grinning at me as he gave me the wrong address for the poker game. How could I have forgotten that grin—with its big gaping hole? Ventura had lost his right front tooth, the same one Ashlee had indicated when she'd described the suspect's gold tooth.

I ran down the list of what else I knew about Ray Ventura.

Ventura was familiar with New York. He had family in the city. And he'd moved out of his apartment in Rhodes several days before someone tried to cash the stolen check.

Ventura had a pea coat like the one the suspect wore. And a heavy beard.

Ventura hung out at the Speakeasy—one of the reasons Dinesh hadn't wanted to go there. Em-T had no connection with that bar, but Ventura sure did. He was there five or six nights a week.

And, unlike any other suspect, Ventura had access to the cabs at Sunbeam.

Jesus, not only that—Plodnick was asking about him.

I thought back to the night of Davies's murder. Ventura had been mugged and ended up in the hospital. He'd lost the tooth when he got jumped near his apartment, a few blocks from Sunbeam. What if Ventura had stashed the cab at the garage, for whatever reason, intending to go back later and dispose of the body—but woke up in the hospital instead?

Trudy was interrogating the wrong guy. Em-T hadn't killed Fred Davies. I didn't have the whole picture yet, but there were a hell of a lot more dots connected to Ventura than to anybody else. If we looked closely at him, the picture would come into focus. I was sure of it.

I had to tell Trudy. I pulled out my phone, then stuck it back in my pocket. Even if I could get a signal, she didn't have her cell phone with her. Maybe I could call the precinct where they'd taken Em-T, leave a message. I started to dial directory assistance.

The bus from Rhodes chose that moment to arrive. As passengers streamed off, people sitting around me stirred. A middle-aged woman struggled to lift her own weight in half a dozen shopping bags. Two college-aged men shrugged into backpacks. A young woman in a long, brightly colored skirt picked up a violin case and went to the front of the line.

I watched the line form, my ticket in hand. Then I turned and went outside. I'd find Trudy and tell her about Ventura myself.

The precinct lobby was a tired-looking room staffed by a tired-looking officer behind a dark wood counter. His eyes were rimmed with red; a profusion of tiny veins radiated from his nose. I smiled, trying to look more cheerful than the average citizen who approached him.

"I'm looking for a deputy from Thomson County. Her name's

Trudy Hauser."

He looked at me like he'd found a real idiot. "This ain't Thomson County, bud."

Patience. This guy didn't have to do a thing for me. I kept the smile glued on. "Yes, I know. But she's here giving a statement. About the kid they arrested for trying to cash a stolen cashier's check. Em-T."

There wasn't a flicker of response to suggest that the cop had changed his mind about my intelligence level.

"He calls himself Em-T," I said. "His real name's Myron Terepka."

"I'll see what I can find out." He lumbered out of the room. I drummed my fingers on the counter while I waited. In a few minutes, he reappeared and heaved himself back onto his stool.

"Terepka's here. No visitors."

"I don't want to see him. I want to see Trudy Hauser. I've got something important to tell her."

"Couldn't find anyone of that name."

Probably he didn't even ask. Come on, I thought. This guy was my only connection to Trudy; he had to be able to tell me something. "She said she was staying in New York tonight at the home of a desk sergeant. A woman. Do you know who that might be?"

He shook his head.

I was running out of ideas. "She was invited to observe when they question Terepka tomorrow morning. When will that happen?"

He shook his head again. Then he looked behind me. "Help you?" he asked past my shoulder. A plump young woman with a toddler in one hand and a squirming baby in the other shoved me over with her elbow. "I wanna get a restraining order," she said.

I looked around the room, willing Trudy to appear, but it was no use. She didn't burst through the back door, chattering in cop-show dialogue, her eyes shining with the excitement of the chase. No matter how much I stared at that door, it wasn't going to open for me. I went out the front door and down the steps.

Now what? I stood on the sidewalk. It was four-thirty in the afternoon. People jostled past me as I considered what to do. Trudy would be here in the morning when they questioned the kid. I'd just have to install myself on the station steps and wait until she walked by.

In the meantime, where was I going to spend the night? I was almost out of cash. An ATM wouldn't do me any good, not with $5.12 in my account. I didn't carry a credit card—back at the Homestead, the attitude had been if you can't pay for it, work for it, or barter for it, you can't afford it. Years later, getting in over my head with late payments and inflated interest rates had reinforced the wisdom of that philosophy. The best plan seemed to be to head back to the bus station. Maybe they'd let me cash in my ticket and I could rent a room at the Y, then catch a ride home with Trudy tomorrow—assuming I found her. Or else I could sleep in the bus station. If some cop tried to move me along, I'd show him the ticket and say I'd missed the last bus. Which I had. And for no good reason that I could see.

Pain shot through my thigh as a stylish woman in a business suit whacked me with her briefcase, then swore at me like I'd plowed into her. "Same to you, sweetheart," I said.

Yet there I stood, an obstacle to everyone rushing by, like a big unwieldy box that had toppled off the back of some truck in the middle of an expressway. There's something disconcerting about being in a strange city as the light dims, knowing you have nowhere to go. Everyone was in a hurry—except me. Everyone had some other place they had to be—except me. Eight million people in this city, and I didn't know a single one.

But that wasn't true. I took a second to plot the route, then joined the current of people, pushing past a few myself as I broke into a jog. If I hurried, I could reach MetroPrimitif before it closed. If I was lucky, Felicia Davies would still be there.

As soon as I opened the gallery door, Felicia approached. "Hello, again. I thought you might come by."

"I was afraid I'd miss you." I looked at my watch. Two minutes past five.

Felicia smiled. "Oh, you had plenty of time. We're open until seven most week nights. Although you're right. Usually I head home around now and let Angelica take over."

I took a minute to recover my breath. "The police recovered Fred's ring. They've made an arrest."

"That's why I was expecting you. The police called, but I had a feeling that you'd want to tell me yourself. You're considerate. It's one of the things I like about you."

The burning in my cheeks came from more than jogging twenty blocks in the cold. I'd come here to beg a favor, and here she was assuming I'd put her feelings first. Considerate—I felt like a jerk.

"I'm surprised that it was Em-T, though," she continued. "Disappointed. Fred really believed in that young man's work. I didn't think he'd be so . . . ungrateful."

"I'm not convinced he was."

She raised her eyebrows and waited for me to continue.

"I think there's more to the story. A lot more." I told her about Ventura—the knocked-out tooth and heavy beard, the connections to the Speakeasy and Sunbeam—all those reasons why he fit the bank teller's description a hundred times better than Em-T.

"But Em-T had the ring," she said.

"That's true. If it *is* the ring."

"It is. I went to the police station and identified it."

"Then maybe there's some connection between Em-T and Ventura that we don't know about. But I'm sure Ventura is involved."

"Part of me just wants it to be over." She sighed. "But when I think about it, that's not enough. I need to know the truth. Fred deserves it. Could we discuss this further—over dinner, maybe? Where are you staying?"

Heat crept up my cheeks again. I hate blushing. "I . . . ah, haven't quite figured that out yet. I was supposed to go back to Rhodes tonight, but I missed the last bus."

She took my arm. "Well, then, you must stay with me. I have a guest room that's too seldom used. What about your friend?"

"Trudy? She's all set." I couldn't keep the bitterness out of my tone. Felicia gave me a searching look, then smiled. She really had a lovely smile.

"Just the two of us, then," she said.

Felicia's Manhattan apartment was in a high-rise co-op with a view across the harbor. The doorman gave me a frowning once-over, then beamed at Felicia. "Evening, Mrs. Davies."

"Good evening, Andrew. This is Bo Forrester, a friend from upstate. He'll be my guest tonight."

"Very good, Mrs. Davies. I'll make a note of it."

Felicia took my arm, and we walked across the mirror-polished granite floor to the elevators. When the doors slid open, I waved her ahead of me with a flourish, stationed myself by the buttons, and asked which floor.

"Forty-eight," she said.

"A penthouse?" I whistled. "I'm impressed."

She laughed. "It's worth the expense. The truth is that I can't bear to have anyone walking around over my head. Especially at night." She glanced at me through her lashes as though weighing whether to make a confession. "I don't always sleep very well."

I felt a little dizzy as the elevator whizzed upward and was glad when the doors opened. We stepped out into a plushly carpeted hallway. The silence was as thick as the carpet, the kind that makes your ears ring just for the sake of something to hear. For the first time all day, I was out of range of the street-level noise: the sirens, the traffic, people shouting over all that racket. At the end of the hallway was a wall-sized window. From up here, the silence and the infinite lights shining in all directions made me feel like I was floating at the center of some unknown galaxy.

Felicia stood beside me. She touched my shoulder. "Let's go inside. The view's even better there."

She wasn't kidding about the view. In the living room, two glass walls showed a nighttime panorama of the city. She let me take in the effect for a minute before she flipped on the lights. The focus shifted from that universe of lights to a spacious living room, decorated with modern furniture: clean, sharp lines and low profiles. There were no paintings on the walls—nothing could compete with that view—but there were several primitive-looking sculptures and a display case full of pottery, like the stuff in her gallery.

"Your room is this way," Felicia said. She opened the second door on the left off a narrow hallway. The guest room held a double bed, a dresser, and a chair beside a well stocked bookcase. A half-open door revealed a private bath.

"Please make yourself at home. I'm going to take a quick shower. It's been a long day." She turned back at the doorway. "Where would you like to have dinner? We should make reservations."

"Doesn't matter to me. Um, there are two things, though, that I should tell you. The first is that I'm vegetarian. The second is I'm out of money—temporarily. I can pay you back in Rhodes."

"I guess that rules out Delmonico's, then, on both counts." She smiled. "But you're my guest, so I won't hear of you paying. And I can be very stubborn, so please don't argue." She considered, tilting her head. "You know, I don't really feel like going out. What do you say we order in? Chinese? I know an excellent place that delivers."

"I never say no to tofu."

We conferred over a takeout menu, and she phoned in our order. While she showered, I scanned the books in the bookcase: a combination of bestsellers and classics, Joyce, Shakespeare, and Austen sharing a shelf with Grisham and Westlake. I sat on the bed, then stretched out. Good mattress. Two hours ago I was resigned to sleeping in the bus station; now here I was in a penthouse. Once in a while, fate twisted the right way.

I must have dozed off because the sound of a door closing awoke me. I got up and went to the living room.

Felicia wore a navy satin robe over lighter blue pajamas of the same material. Her damp hair was combed straight back, and she was barefoot. If I hadn't known she was in her forties, I'd have guessed she was only a few years out of college.

"Please excuse the informality," she said. "It's just that after a day in stiff suits and heels, I like to snuggle in when I get home."

"Perfectly understandable," I said, although other than my dress uniform I'd never worn a suit in my life.

"Would you like something to drink? I don't have much in the place, I'm afraid. Some beer in the fridge, or I could open a bottle of wine."

"I'd love a beer."

"Bock or hefeweizen?"

"Are you kidding? Don't tell me you're a beer connoisseur."

She smiled. "I like interesting flavors."

Her favorites were imported German lagers. The bock was first rate, deep-hued and malty, and I told her about some local hand-crafted microbrews she might enjoy. Both of us seemed reluctant to bring up Fred's murder, so we talked about everything else: the beer, the weather, her recent art-buying trip to Colombia and Ecuador. We were just cracking open our second bottles when the doorman called to tell us the food had arrived.

We ate with chopsticks from the containers. Felicia sat on the couch, her feet tucked up under her. I sat across from her in a leather-and-chrome chair. Neither of us spoke. I watched her push back a strand of hair that had fallen across her cheek, and the thought came to me: This was how her husband had seen her. Casual, relaxed, sharing a simple meal. And beautiful.

Then, chopsticks halfway to her mouth, Felicia broke the spell. "So you really don't believe that Em-T killed Fred?"

"To be honest, I don't know. I just think that the whole thing is a lot more complicated than some spoiled rich kid trying to show the world how tough he is."

"What do you mean?"

I wondered how much I should tell her. Then I decided: everything. She had a right to know. "Well, for starters, I can't prove it, but I think Sebastian Hedlund has been embezzling money from the foundation. And I'm pretty sure that drugs are involved somehow."

She nearly choked on her lo mein. "Drugs? You can't be serious."

I laid out the picture for her, fragment by fragment. If I'd hoped that doing so would give me a new perspective, I was wrong. It was like a crazy quilt or a map of the South Pacific, all these little islands just sitting there, isolated, nothing to connect them. Yet it felt good to talk to her. She listened attentively, nodding and asking smart questions.

When I finished, she shook her head. "I'll tell you one thing. There is absolutely no way that Fred was involved with drugs. He hated them, hated what they do to people. His first wife, you know, was addicted to pain killers. It destroyed their marriage." She placed her empty carton on the coffee table. "Not drugs. Not Fred. When Rhodes was going to cut the D.A.R.E. program from the middle school budget, he stepped in and funded it himself."

"I wish I'd known him."

"I wish he'd known you. I'm sure he would have liked you." She shifted on the sofa. "You've given me a lot to think about. So Sebastian's a gambler. I had no idea. I think I'll have a word with the DFA trustees." She shook her head. "You just never know about people, do you?"

For some reason, Trudy's face flashed across my mind. "No, you never do."

Felicia stood and smoothed an invisible wrinkle from her robe. "I'm getting up early tomorrow. You're welcome to sleep in, of course, and leave whenever you like. But I have to get back to Rhodes. I've got an appointment at one, and I want to stop at the house and unpack first, which means I have to be on the road by seven-thirty at the latest. I'll try not to wake you."

"You won't. I never sleep past six."

She started to say good night, then interrupted herself. "I have an idea. Why don't you ride back with me? I'd enjoy the company."

"I've got to find Trudy and tell her about Ventura."

"She'll give you a ride back?"

"Yeah." My voice sounded doubtful. I wasn't at all sure what kind of reception I'd be getting from Trudy. Not after she'd shoved me away from the investigation with both hands. But at least I had my bus ticket.

As if reading my thoughts, Felicia said, "I hate to think of you riding back on the bus."

She got up and stretched, then came over to my chair. She bent and kissed me on the cheek. Her hair tickled my collarbone as her lips brushed my face. She pulled back a little and smiled, looking deeply into my eyes.

There it was again, that question. It darkened her green eyes and gave them endless depth. But I finally understood what it meant. Felicia Davies was lonely.

I put my hand on hers, the flesh cool and smooth. I don't know how long we looked at each other. It felt like forever—no, not forever, more like a place where there's no such thing as time.

Then Felicia straightened and brushed back her hair. "Good night," she said and glided from the room.

Another forever passed as I watched the path she'd taken, staring until nothing remained of her wake. The room settled into silence. I got up, turned off the lights, and went to bed.

Despite the good mattress, I couldn't fall asleep. I lay there, my thoughts jumping back and forth between the loneliness in Felicia's eyes and tomorrow's reunion with Trudy—if I managed to catch up with Trudy. I pictured how the surprise in her face would harden to disapproval, how she'd remind me that she'd already sent me home, like I was some pesky little brother tagging along behind the big kids. When I did sleep, her voice echoed through whatever dreams tried to emerge, saying, "Have a good trip."

By six the next morning, I'd made a decision. I was showered, shaved, dressed, and ready to go. I left a message for Trudy at the precinct station, telling her to call me ASAP. Then I climbed into Felicia's silver Lexus SUV and once again hit the road—this time in style.

CHAPTER 23

I was back at my apartment by noon. The drive back to Rhodes had been quiet, Felicia thoughtful. She had a lot—too much—on her mind, so I spent the trip looking out the window and checking my phone for messages. No Trudy. No Snake.

I was pretty sure I'd blown it with Snake. Lenny had emphasized I'd have one chance. That chance had come and gone, and I still had no clue where my parents were. Snake's "I'll be in touch" sounded a lot like "Sorry, sucker." I doubted I'd ever hear from him again.

And why the hell hadn't Trudy called?

I knew why, but I snapped on the radio so I wouldn't have to think about it. I turned to my favorite classic rock station to get the echoes of that damn Mozart out of my head. They were playing Hendrix, "Stone Free"—much more my speed. I cranked it up, then turned it down before Mrs. B. started banging on the ceiling with a broomstick.

The weatherman came on to announce that a warm front was bringing in a couple of days of temperatures in the sixties, a heat wave for Rhodes in November. "The rain will diminish by evening," he said, "and we'll have a day or two of Indian summer. Enjoy it while you can—but don't forget those snow tires. Winter's still on the way and will arrive with a bang by Tuesday. Expect temperatures to plummet to the twenties, with a strong possibility of snow."

I opened a window to let the warm air in. It was raining a

little; the smell of damp earth wafted through my apartment. I wondered whether Trudy was getting this same weather downstate—it had been cold at six in the morning. She was probably indoors, anyway, watching the cops interrogate Em-T. They were on the wrong track—I was certain. I wished to hell she'd hurry up and call. After the way she'd told me to get lost, I was kind of looking forward to telling her she had the wrong guy.

It was almost three o'clock when I got a phone call from a number in the 212 area code. Trudy, finally. Eight hours had passed since I'd left her the message to call me.

I flipped the phone open. "Yeah?"

"Hey, it's Trudy. Grab a pen. I'm at a payphone, and I don't have any more change, so let me give you the number and you can call me back."

I actually started scrambling around for a pen before I realized I didn't need one. "I've already got the number. It's in my received calls list."

"Oh, right. So call right back, okay? You're not gonna believe what I've got to tell you."

The line went dead. I watched the second hand sweep twice around the kitchen clock before I dialed the number. I'd waited eight hours for her call. She could stand in front of a payphone for a couple of minutes waiting to hear from me.

She picked up halfway through the first ring and started in without any hello. "That Em-T—Terepka—they let him go!" Her voice was indignant, talking fast. "His parents brought in a whole tag team of lawyers—well, I expected that. And he's got an alibi for the time the check was presented. I expected that, too. You'll love it—that stiff-assed English butler. He'll testify that Terepka didn't come out of his bedroom until two o'clock that afternoon. Big surprise, huh? Like the kid couldn't sneak out."

"Trudy, listen—"

"They even brought in that airhead from the bank to look at a lineup. She wanted Terepka's phone number, but she didn't ID him as the guy who tried to cash the check. I told you she was worthless as a witness. But the end result is that they're not pressing charges. Em-T is out on the streets."

There was silence as she finally stopped for breath. I let it grow before I spoke.

"Did you get my message?"

"Your—? Jesus, Bo, there's a murderer walking around down here just because Mommy and Daddy had the cash to get him off. Yeah, I got your message. I figured you wanted to wish me luck."

"Didn't they tell you it was urgent? 'Hi, Trudy—have fun at the interrogation.' That's not exactly urgent, now, is it?"

"What is wrong with you? I'm telling you that the cops down here have screwed everything up, and you're acting like a big sulky kid."

"Maybe it's not the cops who screwed up. Maybe it's you."

"Why, because I didn't call you the second I got your stupid message? I couldn't. I was on my way to the interrogation room. They weren't going to wait for me. Anyway, I'm calling you now. So get over it, okay?" I could picture her scowling as she heaved an exasperated sigh. "I'm going to stay here a few days and shadow this Terepka kid, and I need you to—"

"It wasn't Em-T."

"What?"

"In the bank photos. It wasn't him."

"Of course it was him. He had the damn ring."

"It was Ventura. A guy who used to drive for Sunbeam. Ryan told me that Plodnick was asking about him, right before we left for New York. Plus he got mugged the night Davies was murdered and guess what—he lost a front tooth."

There was a long silence. I pressed into it: "Did you even look at Em-T's face? He's got a few wispy little baby hairs on his chin. There's no way he could grow the heavy stubble the bank teller described."

"Why didn't you tell me this before?"

It's a good thing you can't strangle a person over the phone. "I tried to tell you. The phone message—remember?"

"You should have come to the precinct. You were a citizen with information related to a criminal investigation."

"I—" I held the phone away and counted to ten, then brought it back to my face. "Just forget it."

But Trudy's voice was thoughtful. "So maybe Terepka was telling the truth."

"What do you mean?"

"About how he got the ring. He said he'd never seen it before yesterday. Claimed somebody left it on his doorstep. The butler opened the front door to get the morning paper, and there it was, wrapped up in a box addressed to Em-T."

"Are you kidding?"

"Terepka said it happens all the time. He gets showered with gifts from his adoring fans." She snorted. "Art groupies. The only unusual thing, he said, was that it didn't come with a love note and a phone number. His parents produced the package. Seems the maid was a little slow emptying the trash yesterday."

Ventura must have known about Em-T's connection with Davies. When he got nervous at the bank, he bolted, then realized he had to get rid of the ring. Delivering it to Em-T's doorstep was a pretty smart way to shift attention away from himself. I was about to say so, but Trudy was still talking.

"So I need info on this Ventura. First name? Address?"

"His first name's Ray. He used to live on Third Street, but he moved, just last week. One of the guys at work thought he moved in with a girlfriend in Trumansburg, but he's got family down around New York somewhere."

"That doesn't give me much to get started with."

"Talk to Ryan at Sunbeam. He'll have Ventura's Social Security number and an emergency contact."

"Um, can you call for me? I'm out of change."

"Ryan's not going to give out a Social Security number just because I asked him."

"Good point. I'll try Mike in Records—he'll take a collect call. He must have a copy of the taxi license on file."

When she mentioned Romeo in Records, I almost offered to go through Ryan's files to see if I could dig up the information she wanted. But I put the brakes on that idea—the last thing I needed was for Ryan to catch me snooping around his office.

"This is great," Trudy said. "When they let Terepka go, I thought we'd hit a brick wall, but now I've got something to go on. Thanks, Bo."

"You're welcome."

Trudy cleared her throat getting ready, I thought, to hang up. But she had more to say. "About dropping you off at the bus station. I wanted to say, um, sorry about that." Something in her voice had shifted, and I saw her in that all-night diner, her hair golden in the light. "When the city cops invited me to observe the interrogation, I felt so pumped. At home, the other deputies shut me out. I never get to do anything more exciting than write speeding tickets and deliver eviction notices. But this was something big, and I was in the middle of it." She paused, and I waited. "Then last night, when I was lying on the sofa trying to sleep, I realized what a lousy thing I'd done to you. I'm sorry."

Her voice cracked on *sorry,* like it cost her something to say the word.

"That's okay." My own voice sounded a little strange.

"Anyway," she said, "I hope the trip back wasn't too awful. What time did you get in last night?"

For some reason, I felt reluctant to answer. "Actually, I came back this morning. I got here around noon."

"Oh, no. You missed the bus? Bo, that's awful. Where did you stay? Please don't tell me you slept in the bus station." I'll admit it—for a second I was tempted to let her believe that's exactly what I'd done. It was the way her voice sounded, warm and full of concern. But I wasn't going to lie to her.

"I stayed with Felicia. She has a penthouse in Manhattan. So I was fine—no need to have worried."

"You *what?*" So much for warm. The icy blast of words almost froze my ear off. "Why in hell did you do that?"

"Because I got stranded, that's why. I *did* go to the precinct. To try to find you and tell you about Ventura. The guy at the desk never heard of you, and since you lost your cell phone I couldn't call you. I'd missed the last bus. I had no money. The only thing I could think of was to go back to Felicia's gallery."

The silence that followed did nothing to thaw matters.

"Jesus, Trudy, what did you expect me to do? Would you rather hear that I spent the night trying to sleep in a goddamn plastic chair, surrounded by winos, after you'd told me to get the hell out of town?" Okay, so the last part was a dig, and I felt like a jerk for saying it after she'd apologized and all. But she started it.

She sighed. "No. It's just . . . Well, anyway, I'll get right on this Ventura thing. I'll call you tomorrow to let you know what I find out."

After we'd hung up, I wished I'd told her to be careful. Ventura was mean, the kind of guy always spoiling for a fight. It was looking more and more like he'd murdered Fred Davies. If he thought Trudy was on to him—she'd better not try to approach him alone. I should warn her. I dialed the payphone number, hoping she was still there. It rang and rang, then finally a voice came on.

"Han-gul?"

Obviously not Trudy. But she couldn't have gone far. "Do you see a woman nearby? Blonde, short hair, early thirties, about five-four? Call out 'Trudy'—if she hears you she'll come over."

"Eh? Han-gul?"

"Never mind."

I hung up, feeling uneasy. I'd just put Trudy on the trail of a murderer, and here I sat, two hundred miles away, while she went after him alone.

Ryan didn't need me to come in until six, and I found myself killing time by pacing the living room, thinking about Ventura. The more I thought about him, the less I liked it. Everything fit: the Speakeasy, Sunbeam, the gold tooth, the cashier's check, the ring. He'd even known about Hedlund's gambling, making me look like an idiot in front of the guy. Like a last gesture of contempt before he blew town.

And I'd sent Trudy after him. Maybe she wouldn't be able to find him. New York was a huge city, and she didn't have an address. Maybe she'd give up and come home.

Yeah, right. If I believed that, I'd quit wearing a rut in my living room carpet.

I needed to distract myself—read the paper, maybe, see what had been happening in Rhodes in the last couple of days. Mrs. B. was probably done with our paper by now. I went downstairs and knocked at her apartment door. No answer. I tried again, but she wasn't home. She was probably out at the grocery store; it was part of her Saturday-afternoon routine. I'd catch her when she got back.

I was halfway up the staircase when I heard footsteps on the front porch. They sounded heavy; Mrs. B. must be loaded down with grocery bags. The footsteps paused at the front door. No sense making the poor woman struggle with bags while she searched her pocketbook for her keys. I went to the front door and opened it.

"Hey, Mrs. B., do you need any help with—"

But it wasn't Mrs. B. A fist the size of a freight train rocketed toward my face. The air exploded into a billion shimmering fragments, then everything went black.

Chapter 24

A light flashed at me, like someone on a distant mountain top was sending a message in Morse code. I squinted toward the dots and dashes, but I couldn't make any sense of them through the fog of pain. My head, twice as big as I remembered it, throbbed all over. My shoulders felt like a ballet troupe of elephants had been dancing a flamenco on them. A voice wrapped in three layers of cotton wafted toward me.

"Bo? You okay? How many fingers am I holding up?"

Fingers? Who was talking about fingers? I blinked at the six faces floating above me. Three Carls. And three Mrs. Bs. I blinked again, and the Morse code signals became the light glinting off her cats-eye glasses. I tried to sit up.

"Hold on there," Carl said, pressing on my shoulders. Damn, that hurt. "I'm not letting you up until you can tell me how many fingers I got."

"I'm gonna take a wild guess, Carl, and say ten. Unless you've got a couple extra thumbs I never noticed."

Carl continued to hold me down; his three heads shook in unison. "Can't say, huh? Not a good sign. See if you can tell me what day of the week it is."

"It's Saturday, okay? Now will you please let me sit up?"

"Help him up, Carl." I was grateful for the cafeteria-lady authority in Mrs. B.'s tone. That is, until she turned it on me. "And Bo, you take it easy. Carl just saved your life."

Halfway up to seated position, I let myself fall backward. If

Carl had saved me, I might as well just die now.

But Carl got me by one arm and Mrs. B. by the other. Together, they dragged me up until I was sitting. I waited for the earth to stop rocking, then realized we were outside in the warm afternoon. The last thing I remembered, I'd been in the front hall, but somehow I'd gotten out onto the porch.

"What happened?" I asked, not sure I wanted to know.

"Well," Carl said, "me and Irene went to the grocery store. When we got back here, the first thing we seen is this guy on the porch. Big guy. He's all hunched over, and he looks like he's pounding the tarnation out of the porch floor."

"He wasn't from around here," Mrs. B. added. "I'm sure I'd never seen him before. The neighborhood isn't what it used to be, but still . . ."

"Naturally," Carl continued, "I was concerned for Irene's safety. Here she comes home from buying groceries to find a drunk lunatic right there on her front porch—"

"He was drunk?" I asked.

"I've been in distilleries smelled less strong."

"And not only that," Mrs. B. cut in. "His suit was terribly wrinkled—it looked like he'd been wearing it for a week—and he slurred his words and staggered around frightfully." She dimpled at Carl. "Once Carl pulled him off you."

Somehow—maybe it was the brain fog—I couldn't quite picture Carl leaping to my defense. But Carl puffed up like a peacock at her words.

"That's right," he said. "I went up to him and asked just what he thought he was doing. He yelled some stuff. I thought he was gonna try to start something with me, seeing as his fists was all balled up, but I guess he didn't dare. He yelled some more, then ran off." Carl's brow darkened. "He said—and I quote—'Where's my wife? What have you done with her, you wife-stealing . . . uh . . . bastard?' " He glanced at Mrs. B., as if worried the word would offend her delicate sensibilities.

She nodded enthusiastically. "Carl's right. 'Wife-stealing bastard.' That's just what he said."

The picture was beginning to come into focus. The huge fist, the drunkenness, the jealousy. Perry Glaser. But why was he after me about his wife? The answer pushed its way through the fog. Nora Glaser hadn't returned from her art history conference.

Carl was shaking a finger at me. Just one. I thought. It was still a little hard to tell.

"It's one thing to take up with that crazy deputy," he said. "You could marry her, though why you'd want to . . . But I swear, Bo, I never would've thought that you"—he made a move like he was going to cover Mrs. B.'s ears, but she batted his hands away, so he dropped his voice to a whisper—"would covet thy neighbor's wife."

Mrs. B. shook her head. "Is it those drugs, Bo? There's a counselor at the high school I hear is pretty good."

"Drugs?" Carl's shocked expression deepened. "I knew about Ronnie—hell, everyone knows about Ronnie—but Bo? I guess I should've known."

I almost wished Perry Glaser were back. If I saw him coming, at least I'd have some kind of defense against him.

"I don't do drugs, and I'm not fooling around with Perry Glaser's wife."

"Then whose—" Carl began.

"I'm not fooling around with *anybody's* wife. I'm not fooling around with anyone at all." Too bad. At least then I'd have something better to do on a Saturday night than get pounded by Perry Glaser, discuss morality with three floating Carls, and then drive a taxi until four in the morning.

When I stood up, the street went on a Tilt-a-Whirl ride. I held onto the porch railing until it stopped. A jackhammer was trying to pound its way out of my skull, and I couldn't see out of my left eye. I touched the swollen lid gingerly while Carl and Mrs. B. filled in more details: When they'd arrived on the scene, I'd been lying unconscious on the front porch while Perry Glaser, my shirt bunched up in his fists, pounded my head against the floorboards, screaming about his wife.

"You're going to have a real shiner," Mrs. B. said. "You got some steak to put on it?"

"I don't keep much steak in the house, Mrs. B."

"Well, here," she said, rummaging through her bags. "Use this. I was going to cook it up for Carl's dinner, but you need it more. He can take me out for a meal instead."

She held out a foam tray with a huge red slab of meat wrapped up inside. Carl stared at it, tongue lolling, looking like a half-starved basset hound.

"Not the T-bone, Irene," he pleaded. "He oughta go to the hospital, anyway, get checked out in case he's got one of them—whadayacallit—contusions."

"You mean a concussion," Mrs. B. corrected. I had plenty of contusions—I could feel each one. She looked at the steak, then at me, her eyebrows raised. I shook my head. My head stopped shaking a few seconds before the surroundings did.

"Well, perhaps Carl's right," she said, handing him the steak. "You probably should have a doctor look at you. You need a ride to the hospital?" I assured her I'd be okay. She clucked at me some, then gathered up her grocery bags and went inside.

Carl was cradling the T-bone like it was a newborn babe. He waited until Mrs. B. had closed the apartment door behind her, then leaned toward me and spoke in an urgent whisper. "While you're out there at the hospital, you have a word with the doctor about your other problem. They got drugs, I hear, that can help. Even a bad case like yours."

The way my head was pounding, I almost didn't ask. "What problem?"

"That sex mania you got. Chasing after anything in a skirt—deputies, married women. Anyone, anywhere, any time of the day or night." He looked down at the steak and tsked. " 'Cause I gotta tell you, it makes me more'n a little nervous to have you living under the same roof with Irene 'til you get yourself under control. If I have to defend her honor—well, don't think I won't do it." He sucked in his stomach and threw his shoulders back, striking what I could only assume was his honor-defending pose. Then he sagged back to his normal pot-bellied posture, gave the steak a loving pat, and followed Mrs. B. into her apartment.

Somehow, I made it up the stairs. In my bathroom, I swallowed an aspirin, but after catching my reflection in the mirror, I took one more. I looked like a wild man, tangled hair flying around my face like a tornado. My left eye was swollen shut. Mrs. B. was right, when it colored up, it was going to be one hell of a black eye. At least I was no longer seeing the world in triplicate. I pried open the lid—no bleeding in the eye. That was good. But my lip was split—I wiped blood off my teeth—and two goose eggs sprouted on the back of my head.

I rummaged in the freezer for some bags of vegetables to slow down the swelling. The way I was feeling, I might as well stick my whole head in the freezer and leave it there for the night. I glanced at the kitchen clock. Quarter to four—I still had two hours to recuperate before I had to leave for work. I lay on the couch, using a bag of frozen corn as a pillow and pressing another of mixed vegetables against my eye.

Damn Perry Glaser. How the hell did he expect me to know where his wife was? She was probably sitting at home waiting for him to return from his drunken rampage. But what if she wasn't? I remembered how her conference talk had been canceled "due to illness," and Trudy's theory that she'd checked into the hotel and then taken off for somewhere else. Ventura was the guy in the bank photos—I was sure of that—but maybe Nora was involved somehow.

I groaned along with my protesting muscles as I got up from the couch to find a phone book. As I flipped through the *G*s, I thought about what I was going to say to Glaser. I couldn't deal with the guy tonight. But tomorrow, on neutral ground, preferably some place with security guards handy . . .

I dialed the Glasers' number, and an answering machine picked up. I kept my message brief. "This is Bo Forrester. I need to talk to you about your wife. Meet me tomorrow—that's Sunday—at noon in the food court at the mall."

Glaser would be there, assuming he came home sober enough to listen to the message. And—against every iota of common sense I ever possessed—so would I. Now all I had to do was figure out where to get a nice suit of body armor, size 40 long.

The mall was crowded. It was a perfect day outside—maybe the last warm one before May—and the citizens of Rhodes had nothing better to do than go shopping. College girls scurried by in packs, carrying three or four shopping bags each. Families dressed like they'd come straight from church browsed store windows or bought hamburgers and fries for the kids. A couple of scruffy teenage boys disappeared into the video game store.

And Perry Glaser staggered through the crowd, as huge and lumbering as Frankenstein's monster on a bad day. I waved, caught his eye, and watched him approach.

He looked terrible. Strands of greasy hair stuck to his forehead, and the bags below his bloodshot eyes sagged halfway down his stubble-gray cheeks. I stood up and offered to shake hands, trying to look friendly. I wanted the guy to talk to me, but I also wanted to be on my feet in case he came at me again.

Five feet away he stopped, ignoring my hand. "Where's Nora?" He clenched his fists, each one the size of a soccer ball. I wasn't afraid of the guy, but I'd rather keep out of range of those things.

I gestured toward the table. "Sit down. Then we'll talk."

His hitting arm twitched, and I got ready. But then he slumped into a seat and splayed his big hands open on the table. I sat across from him. He seemed more or less sober, but he smelled of alcohol, like he was sweating the stuff. He looked at me vaguely, those bloodshot eyes out of focus. Then he jerked himself upright and pounded the table.

"Where is she?" he shouted.

The family at the next table jumped, gave us a quick once over, then picked up their trays and moved.

"I don't know. I swear. I thought you and I could work together to find her."

He stared at me with about as much comprehension as if I'd answered in Swedish. Then he relaxed, his gray face drooping into jowls.

"You'd help me?" Disbelief soaked his voice. This was a guy who'd been fighting the world on his own for a long time.

"Sure. You know, put our heads together. Share what we know."

He squinted at me. "You look like crap. Did I do that?"

I looked like crap? Okay, yeah, I did. But he looked like crap's older brother. We'd be lucky if Security didn't throw us both out. "Let's not worry about that now. When did you last speak to Nora?"

"I thought . . . When she didn't come back, I thought . . ."

He put his head in his hands. I'd been expecting a confrontation, possibly violent, but now I wanted to reach over and pat his shoulder.

I made my voice gentle and asked again. "So when was the last time you talked to her?"

"She went to this conference in Boston. I didn't want her to. I know what goes on at those things." He looked up, and his fist clenched again like it had a mind of its own. "Friday. She called me Friday night and said her talk had gone well. She was supposed to be on the 8:34 flight yesterday morning. I went to the airport to meet her. I brought roses. But she wasn't on the plane. She wasn't on that flight, or the next one, or the next. And she doesn't answer her phone."

"Perry," I said, "Nora never gave her talk."

He looked at me wildly. "How do you know? Were you at that goddamn conference? I told you, I know what goes on at those things! I do!"

"No, you've got the wrong idea. I wasn't there. But the conference Web site said her talk was canceled due to illness."

"Nora's sick?" The poor guy was bewildered. "But she told me two days ago that everything was fine."

Yeah, and she also told him she'd be on the 8:34 flight.

"When you spoke to her on Friday, where was she?"

"In Boston, of course. Or that's what I assumed. She called me."

"Did you ever call her at the hotel?"

"I called her on her cell phone. It doesn't cost extra that way."

So there was still no evidence that Nora stayed in Boston after she'd checked into the hotel. She'd skipped the conference—why? I'd have to tread carefully with my next question.

"Some FBI agents paid Nora a visit last week. Do you know what they wanted?"

For two seconds, his face showed pure shock. Then it hardened into anger. "That's a lie!"

"No, it's true. I saw them at her office."

He slumped back in his seat. "She never said anything about it. What would the FBI want with Nora? Do you think they—?" I waited, but he didn't finish the sentence.

"Do I think they *what?*" I finally asked, but he shook his head and wouldn't answer.

I took a deep breath. "Is it possible, maybe, that Nora could be involved with drugs?"

I thought he'd get mad again, but he just kept shaking his head. "No way. There's a lot of things Nora would do. She has a hard time resisting men. I know that. And we both have a little problem with alcohol. But she wouldn't use drugs." He stared past my shoulder and spoke to himself in a whisper. "Would she?"

"I was thinking more about the distribution side."

Now I'd done it. He was furious. He jumped out of his seat, fists ready.

"That's a filthy, stinking, goddamn lie!"

"Hang on, hang on. I'm not making any accusations. Just asking your opinion. And I think you've made it clear what that is."

"And you better remember it, too." He leaned forward, trembling with aggression. I met his eye and held it. He blinked first, sighed, then sat down.

I had one more question to ask.

"Did she ever mention anyone named Ventura?"

"Who's he? Another boyfriend?"

Without waiting for my answer, he put his head down on the table and stayed that way, absolutely still. I sat there for a minute, uncertain what to say. "Perry—"

He leapt up. "I gotta go." He stumbled away from the table.

I didn't try to stop him. He'd told me as much as he knew. Clearly, he'd never heard of Ventura. And he didn't know where Nora had disappeared to.

I got up and was heading toward the exit when a commotion at the other end of the food court, over by the ATM, made me turn around. Someone was screaming obscenities and kicking the cash machine. Glaser. I ran over, arriving just behind two security guards; each struggled to hang on to an arm. Glaser shook them off like fleas, then lunged at the bigger one, knocking him down and pounding his head against the floor.

The smaller guard jumped on Glaser's back and clung there like a monkey while Glaser continued to batter his colleague. I tugged at Glaser's arm, talking to him, trying to calm him down. Another mall customer, a big guy in a T-shirt and jeans, shoved at Glaser from the other side. Between the three of us, we knocked him off balance and got him down on the floor, still bellowing but no longer struggling. The little guard kneeled on his back while the guy in the T-shirt twisted his hitting arm in a wrestler's hold. The bigger guard was moaning and holding his head. I knew how he felt.

Sirens wailed over the shouting. Someone had called the cops.

"Perry, what happened?" I asked. "What's wrong?"

He looked up at me sideways—he couldn't move his head much the way his captors held him pressed against the floor. Then his face crumpled, and he started to cry.

"That . . . goddamn . . . bitch" came out between sobs. "Oh, Nora . . . oh, that bitch. She's not coming home. Look." He shifted his gaze toward a slip of paper lying on the floor. I picked it up. It was an account balance from the ATM. Thirteen dollars and twenty-three cents.

"Insufficient funds," Glaser said. "She cleaned out our bank account. Didn't even leave me forty goddamn bucks."

The cops arrived. I felt kind of sorry for the guy as they led him away in handcuffs. Everyone was staring—little kids pointed and whispered to their mothers, salesgirls stepped out of their shops and craned their necks. Glaser, head down and shoulders slumped, seemed oblivious. Maybe a few days in the county jail would be the best thing for him. He could dry out, get cleaned up. At least they'd feed him. His wife hadn't left him much grocery money.

When Trudy called around four, I told her about Glaser. But I wasn't sure she heard me, she was so hyped up.

"I've located Ventura. But I want your confirmation, just to make sure."

"I can't afford another trip to New York."

"You don't have to. I got a photo. I'll fax it up to Mike in Records. He's off today, so I'll do it first thing tomorrow. As soon as you can, stop by the station and take a look."

"I'm driving the morning shift."

"Afternoon's fine. Just make it some time tomorrow, okay?"

"All right." I still didn't like the idea of Trudy chasing after the guy. "Listen, keep your distance from Ventura. He's a mean son of a bitch—really dangerous. We're thinking he killed Fred Davies, right? And he could be the one who shot at me at Oneida Falls. Maybe you should turn over what you know to the local cops."

"Are you kidding? And have them screw up again? No way. I'm going to make sure we've got something solid on this one."

"Trudy—"

"Don't *worry.* I'm just tailing him right now. He has no clue I'm around. He—Hey, wait. I've gotta go. I'll call you later. Around seven."

She hung up without saying goodbye.

A little later, I went to Donovan's for a beer. Ryan and Dinesh sat at the bar.

"Man," Dinesh said when he saw my black eye. "You look

worse than Trina." The pudding wrestling finals had been tough on Trina—she'd slipped in a wading pool full of butterscotch and gone down hard, knocking an eye against her opponent's elbow and breaking her wrist. She was home in Connecticut recuperating until spring semester.

"Her parents are suing Overton," he said and shrugged. "So no more wrestling. For this year, anyway."

"Why do they call it butterscotch?" Ryan wondered out loud. "It doesn't taste like butter or scotch."

"What I'm into now," Dinesh said, "is water polo. It's a real sport. Trina's roommate is on the team; she gets me into practices. You should see the way they splash around in those little bathing suits. Did you know that last year the Overton women's water polo team was number three in the entire nation?"

"So how many women's water polo teams *are* there in the nation?" Ryan asked. "Four? You wanna talk about a 'real sport,' let's talk football."

"Ha, you mean Overton's record losing streak? What did they win, like one game this season?"

"Three. But next year they're gonna make a comeback—"

I swallowed some ale and listened to them argue. It felt good to be part of a normal conversation again. No mention of murder or drugs or stolen checks. There I was, a guy having a beer with my buddies, talking about women and sports.

Next thing I knew, it was quarter to seven. I didn't want to take Trudy's call in the bar, and I just had time to make it home. I paid up, left a tip, said goodnight. Then I hurried back to my apartment.

I burst into my living room at two minutes to seven. Made it. I sat down to wait, trying to organize my thoughts. I really wanted Trudy's input on Nora's disappearance and any connection she might have to Ventura. And I wanted to warn her again to keep away from that guy. I double-checked to make sure my phone was on.

But the call never came. Not at seven, not at eight. Not even at midnight, when I finally went to bed. There's a limit, after all, to how long a man is willing to wait.

Chapter 25

The next afternoon I dropped off my cab at the garage and, since it was still unseasonably warm, walked downtown to the Rhodes police headquarters. It was a weird sensation trotting up the front steps of the building I'd spent the past couple of weeks trying my damnedest to stay out of. I hoped this wouldn't take long. The place gave me the creeps.

All I knew about Mike in Records—aside from the fact that he had a major crush on Trudy—was that he'd earned a degree in library science before attending the police academy. I pictured some weedy little goofball, plagued by a bad case of adult acne, with side-parted hair and thick glasses held together by tape above the nose.

Man, was I wrong.

The guy who came out from the back and almost broke my hand shaking it could be summed up in one word: buff. He was my height but had at least twenty pounds on me, every ounce of it muscle. Massive biceps exploded from his uniform's short sleeves. His hair was a sandy crewcut. And what the hell was he doing with a tan in the middle of November?

He winced when he saw my face. "Ouch," he said. "Quite the shiner you got there."

I shrugged. Next to this guy, I felt like someone who'd forgotten to take off his Halloween ghoul costume.

"Great to finally meet you," he said, his smile gleaming like a toothpaste commercial. "Trudy's told me so much about you, I feel like we're old friends."

All I could think of was how *little* Trudy had told me about this guy.

He was waiting for me to say something, so I stopped staring and made my mouth move.

"You've got a photo for me to look at?"

"Sure do. Trudy faxed it up yesterday. It was waiting for me when I got in this morning." He waved the photo at me but didn't hand it over. "Pretty amazing, isn't it, the way she just keeps going on this case? And all on her own time." He shook his head. "What a gal."

I cringed. I've always hated the word *gal.* Makes me think of some perky cowgirl in a fringed skirt, singing *Oklahoma!* and twirling a lasso. Hah, I thought. That showed how little this jerk knew Trudy. I couldn't think of a worse word to describe her.

"She's something, all right." I reached across the counter and snatched the photo.

There was no question: The snarling punk dead center was definitely Ventura. He stared straight into the camera, gold tooth gleaming, an ugly sneer on his face. No sunglasses or hat, but he was wearing a peacoat like in the bank photos.

"That the guy?" Mike asked.

None of your damn business, I thought, but I said, "Yeah. Do you know him?"

"Never saw him before. I checked, and he has no record. Clean as a whistle."

There was something about the photo that bothered me. Something in Ventura's expression. Anger, maybe. Or contempt. Jesus, I wondered, did he recognize Trudy? Did he know she was taking his picture? Suddenly, Trudy's failure to call me last night seemed like more than an oversight.

"So, Mike, when did you last hear from Trudy?"

"Yesterday—about four, four-thirty. She said she'd call again later, but she must have gotten too busy chasing this bozo around."

So she hadn't called either one of us. A feeling of uneasiness began to ball itself into a lump in my stomach. "Do you have a number for her in New York?"

"No. She lost her cell phone again." He laughed. "That little gal must know every gosh darn payphone in Thomson County. Probably in New York City by now, too." He was still chuckling, shaking his head like losing her phone every five minutes was cute. "I did have the number of a policewoman she stayed with for a couple of days, but she's not there now."

She never gave me that number, damn it all to hell. I gritted my teeth and asked, "Do you still have it? I might call and see where Trudy went from there."

His eyebrows went up. "She didn't give it to you? Gee, that's too bad. When I found out she wasn't staying there anymore, I threw it away."

Some record-keeper. Even with a master's degree, he couldn't hold on to one lousy scrap of paper.

"She must be on her way back up here, though," Mike said. "Maybe she's already home. Do you want me to try her there?"

"I've *got* her home number, thanks." I reconsidered as soon as I'd said it. "Yeah, sure, why not?" I glanced down at the photo of Ventura. I'd feel a lot better knowing where she was.

Mike dialed the phone, humming. He listened, then said to me, "Answering machine. Should I leave a message?"

"Tell her to call me."

He gave me a thumbs-up, then turned his attention to the phone. "Yeah, hi, Trudy, it's Mike. I've got your friend Bo here with me at the station. He gave a positive ID on the Ventura photo. He also says he'd like you to call him when you get a chance. Oh, and let me know about dinner on Friday. Okay, bye."

That comment about dinner did not go unnoticed, but other concerns pushed it to the edges of my thoughts. Where was Trudy? I'd warned her that Ventura was dangerous. She'd promised to keep her distance. Surely she wouldn't be foolish enough to confront him head on. Oh, God, what was I thinking? Of course she would.

"You know what?" Mike said. "I bet she's home. I bet she drove back from New York late last night and is tucked into bed right now catching up on sleep. Probably unplugged the phone."

"You could be right. I think I'll drive out there and check."

"Good idea. If you see her, ask her to give me a call."

Fat chance, I thought as I nodded. "And if you hear from her, let me know, okay? Got a pen? I'll write down my phone number."

"No need. I can look it up in your file."

My file. I remembered why I didn't hang out at Rhodes police headquarters. But that wasn't why I needed to get out of there now. I had to get to Trudy's place and make sure she was all right. I said goodbye to Mike and walked through the lobby.

With each step, my thoughts swung back and forth: She'd keep back from Ventura. She'd go after the guy. Keep back. Go after him. I picked up my pace. The sooner I got out to her trailer, the better.

I'd almost made it to the front door when a hand clamped down on my shoulder. "Forrester. Nice of you to save me a trip."

I turned to see Plodnick, a smug grin stretching out his pencil moustache. His eyes widened when he saw my beat-up face.

"Whoa," he said. "What happened to you? Overcharge the wrong passenger?"

"Leave me alone, Plodnick. I've got something important to do."

"*Detective* Plodnick. That's the trouble with you, Forrester.

No respect for the law. An attitude like that gets people in trouble—arrested, even." His grip on my shoulder tightened. "Sure you can't spare a few minutes to talk to me? Voluntarily, I mean."

"No." I shook his hand off and turned back toward the door. In two seconds he was in front of me, blocking my way.

"Do you *want* me to arrest you? Is that what you want? I could, you know. Right now. But," that grin again, "it's up to you."

Just past his shoulder, not four feet away, stood the front door. I could almost touch it, but it was so goddamn far out of reach. And somewhere beyond it was Trudy. The only way I could get out there and find her was to deal with Plodnick first. I looked him in the eye.

"All right," I said, "let's talk."

I sat on the wrong side of a closed door marked Conference Room. The dull-green room wasn't big, maybe ten by twelve; it felt smaller with the door closed. Metal chairs with cracked vinyl seats surrounded a gray metal table. Plodnick pulled out a chair, then paused.

"Coffee?" he asked.

"No, I don't want any goddamn coffee. I want to get the hell out of here. So stop screwing around and ask me whatever it is you want to ask me."

He sat down across from me, then leaned back in his chair and tented his fingers, making it clear he intended to take his time. I suppressed the urge to turn over the table into his lap and knock him against the wall. My only hope of getting out of there quickly was to stay cool.

Plodnick messed around with a tape recorder, plugging it into one outlet, then another. He put in three or four different tapes and pressed the fast-forward and reverse buttons. I was about ready to break the damn recorder over his head when he pushed it aside. "We don't need that," he said. "This is just an informal, voluntary chat, right?"

Voluntary, my ass. "So start chatting already."

"Tell me about your relationship with Ray Ventura."

"No relationship. I worked with the guy for a few months."

"Worked with him where?"

"At the Sunbeam Taxi Company. You know that. We both drove for Sunbeam. He quit over a week ago. I'm still there."

"And that's your only association?"

"Yes."

"You never socialized with Mr. Ventura?"

"No."

"You didn't work together on any—how should I put it—freelance projects?"

" 'Freelance projects'—what the hell is that? Damn it, Plodnick, if you want to ask me something, ask it straight out. You're wasting my time."

"Sure. Let me clarify." He leaned forward. "How long have you been selling drugs with Ray Ventura out of a bar called the Speakeasy?"

Jesus. Is that what they thought? "I've never sold drugs. And I don't hang out at the Speakeasy."

"Really? You've been observed there several times."

"I only went there to—" To what? To follow George Boutros's whacked-out clue in my quest to find the real murderer? Somehow I didn't think that would go down too well, even if Plodnick believed me. I sat silently, aware that he believed he'd cornered me—and without any idea how to correct his impression.

He smiled like he was suddenly my best pal. "It's in your own interest to cooperate. Has Ventura tried to contact you recently?"

"No. The last time I saw Ventura was the day he quit Sunbeam."

"Is that right? I've gotta tell you, then, that I don't believe you. I think Ventura was the reason you went to New York." I must have gaped at him, because he smiled and said, "Oh, yes. I know all about your little road trip. For a professional driver, you seem pretty ignorant of where the county line is." He laughed at his joke. Then his chuckle crystallized into a mean-eyed stare. "So did you hook up with Ventura in New York? You must have had a thing or two to say to him. It had to be a big disappointment when your partner messed up cashing the stolen check." He stood and walked around the table, stopping right behind my chair. His voice buzzed in my ear. "We're watching you, Forrester. If Ventura contacts you or wants you to meet him, you'd better let us know."

"Meet him? Wait—are you saying he's in Rhodes?" What an idiot I was. I'd been hoping, thanks to Mike's suggestion, that Trudy had come back upstate and left Ventura far behind in the big, bad city. Of course she'd never let his trail go cold like that. If she was in Rhodes, it was because she'd followed him here. Instead of kicking my heels against this damn chair, I should be out there making sure she was okay.

"Stop playing games," Plodnick said. "You know perfectly well—" A knock rapped on the door. The detective looked annoyed at the interruption, but when a uniformed cop beckoned him, he went into the hallway.

Ventura was in Rhodes. Why? With a sick lurch of fear, I knew, just *knew,* that something had happened to Trudy. Something bad. Jesus, maybe that was what the sergeant was telling Plodnick out in the hallway right now.

I went to the door and tried the knob. To my surprise, it wasn't locked. I pulled the door toward me a crack.

Plodnick and the uniform were right outside. The uniform

was saying, ". . . out at the county jail. He asked for you by name."

"What the hell does he want with me?"

"He wouldn't give any details. He won't talk to anyone but you. All he said was he wanted to confess."

"Well, I'll be damned. Glaser, huh? I'd better get out there before he changes his mind."

I barely made it back to my seat before Plodnick threw open the door. He was trying to look cool, but excitement lit up his eyes.

"Okay, Forrester, I believe you got the message. Think about what I said. If you hear from your buddy Ventura, give me a call."

Of course I'd call the cops if I saw him. I wanted Ventura locked up even worse than they did. At least until I knew Trudy was safe.

The last of the daylight faded as I skidded onto the dirt road to Trudy's place. I flew over the ruts at a speed that wasn't doing my suspension any good. Ever since I'd left the police station, I tried to be rational: Trudy didn't always call when she said she would. Just because she hadn't called last night didn't mean something terrible had happened to her. She was a trained police officer; she wouldn't try to apprehend a murder suspect on her own.

But that rational voice kept getting shouted down by the one yelling, "Find her! Now!" I pressed the accelerator.

At the trailer, my headlights flashed across Trudy's pickup truck, parked in its usual spot. I hit the brakes and stared, half-afraid it would shimmer away into nothing like a mirage. But the truck was really there. I heaved such a sigh of relief that it felt like I'd been holding my breath all the way from town. Mike in Records had been right after all. She'd driven back late last night or early this morning and was inside sleeping.

Without even bothering to let me know she was home. Now that my heartbeat had slowed to its normal speed, annoyance seeped in. Didn't she know people worried about her?

Time for Sleeping Beauty to wake up. I had a thing or two to discuss with her.

No lights were on inside, I noticed, as I climbed the front steps. I rang the bell a couple of times and waited, then rapped on the storm door and called her name. No sound of approaching footsteps. No sound at all. Man, she was a deep sleeper. I opened the storm door to pound on the solid one behind it. That should get her attention.

That's when I saw that the front door wasn't closed.

I tried the knob. It was locked, but the latch hadn't caught, leaving the door ajar. A nudge pushed it open.

I put a foot on the threshold but stayed outside, as I yelled through the doorway. "Trudy? It's Bo. Why the hell didn't you tell me you were back?"

No answer.

Was she avoiding me? Hiding in here with the lights out so she wouldn't have to talk to me? Not for long, I thought, opening the door all the way and stepping inside. I flipped on the light—and gasped at what it revealed.

Trudy's trailer had been ransacked. To my right, someone had pulled the kitchen to pieces. Empty cupboards gaped; dishes and cans and cereal boxes covered the counters, the table, even the floor. I rushed down the short hallway to the living room. Same thing. A suitcase lay open on the sofa, its contents thrown around. The sofa cushions were crooked, like they'd been pulled up and tossed carelessly back into place. CDs and books, yanked from their shelves, were scattered everywhere. A sock draped itself across the nose of the big buck's head over the couch.

"Trudy? Trudy!" I ran from room to room. There was no sign

of her, but the chaos continued throughout the trailer.

Her closed bedroom door brought me to a halt. I put a hand on the knob. Please, I thought, not knowing who or what I was beseeching, if she's in there, please let her be all right. I took a deep breath and opened the door, groping for the light switch.

The bedroom was empty.

And as much a mess as the rest of the trailer. The sheets had been torn off the bed, the mattress pushed half off the box spring. Open drawers looked like someone had pawed through them quickly.

I pulled the mattress back in place and sat on the edge of the bed, trying to think. What the hell had happened here? No sign of Trudy, but every sign of a break-in, a search, maybe a struggle. What did she have that someone wanted so badly? Was Ventura after that photo she'd taken of him? The trailer was empty, but her truck was parked outside. So where was Trudy?

I looked around like Trudy would materialize if only I stared at the right spot. On her dresser was the jewelry box that held Mozart's hair ribbon—the only thing in the place that hadn't been disturbed. I picked up the box and opened it. There was the ribbon, blue on gray velvet, just as she'd shown it to me. I closed the box gently and laid it back on the dresser.

The phone next to the bed had a built-in answering machine. Its digital display said zero messages, but I'd watched Mike in Records leave a message an hour ago. So someone had played whatever messages it held. Did that mean that Trudy knew I was trying to get in touch with her? Or had someone else—the same someone who'd trashed the place—learned from Mike's call that I'd confirmed Ventura's ID?

Trudy had followed Ventura back to Rhodes. If I wanted to find her, I had to find him. He'd left his old apartment, so he could be anywhere, damn it. But there was only one place to start looking. I got in my car and headed for the Speakeasy.

Chapter 26

Cars and motorcycles crammed the Speakeasy's parking lot. I jolted to a stop on the walkway in front of the door. Inside, the place was packed. In the dim light, all I could see was a solid mass of bodies. I was aware of loud country music, shouted conversations, the smells of stale sweat and staler beer.

I plunged into the crowd. After a few seconds, shapes took form: leather vests, tattooed necks and biceps, greasy beards. Ventura was short, and the room was crowded. I'd never find him. I shoved my way through the throng, ignoring shouted protests and spilled beer. Ventura had to be here. He had to.

Then I spotted him. He stood in a back corner near the pool table, holding a cue in one hand and a beer in the other as he leered at a blonde in a halter top. It was the leer that got me. Had he looked at Trudy that way? Here he was, drinking and playing around, and Trudy had disappeared. I clenched my fists. He was going to tell me where she was or eat that pool cue.

Ventura went on laughing and chatting with the blonde, never even glancing at me. When I was about four feet away he spun, swinging the cue at me like a bat. I jumped back just in time, then rushed him and landed a solid right hook to his jaw. He staggered. His eyes went white, and he collapsed into a heap of laundry on the floor.

I bent over him, pulled him up by the shoulders and shook. "Where is she, you bastard?" I yelled. But it was no use. He was out cold. Whatever he knew had just gone with him to la-la land.

As I watched his face for a twitch, an eyelid's flutter—any sign he was coming to—I could hear a twangy voice singing about being lonesome. Otherwise, the bar was silent. Then came the crash of a bottle breaking. I straightened slowly and found myself facing a rampart of very angry bikers.

This was it. There was no way I could take them all on. If I was incredibly lucky, I'd wake up in the hospital in a couple of weeks and start learning how to gum my food.

Maybe, just maybe, I could convince them that my beef was with Ventura alone. Which would probably be easier to do if my face didn't look like fighting was my favorite pastime.

"Listen, guys, this is between him and me." Nobody blinked. I remembered how the bartender in the poker den mistook me for an undercover cop. Maybe I could pull that off here. "This man is the subject of an ongoing criminal investigation. I'd advise you not to interfere."

"Don't you listen to him!" the blonde behind me yelled. "He ain't a cop. He hurt Ray. Ray didn't do nothing to him. This guy just flew at him like some kinda lunatic."

Another bottle broke. A long-haired guy in a Metallica t-shirt stepped forward. "You come in here spoiling for a fight. Don't look like you got much of one. We're happy to oblige."

I stepped back and picked up the pool cue Ventura had dropped. Might as well go out swinging.

There was a long moment of tense silence, both sides coiled and waiting to see who'd make the first move. Then some kind of disturbance started up at the back of the crowd. I couldn't see what was happening.

"Out of my way, damn it! Let me through!"

Some woman was trying to push her way to the front. Then

the same voice said, "Don't mess with me, asshole. This is the police."

It couldn't be.

But it was. A moment later, Trudy's face appeared around Mr. Metallica's shoulder. She shoved him aside and stepped into the no-man's land between me and the bikers. She wore her deputy's uniform and brandished her gun. Her chest heaved with the effort of getting through that crowd. Sweat plastered her hair to her forehead. I'd never seen a woman so beautiful.

She turned to face the bikers. "Okay, boys, game over. I'm taking this man into custody. Anybody who'd like a ride to the Sheriff's office is welcome to get in my way."

She grabbed me by the arm and said, "Let's go."

The bikers grumbled as they shuffled away. I got knocked by a couple of shoves on our way to the door, but no one made any real trouble.

Out in the parking lot, I leaned against my car, shaking the way you do when a big jolt of adrenalin comes to nothing. The temperature was dropping, and the cool evening air felt good against my face. I smelled wood smoke and realized November was back. Trudy holstered her gun. She looked a little shaky, too, the way she took a deep breath and squared her shoulders, like she was trying to get herself under control.

After a moment, she looked at me and grinned. "Aren't you going to thank me for saving your ass?"

"We've got to go back inside."

Her grin turned into a disbelieving stare. "You got some kind of death wish? They're not going to let you walk out of there twice."

"That's Ventura on the floor in there."

"So?"

"Aren't you going to arrest him?"

"What for? Falling over when you punched him? I told you,

I'm trying to get something solid on him. Last night around midnight he picked up a car from this salvage yard in the Bronx, then drove straight up here. I'm betting that car's loaded with drugs, and I want to see what he's going to do next. So thanks for screwing up my surveillance." She glared at me. "Your ass is the one I should be hauling off to jail. What the hell did you think you were doing?"

"I thought . . ." All my previous fears flashed before my eyes like the life of a drowning man. "I thought he'd done something to you. Mike in Records guessed you were back in town, so I drove over to your place to check. Your truck was there, but you weren't, and—"

"I rode my bike to work. It's supposed to turn cold tonight, so I figured this would be my last chance until May." She rubbed her arms. "They say snow tomorrow, maybe."

"You pedaled a bicycle from your place all the way out to the Sheriff's office?"

"My mo-tor-cy-cle." She enunciated each syllable like she was trying to teach the word to someone who didn't speak English.

"Oh." For a minute I couldn't think of anything else to say. Then I remembered. "But someone trashed your place."

"What?"

"The front door was open. I went inside to make sure you were okay. The place looks like it got blown apart by a hurricane. That had to be Ventura. Who else would search your trailer?"

She was looking at me with an odd expression. "You went in my house?"

"To make sure you were okay," I repeated. "When I saw the condition it was in, I thought you'd been kidnapped." Or worse. But I didn't say that part.

"Didn't Mike tell you I was back? I stopped off at my place

during my dinner break and got his phone message. I called to let him know I was home. It was like five minutes after he left the message—I figured you were still there." I'd been trapped in that damn conference room with Plodnick by then.

"You called Mike in Records, huh? So why didn't you call me? He said in his message to call me."

"I was going to." *When,* I wondered, but she was still talking. "Jesus, I can't believe you just strolled into my house! I'd never let you—anyone—see it like that." She slapped the roof of my car. "Okay, you got me. I made that mess. I drove half the night and then overslept. I had to get to work and was running really late, and I dug some stuff out of my suitcase."

"No, you don't understand. Your whole place was a disaster area. The kitchen cupboards were emptied, drawers pulled out, magazines and CDs thrown all over the floor. Trudy, you've got to see it. You can't tell me that's unpacking."

She was silent for a long time, chewing on her lip. Then she slapped my car again. When she finally spoke, there was something low and dangerous in her voice. "I was looking for my cell phone."

"You were . . ." I watched her eyes narrow and her chin jut out, like she was daring me to make some smart remark. I couldn't. I was laughing too hard.

"Anyway," Trudy said, "any rookie would have known that if the bad guys really wanted to work my place over, they'd have done a better job. Did you notice the rugs pulled up? The sofa cushions sliced open?"

Wiping my eyes, I admitted that I hadn't. "So did you?"

"Did I what?"

"Find your cell phone."

She didn't have to say anything. The blush that spread from the nape of her neck all the way up to the roots of her hair answered for her.

"Maybe we should go back and slice up a few sofa cushions," I said. "Just to be thorough."

"Ha ha." She glanced at the door of the Speakeasy. "What we should do is get out of here before your dance partners in there find out I'm not arresting you."

"Okay. Listen, we've got a lot to discuss. When do you finish your shift? Can we meet up somewhere?"

"I'm off at eight. Come by my place about eight-thirty." She shot me a look. "Since you've already seen it, you can help me clean."

We got into our cars. I pulled out onto the road first, heading back toward Rhodes. Trudy drove behind me for a while, then gave a short siren blast when she turned off, just before the city limits. I beeped back. Never before had I felt so damn happy to have a cop on my tail.

At eight-thirty, I sat on the plaid couch beneath the antlered head. A sock still dangled from its nose. Poor Buck. Seems like there'd be enough indignity in having your head separated from your body and mounted on a wall without someone throwing laundry at you. I reached up and removed the sock, then dropped it on a random pile of clothes.

Trudy was banging around in the kitchen. "You need a glass for that beer?"

"No, I'm fine." I'd brought a six-pack of Grail Ale so I'd have something to drink. She appeared in the doorway, holding some kind of lite beer and a mug.

"Oh, God," she said. "Look at this place." She cleared a space on the coffee table by sweeping the piled-up magazines onto the floor, then set down her mug. She poured her beer—how can something that sickly shade of yellow be called beer?—and sighed. "It's gonna take forever to clean up."

"Let me help," I said. "What can I do?"

"Would you mind folding that pile of clothes?"

I looked at the chaos of clothes around me. "Um, which one?"

"Right there beside you on the couch. The stuff on the floor needs washing." She scooped up an armload of clothes and disappeared into the bathroom. A few minutes later, I heard a washing machine filling.

I grabbed a sweatshirt and folded it. Trudy's scent—soapy and kind of sweet—wafted from the fabric. I pressed it to my face and took one long, deep breath, then set the shirt down on the coffee table and started folding a pair of jeans.

A piece of paper, half caught in the jeans, fluttered to the floor. I picked it up. It was a photocopy of both sides of a check. The front, made out to cash, was for $150,000. The back was blank except for the standard printing you find on the back of a check.

"Hey," I said. "Is this the missing cashier's check?"

Trudy appeared in the doorway. "Yeah, I was going to show you that. I held the real one in my hands—inside a plastic sleeve of course, but it was still the check. The same damn one every cop in Rhodes was after. How cool is that? My friend the desk sergeant let me make a copy of it."

"Any prints?"

"Tons. But most belonged to that airhead bank teller, obscuring the others. They were still working on the prints when I left."

I looked at the signature line. *F. Davies.* The handwriting was strong and self-assured, bold letters slanting strongly to the right. When he signed this check, Fred Davies never imagined that it would become evidence in his murder investigation. Weird.

I placed the paper on the coffee table and went back to folding.

"So you think Ventura transported a load of drugs last night?"

"I'm sure of it. He picked up this car, like I told you, then drove north, all slow and careful. The whole trip I'm thinking, 'If only I had some reason to pull him over.' I bet he's got a fortune in heroin or cocaine crammed inside the door panels of that car. But I don't have any grounds—yet—for a search. Not that would stand up in court. I'm gonna stake out his girlfriend's place in Trumansburg to see what he does next."

She picked up the pile of clothes I'd folded and took them into the bedroom. When she came back, she said, "Chief Ianelli believes the drugs are coming in through New York. Last night, I think Ventura was making a mule run."

"How long did it take you to find him in New York?"

"Not long. The hardest part was getting ahold of Mike. I called him at home to tell him what I needed. He went in to Records—on the weekend—to look it up for me. Nice, huh?"

Yeah, old Mike was a real sweetheart. "Big deal. I took two days off from work to go to New York with you."

She gave me a strange look, like *what has that got to do with anything.* Nothing, probably. I picked up my beer and studied the label. "Well, I did."

"Anyway," she said, "Mike pulled Ventura's taxi license application and got his previous address off it. Place on Staten Island. Then he did a reverse lookup to get the current name and phone number for that address. The name wasn't Ventura, but I tried the number, anyway."

"So what happened?"

"A woman answered the phone. Turns out she's his aunt, but I didn't know that then. Kids screamed in the background. I said I was looking for Ray Ventura—remember, at this point I didn't even think he was staying there—and she said, 'I just told you, hon, he's not in. He didn't come back in the last two minutes, honest. Four times you've called, and I'm trying to make dinner here. He'll call you, I promise.' I thought she'd hung up, but then she said, 'Ray says he's goin' back upstate in a day or two. So don't worry, hon. You can see him then.' " This was interesting. "So somebody—a woman from around here—was eager to talk to Ventura."

"It could be that girlfriend in Trumansburg. But I'm thinking Nora Glaser."

"Which brings us to my news," I said. "Thanks to Nora's husband Perry, Plodnick went running out to the county jail this afternoon. Glaser wanted to make a confession." I explained the hallway conversation I'd overheard at the station.

"Jesus! Why didn't you tell me that before? I've gotta call Mike." She looked around, then put out her hand. "Give me your cell phone."

I was not giving Trudy my phone so she could ring up that muscle-bound librarian. "You've got a phone in your bedroom. Use that one."

She scowled at me, then disappeared into the other room, closing the door behind her. I didn't know why the hell she had to close the door just to get information from Mike. If she—

The washing machine buzzed. Since I was making myself useful, I went into the bathroom and moved the clothes into the dryer.

When I came back, she'd returned to the living room. "So what's up with Glaser?" I asked.

She shrugged. "They're being totally closed-mouthed. I couldn't find out what Glaser had confessed to, let alone whether they're buying it. Mike said it's classified, but it's obvious he doesn't know. Damn it!" She smacked her fist against her palm. "How can we find out?"

She didn't wait for an answer. "Do you think Glaser confessed to Davies's murder? Glaser?" She glanced at me. "Jesus, you're lucky he didn't have a gun when he stopped by your apartment looking for Nora. But *Glaser*—it doesn't fit. Not with everything else we've found out. Unless . . ." she rubbed her chin, thinking. "Unless he's connected with drugs out of the Speakeasy in some way."

"Doubt it. You should've seen him when I asked if Nora might sell drugs. He got shocked, then angry. Almost went for me." And that was just one *almost* out of several. I paused, becoming aware of a noise that had been going on in the background. Some kind of thumping. "Do you hear that?"

"Hear what?" Trudy was pacing. Kind of a difficult maneuver since it required frequent high-stepping over various items on the floor. I started putting books back on the shelves, scooping them up as she went past, to clear her a path.

"If Glaser's the killer, was it jealousy? Or—" She stopped abruptly. "I just thought of something. I've gotta call Mike again. Can I—oh, hell, never mind." She spun around, went into her bedroom, and closed the door. Again.

I kept hearing that thumping noise. Maybe I was still spooked from finding Trudy's trailer open and trashed earlier in the evening, but it bugged me. Was someone trying to get in? If so, they were doing a damned noisy job of it. I followed the sound. At first, I thought it was coming from outside, somewhere in back. Raccoons? I went out with a flashlight but found nothing. I could still hear the noise, but it was fainter out there. Definitely inside the trailer.

I went back in and listened. It seemed to be coming from the bathroom. To be more precise, from the dryer. I opened the machine's door and rummaged around.

I was back on the sofa by the time Trudy had finished her phone call. When she came out of the bedroom, I held out my hand before she had a chance to speak.

"Here."

"My phone! Where'd you find it?" She reached out to take it, then frowned. "Why's it hot?"

"It was in thumping around in the dryer."

"You put my phone in the dryer? You ruined it!"

"Hey, only after you put it through the washing machine."

"Oh." I could see her disappointment that she couldn't pin this one on me. Then her face brightened. She dropped the phone on the coffee table, where it was promptly buried under an avalanche of laundry. "Okay, listen. I found out two things. Nora Glaser is now officially a missing person—she didn't show up at work today—and the Feds are due back in town tomorrow."

"And as far as we know, the FBI isn't involved in the Davies murder investigation."

"Right. As far as we know. So either now they are, or else Glaser's confession is about something else."

"You know, that could be true," I said. "I know his type. As soon as he sobers up, he feels guilty as hell, like the weight of the world's on his shoulders. So he could be confessing to anything from killing Davies to being a bad husband to running over Plodnick's puppy."

"Plodnick hasn't got a puppy."

"You know what I mean. It's probably nothing. If it's anything important, it'll be in the paper in a couple of days."

"You're right. But damn it, I hate not knowing." She started pacing again, then stopped abruptly. "Jesus. Do you think he finally snapped and killed his wife? Nobody's seen her. How do we know she isn't dead?"

Nora might be dead, but it wouldn't have been Perry who killed her. Perry was a helpless, slobbering mess without his wife. And it really looked like she'd given him the slip, vanishing from Boston with all their funds in tow. Perry wasn't smart enough to fake that.

"Would Mike tell you she was missing if the cops knew Glaser had killed her?"

She considered. "He might. But he's a terrible liar. No, if they knew Nora was dead and he tried to convince me she was just missing, I'd know. I can see right through him." She chewed her lip. "But we're still stuck on the same question. Mike has no clue. Plodnick won't give me the time of day. How do we find out what Glaser confessed to? Maybe I can get Mike to distract Plodnick while I—"

"Why don't we just ask him?"

"I *told* you. Plodnick would never let me in on his investigation."

"Not him. Glaser. Why don't we drive out to the jail and ask him? They won't let me see him, since I'm not family or his lawyer or anything, but you can say you need to question him in relation to an ongoing investigation. Or whatever copspeak you'd use to say it."

She grinned. "You're brilliant, you know that? Sometimes I could just kiss you."

I looked up quickly, caught her eye. For a long moment, we just looked at each other. Neither spoke. Trudy reddened, then looked away.

My own face felt hot. "Uh, thanks." I wiped my palms on my jeans. "But right now I'd settle for another beer."

Chapter 27

When the phone shattered my sleep, my first thought was that I'd overslept and Trudy was calling to report on her conversation with Glaser. But the room was dark, and the glowing red numbers on my bedside clock showed 4:47. She couldn't have seen Glaser yet. The ringing continued. Snake—maybe it was Snake. I groped around for my phone and snapped it open.

"Yeah?"

"Where did you go after you left here last night?" It was Trudy. She sounded strange, like a voice from an old movie with a scratchy soundtrack.

"Where did I go? Home."

"That's it?"

"Yes. Straight home from your place; Then I went to bed." My pulse was calming down a little, and I brayed out a half-laugh. "Worrying about you wore me out. Why?"

"Ventura is dead."

"What?" I struggled to sit up. The last time I'd seen Ventura, he'd been passed out on the floor of the Speakeasy. But alive. I was sure he'd been alive.

"He's dead, Bo. He was killed in a hit and run at approximately 2:30 A.M."

"Jesus." So it hadn't been my sucker punch that did him in. Thank God. But why was Trudy asking where I'd gone? "Wait a minute. You don't think *I* killed him."

She didn't answer right away. "It doesn't matter what I think.

Plodnick thinks you did, I can promise you that."

"But why—?"

"For starters, you picked a fight with the guy in front of a couple dozen witnesses."

"I thought he'd hurt you." And Ventura had swung first. Some of those witnesses must have seen that. "Fights happen every night at the Speakeasy. Just because I hit him doesn't mean I killed him."

"There's more. A witness placed you at the scene of the crime."

"How in hell is that possible? I was asleep in my bed."

"That floozy from the bar was there. Ventura's girlfriend. She wrote down the license plate of the car that flattened him. It's your plate, Bo. There's a warrant out for your arrest."

I got out of bed and went to the window, clutching the sheet around my waist. A lime-green VW bug glowed under a streetlight—exactly where I'd left the Corolla. "Somebody stole my car! It's gone. That proves it, right? I couldn't run him over if my car was stolen."

"Did you report it?"

"How could I? I just found out it's gone."

In the silence that followed, I could picture her shaking her head, her lower lip caught between her teeth.

"I don't know all the details," she said. I wondered: doesn't know or won't tell me? "What I do know," she continued, "is that Plodnick is on his way over there, carrying a piece of paper with your name on it."

"He's coming here? Now? But—"

"We need to talk, but there's no time. You've gotta get out of there. Meet me at the bandstand in Lakeshore Park. Can you be there at seven?"

"Seven." In just over two hours—and four or five lifetimes away. "I'll be there."

"Now get the hell out of that apartment," Trudy said. "Plodnick will try to bust in and nab you while you're asleep."

I had zero time, but I couldn't hang up. Something—something other than the obvious—was wrong.

"Trudy?"

"What?"

"I didn't do it."

"You don't have to tell me that."

There. It was the way she said it, the way her voice split open on the last word. "Yes," I said, "I think I do."

"Just go," she said and hung up.

I threw on some clothes, grabbed my wallet and keys from the dresser, and was out the door in less than three minutes. I unlocked the backyard shed and wheeled out my bicycle. It had turned cold; with my scarf around my face and my helmet on, I'd look like one of the college kids or Rhodes eco-nuts who rode their bikes year round, through rain or wind or cold-ass days like this one.

Halfway down the block, I skidded to a halt. There was the Corolla, parked four spaces down from where I'd left it the night before. A streetlight lit up the car I owned, but it wasn't the car I'd parked earlier. Jesus. What a mess. The front bumper was torn, and a dent creased the hood. Brownish spots spattered the paint and windshield.

I didn't have time to inspect the damage further. In the narrow gap between my neighbors' houses, I saw three cars turn onto Melrose Street a couple of blocks over, headed my way. A black sedan and two police cruisers. As they neared the intersection, each car's headlights flicked off. Before the first one turned the corner, I zipped off in the other direction, then cut down a driveway and through someone's back yard, trying like hell to disappear into the darkness.

★ ★ ★ ★ ★

The predawn chill chased out all traces of sleep. I rode without thinking where I was going. All I wanted was to put some miles between me and those darkened cars gliding silently down my street. I imagined Plodnick and his uniformed backups tiptoeing up the stairs, then smashing down my door. Five minutes earlier and they would have got me. Hell, my sheets were probably still warm.

Questions spun through my brain as fast as my feet pumped the pedals. What was going on? Someone had stolen my car, used it to kill Ventura, and then returned it. An obvious frame-up. Why? Was I getting too close? To what? I didn't feel close to one goddamn thing. I still didn't know who'd killed Davies—and now probably Ventura too. But maybe it had nothing to do with getting close. Maybe I was just a convenient scapegoat for whoever wanted Ventura out of the way, for whatever reason. I couldn't prove I'd been home sleeping all night. And there was my car, looking like a loser in a demolition derby.

I was working up a sweat now, going steeply uphill, leg muscles burning. The air cooled my face, though my fingers felt like frozen claws gripping the handlebars. Where was I? The sky ahead of me was still dark. I glanced over my shoulder and saw the sky beginning to lighten to gray along the hilltops. So I must be climbing West Hill toward Enfield. A few more miles up the road was a twenty-four-hour gas station with a convenience store, across from Carl and Ronnie's trailer park. I could warm up there, get some breakfast. I put my head down and concentrated on the road.

At the gas station, I wheeled my bike between a dumpster and the back wall. There was nothing to lock it to, but no one was going to steal it way out here at quarter to six in the morning. One car, a rusted-out station wagon, sat in a corner of the lot;

the lights of two or three early risers shone in the trailer park across the road. I went inside to use the men's room and think about my next move.

The clerk behind the counter looked up from his paper and nodded as I walked by. I froze for a second, seeing that paper, then realized the hit-and-run had happened too late to put my face on the morning edition's front page. Country music twanged over the sound system. I cleared my throat, said, "Morning," and went to the short hallway at the back of the store that led to the restrooms and payphone. I knocked on the men's room door. No response. I pushed it open and went inside, then locked the door behind me.

For a full minute, that men's room was the only place in the world I wanted to be. Gray footprints dulled the white tile floor, there was grime in the corners, and the sink was cracked. The place was stuffy with that sweet-ammonia smell of chemical air freshener. But I didn't feel even a little claustrophobic. The room was warm, and it was safe. No one knew I was here.

I rinsed my hands in tepid water and held them under the hot air blower, feeling warmth creep back into my fingers. I figured I just had time to grab something to eat before heading back into town for my meeting with Trudy. I wished we'd picked a rendezvous site out in the country. It felt crazy to be cruising the streets of a town where every goddamn cop on the force would be looking for me. But there'd been no time to argue or to figure out a plan B.

As I was turning the knob, I heard a voice on the other side of the door. Whatever instinct activates when you're forced to flee from your bed before dawn made me cautious. I inched the door open and peered through the crack. I could see a woman with short blonde hair and a black jacket and jeans, her back to me, speaking into the payphone. She made an emphatic gesture that I knew as well as I knew that voice. Trudy! Her cell phone freshly washed and dried, she'd stopped to make a call. As Mike had said, the woman knew every payphone in Thomson County—and thank God for it. Now I wouldn't have to chance playing cat and mouse with the Rhodes cops. Seeing her, for the first time that day I felt hopeful. Together, she and I would crack this thing.

A second before I threw open the door, something stopped me: Trudy's voice saying the last name I wanted to hear. "Shut up a minute, Plodnick," she said. "We're doing it my way."

Plodnick? What the hell was she doing talking to him?

"I'm telling you, I don't know where he is. If I did, we'd have him in custody by now."

I was hit by a chill that had nothing to do with the temperature outside. She couldn't be talking about me. Not Trudy. Not to Plodnick, for Christ's sake.

"Haven't I said all along he was guilty? Right from day one? Exactly. You keep that in mind next time you're handing out commendations."

She paused, listening. I could hear a voice buzz over the line, but not what it was saying. But Trudy's words came through loud and all too clear. Each one hit me like a punch in the kidneys.

"Yeah, well, that was to gain his confidence. It worked, didn't it? Don't worry. I'll bring him in."

I pulled the door shut and carefully relocked it, making the telltale *click* as soft as possible. My safe haven of a minute ago now looked like a cell. My head pounded. I'd heard her words, but I couldn't process them. Not that I needed to—the feeling in my gut told me everything I had to know. Not three feet on the other side of that door, Trudy was setting me up.

I rubbed my temples. It didn't make sense. Why would she wake me up with a warning if she was working with Plodnick? Even before the question had fully formed itself in my mind, I knew the answer. She wanted the arrest for herself. I remembered the fanatical light in her eyes that first night on the Crossing, after she'd followed me into the bookstore: *I'm going to follow you, and I'm going to watch you, and when you trip up, I'm going to be the one who slaps the cuffs on you.* I thought she'd changed her mind about me, that she believed me, but all along she'd been playing me for a sucker, waiting for me to make that mistake.

The only mistake I'd made was trusting a deer-killing, Mozart-loving, lite beer-drinking, vigilante deputy. God damn those big brown eyes.

I pressed my ear against the door. I could hear faint strains of country music; other than that it was quiet. I cracked open the door—no one stood at the phone. Very slowly, I pushed the door open, taking in more and more of the view. Nothing. I took two steps down the hall and craned to see around the corner. High up where the wall met the ceiling, one of those convex security mirrors showed me that the store was empty, just me and the clerk, still engrossed in his paper. I scanned the parking lot, checked the gas pumps. There was the same rusty station wagon I'd seen earlier, but that was all. At that point, I remembered to breathe.

The convenience store had a few tables and a microwave customers could use to warm packaged foods. I heated a frozen egg-and-English-muffin sandwich and bought some coffee, thinking I'd choke it down for the warmth and some caffeine to clear my spinning head. I took a seat; the table wobbled, but I had a clear view of the parking lot. Unless Trudy had to make another phone call or felt a sudden craving for preservative-packed food wrapped in cellophane, the place she'd just left seemed the safest place I could be. For now. I had to figure out where to go next. I sure as hell wasn't going to be sauntering up to the bandstand at Lakeshore Park in an hour. The spider could wait in her goddamn trap, wondering where the fly had buzzed off to.

Sitting in that convenience store, a cup of coffee cooling between my hands, I stared out the window as the scenery slowly lightened. A few cars went by, early commuters on their way to work. People driving half-asleep into an unremarkable day. Man, did I envy them.

I didn't have much time. Wherever I went, the cops would find me soon. Closing my eyes, I felt a strong urge to get back on my bike and keep riding north and north and north until I got to Canada. That must have been how my father felt thirty-five years ago, after he'd burned his draft card. Canada seemed like sanctuary. A place where you could start over and leave behind whatever mess you were caught up in.

The trouble was, a mess this big would never stay behind me. I'd graduated from "person of interest" to a name on a bona fide arrest warrant. This wasn't going away. The cops wouldn't rest until they could lock me up—*then* they'd forget about me.

The news came on the radio. Ventura was the top story:

> *Police are seeking the driver of a 1995 Toyota Corolla that hit and killed 34-year-old Raymond Ventura. The incident occurred at two-thirty this morning in the parking lot of the Oneida Falls overlook. Despite attempts to revive him, Ventura was pronounced dead at the scene. According to eyewitness Traci Mottola, the driver of the Toyota deliberately hit Ventura, who was on foot, running him over several times before departing the scene. Police are treating the incident as a homicide and appealing to the public for information. Anyone who witnessed the incident or who has information regarding the whereabouts of Mr. Bo Forrester, thirty-eight, of Second Street in Rhodes, should contact the Rhodes Police Department.*

Shit. The appeal to the public was bad. Not only did I have

to worry about avoiding the police, I had to stay out of sight of anyone who knew me. Instead of waving and asking, "Hey, Bo, how's it going," they'd be flipping open their cell phones and pressing 911 as fast as their fingers could hit the buttons.

I kept sitting because I couldn't think of anywhere else to go. A strange inertia had taken hold—if I stayed there, at that rickety table, clutching this cup of coffee, I was safe. But as soon as I got up and started moving, the trouble would begin. So I sat. People drove up to the gas pumps, filled their tanks, and left. Occasionally someone came in for coffee or a newspaper. Everyone was in a hurry to start their day. And still I sat there. The radio played songs about trucks, love, and being a Mississippi girl, interrupted by car-dealer ads and—every twenty minutes—another news bulletin.

After listening to the news story a couple of times, I could picture the scene: the Oneida Falls parking lot, as cold and still as it had been on the night I'd gone there to get shot at. I could see Ventura pull in and park, leaving the blonde in the car as he got out to take care of whatever business he had there. Then the other car—my car—accelerating fast straight at Ventura, lifting him off his feet and tossing him onto the hood, then, when he rolled off and hit the asphalt, backing up to aim for him again. Ventura moaning, the crunch of bones breaking under the wheels . . . The images were so vivid I almost felt like I'd been there. I could even see Ventura's face, its surprise and fear and anger caught in the headlights as the car came at him. Jesus, I'd better cut that out before I convinced myself I'd done it.

When the seven o'clock bulletin came on, I was still sitting in the same spot. Trudy would be at the park by now, pacing back and forth across the bandstand. I wondered how long she'd wait before she got it through her head I wasn't coming. And what she'd do then. Plodnick would be furious—I wished I could overhear *that* phone call, when she had to admit I hadn't walked up to her and said, "Hi, Trudy, please arrest me." I almost smiled, picturing the way her chin would jut out defiantly as she tried to explain.

A movement outside caught my eye. Someone was stepping around the potholes in the parking lot, passing the gas pumps, coming toward the store. I recognized that trucker's cap—oh God, not Carl. Not now. I jumped up and bolted down the short hallway toward the men's room just as he pulled open the front door. I stood there, half-in and half-out of the men's room, ready to slam the door and lock it if he came my way.

"Hiya, Tim," said Carl's voice. "Got any of them cherry Danish left?"

"I think there's a couple."

"Great. I'll take 'em both. Ooh, there's three. Even better."

I edged down the hallway, until I could see the two men in the convex mirror. Carl paid for his Danish, then ripped open the cellophane, and stuffed half of one into his mouth.

"You hear about that hit-and-run over at Oneida Falls?" he asked, brushing crumbs off his jacket.

"Yeah, it's been on the radio all morning."

"I know the guy they're looking for. The one the cops think did it."

"You don't say."

"Yeah. Used to pick me and Ronnie up in the taxi. Sure had me fooled," he took another bite of Danish. "I thought he was an okay guy. Then there's a dead body in his trunk, and *then* I find out he's a sex maniac, all mixed up with drugs."

Tim shook his head. "And a killer, sounds like from the radio."

"Could be. Or maybe just a bad driver. I never did feel safe in his cab."

"What's he look like? Case I see him, I wanna let the cops know."

"He's pretty tall, 'bout like so. Medium build, maybe a little on the skinny side. Got brown hair, wears it in a ponytail."

"One of them hippies, huh?"

"Yeah, I guess so. The hair, the drugs, the free love. Ya know, he lives right upstairs from my sweetie Irene. I'll breathe easier when the cops lock him up, I can tell you that." He crumpled an empty cellophane wrapper and dropped it in the trash. "Well, I better get goin'. Taxi'll be here any minute. Say, Tim, you don't think he'll be driving it, do you?"

"Tell you what, Carl. If the taxi gets here and this hit-and-run guy is driving, you wave to me. I'll be watching. I see you wave, I'll call the cops."

I retreated down the hallway as Carl turned from the counter. The bell on the front door jingled. Carl was gone, but now I was stuck in this back hallway. There was no exit here; I'd have to go through the store to get out. But Carl had described me to the clerk, who was now on super-alert lookout for a drug-crazed, pony-tailed maniac looking for women to rape and men to run down. I wouldn't get two steps before he was on the phone to the cops.

Still, I had no choice but to try. I wound my scarf around my neck, bringing it up high in the back to cover the ponytail. Then I watched the clerk, Tim, in the mirror. His gaze was glued to the driveway of the trailer park across the road, with the intensity of a football fan watching the Superbowl. Time to make my move.

Tim didn't glance at me as I walked through the store. As I reached the front door, a Sunbeam taxi arrived for Carl and Ronnie. Carl looked at the driver, saw it wasn't me, gave Tim a thumbs-up, then waved goodbye. Oh, shit. He *waved* goodbye. In less than a second Tim had the phone in his hand. Carl, realizing what he'd done, smacked himself on the forehead, then shook his head and waved both arms around. Tim nodded, held up the phone, and pointed to it. Carl added hopping to his head-shaking, arm-waving routine.

I ran for my bike.

The cops would arrive in minutes, and I'd better be as far away as I could get. I took off down Holleyville Road, toward Oneida Falls. It's a straight road that runs along a ridge; pedaling hard, I moved fast. Even so, I'd gone no more than a mile when a deputy's car shot past me, lights and sirens going like mad, speeding toward the convenience store.

I wondered who was driving the cab—not Dinesh, I hoped. I knew how much fun it was to be questioned by Thomson County deputies.

Another cruiser raced past. At least I was going in the opposite direction. My inertia had been broken; I was on the move. And I knew now where I was headed—to Oneida Falls, for a look at the scene of my supposed crime.

Chapter 28

If I expected to stumble across some clue that would clear my name and solve the case, I was kidding myself big time. The parking lot was deserted—the cops had finished with the scene and gone. They hadn't left anything for me to find. No engraved lighter or embroidered handkerchief with the crucial initials. No dropped glove or muddy footprint. Not even a gold tooth gleaming as a memorial to Ventura. The only thing there was a reddish brown stain on the asphalt, marking the spot where he'd died.

I stood on the overlook platform, watching water pour over the falls. The gray sky pressed down on the cliff and the skeletal trees that clung to it. Mist rose from the water and plastered the rocks, coating them with frost. It started to rain, and the icy drizzle stung my face. A burnt smell hung in the air. I tried to get a sense of the violence that had taken place here hours before, but there was nothing. Just water falling over rocks in the rain.

My phone rang, and I pulled it from my pocket. It was a local number, probably Trudy calling from a payphone, wanting to know why I hadn't shown up. I almost answered—I would've enjoyed the satisfaction of telling her I knew about her conversation with Plodnick, her failed Operation Betray Bo in the park—but then I remembered I'd read somewhere that the phone company can track your position when you use a cell phone. That's how they rescued a hiker lost in the woods up in Maine—

kept him talking on his cell until they pinpointed his exact location. Well, nobody was pinpointing me. The ringing stopped, and I turned off my phone.

As it shut down, I thought about Snake, how I'd been so desperate to keep the phone on in case he called. I knew now he wouldn't call. But I felt like I'd just severed my last tie with my parents.

In fact, standing there alone in the middle of nowhere, as the falls roared and freezing rain seeped inside my collar, I felt like I'd severed every tie with anyone I'd ever cared about. I was on my own.

On the far side of the parking lot, across from the falls overlook, was a picnic area. It was empty, but there was a shelter—a roof held up by four posts, no walls—over a cluster of picnic tables. Might as well get out of the rain. I wheeled my bike toward the shelter, feeling hard asphalt give way to spongy earth under my feet. I leaned my bike against a post and sat on a picnic table, my feet on the bench. Out of the rain, I didn't feel a bit drier. Or warmer.

Now what? I'd spent the morning running from the cops. I couldn't let them keep pushing me like that; sooner or later they'd get me. If they picked up my trail, I'd never outrun a police car. I could go deep into the woods and hide there—I'd learned cold-weather survival skills in the Army—but I hadn't had time to grab the most basic of supplies. I didn't even have a decent coat; on my way out the door, I'd put on the light jacket I'd worn for the warm spell.

The sound of the rain sharpened to a hiss, as sleet mixed with snow mixed fell on the wet grass. Great. I did not want to sleep outside in this shit, gradually turning into a snowdrift. Besides that, goddamn it, I didn't want to run and hide. I wanted to end this thing.

Ventura still seemed to be the key. So what did I know about the guy? One, he'd tried to cash the stolen cashier's check while wearing the missing ring. That definitely tied him to Davies. Two, he dealt drugs out of the Speakeasy. Hang on, did I really know that? It seemed a reasonable assumption, but what was I basing it on? I counted off the reasons. He hung out at the Speakeasy. Plodnick suspected him of dealing. Trudy had thought that the car Ventura drove up here from New York was packed full of hidden drugs. Knowing Trudy, that was probably just wishful thinking. She had too much imagination for a cop.

The thought of Trudy made my gut clench, like something was burning inside. I pushed her out of my mind.

But she came right back, sitting on the plaid chair in her living room, surrounded by piles of laundry and CDs, swigging her lite beer and telling me that Chief Ianelli suspected the drug pipeline ran up to Rhodes from New York City. Ventura had made multiple runs between Rhodes and New York—he'd requested those trips. Maybe that was how he'd brought the drugs into town, using Ryan's cabs to transport them. Easy enough to put a false back in the trunk or hide the junk in the spare tire well.

Ventura had done lots of those New York runs. Was there a pattern to his trips? I thought back over the weeks and months I'd driven for Sunbeam, but the days all ran together. I remembered someone—was it Dinesh? One of the other guys?—commenting that Ventura sure liked to drive to New York City. "Who wants to drive all that way and back just for one fare?" he'd said. "You get stiffed on the tip, you're out of luck." But I couldn't remember specific days or even how often he'd made the trip. I'd never paid much attention to Ventura.

Ryan's records would have the information. But the cops would be watching Sunbeam—trying to sneak into the office and go through Ryan's files would be like marching into the lobby of Rhodes PD.

I jumped off the table and paced the length of the shelter to warm myself as much as to think. But it didn't do any good. Over and over again, I kept coming to the same conclusion: To get the dates of Ventura's New York runs, I'd have to ask Ryan.

Could I trust him? He'd given the cops information behind my back. But he'd also told me when Plodnick had come around asking more questions. He didn't have to do that. Jesus, though, the guy had a family to think of, not to mention his business. He couldn't afford to mess with the cops. Undoubtedly Plodnick had told Ryan to let him know if I called him. So the question boiled down to this: Would Ryan help me, or would he turn me in?

The snow was starting to stick; flakes clung to the grass. It was coming down hard, falling fast and heavy like rain. I suppressed a shiver, then made up my mind. I'd risk it.

There was a payphone, I thought, near the park office. I steered my bike back onto the road and coasted down the hill, keeping my head down to minimize the icy wind. The sleet stabbed at my face like needles. As I turned into the office driveway, my back wheel spun out on the slick road, tilting me sideways and knocking me off the bike. I hit the ground hard, the bike on top of me. I was okay, just mad. I threw the bike off and got up. This was no weather to be riding around on a goddamn bicycle. I brushed the dirt and snow from my clothes, then walked the bike toward the log building that housed the park office. There was the payphone, on an outside wall around the corner from the office door. Good. No one inside the office could see it. A snow-dusted Park Police car sat in the driveway, but I didn't see anyone around.

I dialed the number for Sunbeam and listened to it ring, wondering if I was making a stupid mistake. Ryan picked up on the third ring.

"Sunbeam Taxi."

"Ryan, it's Bo."

"Yes, ma'am," Ryan said in his professional voice, just a shade too brightly. "We can send out a driver right away."

"The cops are there." I wondered who it was. Plodnick, probably, standing over Ryan's desk, stroking that skinny moustache. "So I guess you know I'm in trouble."

"You betcha."

"I didn't kill Ventura, I swear. Someone stole my car. I can explain it all later, when you don't have company."

"Well, I can't say I'm sure when that'll be. What's the address?"

"Okay, I know we can't keep this up long. Listen, I need your help. Can you put together a list of all the trips Ventura made to New York City, going back three or four months?"

"Yes, ma'am, I believe so."

"Great. What time will it be ready?"

"You need to schedule a return trip at eleven-thirty? Not a problem."

"Eleven-thirty. Okay." I checked my watch. It was nine-thirty now. "I was thinking you could leave it some place where I could pick it up later, like maybe—"

"Yes, ma'am, I *understand* that you need a car. That's our business here at Sunbeam." His voice grew muffled, as though he'd put his hand over the phone to talk to someone in the room. "These old ladies. Half the time they forget what they're talking about."

It took me a second to realize what he was offering. A car. My Corolla smashed, he must've figured I was without wheels. Jesus, a *car.* I wouldn't have to ride my bike in the snow. I could even sleep in a car if I had to.

"You're saying you've got a car I can use, right? That'd be unbelievable."

"So we'll send a driver out to pick you up at the county hospital at eleven-thirty." He paused. "Yes, ma'am, of course he'll be on time."

"Thanks, Ryan. I mean it. You're the best."

"Mm-hmm. You, too, ma'am. Thank you for calling Sunbeam."

The hospital was on Route 96, about five or six miles from where I was standing. I'd have to slog back up the hill, but from there it was an easy ride, and I had nearly two hours. As a rendezvous site, the hospital wasn't bad. It had a big parking lot, and it was far enough out of town that I probably wouldn't bump into anyone who knew me. Of course, if the cops thought I'd injured myself running over Ventura, they might be watching the hospital, but—

And then the temperature dropped ten degrees. Or so it felt. What if Ryan's offer of a car was a setup, a way to draw me out into the open so the cops could pounce? As soon as the thought appeared in my mind, I was half-sick with the certainty of it. Another betrayal.

Or maybe not. With Plodnick right there, why hadn't Ryan simply tried to find out where I was? He never even asked. Unless—oh, Jesus, what if they'd put a trace on his phone? If that was the case, they already knew where I was. And they'd be here faster than I could dream of getting away.

I listened for sirens. Instead, I heard the screech of rusty hinges as the door to the Park Office opened. A uniformed park ranger came around the corner. Shit, Plodnick had called the Park Office to have someone grab me. Did park rangers carry guns? I couldn't remember. I tensed, ready to take the guy on.

He stopped when he saw me. Then he smiled. "Lousy day for a bike ride."

I forced myself to smile back. "That's for sure."

"I hope you don't think you're going trail riding. All the trails are closed. We just got a report that some idiotic hiker climbed over a barrier, right past the Trail Closed sign. Now he's traipsing along the Rim Trail somewhere. I've got to find him before he falls off the cliff. Icy weather like this, he'll be lucky if he just gets a ticket, 'stead of a broken neck."

I nodded, and the ranger walked past me to his car. He brushed the snow from the windshield, then got in and drove away.

I leaned against the rough log wall, waiting for my heart to quit pounding so hard. The woods were quiet, the only sound the swoosh of wind blowing snowflakes through the pines. No sirens. The cops didn't know I was here. Maybe Ryan was being straight with me.

But I wasn't sure. The car drop-off could still be a trap. The wind hurled a fistful of snow into my face. I needed a car, plus that list of Ventura's trips to New York. Okay, I'd be at the hospital at eleven-thirty. In fact, I'd be there an hour early to check the place out. I wasn't going to break cover unless I was certain.

Manitoah Medical Center overlooks the lake it's named after. To get there, you turn off Route 96 and follow the long driveway down a gentle slope. The driveway curves past the Physicians' Professional Center, a flat-roofed, single-story complex of doctors' offices and private labs. At quarter past eleven, I lay on the roof of the Professional Center, watching the parking lot. I'd been there for an hour, gradually turning numb from the cold.

I had a clear view of the main hospital entrance and the entire parking lot. So far, I'd seen nothing unusual—cars came and went; an ambulance, lights flashing but no siren, rolled around to the Emergency door. There'd been a cop car parked in front when I first arrived, but the cop had emerged from the hospital and driven away.

At eleven-thirty exactly, a yellow Sunbeam cab cruised down the driveway. It stopped near the hospital's front door, parallel to the curb and next to a red-and-white No Parking sign. A few seconds behind it came a dark sedan, two figures in the front seat. I wasn't sure, but the sedan reminded me a hell of a lot of the car Plodnick had put on my tail.

The driver of the cab—Letzger, it looked like—got out and leaned against the fender to light a cigarette. The sedan backed into a parking space not far from the taxi. No one got out.

So it was a setup after all. I was supposed to see the Sunbeam taxi and come running over. That's when the detectives would jump out of their unmarked car and start waving their guns around. Jesus, I *knew* I couldn't count on that goddamn Ryan.

Something else was going on down there. A small, bent woman came out of the hospital, leaning on a cane. She gestured at Letzger, who stamped out his cigarette and went up the stairs. He took her arm, helping her down the steps and to the cab. She settled herself in the back seat, and the cab took off. Ten seconds later, the sedan pulled out of its parking space. Both cars turned left out of the driveway, back toward Rhodes.

What had I just witnessed? A passenger pickup identical to the one Ryan pretended to arrange while talking with me on the phone. As I stared at the spot where Letzger had parked his taxi, trying to figure it out, another car came down the driveway. This one was a shit-brown '78 or '79 Chevy Nova, lacy with rust. Judging from the cloud of black exhaust, it was burning more oil than gas. The car parked near the edge of the lot, and the driver got out. He stretched, looked around, took off his Yankees cap to scratch his black hair. Dinesh strolled across the lot and disappeared inside the hospital.

I watched. No other cars arrived. As far as I could see, no bored-looking passengers sat waiting in any parked cars. Ryan had used the cab as a decoy—and Plodnick fell for it, leaving the coast crystal clear.

I went over the roof's edge and dropped to the ground. Leaving my bike where I'd hidden it—I'd dig it out when this was over—I walked to the Nova, trying to appear nonchalant. The door was unlocked, the key in the ignition. There were two keys on the ring. I got in, turned on the engine and blasted the heater as high as it would go. The gas tank was full. I opened the glove compartment. Inside were a couple pieces of paper. I could see the columns of a computer printout on the top sheet: the list of Ventura's New York trips. I owe you one, Ryan, I thought. Big time.

Dinesh came out the front door and walked to the bus stop; he sat on the bench inside the three-sided glass shelter and turned up his collar. He didn't wave as I drove by, but he watched me go.

The Nova's wheels spun on some ice as I turned right onto 96. I got control of the car and headed away from Rhodes. In front of me, behind me, as far as I could see, I had the road to myself.

I drove aimlessly for a while, mostly back roads, keeping one eye on the rearview mirror. When I was sure no one was following me, I pulled off the road, into an unplowed driveway leading to an abandoned barn. The Nova slid to a stop in the snow. I was starving—my breakfast at the convenience store, not much to start with, had been hours ago. But food would have to wait. I wanted to look at Ryan's list.

I turned off the engine and opened the glove compartment, removed the two sheets of paper. There was something behind them; it looked like a radio. I pulled it out and turned it on to hear bursts of static and someone saying, ". . . a 12-82 out on Route 227. Car slid off the road." It was a police scanner, tuned to the Sheriff's department. Ryan had thought of everything.

With the scanner crackling in the background, I returned my attention to the papers. The top one was the list, and I scanned its columns. In four months, Ventura had driven nine round-trips for Sunbeam to New York. The trips were evenly spaced—every two weeks, give or take a couple of days. Ryan had listed the date, the pickup and destination addresses, and the name of the person requesting the trip. Usually, we didn't bother with fares' names, but if someone ordered a cab in advance, say the night before, the dispatcher took the name and a phone number.

Out of the eight trips, two passenger names dominated: *S. Hedlund* appeared three times, *F. Davies,* four. I didn't recognize the other name.

Here it was: a connection between Ventura and the DFA. When Ventura had done his New York drug runs, Sebastian Hedlund or Fred Davies had gone along for the ride. Or to put it more accurately, they'd ordered and paid for the trips that enabled Ventura to carry drugs back to Rhodes.

Ryan's list didn't take up a whole page, but there had been two sheets in the glove compartment. I set the list on the dashboard and looked at the second sheet of paper.

It was a letter, scrawled in Dinesh's handwriting. At the top of the page was an address, followed by this note:

> *I'm guessing you don't have a place to stay. Well, now you do. The second key on the ring is for the lake house owned by a friend of mine. He's studying in London this semester, and he said I could use the house while he was gone. We had some great parties there back in September*—I could see Dinesh grinning as he wrote that—*but it's a three-season cottage. And sorry, but winter ain't one of the three. There's no heat, and the water's turned off. But it's better than sleeping in a rusted-out '78 Nova! The electricity is on—there's a couple of lights on a*

timer. Don't mess with those. But at least you won't have to sit in the dark.

I put some beer and a few groceries in the fridge for you. You like hot dogs, right? (Kidding.) Good luck, man. Don't let those bastards get you down.

>D.

I memorized the address at the top of the page, then used the car's cigarette lighter to burn the note. If the cops caught up with me between here and the lake house, they weren't going to find any letter from Dinesh. And I'd swear I stole this car.

Chapter 29

I was eating the takeout vegetable biryani Dinesh had left for me in the refrigerator. He'd stashed a week's worth of food in there, everything from a twelve-pack of Saranac beer to three loaves of bread to a block of cheese big enough to use as a doorstop. Gallon jugs of water—five of them—lined up on the counter, with two more in the bathroom. The place was chilly, but I had a roof over my head and food in the fridge. Lap of luxury.

The house lay on the west shore of Manitoah Lake, in a section of cottages crammed together on small lots, most of the houses shut up for the winter. This place was basically two big rooms: kitchen-living room-dining room combo downstairs and a sleeping loft upstairs. A desk with an ancient computer faced one of the huge windows overlooking the lake. That's where I sat now, eating the biryani and going through the archives of the *Rhodes Chronicle.* Miraculously, the phone was connected, so I used the computer's modem to get online. It was slow, but it worked.

I'd discovered that three of the four recent overdoses happened within two days of a Ventura New York trip. The fourth OD, George Boutros, didn't fit. The day he died—the day after Ventura quit—Ventura hadn't done a New York run for more than two weeks. He hadn't done one, in fact, since Davies's murder.

I sat back and rubbed my eyes. It looked like Davies and

Hedlund, working with Ventura, had brought hard drugs into Rhodes and used the DFA to launder their profits. I thought Ventura had murdered Davies—over money, probably—then Hedlund killed Ventura in retribution.

But my lists of dates weren't enough to prove it. I needed more. Davies had worried about an audit right before his death. If I could get access to the DFA's books—and do what? I could balance my own checkbook, but I'd have no clue how to find evidence of money laundering in financial records. All those numbers would be gibberish to me.

I sat bolt upright. I knew someone who could decode that stuff. Someone who worked at the same bank where Davies had his accounts. I found Sharon Barton's card and called her work number from the house phone.

"Sharon Barton," she answered in a professional tone.

"Sharon, it's Bo Forrester."

"Oh." Her tone said it all. She'd obviously heard the news.

"Wait. Don't hang up," I said. "Please."

She stayed on the line.

"I didn't kill that guy. Someone stole my car and used it to—Sharon, you know me from way back. You've got to know I wouldn't do something like that."

"You were in the Army . . ."

"And I left it. Honorable discharge and everything. For God's sake, Sharon, the Army doesn't train you to run over people."

She considered my point. "You're really a vegetarian, right?"

"That's right. It's like your daughter, like Tiffany, said. I hate killing."

"Amber." Her voice sounded stiff.

"What?"

"Amber's the one on a vegetarian kick."

Damn. Whatever, I wanted to say. This isn't about your kids. But I took a deep breath and kept my voice smooth. "The police have got this thing all wrong."

Silence buzzed along the line. Don't hang up on me, I thought. Please don't hang up. Finally she spoke. "Bobby did say you're too much of a wimp to kill anyone."

Thank God for Bobby. I'd have to remember to buy the old tub of lard a beer next time he fell off the wagon.

"Why are you calling me?" Sharon asked. "I can't hide you from the police."

"I wouldn't ask you to. I just need some information about Fred Davies's bank accounts. I'm starting to understand why someone might've killed him, but I need to look at his financial records."

Another long silence. "I'm sorry. But that would be a breach of confidentiality. I mean, even if you weren't wanted for murder. It's against all the bank rules."

"This is important, Sharon. More important than the rules. We're talking about murder." And keeping me out of prison.

"I'd like to help you out. Really I would. But I can't. I've been here twenty years. I can't break the rules like that."

"But—"

"I have to go. My boss just stuck his head in the door." She whispered, "Good luck," and hung up.

I stared at the phone in my hand. It might as well have been a big Dead End sign.

An hour later, I was stuck. I'd gone through every reference to the DFA, Sebastian Hedlund, and Fred Davies in the *Chronicle*'s archives. I'd even pulled up Davies's obituary. His photo gazed confidently at me from the screen: Frederick Roland Davies, 1949–2005. The man didn't look like a drug kingpin, but how could you tell?

I got up and moved restlessly around the room. I opened the fridge door, then closed it. I wasn't hungry. I went to the window and peered outside. The scene looked like a snowglobe gone insane. It was great to have a safe haven, but I was feeling cooped up. What could I solve, sitting here on my ass? Nothing. I picked up the phone, put it down again. There had to be some way Sharon Barton could let me know whether I was on the right track without breaching confidentiality.

I dialed her at the bank again. This time I got her voicemail. "It's me again," I said. I didn't want to leave my name—Sharon didn't need any messages from a murder suspect on her work number. "Thanks for not hanging up on me earlier. About that information we discussed—if I told you the sort of thing I'm looking for, could you just let me know if I'm close or else way off base? Without giving away any details, I mean. Just a yes or no. Think about it, all right? You've got my number."

I broke the connection, then used the house phone to dial my cell. Leaving voicemail for Sharon made me think maybe I should check my own.

There were eight messages—all from Trudy. The first one, left an hour after our meeting time at Lakeshore Park, was short and simple: "Bo. Trudy. Call me." The next two sounded worried; after that, she started working her way through various shades of annoyed to mad as hell. Plodnick must really be putting the pressure on her. Good.

The last message, left at 1:04, was different. She said, "I'm at the county jail. I just talked to Perry Glaser. You want to know what he said, you call me."

Glaser. Damn. I'd forgotten all about him.

I checked my watch; it was ten past three. I started to dial Trudy's number, then cut the connection. There was probably a trace on her phone. Even if there wasn't, all it would take was caller ID and a quick reverse lookup to nail this address. And I couldn't risk using my cell phone. I'd have to go back out into the snow and find a payphone. At least I'd be moving again.

I drove toward Rhodes until, on the outskirts of town, I spotted a gas station with an outdoor phone. I wound my scarf around my face and got out to make the call.

She answered on the first ring.

"It's me," I said.

"Where the hell are you? I've been worried sick."

Yeah, I thought, worried about your career. "What did Glaser say?"

"Are you okay? Where are you? It's practically a blizzard out there. Do you have a place to stay?"

"I'm fine. I just want to know what Glaser told you."

She didn't respond at first; when she did, her voice took on a crafty tone. "Not over the phone. I'd better tell you in person."

"Damn it, Trudy." I almost hung up. But I needed to know what Glaser said. If he'd admitted to killing Davies, it blew my whole theory. "Okay, I'll meet you. But—"

"Great! How soon can you be here?"

"How the hell do you think I'm going to get all the way out to Jacksonville? The cops have my car. You expect me to ride my bicycle to your place in a snowstorm?" Yesterday, I'd have done it in a heartbeat. But that was yesterday. "I'll meet you, but I'm calling the shots."

"Meaning what, exactly?"

"Meaning I choose the time and the place. And you leave your gun at home."

"What the hell is with you? I'm on your side, remember?"

I didn't answer.

She sighed loudly. "So when and where?"

I had an inspired idea—a little poetic justice was in order. "You know that convenience store in Enfield, the one at the corner of 79 and Holleyville Road?" I knew damn well she did. It was where I'd seen her talking to Plodnick that morning.

"Yeah, I know it."

"Be there in ten minutes. There's a payphone in the back of the store. I'll call you on that phone to tell you where we'll meet."

"Come on, Bo. Don't play games. Just—"

"Ten minutes. If you aren't there when I call, forget it. I'll read about Glaser's confession in the *Chronicle.*"

"You listen to me—"

"Go ahead and keep talking. It takes about ten minutes to drive there from your place in dry weather. And, as you so considerately pointed out, it's practically a blizzard out here."

"You're more than pissing me off, Bo. You're—I'm—How am I supposed to—Christ!" She hung up.

It would take me almost ten minutes to get there myself. And I needed to get into position before she arrived. The Nova skidded out of the gas station and fishtailed on a patch of ice. Heading for Enfield, I thought of the fury in Trudy's voice. I'd never heard her so angry. You'd almost think she cared.

Chapter 30

By my watch, Trudy was one minute and thirty-four seconds late when her pickup careened into the convenience store's lot. She abandoned the truck where it stopped and ran into the building, leaving the engine running and the driver's side door wide open.

Lucky for her. I'd thought I was going to have to break a window to get in.

I emerged from my hiding place behind a dumpster and slipped into the truck. I debated whether to leave the door open, then pulled it half shut for more cover. Trudy wouldn't remember whether she'd left it open or closed.

I turned off the engine and pocketed the keys, wondering how much time I had. Several minutes, I thought. Trudy would run in and ask the clerk if the payphone had rung. Then she'd pace in front of the phone, scowling at it and willing it to ring. The only part I wasn't sure about was how long she'd wait for a call that wasn't coming.

I opened the glove compartment, where I knew she kept her gun when she drove—I'd seen her stash it there on our trip to New York. There it was now, sitting beside a shiny pair of handcuffs. So she'd really come out to meet me expecting to make an arrest. Well, why did that surprise me? I'd known since this morning she was out to get me. I grabbed the handcuffs and put them on the seat. Then I picked up Trudy's .38.

It had been a long time—years—since I'd held a gun in my hand.

Still, I knew what to do. I checked that the safety was on, then removed the magazine. That went into my pocket. I pulled back the slide to eject the cartridge from the chamber. The cartridge went into my pocket, too. For the moment, anyway, this gun wouldn't hurt anyone.

I crouched down in the floor space so Trudy wouldn't see me until she got in the truck.

I waited less than ten minutes. Trudy didn't even look my way as she climbed into the truck. She fastened her seat belt, then reached forward to start the engine. When the key wasn't in the ignition, she patted her pockets and looked around.

"Hello," I said, pushing myself up onto the seat.

She gave a short scream and put a hand on her chest. "Jesus, Bo, you scared me. That wasn't—"

She stopped when she saw I was holding her gun.

"Put both hands on the steering wheel and keep them there," I said. She glared at me, but she complied. "You know," I said. "I just remembered. That's almost the first thing you ever said to me. Funny, huh?"

"You're committing assault. Aggravated assault with a deadly weapon. And it's worse because I'm a police officer."

"I'm not threatening you, Trudy. Just showing you what I found in your glove compartment. You shouldn't leave something dangerous like that in an unlocked vehicle. Somebody might steal it. You want me to put it back?"

"For your own damn good. Put it back and I'll forget you took it out."

"Promise?"

She nodded, watching the gun.

"Well, I've got a little problem with that. You see, I don't trust you." Her glance flicked up at me, then back to the gun.

"What are you, right-handed?"

She bit her lip and didn't answer.

"That's all right. I know you are. So what we're going to do is take these," I brought out her handcuffs, "and lock your right hand to the steering wheel. Then I'll put your gun away."

"That's false imprisonment. You're digging yourself in deeper."

"What difference does it make? You want to put me away for murder." I raised the gun, but I couldn't make myself point it at her, even unloaded. I aimed over her shoulder. "Don't move." With my left hand, I locked one bracelet around her right wrist, then snapped the other half around the steering wheel. She yanked on the cuffs a couple of times, then swore.

"Happy now?" she said.

"Not even a little. But I'll put the gun away." I opened the glove compartment and stowed the gun inside.

"One more thing," I said. "I need to check your pockets. No—" Her left hand had dropped away from the wheel, and I reached over and grasped her wrist. Her pulse beat under my fingers as I lifted her hand back to the steering wheel.

I held it there while I patted her down with my right hand. I removed her wallet from one coat pocket, a pack of gum and the keys to the handcuffs from the other. There was something in her inside pocket—another gun? For a second my blood froze. We were lucky we hadn't got into a goddamn gun battle, with mine unloaded. But it was too small to be a gun. I fished it out.

"A cell phone!" Under any other circumstances I would have laughed. Trudy, carrying a cell phone. I opened it, and it lit up. A working cell phone, no less.

"I picked up a replacement today. I was going to tell you."

I let go of Trudy's wrist and put the wallet and gum on the dashboard, the cell phone in my pocket. "I'm going to borrow this. You owe me some air time." Besides, I couldn't have her calling Plodnick before I had a fair chance to get away.

Finally, I dropped the handcuff keys out the passenger-side window. They landed in the snow without a clink. Trudy watched as I rolled up the window, her jaw clenched, then looked away.

"Okay," I said. "That's it for the preliminaries. Now, we've got one topic of conversation, and one only: What did Perry Glaser tell you?"

"We've got way more important things to talk about than Glaser."

"Do we? The only reason I broke cover was to find out what he told you. What did he confess? Was it about Davies's murder?"

"Forget Glaser. Glaser's nothing. You've got to turn yourself in."

"Thanks for the advice, Deputy. Sorry if I ignore it."

"I'm not kidding. The longer you run, the more trouble you're in." She tugged on the handcuffs. "Just look at the mess you're making. You've committed at least three felonies in the last five minutes."

I couldn't believe I was hearing this. "Spare me the party line, all right? I asked you a simple question. Either answer it or quit wasting my time."

She didn't say anything. A dozen different expressions flitted across her face as she considered her options. Finally she sighed.

"Okay, Bo. It's like you thought—Glaser's big confession was about something else. Something completely unrelated to Davies or the DFA or anything important. It wasn't even a confession. He just wanted to squeal on his wife."

"Nora? Did she kill—"

"No, nothing like that. She's involved in an art fraud scam. Verifies paintings when she knows they're fake. She was working with an art dealer in Boston who'd buy the real painting, then get a copy made. Nora would verify the fake, and the dealer would sell the copy as real. A few years later, he'd sell the real one. One painting, twice the profit. Nora got a nice cut."

"And that's what the FBI's been investigating?"

She nodded. "You told Glaser the Feds were in town, and he realized they scared Nora off. He kept muttering that she'd be sipping cocktails with Castro or some goddamn thing. They got her this morning; she was arrested in the Bahamas, trying to find a boat to take her to Cuba."

So that explained Nora's disappearance. And my theory was still on track.

"Anyway," Trudy said, slapping the steering wheel with her free hand, "Even if Glaser had signed a confession, wrapped it up in a pretty pink bow, and handed it over on a goddamn silver platter, what good would it do you? Right now, Plodnick's after you for Ventura. He'll worry about Davies later. And there's no way Glaser could have run over Ventura from a cell at the county jail."

I knew that. I leaned back and closed my eyes for a second, feeling goddamn tired. What I really wanted to do was tell Trudy what I'd learned, bounce some ideas off her. I wanted her energy and determination on my side. What I didn't want was to be sitting here like this, forcing her to talk to me like we were enemies. But that's what we were. She'd proved it this morning.

"Bo, listen to me," Trudy said. "You're acting like a total asshole, but I'm still worried about you. There's more going on here than Plodnick screaming for your ass. Think for a minute." She twisted around in her seat to face me. "Somebody wanted Ventura out of the way and pinned it on you. This guy is a killer, a nasty one—you know what a body looks like when it's been run over three times? That same killer is coming after you. Because if you're dead, Ventura's case gets closed and the killer walks away. So right now, he's thinking you'd look awfully good as a corpse. The safest place for you is in custody."

"No."

She sighed like someone trying to be patient with an obstinate child. "Okay," she said, "you don't want to be locked up. I understand that. But at least work with me. I can protect you."

That did it. "Protect me? What a joke." She started to argue, but I kept talking. "I never realized you and Plodnick were such big buddies." She shut up and looked at me, her eyes narrow, like she was trying to guess how much I knew. I mimicked her voice sarcastically: " 'Don't worry, Plodnick. I'll bring him in. I was just trying to gain his confidence.' "

"How—?"

"Never mind how I found out. You're a liar, Trudy. You've lied to me all along. You're not even good at it." I just turn into a gullible sucker, I thought, at the sight of a halfway pretty face. "I never believed you. I was just using you to . . . to get inside information." So I was a lousy liar, too.

"Look, I was only trying to make Plodnick back off. I told him you'd surrender to me."

"I never agreed to that."

"I hoped I could talk you into it."

"Yeah, you must have been real optimistic, bringing a gun and handcuffs along. Tell the truth for once. You wanted the arrest for yourself. Anything else is a goddamn lie." Trudy's face reddened. She opened her mouth, then closed it.

I was done talking. "Okay," I said, "you told me what I wanted to know. Thanks for that. This conversation is over."

"Bo—"

I opened the door and got out of the truck. "The handcuff keys are out here somewhere, although the way this snow is coming down, you'll have to dig a little to find them. Or somebody will. Now, your truck keys," I pulled them from my pocket and jingled them, "I'm taking over to that trailer park. I'll leave them in the parking lot. Might take a while to find those, too. I'd help, but I've got somewhere else I've gotta be." I started to close the door.

"Goddamn you, Rainbow, get back here!" Her face was scarlet with anger. "You can't hide from me. I know where you're staying. I know who you run to when you're in trouble."

"You're bluffing. That's another word for lying, by the way." I slammed the door and ran for the trailer park where the Nova waited near the back. I was halfway across the street when Trudy quit yelling and started leaning on her horn, trying to get the attention of the convenience store clerk. I ran harder. I hurled her keys into a snowbank, jumped into the Nova, and sped out of there. I was too far away for her to read the license plate or, I hoped, to get a clear idea of the car's make and model. But she wasn't watching me; she was staring at the store, waving and gesturing at the clerk.

I turned the wrong way on 79 so I could cut over and double back a mile up the road. Trudy's horn kept blaring. At my last glance in the rearview mirror, the clerk was sticking his head out the door. By the time Trudy calmed down enough to explain and got him to call the cops, I'd be at the lake house.

I listened to the scanner for the report that I'd been sighted in Enfield, heading west on 79, but all I heard was the usual chatter. It took me a minute to realize why. Trudy didn't dare call it in. If the word got out that I'd taken away her gun and left her handcuffed to her own truck, she'd never live it down. And now she'd be even more determined to arrest me herself.

So maybe she wouldn't report her cell phone missing, either. In any case, she hadn't had time to do it yet. I turned on her phone and called in to check my voicemail. Maybe Sharon Barton had called. I steered through the snow with one hand and held the phone to my ear with the other. Using a cell phone while driving—there I went, breaking another law.

Two new messages. The first took me utterly by surprise: a woman's voice, sobbing. *Trudy,* I thought, as a fist squeezed my heart. But it wasn't Trudy. After several seconds of crying, the caller managed to say her name. "It's Sharon Buh—Barton." She hiccupped, then lapsed into another barrage of tears. All I could make out was ". . . gave it to someone else." More sobbing, then "Oh, shoot. I can't do this now. Let me—I'll call back in a few minutes."

In the second message, she sounded calmer. "I'm sorry about my previous message. It's just—" she drew a shaky breath—"I didn't get that promotion, the vice presidency." She paused. "Well, screw 'em, that's what I say. Can you come to the bank? I'm the only one here. Everyone left early because of the snow. I'll wait until five. If you can get here before then, call me." She recited a number.

I repeated the number out loud and started to dial. Wait. I couldn't call Sharon from Trudy's phone. I'd have to go payphone hunting again. It was twenty to five, and the only way I'd make it to the bank on time was to go straight into Rhodes. I took a right, heading for town.

Chapter 31

"I don't know how I'm going to tell Bobby." Sharon Barton's blue-green eyes were bloodshot and puffy, but dry. We sat in her office; she'd let me in the back entrance just before five. She sighed. "We already started spending the extra income. Stupid, huh? Do you know who they hired? Some twenty-eight-year-old MBA from Poughkeepsie who'd never even set foot in Rhodes before her interview. Now she'll be my boss."

"That's too bad." I shook my head, trying to look sympathetic but impatient to move on. Losing the promotion was a blow to her, but it didn't exactly compare with being framed for murder. "Sharon, do you think we could—"

She pounded the desk with her fist. "I'm forty. I've been here forever. And I'll never get promoted. This is it." Her gesture encompassed her small office: the desk with two visitors' chairs, the bookcase, the potted plants, the Impressionist print on the wall. "Some life, huh?"

"Looks pretty good to me." Way better than a prison cell.

She half-smiled, then shook herself. "What am I thinking? I said I'd help you, and here I am moaning about my problems." She removed a folder from a drawer and laid it on the desk in front of her. "I pulled all the bank accounts related to Fred Davies and the DFA. That's what you wanted, right?"

I nodded and reached for the folder. She slid it halfway across the desk, then paused, her plump hand weighing on it like a paperweight.

"I'm not doing this because they passed me over for a promotion," she said. "I want you to understand that."

"Sharon, I don't—"

"No, I mean it. I thought about what you said about people dying. I thought about it a lot. If this information can help you solve a murder, well, that's more important than any rules." She smiled grimly. "I'd feel the same way even if I were a vice president."

She let go of the folder. I pulled it toward me and opened it. On top was a carbon copy of the cashier's check and three pink cards, the kind you fill out when you open an account. Each card held personal information—name, address, date of birth, Social Security number—and the signature *F. Davies:* bold and right-slanted, just like on the cashier's check. Under the signature cards was a stack of papers, dizzying columns of numbers running down each sheet.

I turned the papers so Sharon could see them. "Tell me what I'm looking at. Do you notice anything strange about the accounts?"

She put on a pair of reading glasses, leafed through the pages, then shook her head. "Nothing that jumps out at me. There's a lot more activity in the DFA accounts than the personal one, but that's not surprising. The whole point of the DFA has always been to take in money and give it away again."

"Why does the DFA have two accounts?"

"One's for general expenses; the other, the DFA Century Fund, is for fund-raising."

"So donations go into the Century Fund . . ."

"And from there get disbursed into the general account or to grant recipients."

"I don't suppose it says on there who the grant recipients are."

"No, this is just debits and credits, the amounts and the

dates. But there should be . . ." She leafed through the papers. "Huh. That's weird. All these statements should include photostats of checks written on the account." She put down the papers and tapped a couple of keys on her computer. "They're not in the database, either. Hmm. Here are some internal transfers. Those are what you'd expect—money goes from the Century Fund into the general account. And money from the general account goes into . . ." She tapped some keys and looked over her glasses at the screen. "Fred Davies's personal account. The same amount every other week. Payroll. There are a couple of other biweekly transfers, but they're external. One to Finger Lakes Trust Company, the other to Thomson County Credit Union. Those must be payroll, too. There are lots of other payments, of course, but I can't tell who they're to without those checks."

I picked up the printout of the statement. "Can I keep this?"

Sharon looked horrified. "I'd really rather you didn't."

"Then is it okay if I take some quick notes? I promise I won't tell anyone where I got the information." I wanted to see whether there was any pattern to deposits or withdrawals that might match up with the pattern of Ventura's trips to New York.

Sharon hesitated, then handed me a blank piece of paper. "If you promise," she said. She turned back to her computer while I tried to figure out where to begin. There was so much information: deposits and multiple withdrawals every single day. Getting a pattern to emerge from this statement would be like expecting the wind to sculpt a snowdrift into the Venus de Milo. I started writing down figures, anyway.

"Well, that's funny," Sharon said.

I looked up. "What?"

"I was trying to find those missing checks, but I came across something else: an account called the D*E*A Century Fund." She wrote down a number on a piece of paper. "I'll be right back."

I went to the other side of Sharon's desk to see what was on the screen, but it was just more lists of numbers. I sat down again and waited.

She returned holding another pink card. "This is so strange," she said, handing me the card.

The DEA Century Fund had been opened on June 30, 2004. The person authorized to sign checks was Friedrich Dovis—not Frederick Davies—but his signature was identical to the one on the DFA accounts: a bold *F*, a bold *D*, then a squiggle.

"Who opened that account?" Sharon asked, reaching for the card. "Oh. It's initialed *G.B.* George Boutros. I guess we can't ask him about it." She sat at her desk and looked at the computer. "Lots of activity a couple of weeks ago. Some big cash withdrawals. Wire transfers, too. Looks like the money went overseas, from the number. Where is that?" She went over to the bookcase and consulted a ring binder. "Huh. Guatemala."

A bogus account. Hedlund, I thought, it had to be. He was in charge of the DFA's books. He'd set up this other account to siphon money from the foundation. I wondered how long checks intended for the DFA Century Fund or for Fred Davies himself had been going into the shadow account. At some point, Davies must have found out Hedlund was ripping him off, and Hedlund had killed him. It was Hedlund.

I picked up the pink cards and compared the signatures. "It's a good forgery." I showed the cards to Sharon. "I can't tell the difference at all."

Instead of answering, Sharon stared at the cards, frowning. "That can't be." She took cards and laid them foursquare on the desk in front of her.

"What is it?"

"These cards. They're pink. We didn't start using pink signature cards until 2000. Before that, they were yellow. But most of these accounts were opened back in the '90s. See? The date on this one says April 7, 1998. Fred *couldn't* have signed these cards then. They didn't exist."

"Could the bank have lost the original? Asked Fred to come in and sign a new one?"

"Not for *all* his accounts. Even our administrative assistants aren't that bad." She singled out a card. "Only one is the right color for its date. The DEA Century Fund, the bogus account. It was opened in 2004." She fanned herself with the card, thinking. "Hang on just a sec. Let me check one thing." She turned to her computer and typed furiously. She squinted at the screen, then made a note. "I'll be right back."

Again she left the room. While she was gone, I pondered my next move. Did I have enough to take to the police? Not yet. Even though Hedlund had to be the one behind the phony account, I was speculating. I didn't have anything solid to tie him to it—or to link him to Ventura's murder. If I called the cops now, the only thing they'd want to talk about would be my surrender. And I wasn't going to volunteer to be locked up. I shuddered, hearing a metal door clang shut behind me. The thought made Sharon's cozy office close in like a coffin.

Sharon reappeared, waving a sheaf of legal-sized pages. I took a deep breath and focused on her. "Look at this, Bo. I can't believe it."

"What is it?"

"It's the mortgage note on Fred's house. He bought the place in '97." She slapped the papers down in front of me. "Right there. That's the man's signature."

I looked where her bright pink fingernail pointed. *F. Davies*, in precise, looping cursive, not the dark scrawl on the signature cards. I looked up at Sharon and said, "On the cashier's check, on all those accounts—it's not his signature."

"Someone destroyed the original cards. Just like they

destroyed our copies of the canceled checks. Why would they do that?"

"The cashier's check." I sat up straight in my chair. "The one that was stolen. The cops believed all along that Fred Davies withdrew that money. What if he didn't? Destroying any checks he had signed, and the original signature cards, would disguise that fact."

"But that would mean that someone inside the bank changed the records." We both looked at the cards. All were initialed *G.B.* "But George wouldn't—"

"It must have been him, Sharon."

She looked at her computer again. "The last transaction on the bogus account—it happened the day before George died. There's been nothing at all since then."

"George tried to give me a lead about who killed Fred Davies. He was scared as hell. The next day he was dead."

"But George died of an overdose."

"I think he was murdered, Sharon. I think he helped 'Friedrich Dovis' cover his tracks and then got killed for it."

Friedrich Dovis was Sebastian Hedlund, I was sure of it. That made Sebastian Hedlund an extremely nasty guy—an embezzler, money launderer, drug importer, and murderer. He'd gunned down his boss, given bad drugs to his banker, and run over his driver. And I was about to go after him.

Half an hour later, I was inside Hedlund's office. Breaking in had been simple, a quick trip up the rear fire escape and through a flimsy rooftop door. Now, I worked in the dark, grabbing folders from Hedlund's filing cabinet and scrutinizing their contents by the window. In the first folder—recent contracts and letters signed by Fred Davies—every signature matched the *fake* signature, the bold squiggle on the cashier's check. I kept digging. Several months further back in the files, I started finding

F. Davieses that matched Davies's real signature, the one on the mortgage note.

Hedlund had really covered his tracks. Anyone who came looking to confirm Davies's signature would have to unearth year-old files to find the real thing. And who would go back that far? A quick glance at a couple of letters signed in the month before Davies's death would be enough to allay any suspicions. And unless someone said, "Hey, that's not Fred's signature," there'd be no reason to check in the first place. Something bothered me about that thought, but whatever it was wouldn't rise to the surface. I'd worry about it later, back at the lake house. Right now, I was looking for solid evidence of financial shenanigans at the DFA. Everything I'd turned up so far was routine paperwork: letters, memos, purchase orders—stuff like that.

I sat in Hedlund's leather swivel chair and turned on his computer. While it booted, I studied the blotter-sized calendar on his desk. Hedlund had written appointments and phone numbers in most of the daily blocks and doodled spirals and stars around the edges. His handwriting didn't look any more like "Friedrich Dovis's" than Davies's did. Hedlund printed in tiny, excruciatingly neat capital letters. He'd made a real effort to go to the opposite extreme in developing a bogus signature. Probably practiced for weeks to get it right. I copied down some of the phone numbers to check later, then turned to the computer.

Recently viewed documents seemed the best place to start. The list of files Hedlund had worked on most recently contained spreadsheets and word processor documents. I clicked a spreadsheet, but the computer couldn't find the file. I tried another with the same result. I went down the list of all fifteen recently viewed files—every single one of them was gone. I opened the Recycle Bin, already knowing what I'd find. It was empty. In fact, there were no spreadsheet files anywhere on his computer. Hedlund had been cleaning house.

He must be getting ready to make a run for it, like Nora Glaser. If he was, would he destroy all the evidence? That seemed against the nature of a bean-counter like Hedlund.

I remembered the last time I'd been in this office, handing Hedlund his own address as the site of a high-stakes poker game. Hedlund had sat in this chair, then saved a file on a flash drive he used as a key chain. That was it. If the spreadsheets he'd deleted still existed, that's where they'd be.

I had to grab that key chain. And I had to do it before Hedlund left town—if he hadn't already.

Chapter 32

Hedlund's house, a two-story Tudor on the fringes of the ritzy Manitoah Heights neighborhood, perched halfway up Ingram Street, one of the steepest streets in town. The Nova hadn't been able to make it up the hill from below, its rear tires spinning and slipping on the packed snow, so I'd taken an easier route up East Hill, then crept down Ingram Street from above. I'd passed the house and left the Nova a quarter-mile down the road, in a pull-off at the elbow of an S-curve.

Hedlund had no near neighbors, although lights glimmered through tree branches farther up the hill. I stood in the woods across the street, watching his house. He was home. The whole place blazed with lights, and a silhouette moved back and forth in front of an upstairs window.

I needed a plan. The first thing, I thought, would be to disable his car, maybe sneak into the garage and pop off the distributor cap. From there, I'd try to get into the house. Most people, when they get home, drop their keys on a counter or hang them on a key rack. If Hedlund had that habit, I could slip inside his house, snatch the flash drive key chain, and be gone again before he had any clue I'd been there.

I started across the road but dove back into the woods as headlights swept around the uphill curve. The car—no, it was an SUV—turned in at Hedlund's driveway. The engine stopped; the lights went out. A door opened and closed. And Felicia Davies made her way up the front walk.

If I'd been closer, I'd have grabbed her arm and hauled her the hell out of there. Hedlund was a killer, getting ready to skip town. He wasn't going to let anyone stand in his way.

Felicia rang the front door bell, checking her watch as she waited. The door opened, framing Hedlund in the light from the front hall. I could see two suitcases behind him as he leaned toward Felicia. She spoke to him, gesturing, and he moved to one side to let her in. She stepped on the threshold, then paused. Hedlund moved toward her, and she turned her head, offering her cheek. He kissed it, and Felicia went around him and disappeared inside. He shut the door behind her.

I felt like I'd just watched a lamb trot into a lion's den.

I could see them through a front window. Felicia removed her coat and draped it on a dining room chair. Then they passed through an archway, disappearing into the back of the house. I had to see what was going on. If Hedlund threatened Felicia in any way—well, I wouldn't let that happen.

I crossed the street and skirted the yard to the woods that bordered it. The snow muffled all sounds, but I didn't want to leave footprints that would give me away if Hedlund came outside. It took me a few minutes to go around the long way, then I emerged from the woods into Hedlund's back yard.

The rear of Hedlund's house had French doors that opened onto a terrace. Edging the terrace, low stone walls, surrounded by yew bushes, curved around to three shallow steps leading into the yard. I crouched near the steps, where I could see clearly through the French doors into the living room. Hedlund sat in a leather chair by a bookcase, facing me, holding a drink. I didn't spot Felicia at first, but then she crossed the room, passing behind Hedlund's chair.

Felicia went to a sideboard and poured amber liquor into two rocks glasses. She carried the drinks to Hedlund, took his empty glass, and gave him a fresh drink. They raised their glasses and touched the edges in a toast. Hedlund swallowed his drink in one gulp; Felicia raised her glass to her lips but didn't drink, watching him over the rim. She offered her glass to Hedlund, who took it and tossed it back. He'd polished off three stiff drinks in less than five minutes.

Hedlund said something to Felicia, who laughed and shook her head, then went back to the sideboard. Another minute, another drink. Hedlund dropped his glass on the floor and rose swaying to his feet. He took a step and stumbled, catching himself on the back of his chair. After a second, he started toward Felicia, knocking over a side table. He made a sweeping gesture with his arm; the force of it nearly sent him off balance again. His voice was muffled; it sounded like he was shouting, but I couldn't make out any words through the closed French doors.

Felicia came over, and he gestured again. I stood, thinking he was going to hit her, but instead he threw his arm around her and pulled her toward him. He held her in a tight embrace, trying sloppily to kiss her, although she kept turning her head and pushing at him with both hands. From ten paces outside, I saw the disgust in her eyes even as she smiled at him. I started forward, fists clenched, ready to break through those damn French doors to pull him off her.

But Felicia could take care of herself. She escaped Hedlund's grasp and guided him back to his chair. Then she brought him another drink, a full one, liquor sploshing over the rim. Why was she plying him with alcohol? The guy was obviously an obnoxious drunk, so what was her point in encouraging him? She'd fed him at least five drinks since I'd been watching, and she was already pouring another.

As she stood at the sideboard, her back to me, Felicia took something out of her purse. I couldn't see what she was doing from this angle, so I crept up the terrace steps to get a closer look.

"Freeze, Rainbow!" Trudy's voice rang out behind me. "You are so under arrest."

"Trudy—" I spoke quietly, not wanting our voices to carry inside, and started to turn toward her.

"Don't you dare move until I tell you to. Put your hands up."

I did.

"Now turn around. Slowly."

I turned to see Trudy ten feet back in the snow, just beyond the rectangle of light thrown out by the French doors. Her face was obscured in darkness; only her gun—pointed straight at me—appeared in the light from the house. She wasn't aiming over my shoulder.

"Trudy, listen. I figured out what's been going on—"

"God damn it, Bo, I *listened* when you said you'd call me at that payphone. I'm not listening to you now."

"I'm sorry about that. But I—"

"Shut up!" she screamed. "And lie down on the ground. Face down."

She stepped toward me, moving into the light. I locked eyes with her. "Trudy, don't."

"You think I'm kidding." She came closer; I took a step backward.

"You've got to let me explain—"

Suddenly her head jerked up as she looked past me. Her eyes widened, and she shouted, "Bo! Get down!" Something in her voice—I threw myself onto the floor of the terrace. Glass shattered before I hit the ground. I rolled to the right and went over the low stone wall, then crouched behind the snow-covered bushes. There were a couple of shots, maybe three, and more glass breaking.

Hedlund, drunk and crazy, must have gotten hold of a gun.

He was too smashed to shoot straight, but that didn't mean he wouldn't kill someone.

The yard was quiet. I raised my head to make sure Trudy was okay—and saw blood splashed across the snow where she'd stood. Then the light from the house went out. I saw a dark shape crouching near the stone wall, where I'd watched the house before. It was Trudy. She held her right arm, hugging it against her body.

Footsteps crunched on broken glass. Trudy half-rose from her crouch and fired, but she was holding her gun all wrong, something was wrong with her shooting arm. A return shot knocked her off her feet, and she fell backwards into the snow. "Trudy!" I yelled, leaping up to go to her, but there was a pop and a bullet flew past me, too close, hissing. I ducked and hid. I couldn't help Trudy with a bullet in my head.

More footsteps, but with an uneven cadence—*hard* soft, *hard* soft—like the person was limping. The air was thick with the smell of cordite. I chanced a look. Felicia Davies made her way down the terrace steps, a gun in her hand. She wore gloves but no jacket, and a streak of blood darkened her torn pants leg from thigh to calf. She hobbled toward Trudy, who lay unmoving in the snow.

Damn it, what could I do—throw a snowball? Felicia stood beside Trudy, then bent awkwardly, gasping at the pain in her leg, and picked up Trudy's pistol where it had fallen in the snow. She felt for a pulse, then stood. She stuffed her own gun into her pocket and checked Trudy's.

"She's alive." Felicia scanned the yard, Trudy's gun ready. "But unless you show yourself before I count to three, I'll put a bullet in her head. One . . ." Her voice sounded like a patient kindergarten teacher. "Two . . ."

"Don't shoot her." I stood. "I'm right here."

Felicia turned toward me, aiming the gun. "Move away from

those bushes where I can see you. And put your hands up."

I complied, walking into the yard.

"That's close enough," Felicia said when I was about ten feet away. I could hear Trudy's ragged, shallow breathing. She moaned, trying to raise herself up, then collapsed again. Every muscle in me strained to go to her, but Felicia had the gun aimed steadily at my head.

"Felicia, there's no point. All those gunshots—someone must have called the cops."

"Who'll arrest you the second they get here. Obviously, you've continued your murderous rampage. You, Ray Ventura, and Sebastian, all working together to sell drugs to the good people of Rhodes." She shook her head and tsked at me. "You killed Ray, and Sebastian is in there committing suicide—booze and sleeping pills. The poor man was consumed with guilt over his role in the operation."

So that was why she'd been pouring drinks down Hedlund's throat. "You murdered him."

"Not yet, probably. I'd say he's still got a few minutes."

"Jesus, it was you. You killed your own husband. And Ventura. But—" Suddenly Felicia's role became clear. "Your import business. The gallery. It's a front for smuggling drugs. Ventura, Hedlund, Boutros—they all worked for you."

"Well, aren't you clever? But you know what Euripides said about that."

I didn't reply. My mind raced, looking for a way to disarm her. If I tried to rush her, she'd shoot before I'd taken two steps. There was no way, nothing. Just ten feet of empty space between me and the gun.

"No sirens yet," Felicia said. She cocked her head, listening, then laughed. "These Manitoah Heights snobs. They hate to make a scene. I'll probably have to call the police myself. By the time they get here, you, Sebastian, and your little deputy friend will all be dead. The detectives will look at the carnage and go for the obvious solution: Sebastian committed suicide, and you and the deputy killed each other in a gun battle. My name won't even come up. Or if it does, I'll be long gone."

Her eyes narrowed, and I saw her tense. She was getting ready to shoot. "So aren't you going to ask?" she said.

"Ask what?"

"What Euripides, the Greek playwright, said. About cleverness. I'll tell you, anyway. He said, 'Cleverness is not wisdom.' "

She pulled the trigger.

At the same moment, Trudy lurched upward and threw herself against Felicia, hitting her hard behind the knees. Felicia yelled in pain, and the shot went wide. I charged forward and tackled Felicia. The gun flew from her hand as we both went down hard in the snow.

As soon as she hit the ground, she started screaming. "My leg! Goddamn you, my leg!" I kneeled on her chest and searched her pockets, grabbing the other gun. Then I scrambled off her and hunted through the snow until I had Trudy's gun, too. I turned on the safety and stuck it in the waistband of my jeans. Felicia rolled from side to side, clutching her leg and cursing.

I went to Trudy, who lay still, her skin waxy and almost as white as the snow. She'd taken two shots—one in her right arm and the other in her right side. She was breathing, but there was a whistling noise I didn't like; the bullet must've nicked a lung. I smoothed her hair back from her forehead. Not a flicker of response. Snowflakes stuck to her eyelashes, and her lips were blue. The snow around her was slushy with blood.

I had to get her inside, into the warmth, and get an ambulance here, fast. I glanced at Felicia; she'd stopped yelling, but she still clutched her leg and rocked from side to side. Blood oozed from her thigh wound into the snow. I snatched the handcuffs off Trudy's belt, then I dragged Felicia, struggling and swearing, over to the bushes that lined the terrace. I locked a cuff around one hand, then stretched her arm out so I could snap the other cuff around the bush's trunk. She could stay there until the cops arrived.

I rushed back to Trudy and lifted her gently. She groaned, then pressed her face against me. I carried her into the house.

Inside, a fire burned in the fireplace. I laid Trudy on the Oriental rug in front of it. She sighed, and her eyelids fluttered. I touched her face, and she reached up and grasped my hand. "Don't leave me," she said.

"I won't. I've got to call an ambulance, but I'll come right back."

She squeezed my hand hard, then let go.

When I stood, I saw Hedlund slumped in his leather chair. He was making gurgling sounds as he struggled for each breath. On the table beside him was a single sheet of paper. I scanned it as I picked up the phone. It was the fake suicide note Felicia had typed up for him, claiming remorse for murdering Davies and bringing drugs into Rhodes.

I hit nine-one-one, and the dispatcher picked up on the second ring. "We need some ambulances here," I said. "It's urgent. You've got to send them out right away."

"How many people are injured?"

"Two—no, three," I said, remembering Felicia outside. "Two have gunshot wounds and one OD'd on whiskey and pills."

The dispatcher caught her breath. She asked for my name.

"Just send the damn ambulances. Six-thirty-five Ingram Street." I hung up.

I eased Hedlund out of his chair and got him lying on his side on the floor. I tilted his head back slightly and checked that his air passage was clear. He seemed to breathe easier. I set both handguns on the table next to the phone, then went back to Trudy.

"I'm here," I said.

Even by the fire, she was shivering. I pulled off her gloves and rubbed her hands. They felt small and cold.

She opened her eyes and made a soft, incoherent sound.

"You'll be okay," I said. "The ambulance is on its way."

With the ambulance would come the cops. There was still a warrant out for my arrest. If I left now, I could elude them, then figure out some way to slip into the hospital to see Trudy.

She caught my hand and held it, raised it against her cheek.

A siren wailed in the distance, joined by a second, then a third. I had about five seconds to decide: either take off, knowing Trudy would be in safe hands, or go to jail. Locked up. I couldn't breathe at the thought. Letting the cops catch me wouldn't do Trudy any good.

"Bo," she murmured. Her eyes flew open, and she tried to sit up. I gently pressed her back, told her to lie still. "Bo!" she said. Her voice was urgent, like she had something important to tell me.

"What is it?" I leaned down, my ear next to her mouth. She lifted a hand and turned my head, then kissed me full on the lips. She smiled, then passed out.

When the cops burst in five minutes later, I was still holding her hand.

I sat in the back of a police cruiser, handcuffed and locked in. I didn't resist arrest, but when the cops wouldn't let me stay while the EMTs worked on Trudy, it took four of them to drag me out of there.

Now, I focused on my breathing, fighting the claustrophobia, watching for Trudy. They brought Hedlund out first. He'd gone into convulsions about a minute after the EMTs arrived; it didn't look like he'd make it. As the first ambulance backed out of the drive, Trudy came out on a stretcher. I twisted all the way around in my seat to see her. They'd strapped an oxygen mask to her face, and I couldn't tell whether her eyes were open or closed. One of the EMTs held an IV bag above her; as they loaded her into the ambulance, I saw him hook it to something inside. Then the doors closed and I couldn't see her any more.

I faced front, leaned back, and shut my eyes. My confinement pressed on me from all sides. I couldn't get out, damn it. I couldn't get out, and I needed to be with Trudy. I kicked the partition in frustration, hard. Then again. And again.

Someone rapped on the window, then opened a front door. The cop spoke to me through the wire grille. "Knock it off, Forrester. One of the ambulance guys has a question for you."

An EMT leaned into the car. "You the guy that made the 911 call?"

I nodded.

"The dispatcher said there were three injuries. We only found two. You hurt?"

"No, it's not me. It's Felicia Davies. She's in the backyard, next to the terrace. She's handcuffed to one of the yew bushes."

The EMT gave me a funny look, but I didn't say anything else. I'd have plenty of time to explain. Over and over and over.

He was gone no more than five minutes before the door opened again. It was the same EMT. "We found the handcuffs on the bush," he said. "And we found lots of blood. But there wasn't anybody back there."

Chapter 33

Felicia had disappeared. Her SUV was gone—with all the ambulances and police cars cramming the driveway, I hadn't even noticed that the Lexus was missing. She'd slipped the handcuffs somehow, probably by pushing up her glove and working her hand out of the bracelet. Damn it! She had an escape plan; she'd said she'd be "long gone" before anyone suspected her. If I didn't find a way to stop her—tonight—she'd get away with three murders. Four if Hedlund died.

My mind refused to add Trudy to the potential body count.

The snow had turned to freezing rain, coating everything with ice. The trees in Hedlund's front yard glittered like glass sculptures. I hoped those ambulance drivers knew what they were doing. This would be hell to drive in.

Two cops got into the front seat of the cruiser. I started talking before they'd closed both doors. "You've got to find Felicia Davies," I said. "She was here tonight. She shot Trudy. She poisoned Hedlund. She killed her own husband and Ventura both. Probably Boutros, too. And right now, she's on her way out of the country."

"Shut up, Forrester," said the cop in the passenger seat, as the driver pulled onto the road and steered down the hill. "You can tell your fairy tales after we've booked you."

"It's true. She told me. Listen, she's driving a late-model Lexus SUV. Silver. This storm's got to be slowing her down. If you put out an APB—"

"Didn't you hear my partner?" the driver said. "He said to shut up. Jesus, it's hard enough driving in this shit without listening to you yammering—" He swore and oversteered as the cruiser slid on a curve, sending one wheel dipping over the edge of the steep embankment.

"Christ," said his partner, "keep it on the road, will you?"

"You wanna drive? It's sheer ice."

I'd seen something. I stared out the window, twisting in my seat as the cruiser got fully back on the road. Just past the curve, far down the bank and in the woods, there'd been a glimmer of silver—a vehicle had gone off the road and landed on its side.

It had to be Felicia's Lexus. Who else would try to drive down Ingram Street in this storm?

"Stop!" I shouted. "Didn't you see that? There was a car in the woods back there. It must've slid off that curve. God damn it, you've got to stop."

The cop who wasn't driving turned around. He had dark, mean eyes. "If you don't shut up, I'm going to have to take measures to subdue you. You'll be damn sorry we stopped then."

The police car inched down the road. These cops were just going to ignore me. I had to make them stop and check out that car. I lay back on the seat and kicked at the window with both feet.

"What the hell do you think you're doing?"

With the fifth kick, one foot smashed through the glass. I kept kicking until only some shards remained around the frame, until the driver stopped the car. The mean-eyed cop got out and yanked open the back door. He pressed something against my leg and held it there.

Jagged pain ripped through every muscle of my body in a blinding, eternal flash. I exploded, shattered; I drowned in an ocean of white-hot pain. Everything else evaporated. Then the pain ebbed, tearing itself excruciatingly from my body, leaving me limp-noodle weak. I tried to sit up, but my muscles wouldn't cooperate. I felt like a sack of potatoes they'd tossed onto the back seat. I couldn't remember what I was doing here or why I'd wanted them to stop.

The voice of the cop standing outside drifted in like a dandelion seed on a summer breeze. "Damn it all, he's right. There *is* a car down there. You guard the prisoner. I'm going down to take a look."

My mind floated above the form lying on the back seat. Slowly, a tingling began, giving definition to my hands and feet—good to know they were still there. By concentrating, I could move a couple of fingers. A car—someone had said something about a car. Some of the mist in my brain swirled aside to reveal an image of an SUV, a silver one, lying on its side in the woods. I remembered. I tried again to sit up, moving my head a half-inch off the seat.

"You just lie there." The driver now stood outside and spoke to me through the broken window. "Unless you wanna get zapped again."

No. I damn well didn't. I stayed put.

In a few minutes, the mean-eyed cop returned. "Better call for an ambulance," he said. "The driver's still inside. A woman. She's unconscious, bleeding from the head." A pause. "Damn, I wonder how fast she was going. That thing must've flown off the curve."

I could move now, although any motion felt strange, like my muscles were made of water. The cops helped me sit up. This time, they made sure they buckled me in. "Is it Felicia Davies?" I asked.

"Christ, you never quit, do you?" The mean-eyed cop shook his head, then closed the door. He got in on the other side and sat next to me, behind the driver. When the ambulance and another cruiser arrived, we drove on to the Rhodes police station. I sat still, feeling like a pile of old tires. Nobody said a word the whole way.

At the station, I was searched, fingerprinted, photographed, and officially charged with the murder of Raymond Ventura. They took my belt and shoelaces, my wallet, phone, and keys. They confiscated my jacket as evidence. I didn't realize how blood-soaked it was until I saw it in the officer's hands. Jesus—my jacket, the snow, the rug by the fire. Trudy had lost a lot of blood.

I used my one phone call to telephone the hospital, but the nurse who answered wouldn't release Trudy's condition. I told her I'd made the 911 call, I tried to explain that Trudy would want me to know, I out-and-out pleaded with her, but she wouldn't budge. I'd never sworn at a nurse before.

They escorted me to an interrogation room, different from the conference room where Plodnick had tried to bully me the day before. This room had the same dull green walls and gray metal furniture, but a video camera perched in a corner and one wall was dominated by a huge mirror. One of those one-way observation mirrors, for sure. They sat me down facing it; I wondered how many people watched from the other side.

Plodnick came in, trying to look tough but grinning so widely that his damn moustache was in danger of popping right off his face. He walked around the table and stood across from me; another detective sat at one end and unwrapped a stick of chewing gum. A uniformed cop stood by the door.

"How's Trudy?" I asked as Plodnick took his seat.

He paused, bent over the table, and glared at me, then eased himself all the way into his chair.

"Now, see, I'm the one who's supposed to ask the questions. We got a procedure here. I ask; you answer."

Asshole. I gritted my teeth. "I'll talk all you want. I'll even waive having a lawyer to hold my hand. I've got things to tell you that you won't even believe." I leaned forward. "But I'm not saying another goddamn word until I know Trudy's condition."

He watched me through narrowed eyes, stroking his moustache. The other detective popped his gum. Seconds passed. Finally Plodnick shrugged.

"She's critical. The bullet went through a lung, and the lung collapsed. They've got her on a respirator."

Shit. I leaned my face into my hands. I saw Trudy lying in the snow, her face drained, her breathing ragged, her blood spilling onto my hands.

But Plodnick wasn't finished. "She's in a coma. Lost a lot of blood. Maybe other internal injuries. So . . ." I looked up, the air cool on my cheeks. "So if Deputy Hauser dies, you'll be looking at another murder charge."

I was halfway out of my chair before the uniform clamped his hands on my shoulders and forced me back down. Goddamn Plodnick. I closed my eyes and forced my fists to unclench. Don't lose it now, I thought.

I opened my eyes and stared Plodnick in the face. "I didn't shoot her."

"That's funny. We got your prints all over the gun."

"It was Felicia Davies. She was there. She's the one behind the drugs that have been coming into Rhodes."

"Felicia Davies."

"Yes, she has a gallery in New York, sells South American art. It's a front. She used her import business to smuggle the drugs in. Ventura was a courier. Boutros and Hedlund helped her launder the money through her husband's art foundation." I remembered the hardness in her face right before she pulled the trigger. *Cleverness is not wisdom.* "She killed them all."

"Wow. A one-woman crime wave." Plodnick looked at the other detective, who stopped chewing long enough to smile. "Mrs. Davies wasn't even in the country on the night her husband was killed. So why don't you stop telling me nasty stories about a real nice lady, and we'll get back to that procedure. Remember? I ask; you answer."

"Hedlund has the financial records in a flash drive he uses as a key chain. It'll show you I'm right."

Plodnick acted like he hadn't even heard. "So, you left here yesterday afternoon at approximately five P.M. Where did you go next?"

And for hour after hour, it was the same thing. Plodnick wouldn't hear a word about what I'd uncovered at the DFA—he just kept grilling me about my movements. I told the same story a million times, everything that had happened from the time I'd charged into the Speakeasy looking for Ventura until I'd kicked out the window in the police car. Or most of it. I didn't tell them about ambushing Trudy in her own truck, and I left out the people who'd helped me—Ryan, Dinesh, Sharon Barton—but I described everything else in minute detail. With each retelling, Plodnick tried to confuse me, poking a hole in my story here, breaking a piece off there, pretending he didn't understand when it was perfectly damn clear.

By the time they locked me in a cell, I was so exhausted I couldn't have stated my own name.

I should have been asleep within seconds, but the moment the barred door clanged shut behind me, my body went rigid with panic. Hell isn't a fiery torture chamber; it's a small, tight, airless space with no way out. Like a culvert. Like a cell. *I can't get out* was my only thought. I can't get out.

I started pacing, but that only emphasized the cell's tiny dimensions. Three steps one way, four the other. Six by eight.

One tiny window, high up, barred. Bed, sink, toilet making the space even smaller. I could barely move in there. And I couldn't get out.

The urge to throw myself against the door and scream for the guard almost overwhelmed me. I bit my lip, tasting blood, and forced myself to lie down. The bed was unyielding under a thin foam mattress. To fight down the panic, I closed my eyes and focused on my breathing. I inhaled slowly, counting one . . . two . . . three . . . four, filling my lungs as far as they could expand, then exhaled to the same count. The cell was stuffy, smelled like ammonia and piss. One . . . two . . . three . . . four. In my mind, I pushed apart the bars on the window until the gap was wide enough for me to squeeze between them, out into the cold night. One . . . two . . . three . . . four. I flew over the snowy roads, heading south, until I'd left the snow and the cold, even the darkness, behind. I landed in a grass-filled meadow somewhere, under a wide-open sky. In the distance a lake sparkled. When my feet felt the warm earth beneath them, the iron bands constricting my chest snapped, and I filled my lungs with the sweet-scented air.

I held the visualization for as long as I could, needing to make the scene real, to believe that I was in an open field and not locked in a cage. But it couldn't last. There was too much skittering across my mind: Where was Felicia? How in hell could I get Plodnick to investigate the DFA's finances? And above all, Trudy. Jesus, if I felt claustrophobic in this cell, I couldn't even imagine what it must be like for her, locked into a machine to make her breathe. She'd looked so fragile at Hedlund's house—her face pale, her eyes rolling upward as the lids fluttered. I threw an arm across my face, trying to block out that image, but it remained. Trudy hurt, Trudy bleeding. And nothing I could do to make it stop.

★ ★ ★ ★ ★

I must have slept because when a guard banged on the door I woke up disoriented and groggy. “Your arraignment’s in two hours,” he said. “So get your ass in gear.”

They let me shower and fed me watery scrambled eggs and burnt toast. I asked a guard how Trudy was, but he just shrugged. Either he didn’t know or he wasn’t going to tell me. Then I sat in my cell, staring at the window, waiting. In a few minutes, guards would come down the hall to chain me up like some dangerous animal and transport me to the county courthouse, parading me past a gantlet of gawkers and reporters. I stood up, but there was nowhere to go. Just close-in concrete walls, squeezing the breath out of me. I couldn’t stand it.

A door slammed, and footsteps hurried toward me. I braced myself, tried to resign myself to what was coming.

And then Plodnick appeared.

“I need you to answer some questions,” he said. “Now.”

“I have to go to my arraignment.”

“The arraignment’s been postponed. Hedlund pulled through. He’s conscious. And he’s talking.”

Chapter 34

They let me go the next day. Once Hedlund woke up in the hospital and realized that Felicia had tried to kill him, he wouldn't shut up. It was all Felicia, he said. He claimed that he'd never known about the drugs, that he was just trying to help her hide some of her gallery's profits from the IRS. To secure his help, she'd offered him double his DFA salary; his poker habit wouldn't let him say no. Besides, he said, he was in love with her.

On the day before Davies was killed, a Friday, Hedlund left his office to go to the men's room, then suddenly realized he'd left the wrong spreadsheet—the "Friedrich Dovis" account—up on his computer screen. He rushed back to find Davies standing outside his office door, one hand on the knob. "Oh, Sebastian," Davies had said. "I was going to ask you a question about the audit. It can wait." Davies never said a word about the spreadsheet, but Hedlund knew, just *knew* he'd seen it. In a panic, he called Felicia, who was in Quito on a buying trip. "Don't worry," she said. "I'll take care of it." Thirty-six hours later, Fred Davies was dead.

"Now we can be together, darling," Felicia had told Hedlund. But she didn't act like she wanted to be with him. Not with that Ventura always sniffing around her. Hedlund and Ventura despised each other, competing, Hedlund believed, for Felicia's affections. He was so jealous that he'd picked up the extension once when Ventura had called, hearing this conversation:

Felicia: No, don't worry, the bathroom's fine. You did a good job. There's no trace, even if you know where to look. What I want to know is how you managed to screw up with the car.

Ventura: I couldn't help it. I dumped the gun first, but then I started to feel weird, you know, at the thought of driving around with a body in the trunk. I wanted a gun, my gun. It was only a couple of blocks to my apartment, so I headed there, but then I got jumped from behind.

Felicia: Bad timing, Ray. Incredibly bad. Well, just go back to work as usual. We're going to keep our heads down for a while. I'll let you know if I need you to make another run.

Felicia was F. Dovis, Hedlund said. She'd opened the bogus account and signed all the checks. Although Hedlund kept the books, she had control of the money. She reported the cashier's check as stolen because she didn't know what had happened to it, fearing that Fred had hidden it as evidence of the bogus account. So she'd changed the signature cards at the bank and documents at the DFA.

For the same reason, she was puzzled by the missing ring. Contrary to what she'd told me, Fred didn't wear it all the time. She'd checked the office, his wall safe, his safe deposit box, but couldn't find it anywhere. Ventura claimed he hadn't seen it. But later, when Ventura tried to cash the check, she realized he'd double-crossed her. When she'd left him to clean up her mess, he'd stolen the ring and the check both. She called Ventura in New York, told them they were starting up business again, coaxed him back to Rhodes. And, like Fred, Ventura was dead within hours.

The cops arrested Felicia in her hospital bed, where she lay with a fractured pelvis and broken leg. Even with her injuries, she'd probably have tried to make another run for it if Plodnick hadn't posted a cop in her room. Hedlund's too. I guess the guy had been listening to me, after all.

Once they'd corroborated enough of Hedlund's story to believe it—analyzing the files on his flash drive, discovering spackled-over bullet holes and traces of blood in Davies's master bathroom, finding Felicia's fingerprint on the back of my Corolla's rearview mirror—the police dropped all charges against me. Now, clutching my possessions in a manila envelope, I stood on the top step outside the Rhodes police station, a free man. I breathed in the clear air, so cold it stung my lungs. A pair of cardinals flew across the brilliant turquoise sky. The world spread itself out before me: snow, dirty now in the plowed-up banks along the roadside, covered everything. A block downhill and to the north, the Crossing sparkled in the sunlight.

The door opened behind me, and a voice called my name. Half-fearing some trick that would drag me back to that tiny cell, I turned. Mike in Records stood in the doorway, his tan looking a little faded.

"Bo," he said. "I'm glad I caught you. The hospital just called. Trudy's awake. She's asking for you."

During that first visit, neither of us said a word. Trudy looked so damn sick—her eyes sunken and ringed by dark circles, her mouth a red slash across her face. She was off the respirator but surrounded by clicking, beeping machines connected to her body by a labyrinth of tubes and wires. I sat by the bed and held her hand, as I had that night at Hedlund's house, but her hand was warm, and I could almost feel the strength returning to it.

A burly nurse with iron-gray hair chased me out after five minutes. "I'll be back," I whispered. Trudy, eyes closed, smiled and squeezed my hand.

Over the next several days, I drove my shift and went to the hospital. Even Dinesh understood when I turned down his invitation to a water polo practice. "Yeah," he said. "That's where you need to be right now." Hour after hour, I sat by Trudy's bed, watching her sleep, feeling—no, *knowing*—that I was looking at a miracle.

On the day they moved her out of intensive care, I was there to help her celebrate. It was late afternoon when I opened the door to her room.

Trudy sat up in bed, staring out the window like she couldn't quite believe there was still a world out there. She wore a faded hospital gown with washed-out flowers scattered across a white background. Her right arm rested in a sling. Tubes went into her arm and her nose, and her hair stuck out over her left ear.

"Hey, gorgeous," I said, meaning it.

She started at the sound of my voice, then adjusted her gown and finger-combed her hair. She gave up with a sigh, but she turned to me and smiled.

"Did you bring it?"

"Of course."

I reached into my bag and pulled out the MP3 player I'd picked up at her trailer. I'd checked the music library—20 gigabytes of Mozart, Mozart, and more Mozart. Nothing else.

She grabbed it and put the buds in her ears, then rapidly thumbed the buttons. Her look of concentration, with that cute furrow between her eyebrows, melted into bliss as she leaned back against the pillows and closed her eyes.

After a minute, she opened them again and pulled off the headphones.

"Sorry, that was rude. But I've been going *crazy* in here. Television or AM radio—that's it." She made a face to demonstrate how much she'd suffered. "You're a life saver."

"When are they going to let you go home?"

Her tone turned serious. "No, listen. I really mean it. You

saved my life. I wanted to say thank you."

I cut her off before things got sappy. "You saved mine, too, don't forget. So we're even."

She appraised me with one of her calculating looks, like she was trying to figure out whether saying "we're even" meant I was somehow coming out ahead. Then she smiled.

"I've developed 'a touch of pneumonia,' as the doctor put it. He says it's common with lung injuries. They want to observe me for a few more days. But unless the pneumonia gets worse, I'll be out on Wednesday."

I stood there, just looking at her. I wanted the images that I'd been carrying in my mind—Trudy unconscious on the floor, Trudy motionless in the respirator, Trudy with dark-circled, sunken eyes—to be replaced by this one. Sitting up in bed, smiling, a little pale but so beautiful. I realized I was grinning like an idiot.

"I'd better be going," I said. "I know you need your Mozart fix. Besides, I think that nurse will haul me out by my ear if I stay too long."

"You mean old Iron Pants? Jesus, what a tyrant."

God, it was good to have Trudy back. Instead of leaving, I moved closer to her bed. "I was wrong about something, though. We're not even."

"What?" She scowled, like she was trying to guess how I'd one-upped her.

"I owe you something." I bent down and kissed her on the lips. They were warm and dry and chafed a little. As I stood, her eyes were closed, but they flew open, wide and velvet brown.

"What the hell was that for?"

"You kissed me. At Hedlund's house. I was just returning the favor."

"I did, huh? Must've been delirious."

Then she reached up and pulled me toward her for more.

Chapter 35

"I don't think she has a chance," Trudy said as we walked back from Donovan's on a Friday evening in early March. Felicia's trial would begin on Monday. Thinking about the trial reminded me how lucky I was to be strolling along Manitoah Street, my arm around Trudy, on one of those not-too-cold evenings that almost makes you believe spring might return.

"Not a chance," she continued. "Even with those hotshot lawyers she brought in. Let's look at the facts. One." She ticked her points off on her fingers. "Hedlund's plea deal makes him the star witness. He could nail her all by himself."

"And he can't wait to do that."

"Yeah. I hope I can be in court when he testifies." She held up a second finger. "Two: Felicia's main defense in the Fred Davies murder was that she was out of the country on the night he was killed. The cops have the fake passport she used to fly back early. And now they've also got the Ecuadorian airline employee Felicia bribed to change the records, making it look like she was on the Sunday flight."

"So they can prove she was in the country the night Fred was killed."

"Right, and even establish probability that she was in Rhodes. She flew into New York, then rented a car under the name on the phony passport. When she returned it the next day, she'd driven exactly the right number of miles for a round-trip to Rhodes."

During that trip, she'd surprised her husband in the bathroom as he dressed for the DFA fundraiser, taking him out with the cold-blooded calculation of a professional assassin. Ventura had come over to help her clean up the bathroom. She'd left him painting the spackled-over bullet holes, with instructions to get rid of the body and the gun, and driven back to New York.

Trudy and I stopped to let a car go by before we crossed Manitoah Street. I liked the way she leaned against me while we waited. The car passed, and we walked on.

"And three," she continued, "Mike told me at lunch yesterday—"

I stopped. "Wait. You and Mike had lunch?"

She'd kept walking; now she turned around. "Yeah, you know. Lunch. It's that meal between breakfast and dinner. Most people have it around noon." She waited, jutting her chin, to see if I'd make anything of it. I walked silently forward. She fell into step next to me, close, bumping into my side until I put my arm around her again. "*Any*way," she went on, "Mike said the Rhodes cops can prove how Felicia stole your car."

I didn't ask—I knew she'd tell me. I was still trying to figure out exactly what to think about her lunch date with that meathead in Records.

"They've got a statement from the doorman of Felicia's co-op in Manhattan. When you spent the night with her—"

"Hang on. I did not 'spend the night with' Felicia Davies." We never even had a lunch date, I thought.

"Okay, when you stayed at her penthouse—that better?—Felicia appeared in the lobby at two in the morning, telling the doorman she'd lost the spare key for her car and couldn't sleep until she got another made. She asked him if he knew any all-night hardware stores."

I'd wondered about that. "So she tiptoed into the guest room while I was asleep, stole my keys, and made a copy. I never had a clue." And Ventura never had a chance.

Trudy twisted around and looked at me, that furrow between her eyebrows. "You're sure you slept in the guest room, right?"

"Positive. In the guest room, all by myself."

"I still can't believe you spent the night with her."

"I didn't—"

"Okay, *stayed* with her. She just seems like the worst person to run to when you're in trouble."

"True, but I didn't know that then, and—" A thought struck me. "So that's how you found me. At Hedlund's that night." Trudy had an uncanny talent for popping up in the wrong place at exactly the wrong time, but she'd never explained how she'd known I was at Hedlund's the night of the blizzard. She credited her supernatural tracking skills, developed from years spent stalking defenseless deer through the woods. Now, I realized why she'd suddenly materialized in Hedlund's back yard. "You weren't following me. You were following Felicia. You thought she was hiding me."

Trudy's eyes narrowed, and I knew I'd got it right. "I determined you weren't at her house, but when she came out and got in her car, I figured she'd lead me to you. And she did, just not in the way I'd expected. At Hedlund's, I saw you dart across the street and into the woods. I followed your tracks—"

"And pulled a gun on me."

She shrugged. "For your own good."

I decided not to pursue the logic of that statement.

We stopped in front of my duplex. Trudy's truck was parked at the curb, and she leaned against the door.

"You want to come in?" I asked, running a hand along her arm. "It's early. We could order pizza."

"Better not. I drew weekend duty. I'm on patrol in the morning."

She raised her face expectantly, lips parted, and I bent to kiss her good night. We both jumped when the door banged and a voice called out, "Bo? Is that you?"

Great timing. I stepped back. Trudy was red-faced but smiling. "Hi, Mrs. B.," we said, almost in unison.

"Come up here on the porch. I got something for you." She waved a piece of paper. "A gentleman left it for you this afternoon. He said you'd know what it was."

Trudy walked up the steps with me. Mrs. B. handed me a piece of notebook paper with some kind of drawing on it. Trudy peered around my arm to see it.

Sketched in colored pencil, the drawing showed mountains and several strange doodles. A rainbow arched between two peaks, one of them flying a banner. Near the top of the page, a figure holding a cross knelt by some water. Down a ways and to the right was a heart. Between them, a yellow flower blossomed beside a gleaming box spilling over with coins. Hoisted over the box was a flag made of three fat stripes: blue, white, and red. And in the bottom corner, a serpent coiled around a dagger, looking like a tattoo on a convict's arm.

Mrs. B. lifted her glasses to study the drawing. "Carl thinks it's a treasure map." She pointed. "See? That box looks like a treasure chest. He wanted to make a copy before I gave it to you, but I told him it was your business, not his."

"It does look like a map," Trudy said.

"Yeah, but of what?" I stared at the snake twined around the dagger. A snake. Snake. My heart jumped. Could it be a signature?

"Mrs. B., the man who gave you this. Did he say anything else? What did he look like?"

"He was an attractive gentleman. Snow-white hair, clean shaven. Wore a nice suit." She sighed. "I do wish Carl would buy himself a decent suit." A faraway look passed over her face, as visions of plaid flannel undoubtedly danced in her head. "Funny thing, though. He had a tattoo on his neck. It looked just like that snake on the map, down in the corner. Pity." She shook her head. "Spoiled the whole effect of that nice suit."

I was right—Snake had signed the map. But what did the rest of it mean?

Trudy pointed to the rainbow. "Well, that's you, Rainbow," she said. Mrs. B. made an inquiring sound, but I was staring at the drawing. It was starting to make sense.

"You're right. And the flower's a rose. Rose is my mother's name, and yellow's her favorite color. This box of money here, with the flag? It's a French flag. What's the money they use in France?"

"Euros," said Mrs. B.

"But it used to be francs, right? Get it? Francs—Frank. Frank and Rosie. It's a map to my parents."

Trudy caught her breath. "Jesus, Bo. That'd be great." She'd tried to help me locate them, but nothing in the police databases had panned out. Their last known address was the Homestead. "So where are they?"

That was where things got difficult. The three of us gazed at the map.

"Anyone in your family in the clergy?" asked Mrs. B., pointing to the man with the cross.

I shook my head. I was trying to make out the writing on the banner that flew from one of the mountains. "What does it say on that banner?"

"Looks like P-O-R-E-T-E." said Trudy. "That's not even a word. What's it supposed to mean?"

"It could be a name," Mrs. B. suggested. "Maybe the name of that mountain it's flying from."

"Do you have an atlas, Mrs. B.?" I asked.

She nodded. "Let's go inside and check it," she said. "It's

getting too dark out here to puzzle over a map, anyway."

We followed Mrs. B. inside. My heart was racing. The drawing led to my parents, but none of the clues made sense. Porete, a heart—nothing came to mind. The figure with the cross could be a reference to a church. Mrs. B. beckoned us into her living room.

Her apartment was identical to mine, except chintz and doilies covered everything in sight. The living room smelled like lavender and mothballs. She pulled a massive book from her bookcase, sat on the chintz sofa, and opened the atlas on her lap. She took off her glasses, letting them dangle from the chain around her neck, and thumbed through the index. "Porete . . . Porete," she muttered.

"Look under *M*, too," I suggested. "Maybe it's Mount Porete." Trudy slipped her hand into mine.

"Here it is," Mrs. B. proclaimed. "You're right. Mount Porete, elevation 3,932." She looked up, her finger on the page. "It's in Idaho."

Idaho. Lenny had said they'd gone west, and *west* certainly described Idaho. It must be—what—two, three thousand miles from Rhodes. Idaho was a long way away, but it was a place to look. Frank and Rosie in Idaho. I'd never have guessed, never even thought to look there. In the corner of the map, the serpent twined around the dagger. Thanks, Snake.

"Here," Mrs. B. said, patting the sofa. Trudy and I sat on either side of her and regarded the atlas. "This is the map of Idaho. It matches up. See? Here's Priest Lake—the clergyman by the water. Here's Mount Porete. And this city's called Coeur d'Alene—*coeur* is French for *heart.*"

She was right. Snake's map corresponded perfectly with the one in the atlas. Three points—Priest Lake, Coeur d'Alene, and Mount Porete—formed a triangle around Frank and Rosie.

"Mrs. B., you are one remarkable lady!" I hugged her. She

blushed when I let her go, waving away my praise and looking pleased with herself.

We left. Trudy ran up the stairs, forgetting about her early shift. I followed more slowly, my feet heavy, feeling a little stunned. As I opened the door, my own apartment looked strange, like a photograph whose colors were off.

Trudy dropped her jacket on a chair. "Okay," she said. "First thing I'll do is call the Sheriff's department in whatever county it is out there. They might have an address. And now that we know where to look, we can find out the area code, get their phone number."

I shook my head. "They won't have a phone. They never owned one." I'd hated that when I was a teenager. "Frank used to say, 'If a man wants to talk to me, he can do it to my face.' "

"I'll try anyway. You never know, he might have changed his mind. There must be lots of ways they've changed in twenty years."

It was true, of course. The thought sat like ice in my gut.

Trudy paced, listing her plans. "I'll call the Post Office, too. They might have a P.O. box. One way or the other, we'll find out where you can write to them."

"Trudy—" I caught her arm to stop her pacing, then turned her gently and looked into her eyes. "I don't want to write my parents a letter. I want to go out there and see them. Face to face, like my dad used to say." I owed them that. Hell, I owed it to myself. I couldn't write a letter and then wait for a reply that might never come. A lot of bitterness had grown up between us, and the truth was I didn't know if they'd forgiven me for the way I'd left home. But even if they told me they no longer had a son and slammed the door, I wanted to see their faces again.

"So you're going out there to find them?" Trudy asked.

"That's the plan."

"When?"

"As soon as I can get the money together. Maybe next month." I stopped, calculating how much I had, how much the trip might cost. "I bet Ryan would loan me some cash if I asked him." And I could always pick up a job in Idaho when I got there. Given that all I had to go on was a hand-drawn map, the search might take a while.

Trudy was quiet for a minute, chewing her bottom lip. "Okay," she said, "I think I can get the time off from work. It'll be short notice, but I've got some vacation days coming. And a month gives us time to lay some groundwork." She grinned. "Bo, this will be fun—heading off into unfamiliar territory, chasing after clues together. It'll be just like the New York trip."

Now it was my turn to get quiet. The whole thing was a game to her, another chance to play detective. To me—I was trying to get part of my life back. A very big part that I'd thrown away unthinkingly, leaving a gaping, ragged hole. Trudy's game was one I couldn't play.

"Trudy . . . let's sit down." She sat on the sofa and tilted her head at me. I sat beside her, taking her hand in both of mine and turning to face her. "This is tough to say. Please understand—I need to go out there alone."

"Oh." She looked down at our hands, then slowly pulled hers out from between mine. "Of course. I mean, they're your parents and all." She patted the back of my hand, folded her hands in her lap, then gave me a weak smile. I felt rotten.

"They might not even want to see me, I don't know," I said. "I'll call you. Every day. Let you know what's happening."

She nodded, then stood up. "I'd better go. I've got that early shift."

"Trudy—" I stood too. She made a shushing noise and put her finger on my lips.

"No, you're right." She smiled. "This time. You should go alone. Is it okay if I make those calls? Try to find you a little more to go on?"

"I'd appreciate that." I folded her into my arms, and for a long time we held each other. Her hair smelled like spring. Then she pulled away and put on her jacket.

She paused at the door. "Bo? When you find them—I mean, if the reunion goes okay—are you . . . will you stay out there?"

"Sorry, Deputy. You're not getting rid of me that easily."

"Good. Because if you don't come back, Rainbow, I'm going to Idaho to hunt you down."

After she'd gone, I took out the photo of Rosie, Frank, and me. The long-haired kid still tried to make a muscle; his mother still bent toward him while his father looked at the camera. The way the world had been, for a fraction of a second, thirty years before. All of it was gone. The field where we'd posed now sprouted a dozen homes. The skinny boy had grown into a man in size-twelve shoes. And what about the parents? Had Frank lost his hair? Did Rosie still smell like patchouli? What postures and lines had time imposed on them?

I didn't know. But I was going to Idaho to find out.

ABOUT THE AUTHOR

Nancy Holzner lives in Ithaca, NY, with her husband Steve. She's worked as a medievalist, English professor, high-school teacher, tech writer, editor, and corporate trainer. As Nancy Conner, she's written several popular tech books. When she's not writing, Nancy enjoys visiting local wineries and listening obsessively to opera. Please visit her Web site: www.NancyHolzner.com.